So Much for That

LIONEL SHRIVER

So Much for That

HarperCollins Publishers Ltd

Published by HarperCollins Publishers Ltd

First Canadian edition

HarperCollins books may be purchased for educational, business,
or sales promotional use through our Special Markets Department.

HarperCollins Publishers Ltd
2 Bloor Street East, 20th Floor
Toronto, Ontario, Canada
M4W 1A8

www.harpercollins.ca

Library and Archives Canada Cataloguing in Publication
Shriver, Lionel
So much for that : a novel / Lionel Shriver.

ISBN 978-1-55468-201-0

I. Title.
PS3569.H685S62 2009   813'.54   C2009-905720-4

Designed by Kate Nichols

Printed and bound in the United States
RRD 9 8 7 6 5 4 3 2 1

To Paul. In loss, liberation.

Time is money.

—Benjamin Franklin,
Advice to a Young Tradesman, 1748

So Much for That

Chapter One

Shepherd Armstrong Knacker
Merrill Lynch Account Number 934-23F917
December 01, 2004 – December 31, 2004
Net Portfolio Value: $731,778.56

What do you pack for the rest of your life?

    On research trips—he and Glynis had never called them "vacations"—Shep had always packed too much, covering for every contingency: rain gear, a sweater on the off chance that the weather in Puerto Escondido was unseasonably cold. In the face of infinite contingencies, his impulse was to take nothing.

    There was no rational reason to be creeping these halls stealthily like a thief come to burgle his own home—padding heel to toe on the floorboards, flinching when they creaked. He had double-checked that Glynis was out through early evening (for an "appointment"; it bothered him that she did not say with whom or where). Calling on a weak pretense of asking about dinner plans when their son hadn't eaten a proper meal with his parents for the last year, he had confirmed that Zach was safely installed at a friend's overnight. Shep was alone in the house. He needn't keep jumping when the heat came on. He needn't reach tremulously into the top dresser drawer for his boxers as if any time now his wrist would be seized and he'd be read the Miranda.

Except that Shep was a burglar, after a fashion. Perhaps the sort that any American household most feared. He had arrived home from work a little earlier than usual in order to steal himself.

The swag bag of his large black Samsonite was unzipped on the bed, lying agape as it had for less drastic departures year after year. So far it contained: one comb.

He forced himself through the paces of collecting a travel shampoo, his shaving kit, even if he was doubtful that in The Afterlife he would continue to shave. But the electric toothbrush presented a quandary. The island had electricity, surely it did, but he'd neglected to discover whether their plugs were flat American two-prongs, bulky British three-prongs, or the slender European kind, wide-set and round. He wasn't dead sure either whether the local current was 220 or 110. Sloppy; these were just the sorts of practical details that on earlier research forays they'd been rigorous about jotting down. But then, they'd lately grown less systematic, especially Glynis, who'd sometimes slipped on more recent journeys abroad and used the word *vacation*. A tell, and there had been several.

Resistant at first to the Oral B's jarring cranial buzz, at length Shep had come to relish the slick of his teeth once the tedium was complete. As with all technological advances, it felt unnatural to go backward, to resume the fitful scrub of splayed nylon on a plastic stick. But what if Glynis went to the bathroom when she came home and noticed that his blue-ringed toothbrush was missing, while hers, with the red ring, still sat on the sink? Best she didn't begin this of all evenings with perplexity or suspicion. He could always take Zach's—he'd never heard the kid use it—but Shep couldn't see swiping his own son's toothbrush. (Shep had paid for the thing, of course, along with pretty much everything here. Yet little or nothing in this house felt like his. That used to bug him but now just made it easier to leave the salad spinner, the StairMaster, and the sofas behind.) Worse, he and Glynis shared the same recharger. He didn't want to leave her with a toothbrush that would last five or six days (he didn't want to leave her at all, but that was another matter), its weakening, terminal shudder providing a soundtrack for his wife's lapse into another of her periodic depressions.

So having unscrewed the wall mount only a turn or two, he tightened it back down. Restoring his own handle reassuringly to the recharger, he scrounged a manual brush from the medicine cabinet. He would have to grow accustomed to technological regression, which in a manner he couldn't quite put his finger on was surely good for the soul. Something about backtracking to a stage of development that you could understand.

He wasn't planning simply to cut and run, to disappear himself from his family absent announcement or explanation. That would be cruel, or crueler. He wasn't presenting her with a total fait accompli either, a wave goodbye at the door. Officially he would confront her with a choice, one for which, in the service of credibility, he had paid through the nose. Odds were that he had purchased nothing but an illusion, but an illusion could be priceless. So he'd bought not one ticket, but three. They were nonrefundable. If his instincts were all out of whack and Glynis surprised him, Zach still wouldn't like it. But the boy was fifteen years old, and how was this for developmental regression: for once an American teenager would do what he was told.

Anxious about being caught in the act, in the end he had too much time. Glynis wouldn't be home for another couple of hours, and the Samsonite was replete. Given the confusion over plugs and current, he'd thrown in a few manual hand tools and a Swiss Army knife; in the average crisis, you were still better off with a pair of needle-nose Vise-Grips than a BlackBerry. Only a couple of shirts, because he wanted to wear different shirts. Or no shirt. A few bits and pieces that a man with Shep's occupation knew could make the difference between satisfied self-sufficiency and disaster: duct tape; a selection of screws, bolts, and washers; silicon lubricant; plastic sealant; rubber bands (*elastics*, for N' Hampshire old-timers like his father); and a small roll of binding wire. A flashlight, for power cuts, and a stock of AAs. A novel he should have selected more carefully if he was taking only one. An English–Swahili phrasebook, malaria pills, deet. Prescription cortisone cream for persistent eczema on his ankle, a tube that would soon run out.

Obviating any further inclusions, his Merrill Lynch checkbook. He didn't like to think of himself as calculating, but it turned out to be fortunate that he'd always kept this account in his name alone. He could—he would, of course, offer to leave her half; she hadn't earned a dime of it, but they were married, and that was the law. Yet he would have to warn her that even hundreds of thousands of dollars wouldn't last her long in Westchester, and sooner or later she'd have to do not "her work" but someone else's.

He'd had to stuff the Samsonite with newspaper to keep the paltry chattel from rattling in the British Airways hold. He stashed it in his closet, covering it with a bathrobe for good measure. A packed bag on the bedspread would alarm Glynis far more than a missing toothbrush.

Shep settled in the living room with a bourbon bracer. It wasn't his habit to begin an evening with anything stronger than beer, but habit would have delayed this evening indefinitely. He put his feet up, casting his eyes around the pleasant but cheaply furnished room, unable to mourn leaving behind any aspect of the familiar surround, save the fountain. As for parting with the throw pillows or the nondescript glass coffee table on which it trickled, he felt positively cheerful. By contrast, the fountain had always filled him with that distinctive middle-class covetousness, desire for what you already own. He wondered whimsically if, wrapped in the wadded newspaper that padded his scant booty, it would fit in the Samsonite.

They still referred to it as "the Wedding Fountain." The sterling silver apparatus had substituted for a floral centerpiece at their modest gathering of friends twenty-six years before, twining the bride and groom's labors, talents, and very natures. To this day, the Wedding Fountain constituted the only project on which he and Glynis had collaborated fifty-fifty. Shep had taken responsibility for the technical aspects of the gizmo. The pump was carefully hidden by a sweep of mirror-finish metal around the basin; since the mechanism ran continually, over the years he'd replaced it several times. Wise in the ways of water, he'd advised on the width and depth of sluices, the length of drops from one level to the next. Glynis had dictated the flow of the metal itself, its artistic line, forging and soldering the parts in her old studio in Brooklyn.

For Shep's tastes, the fountain was austere; for Glynis's, ornate; so that even stylistically the construction embodied a meeting of minds halfway. And it was romantic. Melded together at the top, two undulating silver sluices split and intermingled like swans' necks, one supporting while the other broke to spill its liquid into the waiting pan of its mate. Narrow at their apex, the two central lines of their creation splayed and swooped in wider, ever more playful variations toward the basin. There the contributions of the fountain's two tributaries formed a shallow indoor lake, thus *pooling their resources* in the most literal sense. Glynis's workmanship was top-drawer. However busy, Shep had always honored her virtuosity by keeping the water topped up, and by periodically draining the contraption to polish the silver. Absent his conservation, the sterling's accelerating yellow taint might suggest a tarnish on more than metal. Once he was gone, chances were that she'd turn the thing off, and shove it out of sight.

As allegory, the two streams feeding a common pool represented an ideal they had failed. Nevertheless, the fountain successfully integrated their elements. Glynis not only worked with metal (or used to); she *was* metal. Stiff, uncooperative, and inflexible. Hard, refractive, and shiny with defiance. Her body long, attenuated, and angular like the jewelry and flatware she once crafted, in art school Glynis had not chosen her medium by accident. She naturally identified with any material that so fiercely refused to do what you wanted it to, whose form was resistant to change and responded only to violent manhandling. Metal was obstreperous. Were it ever mistreated, its dents and scratches caught the light like kept grudges.

Like it or not, Shep's element was water. Adaptive, easily manipulated, and prone to taking the path of least resistance, he *went with the flow*, as they said in his youth. Water was yielding, biddable, and readily trapped. He wasn't proud of these qualities; pliancy didn't seem manly. On the other hand, the apparent passivity of liquid was misleading. Water was resourceful. As any homeowner with an aging roof or corroded plumbing knew well, water was insidious, and in its own quiet way would find its route. Water had a devious willfulness of its own, a sneaky, seeping insistence, an instinct for finding the single seam or joint you've left unsealed. Sooner or later, water will get in if it wants to, or—more vitally, in Shep's case—it will get out.

His first boyhood fountains, knocked together with inappropriate materials like wood, leaked badly, and his frugal father had chastised him for these "bubblers," as Dad called them, that wasted water. But Shep became more ingenious with found objects: chipped serving bowls, the limbs of his sister's discarded dolls; later creations lost water only to evaporation. The whimsies grew kinetic, using paddle wheels, cups that would fill and flop, jets that kept a suspended object bobbing at bay, sprays that tinkled chimes of seashells or shards of stained glass. He'd kept up the hobby to this day. As a counterweight to the relentless functionality of his vocation, fountains were fabulously frivolous.

This offbeat pastime almost certainly hailed not from some high-falutin metaphor for his character, but from the commonplace associations of childhood. Every July, the Knackers had rented a cabin in the White Mountains, beside which ran a wide, rushing stream. Back then, kids were privileged with real summers, expanses of unscheduled time receding to the hazy horizon. Time whose seeming endlessness was a lie, but the lie was still beguiling. Ripe for improvisation, time you could play like a saxophone. So he'd always linked the lilt of running water to peace, lassitude, and a languid lack of urgency—which, between math camps, get-ahead tutoring, fencing classes, and organized playdates, kids these days never seemed to sample. That's what The Afterlife was all about, he recognized, not for the first time, and poured another finger of bourbon. He wanted his summer back. All year round.

None of the Sunday school classes or Christian youth groups had taken, but the one truly character-forming education that Gabriel Knacker had provided his son was a trip to Kenya when Shep was sixteen. Through the aegis of a Presbyterian exchange program, the Reverend had accepted a temporary teaching position at a small seminary in Limuru, an hour's drive from Nairobi, and had brought his family along. To Gabe Knacker's despair, what made the most intense impression on his son wasn't his seminary students' fervent embrace of the Gospel, but grocery shopping. On their first outing for provisions, Shep and Beryl had trailed their parents to the local market stalls for papayas, onions, potatoes, passion fruit, beans, zucchini, a scrawny chicken, and a great slab of beef of an undifferentiated cut: in all, enough provender to fill five string bags to their maximum capacity. Always fiscally minded—one of his father's objections still was that his son thought too much about money—Shep converted the shillings in his head. The entire haul had cost less than three dollars. Even in 1972 currency, for more than a week's supplies that was chump change.

Shep had expressed dismay at how any of these traders could turn a profit with such miserable prices. His father was keen to emphasize that these people were very poor; swaths of this benighted continent lived on less than a dollar a day. Yet the Reverend did allow that African farmers could charge pennies for their produce because they counted their expenses in pennies as well. Shep had been familiar with economies of scale; this was his first introduction to the scale of economies. So a dollar's value wasn't fixed but relative. Back in New Hampshire, it would buy a box of paper clips; in the Kenyan countryside, an entire secondhand but perfectly serviceable bike.

"So why don't we take our savings and move here?" he'd asked as they lugged their shopping down a farmland path.

In a rare softening, Gabe Knacker had clapped his son's shoulder and gazed across the verdant coffee fields bathed in lambent equatorial sun. "Sometimes I wonder."

Shep wondered, too, and he'd kept wondering. If you could at least survive in places like East Africa on a dollar a day, how well could you live for more like twenty bucks?

In high school, Shep had already been hungry for direction. Much like Zach, alas, in his studies he was competent at every subject, but distinguished at none. In an age that increasingly valued mastery of the abstract—the befuddling world of "information technology" was only a decade away—Shep preferred tasks whose results he could grasp in both his

head and his hands: replacing a rickety banister. But his father was an educated man, and didn't expect his son to work construction. With that heart
of water, Shep was never a rebellious kid. Given his penchant for making
and fixing things, a degree in engineering had seemed apt. As he'd assured
his father many times since, he'd really, really intended to go to college.

Yet meanwhile that whimsy first conceived in Limuru had consoli-
dated to firm resolve. Saving may have gone out of fashion, but surely a
middle-class American income still allowed for salting something away.
Thus with the application of industry, thrift, and self-denial—once the
country's moral mainstays—it should be possible to inflate a robin-sized
nest egg to the dimensions of an ostrich ovum merely by hopping a
plane. The Third World was running a sale: two lives for the price of
one. Ever since coming of age, Shep had dedicated himself to the realization of the second. He was not even sure you called it industry, when
you were working so hard only that you might stop working.

So with an eye to his true purpose—money—Shep had instinctively
gravitated to where America kept most of it, and applied to the City College of Technology in New York. For while Gabe Knacker faulted the character of his son "the philistine" for his worship of the false god Mammon,
Shep believed fervently that money—the web of your fiscal relationships
to individuals and to the world at large—*was* character; that the surest
test of any man's mettle was how he wielded his wallet. Thus a decent,
capable kid didn't tap a father's measly salary as a small-town minister (an
injunction to which Beryl would prove oblivious when blithely expecting
their dad to pay for her film degree at NYU four years later). Ever since
earning his first five dollars from shoveling snow at the age of nine, Shep
had always paid up front, be it for an Almond Joy or an education.

Thus determined to work beforehand and finance his own degree,
he'd delayed his acceptance at City Tech in downtown Brooklyn and
found a one-bedroom nearby in Park Slope, which—hard as it was to
remember now—was a dodgy area in those days, and dirt cheap. The
area's housing stock was run down, and full of families in need of small
repairs but unable to afford the larcenous rates of unionized tradesmen.
Having mastered a variety of rudimentary wiring and carpentry skills

while helping to maintain his own family's eternally crumbling late-Victorian in New Hampshire, Shep posted flyers in convenience stores, advertising his services as an old-fashioned handyman. Word of mouth spread quickly about a young white kid who could replace washers and rotten floorboards for a modest fee, and in short order he had more work than he could handle. By the time he'd delayed entry into City Tech for a second year he'd incorporated, and "Knack of All Trades" was already contracting out for part-time help. Two years after that, Shep took on his first full-time employee. A harried entrepreneur enjoyed little free time, and besides, Shep had just got married. So in the service of sheer efficiency, Jackson Burdina doubled, then as now, as his best friend.

It was still a sore point with Shep's father that his son never went to college, which was ludicrous; Knack of All Trades had expanded and flourished without any benedictory piece of paper. The real problem was that Gabriel Knacker had little regard for manual labor—unless it involved digging wells for impoverished villagers in Mali with the Peace Corps, or patching a pensioner's shingles out of the kindness of your heart. He had no use for commerce. Any activity that could not trace its lineage directly to virtue was destitute. The fact that if everyone devoted himself solely to goodness for its own sake the whole world would come to a skidding halt didn't faze the guy a whit.

Up until a little over eight years ago, Life A had had its merits, and Shep hadn't regarded himself as sacrificing his prime for pie in the sky. He'd always liked physical toil, relishing a distinctive kind of tired you got not from the gym but from building bookshelves. He liked running his own show, answering to no one. Glynis may have turned out to be a handful, and might not have described herself as happy in the big picture, but it was probably safe to say that she was happy with him—or as happy as she was going to get with anybody, which wasn't very. He was glad when she got pregnant with Amelia right away. He was in a hurry, anxious to rush through a whole life in half the time, and he'd have far preferred that Zach had been born pronto and not ten years later.

As for The Afterlife, Glynis had seemed onboard when they met. His status as a man with a mission surely attracted her to him in the first place. Without his vision, without the ever more concrete edifice of Life B rising in his head, Shep Knacker was one more small businessman who'd found a niche market: nothing special. As it was, picking a new target country for every summer's research trip had been an invigorating ritual of their marriage. They were, or so he'd thought until this last year's dawning apprehension, a team.

So when he got the offer to sell up in November 1996, it was irresistible. *A million dollars.* Rationally he recognized that a mil wasn't what it once was, and that he'd have to pay capital gains. Still, the sum had never lost the awesome roundness of childhood; no matter how many other ordinary folks also became "millionaires," the word retained a ring. Combined with the fruits of lifelong scrimping, the proceeds from selling Knack would furnish the capital to cash out and never look back. So never mind that the purchaser—an employee so lazy and sloppy that they'd been on the verge of firing the guy before, surprise, he comes into his trust fund—was a callow, loudmouthed, ignorant twit.

Who was now Shep's boss. Oh sure, it had seemed to make sense at the time to sign on as an employee of what had been his own company—renamed overnight "Handy Randy," a moniker not only tacky but inaccurate, since Randy Pogatchnik was anything but handy. The initial idea had been to hang on for a month or two while they packed, sold off their motley possessions, and located at least a temporary house in Goa. Meantime, they wouldn't spend down their capital, which Shep sank into can't-lose mutual funds to fatten before slaughter; the Dow was effervescent.

"A month or two" had now stretched into over eight years of submission to the sadistic whims of an overweight, freckle-faced brat, who must have got wind of his imminent sacking and had probably bought Knack—you had to give the guy this much—as fiendishly effective revenge. After the sale, standards of workmanship plummeted, so that Shep's "Customer Relations" position for handling complaints, never a post at all during his own tenure as CEO, had burgeoned into a demanding and decidedly unpleasant full-time job.

In retrospect, of course, it had been imbecilic to sell their place in Carroll Gardens a few years earlier—barely out of a recession, and on the heels of a housing crash—then move up to Westchester and rent. Shep would gladly have stayed in Brooklyn, but Glynis had concluded that the only way she could finally focus on "her work" was to remove herself from the "distractions" of the city. (Sure of his weakness, she had made a sly financial case as well: Westchester's high-quality public schools would save them the pricey tuition of private education in New York. All very well, for Amelia. But later, when Glynis thought that Zach needed help—which he did—finding a "better school" was the easiest way to seem to be doing something, and now they were out $26,000 a year for private tuition anyway.) Jackson and Carol had stayed put in Windsor Terrace, and even that ramshackle dive of theirs had soared to a value of $550,000. At least having benefited from the real estate boom himself made Jackson more patient than Shep with Homeowner Smugness; these days, a handyman wasn't in the door five seconds before the wife was crowing about how much the dump was worth now, so watch the wainscoting with that toolbox. It was like that in most big cities now: LA, Miami—a communal hysteria, as if the entire citizenry were on *Dialing for Dollars* and had won the car. Shep was probably just envious. Still, there was something unsavory about that gleefulness, a mania he associated with slot machines. A preacher's son, he failed to see the satisfaction in a jackpot that bore no relation to something good or hard that you had done.

Property in Westchester had appreciated by three times over ten years as well, so, yeah, in hindsight they should have bought—thereby making about as much profit from sitting on his ass as he had from selling a whole company, fruit of twenty-two years' sweat. That was the way people made money in this country now, according to Jackson: ass-sitting. You couldn't get rich on earned income, he railed. Taxes on wages made sure of that. Jackson claimed that only inheritance and investment—asssitting—paid. Shep wasn't so sure. Certainly he himself had worked hard, but he'd been compensated for his trouble. Limuru lay ever in the back of his mind, and he'd earned far more than a dollar per day.

Shep had opted to rent for the same reason that drove every big decision he'd ever made. He wanted to be able to pick up stakes—easily, quickly, cleanly, without waiting for a house to sell in a market whose climate he couldn't foresee. That's what irked him a bit about Home-owner Smugness: all these schmoes with keys to a front door acted as if they'd seen the boom coming, as if they were financial geniuses and not the beneficiaries of dumb luck. He may have regretted missing out on the property windfall; he didn't regret the reason he'd missed out. He was proud of the reason, proud of planning to leave. He was only ashamed of having stayed.

He tried not to blame Glynis. If that meant blaming himself instead, that seemed fair. The Afterlife was his aspiration—the word he preferred to *fantasy*—and any dream was dilute secondhand. He tried not to be angry at her for a lot of things, and to a great extent succeeded.

When they met, Glynis had been running her own small business from home, making jewelry of a strikingly stark, streamlined nature during an era of clunk, slapdash, and feathers. She had contacted Knack of All Trades to build a worktable bolted to the floor, and later, because she liked the proprietor—his broad veined forearms, his wide-open face like a field of wheat—a set of racks for hammers, pliers, and files. Shep appreciated her meticulous requirements, as she appreciated his meticulous execution. The second time he showed up to finish the table, she'd left numerous samples of her work lying casually around the studio (deliberately, she confessed with a laugh once they started going out; she'd dangled the glittering baubles before her handsome handyman "like fishing lures"). Though he'd never considered himself the artistic type, Shep was transfixed. Delicate and morbid, a whole series of elongated stickpins looked like assemblages of bird bones; when she modeled the bracelets for him, they wrapped all the way up her arm, slithering like serpents to the elbow. Sinewy, elusive, and severe, Glynis's creations were an uncanny manifestation of the woman who made them. It was touch and go whether he fell in love with Glynis or her metalwork first, because as far as Shep was concerned they were one and the same.

During their courtship, Glynis was teaching at summer camps and doing piecework in the Jewelry District to pay the rent. Meantime, she was placing single necklaces in second-tier galleries, and her silversmith-ing barely broke even. Yet she fevered long hours, and paid her own phone bill. Surely any man would have assumed that for a self-starter like Glynis—disciplined, ascetic, and fiery—pulling her financial weight in a marriage would be a point of pride. (On reflection, it probably was.) So he'd never expected to have to save for The Afterlife all by himself.

Less compassionate men might have felt they'd been sold a bill of goods. Pregnancy had seemed a reasonable excuse for letting her metal-smithing tools languish, but that accounted for only eighteen months of the last twenty-six years. Motherhood wasn't the real problem, though it took him a long time to figure out what was. She needed resistance, the very quality that metal most demonstrably offered up. Suddenly Glynis had no difficulty to overcome, no hard artisan's life with galleries filch-ing half the too-small price of a mokume brooch that had taken three weeks to forge. No, her husband made a good living, and if she slept late and dawdled the afternoon away reading *Lustre*, *American Craft Maga-zine*, and *Lapidary Journal*, the phone bill would still get paid. For that matter, she needed need itself. She could overcome her anguish about embarking on an object that, once completed, might not meet her ex-acting standards only if she had no choice. In this sense, his helping had hurt her. By providing the financial cushion that should have facilitated making all the metal whathaveyou she liked, he had ruined her life. Wrapped with a slackening bow, ease was a poisonous present.

Yet it wasn't as if she were lazy. Since Glynis still maintained the fic-tion (even in his head, the word pained him) that she was a professional metalsmith, all other domestic activities therefore qualified as procrasti-nation, and thus were seen to with vigor and dispatch. It wasn't as if she'd made nothing, either—metalwork, that is. Spurning jewelry as intrinsi-cally rinky-dink, she'd moved entirely to flatware, and through the years had crafted a handful of dazzling implements: memorably, the Bakelite inlaid fish slice; that exquisite set of hand-forged, perfectly ergonomic sterling chopsticks, whose heavier ends bent slightly, achingly, as if they were melting. Yet each finished project was the product of so much agony and time that in the end she couldn't bring herself to sell it.

So what she hadn't made was money. Were he ever to have observed aloud once Zach and Amelia both entered school that she was still not bringing in a dime, Glynis would have iced over in cold rage (so he hadn't). But her income of zero dollars wasn't an objection. It was a fact. That when they married Shep hadn't imagined he would carry the whole household in perpetuity was also a fact. But he could carry the household, and he had.

Besides, he understood her. Or he understood how much he couldn't understand, which was a start. Making his own geographical inertia all the more perplexing, by and large Shep decided to do something, and then he did it. For Glynis to get from the deciding to the doing was like leaping the stumps of a washed-out bridge. To put it another way, she had the engine, but a faulty ignition switch. Glynis could decide to do something and then nothing would happen. It was an interior thing, a design flaw, and probably not one she could fix.

Having kept his mouth shut for decades, he should never have let it slip out tentatively over breakfast a couple of years ago (during a particularly galling week at Handy Randy) that it was a shame they hadn't been socking away the remnants of two incomes all this time, with which they could have left for The Afterlife long ago . . . Before he had finished the sentence, she'd stood from the table without a word and marched out the door. When he came home that night, she had a job. Apparently all this time he'd have had better luck lighting a fire under the woman not by cajoling but by giving offense. Ever since, she'd been fashioning models for Living in Sin, an upmarket chocolatier whose factory was located in nearby Mount Kisco. This month, the company was already gearing up for Easter. So rather than polish off avant-garde flatware of museum-piece quality, his wife was carving wax bunny rabbits to be cast—aptly—in bitter chocolate, and stuffed with orange cream. The work was part time, without benefits. Her salary made a farcical contribution to their coffers. She kept the job out of spite.

In return, he may have let her keep it out of spite. Besides, she couldn't help herself. They were very good bunny rabbits.

It was disconcerting to be systematically punished for what might have engendered a modicum of gratitude. He did not require the gratitude, but he could have skipped the resentment, an emotion distinctive for being disagreeable on both its generating and receiving ends. Glynis resented her dependency; she found it humiliating. She resented not being a celebrated metalsmith, and she resented the fact that her status as professional nonentity appeared to everyone, including Glynis, to be all her fault. She resented her two children for diverting her energies when they were young; once they were no longer young, she resented them for failing to divert her energies. She resented that her husband and now her thoughtlessly undemanding children had thieved her most cherished keepsakes: her excuses. As resentment produces the psychic equivalent of acid reflux, she resented the resentment itself. Never having had much of substance to complain about was yet one more reason to feel aggrieved.

Shep was temperamentally predisposed to feel fortunate, although he himself had plenty of substance to resent, had he been so inclined. He supported his wife and son. He subsidized his daughter Amelia, though she was three years out of college. He subsidized his elderly father, and made sure that the prideful retired reverend didn't know it. He'd made several "loans" to his sister Beryl that she would never pay back, and had probably not made the last; yet they were officially loans and not gifts, so Beryl would never thank him or feel abashed. He'd picked up the entire tab for his mother's funeral, and since no one else noticed Shep didn't notice either. Every member of a family has a role, and Shep was the one who paid for things. Because every other party took this state of affairs for granted, Shep took it for granted, too.

He rarely bought anything for himself, but he didn't want anything. Or he wanted only one thing. Still, why now? Why, if it had already been over eight years since the sale of Knack, could it not be nine? Why, if it could be this evening, could it not be tomorrow night?

Because it was early January in New York State, and it was cold. Because he was already forty-eight years old, and the closer he got to fifty the more The Afterlife, even if he did finally get around to it, looked like routine early retirement. Because his "can't-lose" mutual funds had only last month recovered the value of his original investment. Because in his idiotic innocence he had broadcast for decades to anyone who seemed interested his intentions to leave behind altogether the world of tax planning, car inspections, traffic jams, and telemarketing. (As his audience had aged, other people's youthful admiration had long ago soured to mockery behind his back. Or not always behind his back, for at Handy Randy Shep's "escape fantasy," as Pogatchnik flippantly tagged it, was a regular source of merciless entertainment.) Because he himself had started dangerously to doubt the reality of The Afterlife, and without the promise of reprieve he could not—he could not—continue. Because he'd tied a carrot in front of his own nose like a goddamned donkey's, soothed by the seduction of infinite delay, never sorting out that if he could always leave tomorrow then he could also leave today. Indeed, it was the sheer arbitrariness of this Friday evening that made it so perfect.

When Glynis opened the front door, he started guiltily. He had rehearsed his opening lines so many times, and now the script had fled.

"Bourbon," she said. "What's the special occasion?"

Still clinging to his last thought, he wanted to explain that the occasion was not special, which was why it was special. "Habits are made to be broken."

"Some of them," she reproached, taking off her coat.

"Would you like one?"

She surprised him. "Yes."

Glynis was still slender, and no one ever pegged her at fifty, though there was a fatigue in her bearing tonight that made it suddenly possible to envision her at seventy-five. She'd been tired since September at least, claiming to run a low-grade fever that he privately failed to detect. Although she'd lately developed a subtle paunch, the rest of her body was if anything thinner; such reapportionment of weight was normal in middle age, and he was too much of a gentleman to pass comment on it.

Their both indulging in hard liquor at barely past seven fostered a warm collusion that he was reluctant to undermine. Yet his innocuous "Where have you been?" came out like an accusation.

She could be evasive, but it was rare for her not to answer at all. He let it go.

Curling protectively around the highball in her usual armchair, Glynis pulled her knees up and tucked her heels. She always seemed enclosed, balled up in another sense, but tonight she seemed uncommonly so. Maybe she intuited his purpose, so long in coming. When he reached into his inside pocket and laid three sheaves of e-ticket printouts silently on the glass table beside the Wedding Fountain, she arched her eyebrows. "Show and tell?"

Glynis was an elegant woman, and he was interested in her—in that way that simple people were so often captivated by the fucked-up. He paused to consider whether, without Glynis, as partner or opponent, The Afterlife might prove desolate.

"Three tickets to Pemba," he said. "Me, you, and Zach."

"Another 'research trip'? You might have thought of that before the Christmas holidays. Zach's back in school."

Though she never used to couch the term in quotes, the sour twist she now gave to "research trip" recalled Pogatchnik's sneering pronunciation of "escape fantasy." He noted how readily she concocted a reason that his caprice was impossible, nimbly dismissing even the brief getaway she mistook it for. In his work, Shep applied his intelligence to solving problems; Glynis applied hers to inventing them, to constructing obstacles to throw in her own path. He wouldn't mind the eccentricity if her path weren't his own as well.

"These tickets are one-way."

He would have expected that when she got it, when she registered the true nature of the gauntlet he'd thrown on the coffee table, her face would cloud, sink into solemnity, or constrict with the wary rigidity of preparing for combat. Instead she looked mildly amused. He was accustomed to ridicule at Handy Randy ("Yeah, sure you're moving to Africa, any day now, you and Meryl Streep"), and sometimes, though it filled him with self-hatred, he'd joined in the fun himself. But from Glynis any suggestion of the same blithe, pitying cynicism slew him. He knew she wasn't into it anymore, but he hadn't thought her attitude had got as bad as that.

"Wasteful," she said calmly, with a thin smile. "Not like you."

She'd correctly intuited that the one-ways had cost more than round-trips. "A gesture," he said. "This isn't about money."

"I can't imagine your doing anything unrelated to money. Your whole life, Shepherd," she announced, "has been about money."

"Not for its own sake. I've never been greedy like that, as you know—wanting money to be rich. I want to buy something with it."

"I used to believe that," she said sadly. "Now I wonder if you've any idea what it is that you really want to purchase. You don't even know what you want out of, much less what you want in on."

"I do," he countered. "I want to buy myself. I'm sorry to sound like Jackson, but he's right, in a way. I'm an indentured servant. This isn't a free country, in any sense of the word. If you want your own liberty, you have to buy it."

"But liberty isn't any different from money, is it? It's meaningless unless you know what you want to spend it on." The observation sounded hollow, even bored.

"We've talked about what I want to spend it on."

"Yes," she said wearily. "Endlessly."

He swallowed the insult. "Part of going is finding out."

Shep could not have contrived a conversation that should have riveted his wife more than this one, but he could swear that her attention had wandered.

"Gnu," he appealed, pronouncing the *G*; the endearment went back to their very first research trip to Kenya, where she had done cracking impressions of wildebeests, hooking her hands over her head for horns and wrenching her long face into a pleading expression that was sad and dumb. The antic had been girlish and beguiling. He used to call her Gnu all the time, and lately—well, lately, he realized with a shock, he hadn't been calling her anything at all. "These are real tickets. For a real airplane, that takes off in one week. I would like you to come with me. I would like Zach to come with us, and if we leave as a family I will drag him down the Jetway by the hair. But *I am going*, with or without you."

Damned if she didn't seem to find his declaration hilarious. "An ultimatum, then?" She drained her glass, as if to stifle laughter.

"An invitation," he countered.

"A week from now you're getting on a plane to fly to an island you've never been to, where you'll spend the rest of your life. Whatever were all those 'research trips' for?"

In her use of *you* as opposed to *we* he read her answer, and he wasn't prepared for the sudden falling sensation in his chest. Although he had tried to be realistic with himself, apparently he had held out hope that she and Zack might come with him to Pemba after all. Still, this face-off was young, so he held out further hope that—for the first time in the history of the universe—he might change her mind.

"I picked Pemba precisely because we haven't been there. That means you can't have already come up with a zillion reasons why yet another option is off the table."

When she said nothing in response, he was able to remember some of what he had recited over the steering wheel earlier this afternoon on the Henry Hudson Parkway. "Goa got the all-clear until you read about that expat Briton who was murdered by a local acquaintance in her house, and then it was too dangerous. One murder. As if people never kill each other in New York. Bulgaria would have been a steal when we first lit on it, and in the Western world, too, if barely, with broadband and a postal service and clean water. But the food was too bland. The *food*. As if we couldn't rustle up a little garlic and rosemary. Meantime, the property prices have already started to escalate, and now it's too late. Ditto Eritrea, which piqued your imagination: proud new country, warm people, espresso on every corner, and the fifties architecture was a kick. Now, lucky for you, the government's gone to hell. You loved Morocco, remember? Cinnamon and terra cotta; neither the food nor the landscape was *bland*. It seemed so promising that I agreed to stay on when my mother had her stroke, and we got back half a day too late to say goodbye."

"You made up for it." Ah, the funeral expenses. If Shep did not resent his family's impositions on his finances, Glynis resented them for him.

"But after 9/11," he plowed on, "suddenly all Muslim countries—including Turkey, to my own disappointment—got knocked off the list. We had a terrific opportunity when the currency collapsed in Argentina. Before that, we could have bought just about anything in Southeast Asia during that financial crisis. But now all those currencies have recovered, and our resources would never stretch for thirty or forty years in any of those countries today. In Cuba, you couldn't live without shampoo and toilet paper. Croatia's residency requirements entailed too much red tape. The slums in Kenya were too depressing; South Africa made you feel too guilty for being white. Laos, Portugal, Tonga, and Bhutan—I can't even remember what was wrong with all of them anymore, though"—he indulged a bitterness—"I'm sure you do."

Glynis exuded an aggressive mildness, and seemed to be enjoying herself. "You're the one who ruled out France," she said sweetly.

"That's right. The taxes would have killed us."

"Always money, Shepherd," she chided.

It struck him then how people who acted above money—arty types like his sister, or his Old-Testament father—were the same folks who never earned any to speak of. Glynis knew perfectly well that The Afterlife had to add up financially or it would solely constitute a long, ruinous vacation.

"But you've paralyzed us at both ends, haven't you?" he proceeded. "Not only is no destination good enough, but it's never the right time to go. We have to wait until Amelia is out of high school. We have to wait until Amelia is out of college. We have to wait until Zach is out of primary school. Middle school. Now it's high school, and then why not college? We have to wait for our investments to recover from the tech-stock crash, and then from 9/11. Well, they have."

Shep wasn't used to talking so much, and babbling made him feel foolish. He may have been as dependent on *resistance* as Glynis, which is to say: hers. "You think I'm being selfish. Maybe I am. For once. This isn't about money, it's about"—he paused in embarrassment—"my soul. You'll say, you have said, that it won't be what I expect. I accept that. It's not as if I nurse a misguided idea about parking myself on the beach. I know sun gets boring, that there are flies. Still, I can tell you this much: I plan to get eight hours of sleep. That sounds small, but it's not small. I love sleeping, Glynis, and"—he didn't want to choke up now, not until he got it all out—"I especially love sleeping with you. But when I say I crave eight hours of sleep, at a Westchester dinner party? They *laugh*. For commuters around here, that's such a preposterous ambition that it's actually funny.

"So I don't care what else I'll do in Pemba or whether the power keeps cutting off. Because if I back down this time? I'd know in my heart of hearts that we're never really going to go. And with no promised land to look forward to, I can't keep it up, Gnu. I can't keep cleaning up the messes that the untrained klutzes at Hardly Handy Randy leave behind. I can't keep sitting in traffic for hours listening to NPR on the West Side Highway. I can't keep running to the A-and-P for milk and getting 'bonus points' on our store card so that after spending several thousand dollars we qualify for a free turkey on Thanksgiving."

"There are worse fates."

"No," he said. "I'm not sure there are. I know we've seen plenty of poverty—raw sewage running in gutters and mothers scavenging for mango peels. But they know what's wrong with their lives, and they have a notion that with a few shillings or pesos or rupees in their pockets things could be better. There's something especially terrible about being told over and over that you have the most wonderful life on earth and it doesn't get any better and it's still shit. This is supposed to be the greatest country in the world, but Jackson is right: it's a sell, Glynis. I must have forty different 'passwords' for banking and telephone and credit card and Internet accounts, and forty different account numbers, and you add them all up and that's our lives. And it's all ugly, physically ugly. The strip malls in Elmsford, the Kmarts and Wal-Marts and Home Depots . . . all plastic and chrome with blaring, clashing colors, and everyone in a hurry, to do what?"

It was not his imagination. She really wasn't paying attention.

"I'm sorry," he said. "You've heard this before. Maybe I'm wrong, and maybe I really will skulk back home a few weeks later all hangdog and sheepish. But I'd rather the humiliation of trying and failing than give it up. Giving it up would be like dying."

"I think you'll find"—her voice was so measured, piped full of some great new wisdom he did not care for—"that it would not in the least be like dying. There is nothing like dying. We use it as a metaphor for something else. Something smaller and silly and much more bearable."

"If this is your idea of getting me to change my mind, it's not working."

"When is this you're planning to depart our shores?"

"Next Friday. BA-179 out of JFK, the 22:30 for London. Then on to Nairobi, to Zanzibar, to Pemba. You and Zach can come with me up until the minute the flight closes. In the meantime, I thought I'd clear off and give you a chance to think." *A chance to miss me* is what he meant. *To miss me while you can still un-miss me.* And in all honesty he was afraid of her. If he remained here, she would be able to talk him out of it. She was that good. "I'll be staying with Carol and Jackson. They're expecting me, and you can reach me there at any time before I go."

"I do wish you wouldn't," she said idly. Having picked up her glass from the table, Glynis rose and smoothed her slacks in a gesture that he recognized as marshaling herself to prepare another ordinary dinner. "Randy is for once entirely handy, and I'm afraid I will need your health insurance."

Later that evening, while Glynis was still tidying the kitchen, Shep slipped upstairs and pulled the bathrobe off his suitcase. He put the two shirts back in the third drawer of his dresser, smoothing them so they'd be in respectable condition for work. He removed the needle-nose Vise-Grips, the screwdrivers, and the hacksaw, then fit them back into the tiers of his battered red metal toolbox. When he was down to the comb, before laying it in its accustomed place beside the cigar box of leftover foreign currency, he ran it through his hair.

Chapter Two

H e'll never go," said Carol, rinsing arugula.

"Bullshit," said Jackson, as he stole a piece of Italian sausage from the sautéed peppers. "He's bought the ticket. I've seen it. Or them. I told him not to waste the money on the other two. She'll never go, that's for sure. I figured it out way before Shep did. Glynis thought it was a game, all those trips. A game she got tired of."

"You always think I mean he's too much of a coward. That's not it. He's too responsible. He'll never leave his family high and dry; it's not in him. Pick up his carry-on and never look over his shoulder? Start a whole new life from scratch, when he's almost fifty? Have you ever known anyone to do that really, and why would they anyway? Even if he does go, to make a point or something, he'll come right back home—Flicka, it's been at least half an hour. Have you put in your tears?"

Their elder daughter emitted a nasal sigh, halfway between a groan and a bleat. Its tonalities were refined, managing to convey both no and yes. She rustled begrudgingly into her sweater pocket for the Ziploc, then dosed both eyes from one of several dozen tiny plastic squeeze tubes of Artificial Tears, whose shape always reminded Jackson of Fat

Man dropped on Nagasaki. As usual, Flicka's eyes were aflame, the lashes caked with petroleum jelly.

"What, tail between legs?" said Jackson. "You got no appreciation of male pride."

"Oh, don't I?" Carol shot him a look. "Where is this 'Pemba' anyway?"

"Off the coast of Zanzibar," said Jackson. "It's famous for growing cloves. Whole island stinks of them, or that's what Shep tells me. I picture my man leaning back in his hammock, breathing in the smell of hot whisky and pumpkin pie."

"I bet he'll go," said Flicka. "If he says he's going to. Shep's not a liar." Though often mistaken for her eleven-year-old sibling's younger sister, she was sixteen; just as one calculated the relative age of pets, her true age in terms of human suffering was closer to 103. The here and now having proved an eternal trial, Flicka was naturally captivated by the idea of somewhere else.

Jackson ruffled his daughter's fine blond hair. They'd kept it close-cropped in her childhood to prevent it from becoming constantly contaminated with vomit, but since the fundoplication surgery she could only dry-heave, and Flicka had been letting it grow out. "There's a girl with a little faith!"

"But what would he do?" Carol pressed. "Make clever water fountains for the Third World? Shep's not the kind of man to be happy lying around in a hammock."

"Maybe not fountains, but, hell, he could dig wells. Shep's *useful*. He can't help it. If I was living in a little mud hut, he's the guy I'd want for a next-door neighbor."

"Flicka, get away from the stove!"

"I'm nowhere near the damn stove," said Flicka in her usual slurred deadpan. She always sounded not only adenoidal but slightly drunk, like Stephen Hawking after a bottle of Wild Turkey. She also sounded surly, and that part was real. It was one of the things that Jackson adored about her. She refused to play the sunny, chin-up disabled kid who lit up everybody's day with her amazing pluck.

"Cut it out!" said Carol, removing the paring knife from Flicka's hand and slamming it back on the counter.

Flicka lurched back to the table with a gait that most people considered awkward but that Jackson always found strangely graceful: her trunk slopping to one side and then the other, while her hands compensated with an elegant little flail, feet placed carefully heel to toe as if walking a tightrope. "Whadda ya think," she said. "I'm gonna lop my fingers into the salad 'cause I mistook them for little carrots?"

"That's not funny," said Carol.

It wasn't funny. When Flicka was nine, she'd tried to help out by making coleslaw, and it was only due to the fact that the cabbage had changed varieties—from green to red—that Jackson had noticed the end of her left forefinger was missing. They'd sewn it back on in the ER, but he'd never been able to stomach coleslaw since. Maybe it seemed a mercy that your kid's limbs were so insensitive to pain that stitches required no local anesthetic, but when he forced his co-workers to really think about it, they blanched. Some of these kids, he'd explain, can break a leg, drag it behind them for blocks, and only notice something's wrong because it keeps getting in the way. For Flicka, of course, banging into things and bleeding everywhere was purely an annoyance, along the lines of tearing a hole in a bag of rice and having to sweep up the floor.

"I've never understood why you seem so eager for Shep to leave the country," Carol resumed. "He's your best friend. Wouldn't you miss him?"

"Sure, babe. I'll miss him like a son of a bitch." Jackson grabbed himself a beer, reflecting that one thing he would not miss would be defending Shep to all the doubting Thomases at Knack. (The company was still Knack of All Trades to Jackson, whatever embarrassing, cheesy, goofball name that fat prick wanted to call it.) Maybe he should have waited until Shep was on the plane, but he hadn't been able to contain himself after lunch today when the website designer made another snide remark. So it was with enormous satisfaction that Jackson had announced, no, actually, Shep had already bought the ticket, *loser*, and would never see the inside of this overheated office as of this very afternoon. That had shut up the cretin pronto. Besides, he hadn't introduced the idea to Carol yet, but he had a notion that they could visit when Shep had had a chance to establish himself. In fact, though it wasn't a picture he was willing to confront yet, he'd a hazier notion of taking his family and joining the guy in Pemba for keeps. Obviously, Carol wouldn't think about it now, but there was looming on the horizon a dark time when a change of scene could be therapeutic.

"Still, somebody's gotta be able to get out of here, to do better than this, right?" he continued after a slug, putting his feet up. "Jesus, let the immigrants have it. I love the idea of the whole native population of this big scam of a country packing up, closing the door behind them, and throwing the *teeming masses* the keys. Moving to these hip, super-ethnic villages in Mozambique and Cancun, into all those houses standing vacant because the owners are cleaning toilets in Cleveland. They want to live here so damn much, let 'em. They can work their butts off and pay half their wages to a government that paves the occasional sidewalk if they're lucky, and invades other countries without asking at their personal expense. Where two-bedroom dumps cost more than they'll earn in their entire lifetimes, and their kids are never taught to count but are masters of 'self-esteem'—"

"Jackson, don't start."

"I haven't started. I've *barely* started—"

"You don't want to get Flicka overexcited."

"I making you *overexcited*, Flick?"

"You *stopped* talking about taxes and spongers and 'Mugs and Mooches,'" Flicka drawled. "About how the Asians are taking over the world. How 'nobody in this country makes anything anymore that doesn't break the first time you use it.' How 'we're turning all our kids into pussies'? Then I'd get *overexcited*, yeah."

The girl may have looked ten years old and sounded semi-retarded, but Flicka was a smart cookie—or "high functioning," an expression that had always struck Jackson as insulting. It wasn't fair, since Carol did most of the parental heavy lifting, but Flicka was always in cahoots with her father. She may have been a pale, scrawny kid with limp hair, red blotches, and—a biological network he'd never heard of before her diagnosis—an "autonomic" system on the fritz, while he was a dark, burly, half-Basque tradesman of forty-four, but their emotional default setting was identical: *disgust.*

"Don't you go repeating that stuff about 'the Asians taking over the world' without adding that your dad said they deserve it," Jackson chided; in the presence of anyone who could decode her slurred whine, that kind of charged racial rhetoric could get Flicka, or more to the point her father, into massive trouble. "The Chinese, the Koreans—they work hard and ignore their teachers' sad-ass advice to wait to learn the multiplication tables until they *feel like it.* They're the real Americans, like Americans used to be, and they're colonizing all our top universities not from some patronizing helping hand of affirmative action, but from *merit*—"

As usual, Carol wasn't paying the slightest attention. Fucking off at Knack, he garnered plenty of little-known information on the Web, but his wife figured she'd heard it all before, and dismissed it. *Some* women would be grateful for a man who brought home new, fascinating (if enraging) factoids every day, and who had an unusual, incisive point of view that made (if depressing) sense of the world. But no such luck with Carol, who would apparently have been more content with a docile drudge who credulously washed out his mayonnaise jars even though most of his "recycling" ended up in landfill, who cheerfully donated to the Patrolmen's Benevolent Association in defiance of the fact that the word *benevolent* didn't belong within five miles of a cop, and who championed the sacrifice of nearly all his disposable income to bureaucratic shysters and incompetents as an act of civic-mindedness. In sum, she'd have preferred a husband who bought into the whole brainwashing hoax of "patriotism," which slyly converted an arbitrary accident of birth into the kind of mindless go-team frenzy of pom-pom waving that had driven Jackson to get stoned in stairwells during pep rallies in high school.

Sure, her politics had always been wet, but otherwise Carol didn't used to be like this. When they met she'd been doing the landscape gardening for a house where he also had a big Sheetrock job; they'd found common cause in the owner's being an asshole, and their both being underlings had put them on the same level. So it hadn't been a factor then that, despite the just-out-of-college scut work, she turned out to have a degree in horticulture from Penn State, or that her father (who always thought his daughter had married beneath herself) wasn't any old seat-of-the-pants "handyman" but a property developer. Back on that job, Jackson had been drawn to a pretty woman who wasn't afraid to get her hands dirty, and who hefted her own thirty-pound bags of peat. But most of all he'd liked that she could spar. She disagreed with him on everything, but had seemed to enjoy disagreeing with him, and over beers after work they'd really got into it. Nowadays it was as if she'd summarily won already so why bother, which was a puzzle, since Jackson couldn't remember losing a single argument.

And she never used to exude this killjoy seriousness. She'd been a hoot before, or she'd at least laughed at his jokes, which gave him an even better feeling than laughing at hers. He put it down to Flicka. The responsibility, it changed you. One of the reasons that Carol hardly drank anymore: at any given time their daughter's life might depend on her mother's mind being sharp. It was like being a doctor yourself but without the golf. You were always on call.

So Jackson returned to the subject that at least seemed to engage his wife. "You don't understand why it's so important to me that Shep follows through with his exit from this travesty of 'freedom.' But let's turn it around. Why is it so important to *you* that he doesn't?"

"I didn't say it was 'important' to me," said Carol. "I said he's a kind, considerate person who would never leave his family in the lurch."

Jackson slammed his boot back down on the blue parquet of their Forbo Marmoleum (and who had helped him to install it? *Shep Knacker*). "You just can't *stand* the idea that somebody might get out! That somebody might not trudge through their life like an automaton and march in lockstep to the grave! That there might be such a thing as a *real man*. With courage! With imagination! With *volition*!"

"So you want to pick a fight? Great, that's a surefire, hundred-percent-guaranteed route to upsetting your daughter. But go ahead, make her tense," Carol murmured temperately, with that calmness she had that bordered on insanity. "You're not the one who has to shove the diazepam up her anus because she can't keep down the oral kind."

At the mention of pharmaceuticals, on cue Heather flounced into the kitchen and demanded, "Isn't it time for my cortomalaphrine?" Jackson had no idea; he could never remember if they were pretending she had to take it before or after meals.

"Heather, I've got to get this dinner ready because we're having a guest, who could be here any minute, so why don't you take them when Flicka grinds her meds after we eat."

"But I'm starting to feel funny," Heather objected, introducing a slight weave to her stance. "Dizzy and prickly and sweaty and stuff. I can't concentrate or anything."

"Oh, all right then; pour yourself a glass of milk." Carol unlocked the high cabinet; keeping sugar pills under lock and key was obviously gratuitous, but part of the theater. So was "cortomalaphrine," a name they'd effortlessly made up after years of the Catapres, clonazepam, diazepam, Florinef, Ritalin, ProAmatine, Depakote, Lamictal, and Nexium that filled out Flicka's pill chart like nonsense rhymes from *Alice's Adventures in Wonderland*. "Cortomalaphrine" and its recommended dosage were printed on formal Rx labels. Jackson had been dumbfounded to learn that pharmacists keep sugar-paste placebos as part of their standard stock, so presumably it wasn't only Heather who was scarfing down little brown vials of Good & Plentys at ten bucks a pop.

As Carol shook out three capsules, Jackson looked away. He didn't believe in this crap. Oh, he took Carol's point that Heather always had to assume a backseat to her sister's ceaseless medical crises. But if Heather needed more attention, a fake prescription wasn't the answer. She should be taught to treasure her good health, to be grateful for it. Sure, back when Carol was pregnant with Flicka the labs didn't have a test for familial dysautonomia, and once they were told that the baby was fine they'd relaxed. (Ha ha, big surprise in the offing. When their pediatri-

cian *finally* stopped hiding behind his lame nineteenth-century diagnosis of "failure to thrive" and identified why their newborn couldn't
suckle, was losing weight, and puked all day, that false reassurance from
the first trimester made the news much harder to take.) But Jesus, by
Carol's second pregnancy a test had just been developed, and they already knew the chances of another FD kid were one-in-four; getting
the results of the amnio, they'd been nervous to the point of stroke.
When the obstetrician beamed a big smile and gave them the all-clear,
Heather's mother-to-be was so relieved she cried. Did Heather have any
idea that if her fetus, too, had carried the two copies of the FD gene she
seemed so foolishly to envy she wouldn't be here? Well, no, you didn't
tell children that they had ever been an inch away from an abortion.

And you didn't let your older kid know that, either, since the obvious implication was that if they'd known they'd have marked Flicka
"Return to Sender," too. He wouldn't go so far as to say that they would
have, or should have, but he'd wondered about it. During some of the
worst of it—once the corrective surgery for scoliosis had barely healed,
they then had to break it to her that it was time for a "Nissen fundoplication" to cure her chronic acid reflux—he'd suspected that Flicka was
angry not just in that why-me way, but angry at her parents in particular, who made her be here. Just be here at all.

However much it cost her, he'd assured Flicka many times—and
thanks to her very refusal to embrace that hackneyed angel-of-innocence
shtick, which would have bored her father senseless—that she really did
brighten their lives. It was his fault that she was a brat—a caustic brat,
an entertaining brat, but still a brat. Yet how could you not spoil the girl,
at least a little? As hard as he tried not to see it, FD was a degenerative
condition, and Flicka was duly deteriorating. She used to be so cute. If
she was still cute to her father, he sometimes recognized that her chin
had started to round upward and jut forward like Popeye's, lending her
face a permanent pugnacity. Her smashed-looking nose was growing in
the opposite direction, its tip rounding downward and curving inward,
as if the nose and chin were trying to touch each other. Her mouth had
grown disproportionately wide, her eyes had migrated too far apart, and

as the chin grew up and out she had started resting her front teeth on the outside of her lower lip. He wasn't concerned about her having grown less fetching; he was concerned that these were outward manifestations of something much more dire happening that you couldn't see, something he still didn't quite understand, although it wouldn't matter if he did.

He'd started out thinking about Heather and then ended up thinking about Flicka again, so maybe Carol was right about Heather's feeling neglected. A few sugar pills were probably harmless enough, and she got to name-drop to her friends about taking "cortomalaphrine." Most of the kids at Heather's primary school were drugged to the eyeballs, and apparently a diagnosis was her generation's must-have, the equivalent of fringed suede jackets in the sixties. But what really floored him about this placebo business was that as soon as she started popping those pills Heather, already on the stocky side, had started to put on weight. It wasn't the pills themselves, which couldn't have been more than five calories apiece; it was pure suggestion. All her classmates on antipsychotics and antidepressants and every other anti-be-difficult prescription were porkwads.

Jackson was disheartened to detect that already at eleven Heather showed signs of being a joiner. He'd never understood this impulse to be just like everybody else when everybody else was a fucking moron. Even as a boy, Jackson had always wanted to stand out; his daughters' peers seemed driven to blend in. The sole exceptions, the only truly ambitious kids determined to draw attention to themselves as a cut above, clinked to school with an arsenal under their trench coats.

On the other hand, maybe he was more of a conformist than he liked to admit. Take Heather's name. They'd picked it because they thought it was unusual. Now there were three other Heathers in her class. What was it with this name thing? You think you've never heard it before, but it's in the air or something, like a smell or a gas, and meanwhile every other pregnant couple on the block is deciding to name their kid Heather because it's *unusual*. At least by some miracle their firstborn's high school wasn't chockfull of Flickas. Thank fuck for Carol's hang-up on stupid horse books as a kid. Look at you, he kicked himself. Flicka again. You can't keep thinking about your second daughter for ten seconds. Still, there was sure to come a time, no telling how soon, when he would have to think about Heather because Heather was the only daughter he had.

"Jackson, should I go ahead and feed the kids? It's getting late."

"Yeah, probably. Shep and Glynis likely got into a thing. If I know Glynis, she won't let him go without a fight. No telling when he'll get here, really."

"Sweetheart," Carol said gently. "You should prepare yourself for the possibility that he gets cold feet. Or sobers up and realizes that he has a son and a wife and a life, and this Pemba thing is ridiculous. Cloves. I mean, really." It was a particularly female form of condescension: men and their juvenile notions, their vain, impractical little projects.

Jackson glared. It was one more of those moments when looking at his wife was an outright torture. She was unbelievably beautiful. It sounded mean-spirited, but he'd been a little exasperated that as she'd grown older she'd remained as sexy as ever, tall—taller than he was—with long amber hair and perfect round breasts the size of halved grapefruits. She never gained an ounce. Not from dieting or jogging either, but from hauling eighty-five pounds of writhing, gagging human flesh to an upstairs bed or emergency room. He was no longer sure whether Carol's face had always been set in that serene, impassive expression, as if carved in marble, or if she had developed that stillness and infuriating composure in order to project a soothing, tranquil presence for Flicka. In any event, for years now she'd been so hard to rile that she inspired him to try.

He was always proud to be seen with her in the company of other men and their washed-out, lumpy wives, but here at home the only adult for Carol to be better looking than was her husband. He wasn't outright ugly or anything, but he worried that they were one of those couples about whom other people wondered in private, *Carol's a knockout, but what did she ever see in him? Why would such a fox pick a short, stocky working-class stiff with hair on his shoulders?* He'd read somewhere that one of the things that made for a successful marriage was that both parties were roughly the same level of physical attractiveness, which had made him nervous. Most men would think him crazy, but he wished she were a shade homelier. The fact that *homelier* and *homier* shared so many letters didn't seem a coincidence.

Jackson laid out plates for the kids, catching Flicka's look of dread. Sausage and peppers was one of Carol's signature dishes, always a crowd-pleaser, but fennel seed and garlic were wasted on Flicka. With little sense of smell and a tongue smooth as shoehorn, she couldn't taste for shit. She may have learned, painstakingly, to fold down her epiglottis to prevent food from leaking into the trachea, but she still chewed every bite so long that she might have been gnawing her way through the table itself, and if her mother turned her back for an instant she'd scrape the remains of her plate in the trash. The weird truth was that she made no association between hunger and food. Accordingly, she found the amount of time squandered on cooking bafflingly disproportionate. The cultural folderol to do with eating—separate salad bowls and fish forks, anguish over orders in restaurants, shared disappointment over a soggy homemade pizza crust that was keen enough to ruin an evening—was as impenetrable to Flicka as the sacrificial rituals of an arcane animist cult. Her chunky sister's stuffing down chocolate when the organism didn't strictly require more calories seemed simply nonsensical, as if Heather were continuing to squeeze the nozzle when gas was bubbling out the cap and running down the side of the car.

"Flicka, I made you a separate portion, without any sauce."

"Keep it," said Flicka sullenly. "I can just load in a can of Compleat."

"I don't want to have this fight with you every night." Carol's delivery was so smooth that anyone listening would have thought, what fight?

"Yeah, yeah, the family that swallows together stays together. Makes a *lot* of sense."

"Your feeding therapist says you have to try to eat something every day, and that serving is very small. Being able to eat even a little bit is important for making friends."

Flicka's intended snort came out more like a gurgle, and she wiped the drool from her chin with the terrycloth sweatband on her right wrist.

Since it was always soaked, the rash underneath had grown chronic. "What friends?"

"We pay for that therapist out of our own pockets—"

"Yeah, well how'd you like some goon sticking their fingers in your mouth all the time? Karen Berkley's not for me, but for you—"

"*Just eat it.*" Good Lord, Carol almost sounded flustered.

After filching into her school backpack for a large battered Ziploc, Flicka pulled herself up with Carol's cornflower-print curtains and lurched to the small pan of undressed sausage and peppers on the counter. Before Carol could stop her, she'd upended the pan in the blender, sloshed in two mugs of water, and turned the appliance on high. The meal churned to an aerated brownish pink that immediately put Jackson off his dinner. With a malignant glint in the Vaseline around her eyes, she fastened the wide-bore syringe to its clear extension tubing, the other end of which she connected to the capped plastic port on her stomach— one not much different from the screw-off pour spouts on cartons of Tropicana. She removed the plunger and drained a measure of the blitzed pink gunk into the plastic syringe. Its clamp released, the tube's translucence made it all too easy to follow the progress of the vomit-colored drizzle. Flick raised the syringe high in her right hand with a victorious look on her face, like the goddamned Statue of Liberty.

Okay, it was hostile. Rubbing salt in the insult, Flicka announced, "I'm eating it."

"That tubing will be very difficult to clean," said Carol, giving in to a hint of iciness as the phone began to ring. "Sweetheart, could you please get that? It seems I have some tidying up to do."

Well, that's that," Jackson announced curtly on return to the kitchen. "He's not coming."

"He's not coming, or he's not going?"

"Neither."

Carol fetched two more plates, and he caught a flicker in her face.

"So what makes you so fucking happy about that?"

"I didn't say anything!"

"You're *glad*, aren't you?"

Carol nodded discreetly in Flicka's direction, and shook her head. He may have been shouting. "I'm glad," she said, her voice like a spatula spreading cream-cheese icing, "for Glynis."

"Don't be."

Though Handy Randy had expanded into other boroughs, the main office and supply warehouse were still on Seventh Avenue in Park Slope, less than a mile from Windsor Terrace. Since he could walk to work, it wasn't hard for Jackson to arrive early the following Monday, hoping to ensure that when Shep walked in the wisecracks would keep to a minimum. He deliberately projected a protective air of pent-up explosiveness and impending violence, which under the circumstances came naturally enough. Still, the atmosphere in the office was of barely suppressed hilarity; the accountant, the Web page designer, the dispatcher—everyone down to the receptionist wore expressions as if they were stuffing fists in their mouths to keep from busting out laughing. When Shep did walk in, he didn't appear to make anything of the fact that the rest of the staff suddenly fell silent, and he glided toward his cubicle with a robotic passivity that seemed familiar; maybe Shep and Carol had something temperamental in common. No matter what life threw at him—"life" was a gentle way of putting it; other people, more like it—Shep absorbed it, like that blithe, look-the-other way shit his family pulled when he paid for his mother's funeral, from casket to pâté, as if covering all those expenses was like farting and you didn't mention it in polite company. When Mark, the website guy whom Jackson had put in his place on Friday, asked archly, "What, no suntan?" Shep returned mildly that the weekend had been overcast. He sat at his terminal and checked his email for complaints; Jackson could tell at a glance from across the room that there were plenty.

It was hot. Jackson had learned to wear short sleeves in the winter months, or he'd have come home drenched. Pogatchnik kept the heat cranked up full blast, if only to irritate Shep, who deplored the waste. According to their dickhead boss, waste was the point: a business that kept its premises tropical in January and arctic in August encouraged customers to feel confident that the enterprise was thriving. It was a sign of prosperity, just as fat used to be a badge of affluence: once you could afford to overeat; now you could afford to overheat. Shep had countered that he couldn't understand why any red-blooded creature would be comfortable at eighty-five degrees in one season and fifty-five in another, but every position Shep ever took with Pogatchnik backfired, and the last time Shep had politely requested that they lower the thermostat the setting went up another two degrees. For that matter, just about every innovation Pogatchnik had installed was specifically tailored to goad Shep Knacker, down to the special seminar on "Getting Along with Difficult Co-Workers," when Pogatchnik himself was the difficult co-worker.

Their boss finally deigned to shamble in at 11:00 a.m. He headed straight to Shep's cubicle. "Seems like you owe me an apology, Knacker."

"Yes, I do," Shep said stonily.

"So?"

"I apologize."

Pogatchnik continued to loom over Shep's desk, as if wanting something more.

"I *humbly* apologize," Shep provided. "I may have had a bad day."

"Just because you used to own this outfit when it was an itty-bitty local operation doesn't give you special rights. I'll cut you slack this time, but any other employee I'd have shown the door. In fact, since you *are* any other employee—"

"I appreciate the second chance. I never expect special consideration. It won't happen again."

Listening to this grotesque public shit-eating from twenty feet, Jackson had a good grasp of why employees were arriving at work with canvas bags full of automatics all across the nation. The "itty-bitty local operation" was particularly hard to take. Shep had sold Knack of All Trades right around the time that the World Wide Web was just taking off big time, and how was he to know that the handyman biz would burgeon online? After Pogatchnik registered the domain name www.handiman .com (www.handyman.com had already been taken, but they got all the clients who couldn't spell; this being America, that hadn't curtailed their business in the slightest), their customer base exploded. Pogatchnik took all the credit, as if he'd invented the Internet itself, like Al Gore. Now the company was probably worth four times what that pond scum had paid for it, and Pogatchnik had started running television ads of himself tunelessly belting an excruciating variation on Sammy Davis, Jr., "The handyman, oh, the handyman can!" that drove Jackson to change the channel with an urgency bordering on hysteria. It had seemed so cool at the time, that check for a million smackers, and now it turned out that selling Knack was the dopiest thing Shep had ever done.

When the two grabbed their customary sandwiches at a café up the street—Jackson could have lived without all the buffalo mozzarella and prosciutto nonsense, aka ham and cheese—he had to ask: "What was all that mea culpa ass-lick with Pogatchnik?"

Shep was always a contained character, but even for Shep his affect all morning had been inhumanly flat, cooperative to the point of non-existence. As if you could run him through the paces of a DUI stop and he'd touch his nose for you and stand on one leg and count back from a hundred by sevens and it wouldn't matter that you weren't a cop and he hadn't even been driving.

"Oh, that," said Shep in a monotone. "When I left Handy Randy on Friday"—the guy never called the company Handy Randy, he always called it Knack; Christ, the poor chump sounded like Paul Newman in *Cool Hand Luke* after he's been in that tiny sweat box for days and he says, *Yah sir, yah sir*, because his will is broken—"I think I said something like, 'So long, asshole.' It was an indulgence. I didn't think I was coming back."

"Okay, I can see saying sorry, but did you have to crawl?"

"Yes, I did."

Jackson thought about it. "Health insurance."

"That's right." Shep took one bite of his sandwich and put it down again. "Correct me if I'm wrong, but I got the impression that my colleagues were aware that I'd originally planned on an excursion. The fact that I came to work today seemed to be the source of some amusement."

"Look, I'm sorry. Last week Mark was being sarcastic again, and—I guess I should have kept my trap shut. But I was so sure you were really going to go this time . . . I'm not making any excuses, but it would have been easier on both of us if you'd kept your grand plan to yourself years ago until you were good and ready to press the Eject button."

"Years ago there was no reason for me to keep it quiet. It was just what I was going to do."

"Still, I wish you'd let me tell the staff at Knack, about Glynis. Not let them think you didn't go to Pemba because you're chicken, or some loony fantasist. They'd give you a lot less grief."

"Glynis doesn't want it out. I got permission to tell you and Carol. But otherwise, it's her business. I'm not going to use her to make my work life more agreeable. It isn't agreeable anyway and it never will be, so really it doesn't make any difference."

"Why do you suppose she wants to keep it a secret?"

Shep shrugged. "She's private. And letting it be common knowledge makes it real."

"But it is real."

"All too," said Shep.

"Listen," said Jackson as they headed back. "You want to swing by the house for a beer before you drive back to Elmsford?"

It was obvious that the prospect of doing anything for fun or for comfort or for any reason that had to do with himself and what he might "want" had become foreign to Shepherd Knacker overnight, but Jackson had asked him to do something, so he would do it. "Sure," he said.

can't stay long," Shep warned as he drove them to Windsor Terrace.

"That's all right. We have to meet with that FD support group at nine anyway. Which I dread. Oh, it would be okay if it were only sharing info on the side effects of medication and stuff. It's the whole Jewish thing that gets a bit much. I mean, don't take me wrong, I'm not one of those 'self-hating Jews.' I'm just not especially, well, Jewish." Jackson was babbling, but with a zombie at the wheel someone had to say something. "My mother isn't observant, and my father has this Basque thing going, which is kind of cool—not that I'd blow up any Spanish politicians over it or anything. And then Carol, well, she was raised Catholic. She had *one grandfather* on her father's side who was Ashkenazi. So we get all this pressure at the support group to stuff Flicka full of gefilte fish, and technically Flicka's not even Jewish.

"And these Orthodox loons . . . When they get married, the couples refuse to get the DNA test. Even after they've had an FD kid, they won't get amnio. There's a family in Crown Heights has *three* of them. Perfect punishment for being that stupid. Because, sure, Jews are down on abortion. But despite that, the rabbis in *every* form of Judaism—reform to ultra-orthodox? They all tell you that if the fetus has FD, get rid of it. Like, God doesn't want them to suffer. It's that bad.

"It just slays me, you know? Supposedly it's the Jewish *faith*, and you'd think you could choose, right, what you believe in? But no. These fucking genes have been stalking me, man, one generation after another. It's like being mugged by a rabbi." Considering, Jackson shouldn't be complaining about anything on his own account, and he shut up.

Carol and Shep hugged, and Carol said she was so, so sorry. Settling in the kitchen, Shep explained that he'd spent most of the weekend on the Internet, and told them what he knew. He said he was taking a personal day at the end of the week, to go in with Glynis and meet with an oncologist, after which they'd be better informed. Carol asked how he thought Glynis was taking it, and Shep said that she was pissed off but that she was always pissed off, so it was hard to tell. Then Carol asked how Shep was taking it, and he seemed to find the question irrelevant. Obviously I'm scared, he said, but I can't afford to be scared, or to be anything else, either. I'm the one who has to keep it together. So it doesn't matter how I am. *I don't matter anymore.* It was the first thing he'd said all day with real passion.

Carol commiserated over Pemba, though Shep knew perfectly well that she'd thought the whole idea was nuts. He said that deep-sixing his "Afterlife" already seemed like small potatoes, like something that happened a long time ago. He said that the only good aspect of this awful turn of the wheel was realizing what was important. Now he didn't have to decide whether to leave or not, because as soon as Glynis told him there was no decision. There was no Pemba. It was as if the whole island had sunk into the sea. You wouldn't think it, he said, but I've never experienced any other moment in my life in which everything suddenly got so simple. Shep wondered aloud whether this thing happening out of the blue amounted to a sick sort of divine intervention. He hadn't wanted to go to Pemba without Glynis and Zach. He shouldn't have gone without them and now he couldn't. It was neat and clear. So in this sense the game changer was a relief. The lack of hesitation. The great, glaring obviousness of what he had to do. And wanted to do, Shep added emphatically. Glynis needs me. Maybe she did before, too, but it wasn't as apparent. When Shep said that your wife needing you, it's a good feeling, Jackson felt a stab of envy that he didn't understand.

Shep wasn't commonly this confiding. He wasn't a heartless person, far from it, but he was like a lot of guys. It was a perfectly decent way of being, in Jackson's view, a dignified way of being: he tended to let other people take his deepest feelings for granted. He didn't name them or wear them on his sleeve. So when he spelled out that he loved Glynis and had not realized until now how much, that now he was remorseful about what he had planned to do when only last week he had cast it as last-ditch self-salvation, Jackson was both offended, and moved. Jackson thought about how much Flicka had changed him and Carol, and how some of that change was bad, like getting so under-slept from the late-night feeding regime that they rarely had sex, but how some of the change was good, too. They had an imperative. They were doing something together that was more vital than sex, and even more intimate, it turned out, which had surprised him. So maybe your wife announcing that she could be about to die would have a similar effect of rearranging everything, focusing everything, and bringing you together in a way that wasn't totally, hopelessly, and unremittingly terrible.

Still, when Shep went on about how glad he was that he no longer had to take responsibility for "abandoning Glynis" and "abandoning his son," Jackson was taken aback; he had never before heard his friend use that harsh and unforgiving word when describing his intentions: *abandon*. Shep said that the diagnosis "took this cup from him," as his father would have said, and Jackson thought, but kept to himself, that the one transformation he was *not* up for was Shep suddenly going all Christian on him. Instead Jackson said that's funny, you get out of responsibility by having it dumped in your lap wholesale. Shep said yes, but I feel more like myself now. More normal. Doing the right thing. Taking care of my wife. I did think, Carol hazarded, that walking off into the sunset wasn't like you. No, said Shep, with a tinge of sorrow. It certainly wasn't like me. Anyway, said Carol. You know what they say about life and making other plans. Yes, Shep agreed, it's surprising that we bother to make them. In sounding so philosophical he also sounded older, and there was a boyishness in his best friend that Jackson noticed only now that it was gone.

But with your better cut of people, trouble reminded them that everyone had troubles, that there was an everyone. So Shep didn't stay on Glynis and Pemba, but asked after Flicka—the girls were upstairs doing their homework—and had the decency to ask after Heather, too. He even asked about Carol's work, which hardly anyone did because it was so dull, and he wondered whether Carol missed landscape gardening. Yes, she did miss it, she said, doing something physical, involved with the earth. Shep said that he felt the same way, that he missed fixing things, making people's lives palpably better and seeing the results of his labor, instead of arranging to clean up someone else's botched job over the phone. He apologized, but he couldn't remember; he knew that Carol went to work for sales at IBM partly because they let her operate from any computer terminal she liked, be that at home or in Tahiti; she could put in whichever and however many hours she wanted, so long she did the work—a policy that they all agreed with a laugh shouldn't be revolutionary but was, that the criterion for performing a job was getting it done. Still, the landscaping had been freelance, with flexible hours, too, and she'd not had a problem, as Shep remembered, being home by the time the girls returned from school, ferrying Flicka to therapists, even rushing her to the ER. Had it really been worth the sacrifice, he asked, for a bigger paycheck? Jackson suppressed an irritation; it bothered him that Carol made more money than he did, as it bothered him that she'd had to give up work that she loved for the reason she had, but everything between men and women was meant to have changed, and this stuff wasn't supposed to bother him.

"Oh, it wasn't really for a better salary that I took the job with IBM," Carol explained. "When Randy took over Knack—you know what a corner-cutter he is, what a bottom-liner—he switched to a cheaper health plan. With all our expenses with Flicka, the therapies and surgeries and bouts in the hospital, we couldn't depend on Jackson's coverage anymore.

"See," she went on, "this World Wellness Group outfit is the health insurance company from hell. They levy co-pays on everything, including the meds, and we have to fill dozens of prescriptions every month. With their whopping deductible, you're out five grand before you're reimbursed a dime. Their idea of a 'reasonable and customary' fee is what a doctor's visit cost in 1959, and then they stick you with the shortfall. They're way too restrictive about going out of network, and Flicka requires very specialized care. Then there's co-insurance on top of the co-pays: twenty percent of the total bill, and that's *in network*. And here's the killer: there's no cap on out-of-pocket expenses. Add to that that their lifetime payment cap—you know, how much they'll fork out in total, ever—is also pretty low, only two or three million, when someone like Flicka could easily exceed numbers like that before she's twenty . . . Well, we had to find other coverage."

"Gosh, I had no idea."

"But you should know, Shep," said Carol. "It's your insurance, too."

Chapter Three

Shepherd Armstrong Knacker
Merrill Lynch Account Number 934-23F917
December 01, 2004 – December 31, 2004
Net Portfolio Value: $731,778.56

While they drove to Phelps Memorial in Sleepy Hollow, Shep kept one hand on the wheel, the other in his wife's. Their clasp was relaxed; her palm was dry. They both stared straight ahead.

"It wasn't necessary," he said, "for you to go through the diagnostics on your own."

"You were off in your own little world," she said. "So I went off in mine."

"You must have felt lonely."

"Yes," she said. "But I had been feeling that way for some time."

By the next exit, she added, "You're a planner, Shepherd. You always look before you leap. Really, you leap before you leap. In your head, you took that plane to Tanzania months ago."

He was relieved that she was talking to him at all. He was willing to be castigated, glad for it.

To his horror, Glynis had already been subjected to abdominal X rays, a CAT scan, and an MRI. Memories fell into place. On two mornings in December she had declined not only breakfast but even coffee, which for Glynis was unheard of. He couldn't recall the excuse, but it mustn't have been persuasive, because the refusal of coffee in particular had injured him; she had spurned one of the sacred rituals of their day. On two evenings, she had kept rising for another drink of water, and yet another. So she'd not been quenching a powerful thirst, but rinsing contrast medium from her veins. Likewise one odd, floating memory finally lodged into an orderly narrative: of walking into the bathroom before she had a chance to flush, and noticing that the bowl was red. It had been awfully early in her cycle, but she was fifty, perhaps getting irregular; aware that she was touchy about the approach of menopause, he hadn't passed comment. Now he realized: that was not her period. He also realized that she had started to wear a nightgown to bed not, as she had claimed, because she was cold; it was to hide the laparoscopy scar on her belly, which he had now seen. Though only an inch long, it alarmed him: a first violation, and not the last. The nightgown had injured him, too. They had slept for twenty-six years skin to skin.

Since that signal Friday evening a week ago, she had shared only bits and pieces about the tests. So her mention that weekend of one small technicality had stood out. Before the MRI, for which all jewelry must be removed, they had to do an extra X ray before sliding his wife into the tube. "Because they learned I was a metalsmith," she'd said. "The imaging is magnetic. Metal screws it up. You can't have any fragments or filings stuck to your body."

He should have recognized why she had told him this: because she was proud. He shouldn't have asked her, "So did they find any?" An effective but infuriating gambit increasing in frequency, she hadn't responded to his question at all, which in this case meant no. They found no fragments or filings. She had worked so little in her studio for months that she could have taken the MRI just like anyone else. Even at such a juncture, he'd had to rub it in.

Your own little world. Her subterfuge would never have succeeded without his corresponding neglect. If he had noticed that despite the recent fullness around her stomach she'd grown thinner, he had made little of the observation, which was as good as not having noticed. He thought, I'd no idea that our marriage was in such disrepair, and then he remembered that until last Friday evening he was planning to leave her.

"That night," he said. "You didn't have to let me go on like that, about Pemba. You could have stopped me."

"I was interested."

"It wasn't nice."

"I haven't been feeling," she said, "*nice*."

"How *do* you feel?" Shep was ashamed. In the last week he'd been so-licitous, perhaps annoyingly so. Yet in the months beforehand he could not remember the last time he had asked her how she felt.

She took a moment. "Frightened. For some reason it was easier when you didn't know."

"That's because you can give yourself permission, now, to be fright-ened." He pressed her hand, just. "I will take care of you." It was a big promise, one he would fail. But he would fail valiantly, and that was the promise he made to himself.

Dr. Edward Knox extended a hand to Shep, his clasp firm and gener-ous. The oncologist gave off the astringent tang of antiseptic, as if he were one of those rare physicians who really did wash his hands. It was a smell Shep associated with anxiety. "Mr. Knacker, I'm so pleased that you could finally arrange to join us."

In this phrasing Shep detected reproof, and his wife's outrageous misrepresentations. In other circumstances, he would have taken her to task for them. Since now he would not, he sensed that taking her to task for anything was now pretty much a thing of the past.

The familiar air with which Glynis took a chair indicated that she had been in this office before. These two had a history together, and though Shep was "finally" here he felt excluded. He got the peculiar impression that for Glynis this office was a seat of power.

As the doctor assumed his swivel chair, Shep adjudged that the oncol-ogist may have been in his latter thirties, although he'd grown ever less certain about ages. While he could still tell the difference between sixty and sixty-five, lately his juniors all entered an undifferentiated category of Younger Than Me, which was odd, since he had been that age before, knew what it felt like and how it appeared in the mirror. But from the perspective of a greater age it always turned out that you hadn't, at the time, understood being thirty-seven at all, what it was, what it looked like. Unfortunately for current circumstances, younger people always seemed callow to Shep now, their confidence, which Dr. Knox radiated in pulses, hollow and unjustified—that is, enviably self-deceiving. Still Shep wanted to believe in this man, and rather hoped that with friends he went by "Edward" and not by the flip, less reliable-sounding "Ed." Fit and trim, Knox probably chose fruit for dessert in the cafeteria and made time for the treadmill in the hospital gym; he practiced what he preached. Personally Shep always had a soft spot for medical practitio-ners who carried twenty surplus pounds and sneaked cigarettes in the staff parking lot. The hypocrisy was reassuring. From doctors, Shep had always sought less authority than forgiveness.

"I apologize that it's taken us so long to arrive at a positive diagnosis," Dr. Knox began, addressing himself to Shep. "Mesothelioma is notori-ously difficult to identify, and we had to rule out a host of other more commonplace explanations for your wife's fever, tenderness, abdominal swelling, and gastric dysmotility." Shep didn't know what *dysmotility* meant, but he didn't ask, because then the doctor would know that this was one more of his wife's symptoms that he hadn't known about, or cared about, or noticed.

"After all, as I'm sure your wife has told you, peritoneal mesothe-lioma is very rare," Dr. Knox continued. "And I won't mislead you. It's also very serious. Because the peritoneum is a very fine membrane sur-rounding the abdominal organs, almost like Saran Wrap, diseased tis-sue can be tucked into corners that are difficult or impossible to get at surgically." Shep admired the doctor's locution, which at least pretended that of course Shep knew what the peritoneum was; Knox was loath to imply that his patient's husband paid so little heed to his own wife's grave medical distress that he wouldn't bother to look up her diagnosis in a dictionary. "And I'm sorry to say that symptoms of mesothelioma don't generally make themselves felt until the cancer is fairly advanced. Nevertheless, we have a range of therapies at our disposal. New treatments, new approaches, and new drugs are being developed all the time. The survival rate has done nothing but improve."

Shep knew all of this from the Internet, but felt it would appear impertinent for him to say so. Besides, it seemed important to allow the oncologist this formal introduction. Shep had already read enough to have registered that most of the nostrums in Knox's grab bag of tricks were poisons. In the face of being able to do so little, it must have been comforting to the doctor to seem to be useful in this discursive way. His manner methodical but warm—he smiled encouragingly and looked Shep in the eye—Edward Knox had struck Shep from the start as very kind.

But even when doctors *acted* kind, the extent of their capacity to *be* kind was often out of their hands. However gently put, many a message that physicians were forced to deliver was cruel, and if it did not feel cruel it was a lie and thus was even crueler. Personally Shep didn't understand why anyone would want to be one. Oh, certainly the tasks of stenting an artery and clearing a bathtub drain were technically akin. Yet a doctor was like a handyman who, some appreciable percentage of the time, had to knock on your door and say, I'm sorry, but I cannot clear your drain. That's all the acting kind was good for: the *I'm sorry* part. And then he walks away and maybe he waves, leaving you with scummy standing water in your bath. Why would anyone want a job like that.

"And I do have some good news," Knox continued. "First, as I assured you last week, Mrs. Knacker, the MRI did not reveal any anomalies in the pleural—in the lungs. Even more critically, I now have the lab report from the laparoscopy. Mesothelioma comes in two flavors, if you will—two types of malignant cells. The epithelioid are less aggressive, the sarcomatoid much more so. In the samples we extracted, only epithelioid cells were detected. That makes the prognosis considerably more optimistic."

Glynis gave a schoolgirl nod, as if she had done something right. Shep was about to ask, so what prognosis is that? He opened his mouth and it was dry. He closed it, and swallowed. Instead he said, wanting to be grateful, to play his part, to enter into the spirit of gung ho that was clearly expected here, "Yes. That sounds like very good news."

At once, he could not help but reflect that only a week ago "good news" comprised the value of his Merrill Lynch portfolio increasing by $23,400 without his lifting a finger. Their son finally passing second-year algebra. Randy Pogatchnik playing hooky at some golf resort, so that for three days working at Knack would be, if not quite the same as the olden days, at least collegial. Glynis being in a playful, indolent mood he could barely remember now, and up for watching an old episode of *The Sopranos*. Now on a dime he was expected to enter a world in which "good news" comprised his wife's abdomen coursing with vicious "epithelioid" cells rather than the even more vicious "sarcomatoid" kind and this information was meant to cheer him.

"As for where we go from here," said the doctor, "you may want to commission a second opinion. It's always possible that other specialists will recommend an alternative approach, but I thought I'd prepare you for the standard course of treatment for epithelioid mesothelioma. Assuming the diagnosis is confirmed, Mrs. Knacker, you'll probably be scheduled for debulking surgery as soon as possible. This is to remove as much of the cancer as can be reached. We've located three patches of diseased tissue in the peritoneum. I'm afraid that the surgeons I have consulted concur that one of those patches is inaccessible. Both to shrink the little bit we can't reach and to discourage further malignant cell growth, chemotherapy will almost certainly have to follow once you've recovered from the operation. To that purpose, a thoracic surgeon will install two ports in your abdomen. This way we can deliver intraperitoneal infusions of heated cisplatin that will wash over your organs, rather than administering chemotherapy through your bloodstream. Unpleasant side effects with this direct application should be markedly less pronounced."

"Does that mean I won't lose my hair?" asked Glynis, reflexively touching her crown, as if to make sure her hair was still there.

A shadow crossed the oncologist's face, a sadness, a pitying, into which Shep could read that such a small damage to his patient's vanity was bound to be the least of Glynis's problems. "Patients react differently to treatments," he said gently. "There's no way to predict."

"Besides, it grows back, doesn't it?" said Shep. This was the role. He was supposed to be upbeat.

A second shadow, and this time one that Shep could not decode. "Yes, once treatments are completed, it certainly does," said Dr. Knox, seeming to rouse himself. "Some patients find it grows back in even more thickly than before."

Shep had the sudden impression that this visit, if not the whole song and dance from the X rays and the CAT scan to all the scalpels and "abdominal ports" and vile medications to come, was a farce, a macabre charade. As helpful and soothing as this doctor was trying to be, Shep felt distinctly humored. In turn, he also felt co-opted into a collusion with the doctor, whereby together they were humoring his wife. The joke was on Glynis. It was a wicked joke, a despicable joke, for which she would pay with every fiber of her being. He did not want to be a part of it. He would be a part of it.

"But before we go any further?" the oncologist continued. "Because this is such an unusual cancer, I have limited experience with the disease. Phelps Memorial has seen only two cases in the last twenty years. However, there's a specialist in internal medicine at Columbia-Presbyterian, who works in tandem with a skillful surgeon. They both have extensive clinical experience with mesothelioma, and have a terrific reputation."

"Are you trying to get rid of us?" said Shep with a strained smile.

Dr. Knox smiled back. "You could say that. Mesothelioma patients come to Philip Goldman from all over the world. You're lucky, because for you two he's effectively right next door. Now, he doesn't come cheap. It's likely as well that he'll be out-of-network for your insurance. You'd need to get permission from your insurer if you want them to fully cover an out-of-network physician, and you'd certainly have a good case. But even if your provider declined, I'd urge you to consider Dr. Goldman.

Your insurer would still pick up most of the bill; I don't know the specifics of your health plan, but you might just be levied a higher percentage of co-insurance. And given the stakes . . . Well, I assume that money is no object."

"Of course it isn't," Shep found himself saying. "We'll pay whatever it takes to get Glynis well again." Given his wife's milk-money income from a chocolatier, the *we* was more farce. That the *well again* might also qualify as farce Shep was not yet prepared to contemplate.

Nevertheless, as Knox wrote out the contact details of this famously expensive shaman of the black arts, Shep considered this quantity now officially of "no object." Of course it had no value by itself. Money was a means. But to ends not readily dismissed as "no object." Food, shelter, clothing. Safety, insofar as there was such a thing, and thus also the capacity for rescue. Efficacy, power, sway. Ease, freedom, choice. Generosity, charity; if not love, for his children, wife, sister, and father, the palpable evidence of love. Education; if not wisdom, its prerequisite of accurate information. If not happiness, comfort, which could stand in for happiness in a pinch. Airplane tickets—experience, beauty, and escape. From the description of their apparent savior in Columbia-Presbyterian, raw, animal survival. For in the face of a virulent cancer, they would not simply follow directions, and marshal their forces of will; they would buy life. They would buy Glynis's life, day by costly day, and in the end you would be able to affix a price tag to every one.

"So far, do either of you have any questions?" asked Dr. Knox.

"The side effects . . ." said Glynis. Of course, there was nothing "side" about them. They were effects—big, brutal, and anything but ancillary.

"Each drug and each patient is different. You'll be alerted what to be prepared for, I promise. Let's get through the surgery first. Not get ahead of ourselves."

In the proceeding silence, Shep looked to his wife, then to the oncologist, beginning to panic. He did not want to shake hands and find himself in the car and have the omission, the elision, the craven evasion, steeping the inside of the vehicle like toxic emission fumes. But he also did not understand why he had to be the one to ask. Glynis might have raised this obvious matter before, but if so she hadn't shared with him the upshot of such a discussion, and that seemed impossible.

When trying to get up to speed about a disease he'd never heard of before last Friday, through the following weekend Shep had spent hours at the computer. Know thy enemy, he figured. Yet on one medical Web page, well into its patient, hand-holding explanations of every test and treatment that mesothelioma patients might expect, he had finally arrived at a section headed "Survival Rates." He had nearly memorized the first paragraph, having stared it down for so long:

> Following on this page is quite detailed information about the survival rates of different stages of mesothelioma. We have included it because many people have asked us for this. But not everyone who is diagnosed with a cancer wishes to read this type of information. If you are not sure whether you want to know at the moment or not, then perhaps you might like to skip this page for now. You can always come back to it.

It was his initial impression that the authors of the text were being patronizing. His first impulse was to scroll down. He had always faced difficulty squarely. But this was different, if only because it was not his difficulty. It was bound, at points, to seem like his difficulty, but he would have to be mindful about that. Still, there was no question that as that paragraph burned on the screen, what bloomed in his gut was terror. He reached for the mouse. He withdrew his hand from the mouse. He did not scroll down. Taking the page's advice, *skip this page*, he had returned to the same point on the same website three other times. He had never scrolled down. He wasn't ready. In this office, with a fellow human being who could speak with all that useless kindness, it was time to scroll down.

"What are her chances," said Shep, so leadenly that he was unable to lift the end of the sentence to imply the interrogative. "How long." This was no juncture at which to be unclear. He formed the question fully. "How long has my wife got to live."

But it was Glynis who spoke. "There's no way to say. Every patient is different, you heard the doctor. Every patient reacts differently, and, as he said, new drugs are coming on the market all the time."

His glance darting between them, Dr. Knox seemed to appraise the couple carefully. "It's important to remain optimistic. I've often been pressed for a specific prognosis, and even when I've relented I can't tell you how often I've been wrong. How many times I've predicted that a patient had such-and-such an amount of time left, and then years beyond the point at which I'd have expected to be sending flowers they're thrashing their best friends at squash."

"And it helps, you said," said Glynis, "that I'm in very good health to begin with. I'm not overweight, my cholesterol is good, I exercise, I don't have any complicating conditions, and I'm barely fifty years old."

"Absolutely," Dr. Knox chimed in. "Committing to a specific doomsday date is like going to war and choosing ahead of time the day on which you plan to lose. In medicine just as in the military, it's a positive attitude that gets results."

Shep was familiar with this talk of illness as armed confrontation: the "battle" with cancer, whose patients are invariably classified as "real fighters," with "an arsenal" of treatments at their disposal with which to "defeat" an invasion of wayward cells. But the analogy felt wrong. His small experience so far was more one of bad weather. So it was as if the doctor had declared they would "go to war" with a snowstorm, or a gale wind.

"Yes, well, I didn't mean to sound pessimistic, and there must be a huge variation . . ." Shep dutifully backed down. Still, he was surprised. Given her ferocity, her defiance, her darkness—of the two, he was far more constitutionally inclined toward the very optimism that Knox was promoting—he would have classed Glynis as the scroll-down type. Doubtless there were more things he would find out about her as this proceeded. Maybe you never really knew anyone until they were dying.

Thus blocked from "getting ahead of themselves," Shep worked backward.

"Asbestos," he said. He found it odd that they had spoken so long without anyone mentioning the word. "Mesothelioma is associated

almost exclusively with asbestos. How could my wife have been exposed to that?"

"She and I have discussed this, and I'm afraid we didn't solve the mystery. She tells me that, to her knowledge, she's never worked with the
material. Nor, I gather, have you ever had the insulation replaced in your
home. But it was once so pervasive . . . and it only takes a single inhaled or
ingested fiber . . . The gestation period for mesothelioma is anywhere from
twenty to fifty years. That makes it incredibly difficult to identify a particular product as the provenance of the disease. Does it really matter?"

"It matters to me," said Glynis hotly. Her demeanor thus far had
been so meek; finally in the flash of anger, she sounded like herself.
"If some stranger on the street stabbed you in the belly with a butcher
knife, wouldn't you want to know who it was?"

"Maybe . . ." said Dr. Knox. "But I'd be much more concerned with
getting to a hospital to be patched up. If the misfortune was the result of
'wrong place, wrong time,' who—or in this case what—was the culprit
would mostly be a matter of idle curiosity."

"There's nothing *idle* about my curiosity," said Glynis. "Since I'm
about to be slit open and gutted like a fish, then pumped full of drugs
that make me throw up and go bald and sleep all day—sleep if I'm
lucky—I would *rather* like to know who did this to me."

The oncologist chewed on his inside cheek. This office must have
seen its fair share of impotent fury. "Maybe I should have asked before.
What do you do for a living, Mr. Knacker?"

"I run—I work for a company that does household repairs. We send
out handymen, basically. Provide the materials . . ."

The eyes of the physician sharpened. "Do you, or have you done, any
of this kind of work yourself?"

Handyman sounded down-market—it had always had a low-class ring
to his father, and Jackson had invented all sorts of clunky euphemisms
to avoid using the word—but Shep refused to regard the occupation as
shameful. If Glynis, too, preferred to describe his more executive capacity at dinner parties, he saw nothing ignoble about physical labor. He was
more likely to find ignoble lolling for years at a desk. "Sure, of course."

"And would you have worked with insulation, or cement products . . . fireproofing, soundproofing, roofing materials . . . gutters, rainwater pipes . . . vinyl flooring, plaster . . . water tanks?"

Shep felt a flicker of wariness, an intuition that this was the point at which savvy criminals in police interviews took the fifth. The innocent, by contrast, believed that they had nothing to hide, and idiotically blabbed their hearts out. Little wonder that *innocent* had two connotations: without sin, and ignorant. "All of the above, at one time or another. Why? I never took Glynis out on the job. If any of those materials had asbestos in them, wouldn't I be the one who got sick?"

"You might have brought fibers home on your clothes. In fact, I came across a story recently about a woman with mesothelioma in Britain, who's suing their Ministry of Defence. Her father was an insulation engineer at a naval dockyard, and she's certain that she was exposed to asbestos from hugging her father as a child."

As a grown man, Shep rarely blushed, but now his cheeks stung. "That seems far-fetched."

"Mmm," said Dr. Knox. "A single fiber, on the hand, touched to the mouth? Unfortunate, but not far-fetched."

The wave of heat was followed by a wave of cold, as Glynis turned to him and her expression was accusatory. First he's so caught up in his "own little world" that his wife doesn't confide that she's being tested for a deadly disease, and now he gave it to her.

Shep finally broke their silence as he unlocked the car in the parking garage on Ft. Washington. "I thought asbestos was banned a long time ago."

"It's *still* not banned," said Glynis, bundling furiously into the passenger seat. "The EPA *finally* banned the shit in 1989, but in 1991 the industry got the ban overturned in court. You can't use it in insulation and some other whathaveyou anymore, that's all, or building anything new."

Shep was immediately struck by the homework Glynis had done on this subject—there was no way that this regulatory timeline had been

long lodged in her head as general knowledge—when she had conspicuously refrained from availing herself of the copious information at her
fingertips about her illness. She was hazy on the side effects of drugs
whose names and downsides were meticulously listed on a host of websites; she would not *scroll down*. Yet her searches on their home computer had apparently regarded not what was happening to her or what
would happen to her next, but who was to blame. The misdirection of
her energies was painfully typical.

"I'm not quite sure how I could have known." He didn't start the
car, though he stared intently out the windshield as if he were driving.
"The materials I used to work with were the same ones everyone used.
Licensed plumbers, professional roofers . . . I never cut corners, or used a
material that I knew other repairmen were careful to avoid."

"You could easily have known, and you should have! Evidence about
the dangers of asbestos goes back to *1918*. The evidence was really beginning to accumulate by the 1930s, but the industry had the research
suppressed. The specific link between asbestos and mesothelioma was
made in 1964. That was before you even started Knack! By the 1970s,
that asbestos could kill you was basically a known fact. I grew up surrounded by these stories, and so did you!"

"Glynis, try to think back," said Shep, keeping his voice calm, reasoning, quiet. "During the early years I was putting in twelve-, sometimes fourteen-hour days getting Knack off the ground. I didn't have
time to read the papers front to back. Much less to bury my nose in a
microscopic list of ingredients every time I opened a can."

"We're not talking about your not having time to follow every twist
and turn of peace talks in the Middle East. You had an obligation to
keep up with health and safety issues that bore directly on your work.
And to do whatever modest research might have been required to choose
safe products over *lethal* ones. Never mind just you—or, by the way,
your wife and children. What about your employees?"

"I no longer have employees," he said quietly. "Glynis, why are you
doing this? Are you getting back at me for Pemba?"

She was not to be sidetracked. "All these companies being sued up the wazoo for decades right and left, but no, you stick your head in the sand and totally ignore it!"

Shep himself had never been a man for causes. It was his nature to see two sides of things; worse, many sides, so that acquaintances often mistook him for having no opinions at all. He was attuned to particularities, complexities, and extenuating circumstances. He wasn't critical of ideologues; he found Jackson entertaining. There were causes whose proponents had prevailed and improved matters. He was glad that his wife could vote, and that blacks no longer had to use separate water fountains. It was clearly a fine thing, too, that some firebrands had demonized asbestos, so that his own co-workers were no longer replacing insulation that could kill them, and wouldn't risk being cast in this terrible role of contaminant by their own wives.

Nonetheless, he had also founded a company, and had a better-than-average understanding of what a company was: neither ogre nor abstraction. It was an amalgam of many people—including the odd slipshod employee or ruthlessly bottom-line zealot who could single-handedly undermine decades of collective diligence. It was an intersection of many products, each of which was connected to yet another company, also of many people, decent people who didn't always feel like going to work every morning and still did, and each with its host of obligations—to stockholders, investors, health plans, and pensions. Yet a company was also an entity that somebody loved. Not that he was excusing poor practice, but corporate malfeasance was therefore both diffuse, and deeply personal. Given the diffusion, he couldn't see the satisfaction in pointing the finger at "a company," much less at "an industry." After all, look at Glynis. In preference to railing at "an industry," she was clearly far more gratified to locate a guilty party whom she could literally get her hands on.

He wondered if Edward Knox had any idea how anguishing was his suggestion that Glynis would have come by her cancer as the result of an embrace.

Yet if it helped her, if she hungered to tell herself a story, acquiescing to the part of villain was a service Shep could perform. Maybe it was a modest service, although it didn't feel modest.

"I'm sorry," he said. "I had no idea asbestos was so deadly. Or that it was in all those materials your doctor mentioned. But you're right, I should have read those articles. Before working with any product, I should have made certain what it contained. I was irresponsible." He choked a little on that last adjective, never in his life one applied to him, by himself or anyone else. "And now you're the one who has to pay for that. It's not fair. I should be the one who's sick. I wish it was me. I wish I could shoulder it for you."

He was not sure that this was true. But he suspected that in due course it would become true, which made it true enough.

When they returned home, Glynis allowed that she wasn't very hungry, but Shep pressed that she had to keep up her strength. Though he knew that the suggestion was a life-long anathema to her, he even hazarded that before the surgery she should probably try to put on weight. After the violence of the Ft. Washington parking garage—no one had raised a hand, but that's what it had been, violence—they were quiet, moving around each other with exaggerated deference. Shep volunteered to make dinner, not his usual duty. He wasn't trying to imply that this was penance; he meant instead to imply that preparation of one meal was merely the beginning of a very long penance, more gestures and sacrifices and many more meals. She was not up for fighting, as she was not, really, up for cooking either, and she let him.

"Dad's making dinner?" said Zach, shuffling into the kitchen. Whether from his age or nature, their fifteen-year-old was at a stage where he strove for invisibility. He turned to his father, who was peeling potatoes. "What'd you do wrong?"

Kids' unerring intuition always impressed Shep, and made him nervous. "Where do you want to start?"

They had resolved not to tell the children about their mother's illness until they were better able to prepare them for what to expect, and they'd confirmed her diagnosis with a second opinion. Or that was the excuse; doubtless they were simply putting off a painful scene. But Zach knew something was up. Since he almost never ate with his parents any-more, this sidle into the kitchen was a spy mission, the nosing through the fridge mere pretext.

Yet Shep was grateful for a third party to cut the tension, and to help manifest the appearance of a normal family—hungry foraging teenager, parents begging in return for some morsel from the well-guarded larder of his private life. A hackneyed tableau soon consigned to the past. In the months to come, Zach would have to learn to be a "good son," and therefore an artificial one.

"You going out?" asked Shep.

"Nah," said Zach—"Z" to his friends. His parents had christened him Zachary Knacker before they knew the boy. They'd liked the as-sonance, the clackety-clack steam-train cadence, which to its bearer sounded "like a character in Dr. Seuss" (*The Cat in the Hat* probably being the last book Zach had read cover to cover). The name was too high profile for a kid desperate to keep his head down, so now he hud-dled at the end of the alphabet in a cryptic single letter.

"But it's Friday night!" said Shep, who knew better. He was merely trying to keep his son in the kitchen. Zach never went out. He stayed in his room. His rare forays were to other boys' rooms. They all lived online, and spent hours at computer games, a diversion of which Shep had ini-tially despaired, until he got it. The attraction wasn't blood and gore, or aggression. In the days he'd had spare time—whenever was that?—Shep himself had enjoyed solving crossword puzzles. He wasn't very good at them, but so much the better; they only served their purpose incom-plete. Comically low-tech in comparison, but the draw was the same. The reward of all these games was concentration, focus for its own sake; it didn't matter on what. You couldn't object to that, and he didn't.

"Just another night of the week to me," said Zach, throwing a pizza pocket into the toaster. Lanky, he could afford the grease. Shep peeled his last potato slowly, appraising his son. The features of the boy's face were growing at wildly different rates, his brow too broad, his lips too full, his chin too small; it was all out of proportion, like a jalopy cobbled together from different cars. Shep yearned to reassure the kid that in two or three years these elements would settle into the same strong, square symmetry of his own countenance. But he didn't know how to say this without seeming to flatter himself, and promising Zach that he would be handsome soon would only mean to his son that he was ugly now.

"Hey, Mom." Zach side-eyed his mother, who sat at the breakfast table at an angle more acute than usual. "You tired? It's only seven o'clock."

She smiled weakly. "Your mother's getting old."

Shep could feel it, that for Zach suddenly the whole happy-family playacting was too much. The boy didn't know that until a week ago his father was about to abscond to the east coast of Africa, and he didn't know that his mother had just been diagnosed with a rare and deadly cancer, much less did he know that as far as his mother was concerned the disease was his father's fault. But these hardly incidental unsaids emitted the equivalent of the high-frequency sound waves that convenience stores now broadcast outside their shop fronts to keep loitering gangs from the door. What dulled adult ears could no longer detect was unbearable to adolescents, and the same might be said of emotional fraud. Zach popped his pizza pocket early from the toaster and took his half-frozen dinner in a paper towel upstairs without even bothering with "See ya."

Roast chicken, boiled potatoes, and steamed green beans. Glynis commended his preparation, but only picked. "I feel fat," she admitted.

"You're underweight. It's only fluid. You have to stop thinking like that."

"Suddenly I'm supposed to become a different person?"

"You can be the same person who eats more."

"Your chicken," she said, "is probably not what I feel so little appetite for." This was surely true. Given the purpose of food, an appetite at meals implied an appetite for the future.

Just then Shep was filled with the useless but overpowering sensation that he did not want this to be happening. It was almost as if, should he refuse to allow it staunchly enough, much as he had sometimes to stand up to Zach and forbid any more computer games until his grades improved, it would go away. It did not go away, and the feeling passed. He stood behind her chair and slid his hands down her shoulders, leaning to nuzzle her temple with the butt of his head like an affectionate horse.

"This is not why," she said, "any self-respecting woman would want her husband to stay."

"Oh, I don't think I'd have been able to go, up against it. Even without this." Another small sacrifice—of his opinion of himself. But then, maybe he really wouldn't have gone to Pemba, in the end. As the Wedding Fountain purling in the next room reminded, he was made of water.

"What if I'd found out a week or two later?" It was understood that they would keep their discourse allusive—never specifying this *what* is not why any woman wants her husband to stay, go *where* up against it, found out *what* a week or two later—in case Zach came back downstairs. Elliptical dialogue that most parents would recognize, it reliably backfired; eavesdropping children filled in the blanks with their worst fears. Little matter. From this conversation, Zach would be hard pressed to infer anything worse than the facts.

"Then you'd have told me," he said, "and I'd have come back."

"You just said that you'd never have gone in any event."

"You were being hypothetical. I was, too. Please, don't hold onto it."

The request was ludicrous. Ten years ago her sister Ruby sent a present of a desktop pen set, and a logo on the base betrayed that it was a freebie from Citibank; Glynis had unfailingly recalled the insult on every subsequent birthday. More recently, Petra Carson, her best friend-cum-nemesis from art school, had foolishly taken at face value Glynis's urging to be critical, and tentatively ventured that her Bakelite-inlaid fish slice was "maybe a little chunky"; the poor woman had been trying to make up for the gaffe with over-the-top compliments on Glynis's flatware ever since, but to little avail. If Glynis couldn't relinquish grievances over re-gifting or underappreciative comments about her metalwork, the likelihood that she'd forgive and forget attempted marital desertion was on the low side.

Depleted, Glynis decided to turn in early, and Shep promised to join her soon. Once she went upstairs, he walked onto the front porch. The golf course across the road lost its prissiness in the dark, and could almost pass for wilderness. It was cold and clear. Coatless, he braved the chill, following the course of an airplane accelerating across the stars, waiting until the distant whine subsided and he could see the red taillights no more. Then he went inside, locked up for the night, and padded upstairs to his study. A line of light still shone from Zach's bedroom, so he closed the door. He unfolded the e-ticket printouts from the bottom desk drawer. They bore today's date. Sheet by sheet he fed them to the shredder. The maw ground the pages with an intestinal growl; in the basket below, The Afterlife curled to crushed confetti. He'd bought the shredder to guard against identity theft; queer that the machine itself was now stealing who he had been.

Finally, he settled before his computer and went to the Web page whose address the search engine brought up after three keystrokes. When he reached "Survival Rates," he refused to pause even briefly; taking the plunge without hesitation had always been the best approach to diving into the icy White Mountains swimming hole of his boyhood. He scrolled down. He read carefully to the end of the section, and then read it a second time. Once he shut down the computer, he tried to cry softly, that he not wake his wife.

Chapter Four

At Randy Handy—a salacious staff sobriquet so obvious that you'd think Pogatchnik would have headed it off with a company name less vulnerable to perversion—Jackson had adopted a new perspective. He'd let his co-workers make all the sarcastic remarks about Shep and his pathetic "escape fantasy" they liked. Eventually they were bound to find out why the former owner was still yes-massahing Pogatchnik, and then they'd feel bad. Really fucking bad. Jackson was looking forward to it.

He'd concede that in the friendship he'd long played something of a sidekick, but starting with the god-awfully stupid sale of Knack, which demoted Shep from boss to fellow schmo, and now with the plain god-awful business of Glynis and the Fall of Pemba, that dynamic had subtly flipped. These days he was Shep's protector. The role came at a price. He couldn't ask for anything. When Shep had been the stoic stalwart, he could lean on the guy. No, he hadn't ever put his hand out (like everybody else in the schmuck's life). Still, what with Flicka, an on-again-off-again predilection for gambling, and a not-unrelated little difficulty with credit card debt, he'd always been the one with the problems who needed advice. Now he had to keep his mouth shut, and for Jackson keeping his mouth shut, ever, about anything, was unnatural.

That said, there was one subject he'd been tempted to raise for some time, and at least on this point he was relieved to have a better reason to put it off than the usual cowardice. It wasn't the sort of thing you talked about with other men, even if it should have been, since you sure weren't going to talk about it with women. Besides, there was something to be said for the restoration of the concept of privacy in a country where at the average bus stop you were as likely to be regaled with the story of some stranger's abortion as asked for a light. He'd set the date anyway, so there was nothing, really, to discuss.

When they left at 1:00 p.m. for their stingy forty-minute lunch break, Shep asked if maybe they could walk instead of eat; intent on getting straight home to Glynis after work, he could no longer make time for their tri-weekly weight-lifting sessions at the Fifth Avenue Gym. (Jackson was a *little* relieved to get out of the team workouts; Shep always showed him up.) Though forgoing his sandwich made him petulant, Jackson had to say no problem. Basically in the face of cancer, even of cancer once removed, you had no rights.

"You know, Glynis would never have been able to keep her secret much longer even if she'd tried," said Shep as they hustled down Seventh Avenue; it was too damned cold for a casual stroll. "The bills have started to arrive."

"Yeah, tell me about it," said Jackson. "Let me guess: it's not one bill, it's dozens, right? Going on for fifteen pages, from every little radiologist and every little lab. And that 'EOB' thing!"

"Explanation of Benefits—or lack of benefits, more like it. It's byzantine."

"Carol does the paperwork for Flicka, and I'm so grateful I could cry."

"What kills me is how near-impossible it is to figure out what you owe. Before I brought in an accountant, I used to do the books at Knack myself, and I'm no slouch in that department. But it took me *hours* to sort out what to send in and where."

"Fucking hell, you'd think they'd make it easy to give them money," said Jackson. "Still, I think it's deliberate. The blizzard of paper, all the numbers and codes. It's a smoke screen. Behind which you get charged three hundred dollars for a Band-Aid and you don't notice."

Jackson shot a ritually despairing glance down the avenue. He missed the old Park Slope—a few failing pizza joints, coffee shops that didn't charge four bucks a pop, hardware stores with barrels of screws instead of little packets of four all wrapped in plastic. "Gentrified"—though he was hard pressed to see how an army of whiny Barnard grads plowing them into the gutter with strollers the size of troop transporters qualified as "gentry"—it was all yoga parlors, organic smoothie bars, and pet therapists.

"And, you know, what Carol mentioned?" said Shep. "But I didn't understand at the time. This World Wellness Group. They cover procedures according to prices that are 'reasonable and customary' in your area. In other words, what the fee *should* be, and not what it actually is."

"This stuff is news to you, pal?" Jackson felt a surge of pitying condescension.

"I did some digging online. The outfit that generates this 'reasonable and customary' figure? It's another unit of the *same company*. They're under no legal obligation to tell you how they arrived at it. And it's in both outfits' interests for that figure to be as low as possible. As far as I can tell, they could be making it up."

"Here's how it works," Jackson explained benevolently. "We're going on a trip, and it's your car, so I've agreed to pay for gas. We stop at a station, you fill up the tank, tell me the gas was fifty bucks, hold out your hand. With an expression on my face like I'm doing you a big favor, I hand you a twenty. You say, what's this? I say, but that's what a tank of gas *should* cost—since that's what it cost when I was twelve. Basically, the insurers live in a fantasy world, and we Mugs are stuck in the real one."

Shep shook his head. "Glynis and I have always kept to a tight budget. Trying to build that nest egg for The Afterlife. We've waited for the two-for-one offer on shampoo. Bought toilet paper in the economy size of twelve rolls, single ply. Got the special on turkey burgers even if we were more in the mood for steak. Now it's five hundred for this, five thousand for that . . . And they never tell you in advance what it costs. It's like going on a spree, piling all this shit on the counter, and none of it has any price tags. We only pick up twenty percent in co-insurance, but that's after the five-K deductible. One single lab bill—that's a hell of a lot of toilet paper."

"Double-ply," said Jackson.

"I'm thinking, why did we ever eat turkey burgers? And then I remember that I'm not supposed to care. Ultimately, I don't care. All that matters is Glynis."

"That's what they're counting on, bud. That's the whole scam in a nutshell. Same with Flicka. It's your kid, right? So what are you gonna say, no we're not going to treat her pneumonia—again—cause we want the kind of DVD that records? And, friend . . . I hate to say it, but for you this is just the beginning."

"I know," said Shep quietly, as they hung a left on Ninth Street and headed for Prospect Park. "Even to cover the last stack of bills . . . Well, you know I've kept this other account, where I put the proceeds of the sale of Knack once I paid off the feds. It's earmarked for The Afterlife, and I've never touched it. But there wasn't enough in our joint checking, so I had to tap the Merrill Lynch. I'd never written a single check on it. Number 101 went for the CAT scan."

"My guess is you're already on 115. Take my advice, and order another checkbook pronto."

"Signing that first one was strangely emotional. Even if it's 'only' money, as my father would say."

"Yeah, 'only' the proceeds from over twenty years building your own business. 'Only' eight years of humiliation with Randy Pogatchnik."

"It doesn't matter. I just didn't realize at the time what I was really saving for."

"You ever think about it? Pemba?"

"No," said Shep, and changed the subject. "I guess we're lucky, though. We live in the States. Hey, we get the best medical care in the world."

"Think again, pal. In comparison to all the other rich countries like England, Australia . . . Canada . . . I don't remember the rest. Look at all the statistics that matter—infant mortality, cancer survival, you name it? We come in *last*. And we pay *twice as much*."

"Yeah, well. At least we don't have socialized medicine."

Jackson guffawed. Shep wasn't stupid, but he could be painfully co-operative. That "socialized medicine" bogyman went all the way back to the 1940s, when Harry Truman had wanted to bring in a national health service, just like the Brits. Nervous that doctors wouldn't keep raking it in, the American Medical Association concocted this inspired cold war buzz phrase, which had struck terror in the hearts of their countrymen ever since. A genius stroke of labeling. Like when supermarkets came out with that "no frills" line, packaging a perfectly standard, decent product in stark, ugly-ass black-and-white, thus ensuring that no one with any class would buy it, at half the brand-name price. It worked. Even Jackson's cash-strapped mother hadn't wanted to be caught dead with no-frills tissues in her cart.

"You realize fortysomething percent of this country is either on Medicaid or Medicare?" said Jackson; history lessons always put Shep to sleep. "All this *ooh-ooh* about how we don't want 'socialized medicine.' Well, we *got* socialized medicine, for nearly half the population. So the other half is paying twice. Your Mugs are paying for your Mooches' CAT scans with confiscatory taxes"—*confiscatory* was a wonderful word Jackson had learned only about a year ago, and he used it at every opportunity—"and a second time for their own damn scans."

"You sound so down on Medicare and Medicaid. But you're not saying that you wish old and poor people didn't have access to health care."

Jackson sighed. That line was so predictable. Shep was a class-A Mug. For the ranks of complacent dupes to which, alas, Jackson also belonged, Shep Knacker could be the mascot. "No, I'm not saying that. My point is, guys with health benefits don't *think* they're paying their own medical bills. They cling to their precious employee health insurance as if it's this great freebie. It's not free! They don't understand they'd be getting, like, fifteen grand more in salary if it weren't for the damned health benefit! It's fucking sad, man."

"Money's gotta come from somewhere, Jacks. Some big national thing would send taxes through the roof. There goes your fifteen grand. Worse, if you earn a decent living."

"It seems like it's all the same dough, but it's not. Think about it. Every piece of paper that just landed in your mailbox cost money. Some officious twit was paid to fill in all those codes, and tick the boxes, and fire off copies to five other places. *Thirty percent* of the money spent on medical care in this country goes to so-called 'administration.' Fact is, there's a wholly fatty layer of for-profit insurance companies larded between Glynis and her doctors, a bunch of bloodsucking greedy fucks making money off her being sick. And not one of them knows how to set a broken arm. Kick those assholes out of the picture, and for the same cost the whole country would be covered, without fifty different bills a week arriving in your mailbox."

"*You* of all people want the government to take over health care?" said Shep, shaking his head with a lopsided smile. "Jacks, you hate government. You're an anarchist."

"These companies are so in bed with government that they might as well be the government," Jackson charged back, irked by Shep's superior bemusement; yeah, maybe he wasn't totally consistent, but at least he read stuff, he thought about things, unlike *some* people, who took everything they were told as gospel. "Why else do you figure that no halfway credible presidential candidate, Democrats included, ever dares suggest eliminating the bloodsuckers altogether? Besides, if the feds wouldn't do it much better, they couldn't do it worse. And the whole concept of insurance is to spread the risk, right? To pool the healthy people and the likes of Flicka together so it all evens out in the end. Well, what could be a fairer 'risk pool' than the whole damned country? Health care is about the only thing the fucking government *should* be good for. And maybe, just maybe, if you could at least go to a doctor without having to take out a second mortgage, people would figure that, okay, they pay taxes but at least they get something back. Right now, you get dick. Oh, sorry"—Jackson kicked a rim of raised concrete—"you get sidewalks. I always forget."

He'd promised himself to shut up, to focus on Shep's problems for once. Still, none of this stuff was off-point. "Hey," he said, as Shep stared dully into the blanched, glaucous vista of the park, which in winter looked like a drawing that had been erased. "This isn't an off-in-the-clouds rant, bud. This is about you and Glynis, right now, what you're going through, and you're not even paying attention."

"Sorry. It's just . . . well, we got our second opinion. From this pair of hotshots at Columbia-Presbyterian. They work as a team, an internist and a surgeon. And don't get me wrong; they were great. In a way."

"In a way," said Jackson, forcing himself to listen. It wasn't his strong suit.

"I wanted them to say something different," Shep said glumly. "This mesothelioma thing, it's incredibly rare. Nobody gets this disease. I didn't realize how much I was counting on their saying it was all a mistake. When they confirmed the diagnosis, I thought I was going to be sick. Honest, my vision went blurry and black around the edges, as if I was going to faint. Like a girl. Glynis was the one who took it like a man. She'd already resigned herself."

"This is some hard shit, pal."

"It's *mainly* hard for Glynis. She's weak, and exhausted, and scared. Alone most of the day, too, so when I come home all I want to do, and should do, is keep her company. No such luck. Like, you think other people will take care of at least the paper-shuffling side, but they don't. Just to get the second opinion, I had to request the pathology slides. The radiology reports. The 'tissue blocks.' The results of every frigging test from each separate hospital department—all in writing. I had to fill out forms giving Glynis's medical history a dozen separate times. I was up til two a.m. every night. Meanwhile I have to cook. Shop. Show up at work and at least look like I'm doing my job."

"Yeah, I meant to warn you. I overheard Pogatchnik grumbling about how many personal days you been using up. You're gonna have to watch the absenteeism."

"I haven't had any choice. I lost two solid days wrangling with the World Wellness Group. The hotshots at Columbia are out-of-network, just like that Dr. Knox warned me. So I had to beg these HMO people to agree to cover Glynis going to the dream team, which meant talking to a human being. You know, ten different automated menus. Then you're on hold for forty-five minutes, listening to 'Greensleeves' several hundred times. I can't get it out of my head; it's driving me crazy. Finally get connected, turns out it's the wrong department. Back to 'Go.' With that open-plan office, I can't sit on the phone for hours at work unless

I'm talking about the fact that, thanks to our *expert* services, some lady's boiler just exploded."

Shep was usually so cool-headed, and Jackson had rarely heard the guy talk so much.

"Anyway," Shep went on, "I can appeal, but. This provider Pogatchnik has signed onto, they're real assholes, and so far they're not budging. Edward Knox has treated one case of mesothelioma in his whole career. As far as World Wellness is concerned, that makes him a mesothelioma whiz. If we go to Columbia, we'll have to eat forty percent co-insurance."

"Forty percent of what?"

"Forty percent of a blank check."

"Jesus. Can you really not use this Knox guy?"

"This isn't a question of putting up with single-ply toilet paper. If these doctors at Columbia know what they're doing, then I'll spring for them. We're talking about Glynis's life—"

"*Jim!*" Shep would usually have found the allusion to Dr. McCoy's sanctimonious refrain in *Star Trek* funny (*We're talking about human life, Jim!*), but he didn't even crack a smile.

"I'm not going to buy turkey-burger medical care."

"At least you're lucky you got a cushion. Most suckers in your shoes would be putting this crap on their credit cards."

"It's a pretty weird version of lucky. But yeah, I am lucky. Shit, I'm rich."

"Not these days—"

"I'm rich," Shep cut him off, and Jackson knew this preacher's son well enough to know that he wasn't bragging. He felt guilty. Shep may have been a lapsed Presbyterian, but with this deep-down stuff there was only so lapsed you ever got. "You haven't traveled enough."

"Well, *excuuuse* me. I plumb forgot to put in my ten years with the Peace Corps in Malawi."

"I shouldn't be talking about money at all. Maybe I'm just getting this out of my system, because in comparison to Glynis . . . I have no business complaining. You should always remind me of that."

"I hardly ever heard you complain about anything. I'd recommend you get more practice. It's not good for a man to take every lump of shit life throws at him lying down."

"We both take it lying down, Jacks. You just lie down with a mouth."

"Speaking of which, I came up with a new title for my book," said Jackson, hoping to lighten the tone. "Ready? *FLEECED: How Shrewd Spongers from Vagrants to Vice-Presidents Are Living Off Us Poor Spunkless Sheep*."

A half-smile. "Not bad."

"I liked the *fleeced* and *sheep* thing. You know, keeps up the metaphor."

"But the 'spongers' doesn't quite fit in. Do you sponge sheep?"

"I'll work on it."

"That 'spunkless.' Ever notice how almost all your titles have something to do with dicks?"

Jackson shot an uneasy glance at his friend. "As in, having mine cut off? Like, every day? Obviously the experience is central to my thesis."

"The castration thing is . . . well used. My favorite of yours is cleaner."

"Which is?"

"*Democracy Is a Joke*."

"Yup. Nice and punchy," said Jackson with satisfaction. "Good thesis, too. It's theoretically possible for fifty-one percent of the population to soak the other forty-nine percent for everything they're worth. This guy in Venezuela, who's it's, Howard Chavez or something. That's how he does it. Really, he just sends the underclass checks. You give the Mooches other people's money, and then they vote for you."

"Think you'll ever write it?"

"Maybe." Jackson was noncommittal. "But the key is the title. Get that right, and it doesn't matter what's inside. You could sell a pile of blank paper called *How the Irish Saved Civilization*. All those micks are so flattered they'll pay twenty-five bucks to put it on their coffee tables even if they never read past the copyright page."

"Maybe that's the trouble with your titles. *PENISES AND PRICKS*," Shep remembered. "*How We Gutless Weenies Are Being Bilked Dry While the Other Half of the Country Is on the Tit.* You couldn't call that complimentary."

"The idea is you make your book buyer feel like a little less of a sap because he knows he's a sap, unlike everybody else, who're such incredible saps that they don't even know it."

"I bet they'd prefer to save civilization."

"Not my book buyers. They'd rather light it on fire."

On the way back, Shep put his collar up and huddled into his scarf. "Anyway. Glynis is scheduled for surgery in just under two weeks."

Jackson grunted. "Been there. Flicka's operation for scoliosis was terrifying. Personally, I didn't want a knife within a mile of my kid's spinal cord." He would have to watch himself, always claiming seniority in the medical nightmare department.

"Actually, I've been meaning to apologize," said Shep.

"What the hell for?"

"All you've been through with Flicka. I don't think I've been sympathetic enough. I didn't have a feel for what it must have been like for you guys until I sank up to the neck in the same shit myself. I should have been a lot more understanding."

"Balls, my buddy. You been plenty sympathetic. And how you supposed to be 'understanding' til you understand it?" Still, the exchange was gratifying. Shep hadn't had any idea, and the truth was he still didn't.

"Anyway, I've heard about people 'going in for surgery' my whole life. I never thought about it. Now it seems medieval. Like taking your wife to a slaughterhouse."

"It really wipes you out. You think the hard part's going under the knife, but the real hard part's after. Takes forever. Flicka said she'd lie around and have to think for, like, an hour about whether it's really worth the trouble to ask her mother to hand her a magazine from the dresser. Not to go get it herself; just to *ask* for it. It's like you been taken out back of some bar and had the crap beat out of you."

"Thanks," said Shep sourly. "That really helps."

"Look, whadda you want, I should tell you fairy stories? Glynis is a 'tough cookie' who's gonna 'pull through in no time' and be 'right as rain'?"

"Sorry. No, I'd rather know. We might as well be prepared."

"Don't bother. You won't be."

Jackson shot a contemptuous glance at the heavy jogger (whom they *walked* past) clutching his Evian with that distinctive sense of righteousness conveyed by bottled water. It was a wonder how the Western frontier was ever crossed, their forefathers trudging between watering holes hundreds of miles apart, when after five minutes without a chug modern Americans like tubby there were parched.

"I wondered if you and Carol might come to dinner," said Shep. "Next Saturday, if you can find a sitter. Just the four of us. It's a last . . . It'll be our Before Picture. I know it sounds inconceivable, but I'd like us to try and have a good time."

"We'll do better than try. Wouldn't miss it," said Jackson, calculating that the timing was not ideal. "Though if you want it to be all happy as Larry—should we be sure and avoid the asbestos thing? Get the feeling it's a sore subject."

"If we avoid sore subjects, we won't talk about anything."

"She still holding that against you?"

Shep snorted. "What do you think?"

"That it keeps her warm at night."

"Toasty. Far as I can tell, cancer doesn't change people."

"You wouldn't want her to change."

"I walk around feeling awful. I'd feel awful anyway, so it's hard to tell how much of the awfulness is this whole thing being all my fault. I was sloppy. Inconsiderate. I'm starting to understand how gays feel, when they give their partners AIDS."

"Plenty of those sausage-stuffers know damn well they've got HIV and keep porking away without a casing. But you didn't know. It's not even certain that the fibers were from you, that doctor said. You're fellating . . ." Jackson said unsteadily. "I mean, whipping yourself. Because you feel guilty about Pemba."

"Glynis is determined to sue, to make 'them' pay. But we can't go for any company if I can't remember what I could have worked with that was contaminated. How am I supposed to remember the brand of the cement I poured in 1982?"

"Yeah, I've done like you asked and put my mind to the same thing, but I can't remember, either. That whole list of products you gave me—a brand of roofing tile, well, it's just not the kind of thing that sticks in your head twenty-five years later."

"But if she doesn't get her hands on a corporation, she's going to keep wrapping them around my neck. I'd bear up if having someone to blame really seemed to help. But I've apologized until I'm blue in the face, and every time, after I've finished, she still has cancer."

They were good friends and all, but it hadn't been the form for Shep to get all choked up, about anything, so Jackson did him the favor of watching a cyclist ride the wrong way around the park while the guy got himself together.

"Nuts," said Shep, in hand again. "Between now and Saturday, I've got to tell everyone."

"About the surgery?"

"About the fact that Glynis is sick at all. Nobody knows yet, except you and Carol."

"You don't think Glynis should do the honors?"

"Nah. It's better for everyone if I do it. Especially with her family in Arizona. You know Glynis. She'd probably call up and lean back and let her mother go on for half an hour about how the Mexicans next door have five pickups and don't separate their recycling. Once her mother had hung herself good, Glynis would call her a racist, so Hetty'd get huffy and offended and say something insulting back. *Whoom*, in for the kill! 'Is that so? Well, I just wanted you to know that I have cancer!' *Bang*, down with the receiver."

"I can hear it!" Jackson chuckled. "God, I love her."

"Yeah. I do, too."

Nearing Handy Randy, Jackson started to whistle "Greensleeves."

"You fuck!" Shep exclaimed, though at least Jackson had made him laugh. "I'd finally got rid of it!"

Chapter Five

Shepherd Armstrong Knacker
Merrill Lynch Account Number 934-23F917
January 01, 2005 – January 31, 2005
Net Portfolio Value: $697,352.41

After work, Shep had to swing by and pick up Beryl, who'd called earlier in the week hoping to come up to Elmsford and "hang," meaning invite herself to dinner. The timing was bad in one way—that is, as the timing of anything was bound to be bad for the indefinite future—and good in another. Since Zach was spending the night in another boy's rank, cable-strewn bedroom again, Shep could practice delivering the news in person to Beryl. They'd resolved to tell the kids tomorrow, and he wanted to work on the wording. He was still unsure whether to share the prognosis when he hadn't discussed it with Glynis herself.

"Swing by" was an inaptly carefree expression, since picking up his sister in Chelsea meant crawling from Brooklyn into Manhattan during rush hour. It would never occur to her to take the train. (Were the situation reversed, of course, Beryl would never have offered him a lift, nor would Shep have expected one. But he was resigned to the fact that he gave and his sister took, as if they simply had different jobs. It was

Jackson who railed about how his friend was constantly doing favors for people that Shep himself would never demand of others in a million years. But he'd rather the double standard work that way than the other way around.) For that matter, Beryl's volunteering to take time away from her busy creative schedule to slum with her boring brother meant that she wanted something. Something more than dinner.

Mesothelioma kept frustration with his sister at bay, likewise whatever sense of mourning he might otherwise have felt about Pemba. He had not been lying to Jackson. He didn't think about it. He thought about one thing and put all his energies into one thing only. Glynis's cancer facilitated the same laser-like focus that Zach found in computer games, perfectly replacing the driving single-mindedness previously provided by The Afterlife. Merely relinquishing Pemba with nothing to put in its place would have left him lost, fractured, at sea, and for once in his life maybe angry. As it was, he still hewed to a prime directive. He would do anything to make Glynis more comfortable, or to keep her from going to any trouble. He would do anything to save her.

With Beryl coming over, he'd stayed up until 3:00 a.m. the night before assembling a pan of lasagna and washing salad greens. He had never cooked very much or been interested in cooking, but now his interest didn't matter. He looked up recipes. They suited a man who was constitutionally obedient, and he followed them to the letter.

Because for now there was nothing left to contemplate that served the prime directive—he'd already read a dozen Web pages on how best to prepare Glynis for surgery in two weeks' time—while eking over the Brooklyn Bridge Shep allowed his mind to slide to Jackson and his goofball book. Even Jackson didn't believe he'd ever write it. After all, he was one of these guys who were remarkably lucid in conversation, but who seized up at keyboards. It was weird how some people could be so garrulous and articulate when blah-blah-blahing down the street, yet couldn't write a meaningful sentence to save their lives. Their reasoning went spastic, their vocabularies shrank to "cat" and "go," and they couldn't tell a coherent story of a trip to the mailbox. That was Jackson. This afternoon, he'd liked that idea of a title on a pile of blank pages because titles were all he was good at. Still, *CHUMPS: How Behind Our Backs a Bunch of Bums and Bamboozlers Turned America into a Country Where We Can't Do Anything or Earn Anything or Say Anything When It Used to Be a Damned Nice Place to Live*—well, at titles he was very good indeed.

As for his friend's half-baked theories, Shep had never been sure whether he himself bought into them even slightly. (It was difficult to attach these views to a political party, since Jackson thought not voting was a political party.) They went something like this: Americans were divided between folks who played *by* the rules and folks who simply played the rules (or ignored them altogether). Jackson spoke of one "half" leeching off the other for ease of reference, but allowed that the proportions were likely far more dire; the fraction of the population that was being soaked by the savvier sorts who knew the ropes may have been closer to a third, or a quarter. Over the years, Jackson had christened these two classes with a series of homespun shorthands whose children's-book alliteration Shep remembered with affection: Patsies and Parasites. Freeloaders and Fall Guys. Saps and Spongers. Slaves and Skivers. Jackals and Jackasses. Lackeys and Loafers. He'd used Mugs and Mooches for three or four years now; maybe the tags were going to stick.

According to Jackson, the Mooches comprised first and foremost anyone in government, and anyone who lived off government: contractors, "advisors," think-tankers, and lobbyists. He reserved special contempt for accountants and lawyers, both of whom slyly implied that they were on your side, when this bloated, parasitic caste of interlocutors effectively constituted a penumbral extension of the State, their extortionate fees amounting to more taxes. Other Mooches: welfare recipients, obviously, though Jackson claimed they were the least of the problem, and as much victims as perps. Marathon runners with sprained thumbs on disability. Bankers, who manufactured nothing of value, and whose money-from-money deployed the suspect science of spontaneous generation. On the opposite end of the spectrum: any mastermind who refused to earn any appreciable income—why bother, only to be robbed of fifty cents on the dollar? (Jackson was indignant at having been raised on anticommunist propaganda. When for half the fucking year, he said, you were working full time for the government, your country *was* communist.) The recipients of inherited wealth, which covered Pogatchnik. Illegal immigrants, who would remain "undocumented" in perpetuity if they knew what was good for them; synonymous with becoming a card-carrying Mug, citizenship as an aspiration was pathetic.

Criminals were Mooches, too, of course. Yet while Jackson scorned establishment Mooches, who concealed their rapacity behind a façade of rectitude, or even, gallingly, of self-sacrifice (the expression "public servant" drove him wild), ordinary decent criminals won only his admiration. Drug dealing, Jackson claimed, was an intelligent, well-considered career path for the average young person, enterprising self-employment sans the Schedule C. He esteemed anyone who worked off the books or serviced a black market. He had a soft spot for Mafia movies, and had seen *Goodfellas* five times. To Jackson, criminals embodied the seminal American spirit.

As for the Mugs, Jacks cheerfully confessed to his own lifetime membership. They comprised all the remaining schmucks who got with the program, but mostly because they had no guts, and lacked imagination. Mugs exhibited neither resourcefulness nor innovation, ostensibly core traits of the national character. Having never undergone proper adolescent rebellion, Mugs were developmentally retarded, and as grown-ups were still figuratively setting the table and taking out the trash. They may have learned to say "fuck" in front of their fathers, but they could never bring themselves to use the word with the IRS. Even on the five-point scale of moral reasoning (where Jackson had dug that up Shep had no idea, but its exposition had consumed one of their ritual foursome get-togethers last summer), Mugs were stuck at the bottom. For Mugs weren't motivated by virtue, but by fear. They sweated bullets over their taxes, adding up tattered receipts for $3.49 and $2.67 and getting flustered when the calculator didn't produce the same result to the penny on a second tally—despite the fact that the recipients of their fervid bookkeeping would blithely drop $349 *million* through the cracks in the GAO floorboards or fritter $267 *billion* on a dead-end war in a sandpit, a dizzying shuttle of decimal points that never struck Mugs as unfair or bitterly hilarious. They got their car insurance payments in on time; able to afford only collision, these were the same suckers who'd be T-boned by an uninsured Guatemalan running a solid red light and get stuck with the bill. They didn't put extensions on their houses without getting a building permit, belying that they really owned their houses to begin with. To the degree that these poor flunkies were not tippy-toeing through their lives abdicating everything they ever worked for out of terror, they were stupid.

But it wasn't meant to be this way, Jackson insisted. Sneakily, little by little, the Mooches had hijacked a system that hadn't started out half bad into a situation that would have mortified the founding fathers, who'd never intended to create a monster. Nor did they design democracy as an evangelical religion or a self-destructive export business, whereby it actually cost you money to sell your product abroad. What Thomas Jefferson's crowd had in mind was a country that left you alone and let you do whatever you fucking well wanted so long as you didn't hurt anybody—in short, "a cool place to hang out," and not "this big drag."

For government was now, in Jackson's view, a for-profit corporation, although a sort of which the average industrial magnate could only dream: a natural monopoly that could charge whatever it wanted, yet with no obligation to hand over a product of any description in return. A business whose millions of customers had no choice but to buy this mythical product, lest they be locked in a small room with bad food. Since all politicians were by definition "on the tit," none of them had any motivation to constrain the size of this marvelous corporation that didn't actually have to make anything. Occasional conservative lip service notwithstanding, sure enough, over the decades USA Inc. had done nothing but expand. Jackson predicted that at some point in the near future the last remaining Mugs would get wise and sign on. Once the entire American populace was either working for or living off the government, the country would shudder to a halt. It was happening in Europe, he said, already. With a ratio of all-Mooch to no-Mug, there'd be no one left to squeeze dry, and presumably they'd all sit around waiting to die, or kill each other.

Shep was reluctant to believe that he got nothing from government. Roads, he'd point out. Bridges. Streetlamps and public parks. Admittedly, this is what Jackson meant by the umbrella term "sidewalks." The nominal infrastructure required to conduct ordinary life was largely provided by municipal authorities, which commanded such a tiny sliver of the pie that on a plate it would fall over. As Jackson frequently observed, if every citizen threw the same ante into the pot, they could cover all their primitive communal needs with "chump change"—and that was what George Washington had in mind, as opposed to "this obeisance to the king bullshit."

While Shep enjoyed the game of coming up with another vital service from on high that was worth the price of admission—drug testing, air traffic control—he conceded that citing the palpable benefits that his taxes accrued to him personally was surprisingly difficult. Yet he also felt that the totality of the many agencies that controlled his life still approximated an order. Even a rough, inequitable order, as opposed to the gory havoc of animals running in packs, was priceless.

Besides, even if he accepted Jackson's cartoonish categories, he'd still rather be a Mug than a Mooch. Someone on whom others depended, a man as he understood the word. Although he believed in an implicit social contract—that you agreed to take care of other people so that when the time came they would take care of you—he didn't keep up his end of things in order to incur a debt he'd any intention of calling in. He would remain a resource rather than a drain to the end of his days if he could help it, if only because being reliable, self-sufficient, and capable *felt good*. This big, round, grounded solidity surely beat the thin, tittering tee-hee of putting one over on people. It beat the sneering self-congratulation of a confidence trickster and the huddling sneakiness of a cheat. There was nothing enviable, either, about the resentful gratitude of the beholden. Curiously, although forever ridiculing the gullible stalwart who was responsible, dependable, and steadfast, Jackson had long admired Shep Knacker for embodying these very qualities.

More perplexing still was why Shep's best friend would lavish so much effort on a paradigm that cast himself as weak, powerless, and craven. It was thanks to Shep's stipulations on selling Knack—an assurance in writing from Randy Pogatchnik that the workforce manager would get a six-figure salary, replete with an elevator clause—that

Jackson made enough money to begrudge the taxes he paid on it, and sometimes Shep wondered if he'd done the man any favors. What was it about his life that made him feel so taken advantage of, so diminished?

Miraculously, Beryl was peering through the window of her lobby, so he wouldn't have to do circuits of Sixth and Seventh Avenues waiting for her to come down. She bundled into the front seat in nubbled layers of cape, sweaters, and scarves, clunking in jewelry of the rocks-and-feathers school that Glynis detested. Though no thrift-shop confabulation—he suspected that she paid through the nose to look that casually rumpled—Beryl's faux bohemian dress was typical of a generation that just missed out on the sixties. Although her older brother had almost missed the era himself, Shep encountered enough of its tail end not to be nostalgic about the hippy thing. Now, *those* guys were Mooches. Always borrowing money, or stealing it, promoting free this and free that, parroting a lot of anticapitalist twaddle only made possible by the hardworking parents they lived off. He was sorry about the boys who died in Vietnam. The rest of it was a crock.

Beryl kissed his cheek and cried, "Shepardo!" the neo-Renaissance nickname from childhood still imbued with a measure of affection. "God, I hope no one sees me in this SUV. You remember I did that film on SUV-IT, the activist group that smashes these things up as a political statement about global warming."

Were Beryl truly concerned with carbon emissions she'd have volunteered to take the train. "This one's a Mini Cooper," he said mildly, "compared to the new ones."

She asked perfunctorily how he was. He was relieved that she didn't notice when he declined to say.

"So what are you working on now?" he asked. It was safest to return to the subject of Beryl. She never inquired about what was up at Handy Randy; the assumption ran that nothing was ever up. It was a business, a prejudice against which she had unquestioningly inherited from their father.

"A film on couples who decided not to have kids. Particularly homing in on people in, you know, their mid-forties, right on the cusp of not having any choice. Whether they're content with their lives, whether they think they're missing anything, what put them off about having a family. It's really interesting."

Shep made a ritual effort to care, but it was harder than usual. "Are most of them resigned, or regretful?"

"Neither, for the most part. They're perfectly happy!"

As she went into the particulars, Shep reflected that his sister's body of work might seem incoherent from the outside. The one documentary that she was known for, insofar as she was known at all, was a paean to Berlin, New Hampshire—pronounced *Ber*-lun, a provincial mangling of its European roots that he'd always found strangely sweet, and hailing from a patriotic disassociation from Germany during World War I. Using interviews with residents of its dwindling population, many of whom used to work for the paper mills that were now nearly all shut down, Beryl's film *Reducing Paperwork* had captured something archetypal about New England's declining postindustrial towns that was reminiscent of Michael Moore without the smirk. It was warm, and he'd liked it. He was truly pleased for her when the hour-long elegy made it into the New York Film Festival. She'd done a quirky documentary on people who don't have a sense of smell, and a more serious one on graduates saddled with crushing debt from higher education.

But her subject matter only seemed all over the map until you realized that Beryl's lunatic then-boyfriend was a member of that group that shattered the windshields of SUVs, and that Beryl herself resented cars of any description because she couldn't afford one. Beryl was in her mid-forties, and Beryl didn't have children. Like Shep, Beryl grew up in *Ber*lin, New Hampshire. Beryl was born without a sense of smell—rather impairing a full grasp of her signature material, since throughout his boyhood Berlin reeked—and Beryl still hadn't paid off her student loans. The self-referential nature of his sister's work reached its apogee when last year she made an independent documentary about independent documentary makers, a project tainted with a whiff of self-pity that involved most of her friends.

In general, the feisty, spunky determination that was driven by inspiration when she was younger had aged into a grimmer, glummer resolve that was driven by spite. She would "show them," whoever *they* were, and churning out yet another film project on a shoestring now seemed as much habit as calling. Too old now to be an aspirant, Beryl hadn't established herself sufficiently to qualify as anything but. Oh, she did get the smell doc on PBS, and she'd won the odd grant from this or that arts council. But the New York Film Festival coup was years ago. The technological advances in compact cameras that enabled her to keep going with minimal funding also meant that plenty of other wannabes could buy the same cameras, and she faced more competition than ever. Maybe he was too conventional, but her hand-to-mouthing it in middle age was starting to look less like a gifted woman sacrificing for her work, and more like failure.

"You give any more thought to participating in a documentary about people who dream about quitting the rat race?" she asked as they sat, stationary, on the West Side Highway. "I was even thinking about calling it something like *Belief in the Afterlife*."

He rued having shared the private argot. "Not really."

"You'd be surprised. It's a pretty common fantasy."

"Thanks."

"I just mean you've got company. Like, it's kind of a club. Though I've had a hard time finding anybody who's actually done it. With the two cases I've stumbled across, they both came back. One couple went to South America and the woman practically died; another guy sold everything he had and moved to a Greek island, where he got lonely and bored and didn't speak the language. None of them lasted more than a year."

Shep was determined to avoid any entanglement with her projects, which had already cannibalized most of her life and would hungrily move on to her kin. Thank God he'd kept his mouth shut with Beryl about Pemba.

"But anyone you run into," he observed, "has obviously come back. The people who've left for good aren't here." It was theoretical for him now, but stuck in this agonizing creep of cars he still wanted The Afterlife to be possible for somebody.

"Hey," she asked. "You made any new fountains lately?"

A safer subject. Unlike his own family, Beryl thought his fountains were charming.

When he turned onto Crescent Drive, Shep realized that he could have told his sister on the trip up, and that might have been nicer. Yet he understood what Glynis had meant by "I haven't been feeling *nice*." For some reason he was inclined to make this as difficult for Beryl as possible.

His wife and sister greeted each other coolly in the kitchen. In the absence of a theatrically commiserating embrace, Glynis could tell that he'd kept quiet about her diagnosis in the car; a shared glance confirmed that she approved. They had a secret, and when they decided to impart it was their business. In fact, as the uncomfortable evening got under way—uncomfortable for Beryl—he began to understand what his wife might have got out of keeping all those tests and appointments to herself. There was something powerful in the withholding. Like walking around the house with a loaded gun.

Glynis had been fussing with the foil on the lasagna. Shep chided that he would take care of the food. Beryl was too unobservant to find this odd, since in times past dinner would always have been her sister-in-law's province. She didn't seem to note, either, the care with which he led his wife gently to a chair in the living room and settled her with a drink. Glynis wouldn't be having wine in two weeks' time, and he hoped that she remembered to enjoy it. Beryl hadn't brought a bottle. She never did.

As they waited for the main course to warm, Beryl helped herself to a top-up glug and began noshing through olives in the living room, ignoring the bowl provided and laying the pits on the glass coffee table beside the Wedding Fountain, where they left a smear. She seemed nervous, which put Shep at a contrasting ease.

"So, Glynis," she said. "Done any new work lately? I'd love to see it." To the degree that the inquiry was not knee-jerk conversation filler, Beryl was betting on the high likelihood that her sister-in-law hadn't visited her studio in months. Glynis and Beryl hated each other.

Ordinarily Glynis would have bristled, but she had a smug feline purring about her this evening. "Not since you asked me that last time," she said. "I've been distracted."

"The house and shit?"

"A house of sorts," said Glynis. "And shit. Lots of shit."

"You still making molds for that chocolate shop?"

"Actually, I recently retired. But if you mean do we still have the usual box of rejects on hand, yes. A little deformed, but they're fresh. You're welcome to take home as many truffles as you like."

"Well, that's not what I meant . . ." It was. "But if you're offering, sure. That'd be great."

Shep put the box from Living in Sin by the door as a reminder. Glynis had admitted to missing her ridiculous part-time job more than she'd expected. Because even Glynis could see that the quality of chick-shaped molds for raspberry creams was inconsequential, the work had been her first experience in decades of creation without fear. Sadly, had she embraced the same liberated playfulness in her attic studio, she might now be a metalsmith of some renown.

He refilled his sister's glass. Keeping the evening's main agenda under wraps may have been cruelly gratifying, but it might soon seem impossible to raise the subject at all.

"Hey, you know I took the bus up to see Dad last week?" said Beryl, who rarely headed to New Hampshire without getting a lift from her brother. "I'm a little worried about him. I don't think he's going to be able to live on his own much longer."

"He's managed pretty well so far. And his mind is—almost horribly—sharp as ever."

"He's almost eighty! Most nights he sleeps in that chair in the den to keep from tackling the stairs. He eats nothing but grilled cheese sand-wiches. His former parishioners help with the shopping, but most of them are pretty old by now, too. And I think he's lonely."

Routinely visiting Berlin three times more often than his sister, Shep knew about the chair, more a matter of lassitude than incapacity. Dad fell asleep reading detective fiction—thankfully not the Bible—and he *liked* grilled cheese sandwiches. Still, Shep should be glad for his sister's concern. "What did you have in mind?"

"We should probably consider putting him up in one of those assisted-living places." His sister had a funny way with pronouns.

"You know they're not covered by Medicare."

"Why not?"

"It doesn't matter why not," Glynis said with exasperation. Beryl imagined that if you established why something *should* be otherwise then you changed the way it was.

"Technically, they're not medical facilities," Shep said patiently. "I've looked into it. These places run to seventy-five, even a hundred grand a year. Dad has no savings, since he gave away anything he ever had to spare, and his pension is peanuts."

"Shepardo! Typically, I bring up something like our father's increasing infirmity, and you immediately start talking about money."

"That's because what you're suggesting involves a good whack of it."

"A good whack of *our* money, more to the point," said Glynis. The fact that Shep had "loaned" his sister tens of thousands of dollars had always outraged his wife, whose minimal income made her only more proprietary about his. "Or were you planning to make a contribution? He's your father, too."

Beryl raised her hands and cried, "Blood from a stone! You think the day I won the lottery you just forgot to read the paper? I've already run through the grant for this childlessness documentary, and I'm finishing it with my own money—what little there is of that. It's not that I'm some kind of asshole. I'm completely strapped."

Poverty had its stresses, but for a moment Shep envied his sister its relaxing side. Penury reprieved Beryl from responsibility for a host of matters, from maintenance of the Williamsburg Bridge to his father's care. But then, if in legalese Beryl was "judgment-proof," that did not necessarily reprieve her from judgment of other sorts, and it seemed important right now to side decisively with his wife. "It's your idea to put Dad in a retirement community, but you expect us to pick up the bill."

"Didn't you sell Knack of All Trades for, like, a *million dollars*? Jesus, Shep!"

In his next life, he would keep his mouth shut. "My resources aren't infinite. I have—other commitments. And if Dad stayed in decent health for another five to ten years, what you're suggesting could leave *us* completely strapped."

Beryl's eyes smoldered; she obviously pictured his *other commitments* along the lines of an iPod for Zach. "Well . . . what if Dad moved in here? There's Amelia's old bedroom."

"No," Shep said flatly, irked with himself, since breaking the news in the car would have obviated much of this discussion. "Not now."

"What about your place?" said Glynis. "It's palatial, in Manhattan terms. And if you can't do your part financially . . ."

"True," said Shep, playing along. "And then I could help you out with incidentals."

Of course his sister's newly forged filial concern would never extend to her personal inconvenience, but he thought they'd cornered her sufficiently to at least make her squirm. Instead, her eyes lit from sullenness to rage.

"Sorry, won't fly," said Beryl, her tone clipped, victorious. "That's one of the things I wanted to talk to you about."

It was, Shep intuited, *the* thing she wanted to talk about. They moved to the kitchen, where the lasagna was starting to burn.

For many years Beryl had lived in a vast, high-ceilinged apartment with all the original fixtures on West Nineteenth Street for which she paid a pittance. Possession of the three-bedroom walk-up had delivered her disproportionate power in her many volatile romances. She could always threaten her partners with exile from a residence whose pantry was larger than the apartment they could afford outside her door. Shep wouldn't claim that her swains loved her for her lease, but even if they did fall in love with Beryl, they fell in love with her apartment first.

For hers was one of the diminishing number of buildings still covered by an anachronistic regime of rent control brought in after World War II. So desperate were owners of these protected buildings to dislodge sitting tenants, thus restoring the apartments to "fair market" rents, that whole codes in the statutes addressed the rules of vacancy and re-inhabitation when landlords set their own buildings on fire.

"Every time a tenant has died," Beryl regaled them, stabbing her salad, "and I mean, while the body is still warm—*whoosh*, in sweep the work-men to 'renovate,' and never mind ruining those glorious old cornices and chandeliers! They rip the guts out. The landlord's completely redone the lobby, though it was in mint condition, and converted the basement to disgusting little studios, so we don't have laundry facilities anymore. Anyway, he finally got his hands on my neighbor's place down the hall—AIDS—and that did it. Seventy-five percent of the building is now offi-cially ruined, which qualifies as 'substantial renovation.' That takes it out of rent stabilization, totally. I don't know what I'm going to do!"

"You mean he can now charge you what your apartment is actually worth?" asked Glynis.

"Yes!" Beryl fumed. "Bingo, my rent could go from a few hundred bucks to thousands! Thousands and thousands!"

"I'm surprised," said Shep. "Sitting tenants under that regime are usually protected like endangered species."

"We *are* an endangered species. I might have been okay, except the *moment* my landlord hit that seventy-five percent mark he hired some goons to go on a witch hunt for illegal subletters. The guy who's purely as a technicality on my lease and lived there, like, five tenancies ago, back in the Stone Age, moved to New Jersey. I paid him a *fortune* in key money, too. But the idiot changed his voter registration, so they found out."

"You mean it's not even your lease?" said Shep.

"Morally, of course it is! I've been there for seventeen years!"

Despite Shep's intuition that Beryl's headache was about to become his as well—her problems often exhibited a transitive property—his sis-ter's real estate welfare coming to an end was insidiously satisfying. "On the open market," he observed, "that place might go for five or six grand a month."

Glynis didn't look *insidiously satisfied*; she looked delighted. Ever since her diagnosis, she'd seemed to relish anyone else's misfortune; so much the better if it was Beryl's. "So what's the game plan? Don't tell me *you* want Amelia's room."

"I'd *like* to *sue*."

"Whom for what?" asked Shep.

"That guy has been scheming to reach the seventy-five-percent threshold for years, and practically none of that 'renovation' was necessary."

"It is his building."

"It's *my* apartment!"

"Only if you can afford the rent. Listen," Shep forked a black rippled edge from a noodle, "maybe you should think 'glass half full' here. About how lucky you've been. What a great situation you've had all these years. Okay, it's over—" His voice caught. *How lucky you've been; what a great situation you've had; okay, it's over.* He could've given the same speech to himself.

"Nobody feels *lucky*," said Beryl, "when their luck has just run out."

"You can say that again," said Glynis. Rare accord.

Shep served second helpings. He'd broken out Glynis's famous sterling fish slice for the meal, a little unwieldy for lasagna, and admittedly incongruous with the beaten-up aluminum baking pan. But he wanted his wife to feel accomplished, to take advantage of a rare opportunity to show off on her behalf. When they'd first sat down to dinner, the lithe line of the silver, the oceanic Bakelite inlay of sea green and aquamarine, had obliged his sister to admire the very metalcraft that she was loath to concede Glynis ever got around to fashioning. The transparent insincerity of Beryl's compliments provided his wife a backhanded pleasure.

Glynis declined another serving. Please, he whispered. *Please.* He placed a small square on her plate anyway, mumbling, *You don't understand. It's not about food anymore, about whether you want it.* Beryl was too caught up in the loss of her rent stabilization to infer what the exchange might mean. With no idea how to bend the evening's subject matter around to the real issue, he tried to shift it by degrees.

"You know, speaking of bum luck," Shep raised offhandedly, "do you carry any health insurance?"

"I'd hock my firstborn child, but I don't have one."

"So what would happen if you were in an accident, or got sick?"

"Beats me." Beryl's manner was defiant. "Don't emergency rooms have to take you in?"

"Only for immediate care. And they still stick you with a bill."

"Which they could shove where the sun don't shine."

"That could ruin your credit rating," he said, cringing inside; the likes of *credit ratings* were exactly what he had yearned to flee in Pemba.

"That's your world, big brother. Out here in mine, I could give a shit." Apparently Beryl's furious resentment had leached from her pending eviction to encompass her staid brother, his conventional house in Westchester, his gas-guzzling SUV, and his spoiled dilettante of a wife.

"But if something terrible happened to you . . ." Shep ventured. "Well, the person who would really end up paying for it is me, right? Who else, with Dad on a pension? In fact, that's why I pay for Amelia's insurance."

"I'm not stopping you, if you want to buy me health insurance, too. Since from the sound of it you're not really worried about me, but about yourself."

"An individual policy at your age could run to a grand a month."

"QED," said Beryl. "Some months I don't net more than a grand. So, what, I'm living on the street out of garbage cans, but, boy, do I have the best health insurance that my entire annual income can buy!"

"When you're not covered," said Glynis, "hospitals charge twice as much."

"Which makes a *lot* of sense," Beryl fumed. "Double charge the folks who can least afford it."

"I didn't make the system," Shep said quietly. "But you're getting older, things happen, and this is something you should start considering."

"Look! Fortunately right now I'm not about to keel over, because I've got a problem a lot more pressing, okay? If you're really worried about me, then, yes, you can help. Assuming I'm not going to fight this thing—which I also can't afford—I'm going to have to move. I thought for the time being I could haul my crap up to Berlin; Dad says that'd be okay. Maybe even hole up there a while, to save on expenses. But to get another lease in New York I'd still need help on a security deposit. That's three months' rent up front. And you know what's happened in Manhattan—a studio the size of a Porta Potti goes for three thousand a month! So, look, I hate having to do this, but . . . Well, doesn't it make more sense for me to buy something? Instead of pouring all that rent down a rat hole? If you could just cover, I don't know, maybe a hundred grand or so for a down payment . . . Think of it as an investment."

"You want me to give you a hundred thousand dollars. *Or so.*"

"I never want to be in the position again where some prick landlord can kick me out of my own home. I mean, this is an emergency, Shepardo. I'm begging here."

Shep reached for Glynis's hand under the table. They'd had some dreadful rows over Beryl's *loans*; a glance reassured her that this time he wouldn't slip his sister a check when Glynis wasn't looking.

"Beryl," he said evenly. "We are not buying you an apartment."

Beryl looked at her brother as if confronting a hitherto reliable appliance that suddenly wouldn't turn on. She tried the switch again. "Maybe you'd like to think about it."

"I don't need to think. We can't do it."

"Why *not*?" As usual, presumably an unsatisfactory justification would effect a reversal of policy.

Nevertheless, this was the opening that Shep had been waiting for. He took a deep preparatory breath, one just long enough for Beryl's temper to rev. She seemed to register that, unlike the intrinsically ambiguous matter of sexual consent, with money "no" really does mean "no," consternation at which drove her recklessly to burn her bridges.

"Don't tell me," she said blackly. "You have to keep my down payment salted away for *The Afterlife*. You have to keep stashing away millions and millions of dollars for some fantasy Valhalla, and meantime your own sister is thrown out on the street. You have to go on expensive vacations year after year, on the pretense that you're doing 'research.' But get real! If you were ever going to decamp to a Third World beach sipping piña coladas, wouldn't you have gone already? You could make a huge difference to my life right now, but no! We all have to pay for your delusion, for this hubristic idea of yourself as special and above the common ruck, when the truth is you're an ordinary corporate salaryman like practically every other drudge in the country. I've tried to do something interesting with my life, and make challenging, imaginative films that make a difference to people's experience of the world, and it's not my fault that doesn't pay much. I work just as hard as you do, and maybe harder, a lot harder. But I've got nothing to show for it, and now I don't even have a place to live—thanks to rich capitalists just like you who have to get even richer. Meanwhile, you drive around in a fat car and live in a fat suburban house with a bank account that's busting at the seams—for what? You're only going to see one *afterlife*, my brother, and it's going to be a pretty scorching experience if while you were alive you weren't a little more charitable toward your own family!"

Assessing that Beryl appeared to have finished, he gave his wife's hand a gentle squeeze before interlacing his fingers on the table squarely opposite his sister.

"You're right," Shep said calmly. "Despite how long I may have hoped to, we are not likely at this point to start a new, fascinating, relaxing life in a more affordable country. I'm sorry about that. I'm far sorrier for the reason."

"And what's *that*?" Beryl sneered.

"We just found out that Glynis has cancer. It's a rare and virulent disease called mesothelioma. I may have given it to her myself from working with products that contained asbestos. I will need to conserve both my energies and my funds. Between Glynis's health and buying my sister property in the most inflated real estate market in the country, I have to opt for saving my wife's life."

It wouldn't have been appropriate to smile, but he did have to suppress one corner of his mouth from rising in a curl of recognition. He'd told Jackson in the park this afternoon that he wanted to "do the honors" and inform his in-laws about his wife's condition, since Glynis was sure to bait her relatives into saying something nasty and then to cut them to the quick with her zinger bad news. Maybe the two of them weren't such different people as Shep had often feared.

know this is perverse," said Glynis, languishing in a chair while he washed up. "But I had a wonderful time tonight. I never realized that having cancer could be so much fun."

"She's always thought that, you know. That The Afterlife was a 'delusion.'"

"Beryl's the creative one, and you're the dullard. People get very attached to these designations. She wouldn't want you to be capable of doing anything brave or strange."

He turned to her from the sink. "Would you?"

"Maybe," she considered. "But not without me."

"Be honest," he said. "Without—this. Would you seriously have considered dropping everything and coming along?"

"According to you, you never would have gone."

"Moot point." He went back to scrubbing the blackened crust from the lasagna pan.

"It isn't moot," she said, "whether you love me."

He stopped. He rinsed his hands, and dried them on a towel. He knelt by her chair, and took her face in both hands. "Gnu. In the next few months, you will discover," he promised, "how much I love you." He kissed her, and let his lips linger until he could feel her spirit still.

He returned to the task at hand. It took a minute for the water to make it to the sink again. When it first became apparent that they had moved into their Elmsford rental "temporarily" in the adult sense of the word—i.e., as a synonym for *forever*—he had consoled himself by constructing a fountain at the kitchen sink. It was a whimsical contraption, with a culinary theme: the water ran from the faucet up a rubber hose that ended in a turkey baster, whose jet spray spun a round metal whisk, then cascaded down a chipped delft teacup, a bent soup ladle, an old-fashioned glass lemon juicer, a cow-shaped coffee creamer, and a wooden-handled ice-cream scoop he'd picked up at a stoop sale that must have been a hundred years old, finally landing in a tin funnel that directed the water back into the sink. Pleasingly, the water maintained roughly the same flow and pressure provided without the journey he imposed upon it, even if the hot water did drop a few degrees along the way. The mechanism was a kooky, childlike affair reminiscent of the game of Mouse Trap he'd grown up playing with Beryl. Yet his fondness for this homemade toy had taken a blow when he and Glynis came back from Puerto Escondido several years ago. In their parents' absence, the kids had disconnected the hose. Presumably they dispensed with the nonsense over the kitchen sink whenever they had the house to themselves, and reconnected the hose when their father was due back; for the first time they'd forgotten. He didn't tell the kids they'd hurt his feelings. Naturally he would have liked them to cherish the product of his playful side. But he couldn't force his children to treasure in their father what he treasured about himself.

"I wonder, did you put it all together, that business about Berlin?" Glynis asked, once he had resumed battle with the pan. "While you were busy buying her a new apartment, she was planning to move all her stuff into your father's house. Meantime, you were supposed to put him in an assisted-living facility so she could live there without the bother of his company."

"Losing the rent-stabilized place—she's not thinking straight, and she's panicking."

"You're too kind."

"Lucky for you."

"God, the indignation! As if rent stabilization were a *human right*. And what was all that about how hard she works and how it's 'not her fault' she makes no money? She made her choices. It's called making your bed. So you lie in it."

"We're better off than she is," he said, adding, "monetarily anyway. She's jealous."

"But she holds you in contempt."

"It makes her feel better. Let her."

"I mean, the nerve! A hundred grand! Which would just be the beginning, since she wouldn't have made the mortgage payments, either. I warned you a long time ago that if you kept giving in on the smaller amounts, it would only get worse."

"I didn't mind helping her out now and again." A doubt crossed his mind over whether in different circumstances he might have been amenable to his sister's proposition after all.

"Did you get a load of that 'millions and millions' crack? Where'd she get that idea?"

"Beryl's like a lot of people who've always been hard up. They think there are people like them, and then everyone else is unimaginably wealthy. Some money is the same as infinite money. She doesn't have kids, and she doesn't know what things cost. Zach's tuition. Car insurance in New York. Taxes—"

"You can bet she doesn't pay any. And it's people like your sister who think people like us should pay even more."

"Well, I hate to sound like Jackson. But Beryl is completely unaware that her life is subsidized. That her trash is collected, that she can go for a walk in a park, that emergency rooms really will treat her without insurance if she's bleeding—it's all paid for by someone else. I'm dead certain that thought never enters her head."

"To the contrary," Glynis agreed. "She doesn't feel like a beneficiary, but like a victim. She has a chip on her shoulder the size of a redwood."

That the same might be said of Glynis Shep kept to himself.

"My favorite part of the evening wasn't even your announcement," she continued. "It was the crocodile tears afterward. All that histrionic solicitation and despair. So fake! Just like all that overdone fawning over the fish slice. She's a terrible actress. She was mostly aggrieved that from now on she can't put her hand in your cookie jar."

"Well, I guess the expectation is that in the face of serious illness, all the—friction—between people, like you and Beryl—"

"*Friction?*" Glynis laughed, and the sound was wonderful. "She detests me!"

"Okay, but even that—it's supposed to go away. She can't feel that way about you anymore, and then she still does and it's awkward."

"There's something delicious about it. I can't explain it, but I loved watching her so obviously play pretend. I get the feeling there are just a few bits and pieces of this mesothelioma thing that I'm going to enjoy."

As he lovingly dried the fish slice, the fact that Glynis roused herself to get up and wrap her arms around him from behind was strangely moving. She was so depleted that small gestures of affection must have cost her an extraordinary outlay of energy.

"Oh, and did you notice?" Glynis mumbled into his shirt, laughing again. "She still remembered to take the chocolates."

Chapter Six

The timing of the Before Picture dinner up at Shep's was even worse than Jackson had foreseen. The night before, the Saran Wrap that Flicka wrapped around her eyes to seal in the Vaseline had come off while she slept—he should never have bought that off-brand surgical tape—so that morning her eyes had been flaming. While he was out for a few hours, she apparently got—well, "irritable" was an understatement.

For while Carol was always urging him to avoid subjecting Flicka to "stress," by far and away the biggest source of stress for their elder daughter was the very condition that made her so sensitive to it. She didn't mind her father's familiar mouthing off about isn't it a coincidence how every sanctimonious new "green" law legislators proposed, like a *tax* on plastic bags, a *tax* on airline carbon emissions, just happened to make the State more money. She did mind waking up with puffy red eyes halfway to conjunctivitis before breakfast. She did mind not being able to talk right when she had plenty to say. She did mind drooling all the time, and sweating all the time; even if the kids at school had been lectured on not making fun, she might have preferred a little regular-kid teasing to the outsized politeness and looking-the-other-way she put up with instead. She got sick of having to pour that water-sugar-and-salt solution into her g-tube every hour and a half, which produced none of the gasping satisfaction she witnessed in her sister after a deep, thirsty quaff of Coke. She got tired of wearing that big black "airway clearance system" vest for fifteen minutes every morning and night, as if bracketing her sleep with two rounds of boxing.

Flicka might have been grateful that the Vest now spared her parents' uncomfortably intimate double-fisted pounding on her back while astraddle her buttocks. She might have been grateful, too, that they'd given up on the chest drainage sessions that had tyrannized her childhood: the tube worked unpleasantly down her nose, the pump's sickening gurgle and slurp, the grotesque accumulation of mucus in the waste container; it had always amazed Jackson how much thick, viscous gunk could derive from those two tiny lungs, and though Carol had always dispensed with the effluent with her usual no-nonsense officiousness, he could not have been the only one to have found the gloppy, stringy substance nauseating. But if he himself was grateful that dislodging her congestion had grown less revolting, for Flicka gratitude was a foreign sensation. She suffered so many other annoyances that she simply transferred her vexation to something else: chronic constipation from all those meds, the humiliating enemas.

Moreover, the biggest trigger of a dysautonomic crisis was surely sheer dread that, for fuck's sake, she was about to have another dysautonomic crisis.

The signs would have been falling into place in his absence, while Carol was making a German chocolate cake to bring to tonight's feast at the Knackers'. He knew the drill. Flicka had endured more medical indignity by sixteen than most folks abided over a lifetime, and her true nature was stoic. Sure, she grumbled plenty, but if she ever got outright whiny, that was a red flag; "change in personality" and "emotional lability" were textbook indicators of a crisis. The thing was, most kids with Riley-Day—an older tag for familial dysautonomia that sounded like a pop duo who sang perky numbers on Christian

radio—would "whine" that their sister was hogging the family computer. But Flicka had an existential streak a mile wide, and her personality never altered as much as all that. Her version of "lability" was a
lot harder to take. She would "whine" about the fact that she hated her
life and hated her body; about how she had nothing to look forward
to besides submitting to more bouts in the hospital, ending up in a
wheelchair, and having her whole cornucopia of symptoms—the wild
blood pressure fluctuation, the chronic congestion, the lousy balance,
the cornea infections, the seizures—get *worse*. Flopping and perspir-
ing about the kitchen, she'd "whine" that she'd rather be dead. That
was rough for any parent to listen to, since the declaration couldn't be
put down to regulation teenage histrionics. She meant it. This wasn't
a kid who "didn't understand the concept of death," either—the likes
of whom Jackson had never met anyway. Like most children, Flicka
understood perfectly well what death was, and on days like this she
thought it sounded wonderful.

Sure enough, he could hear the girl's nasal screech from the back
of the house while he was still out on the stoop. ("No, I didn't wear
the Vest, I hate it, I hate everything, all this stuff about how great it
is at least to be alive, I don't know what you see in it!" Brief lulls were
doubtless filled in with Carol's ritual assurance that she shouldn't talk
like that, that "life was a precious gift," sentimental homilies guaranteed
only to further their daughter's rage.) He was still feeling afloat and
unfocused himself; he'd been warned not to drive, and had ignored the
injunction. The sedative seemed to have brought on an after-high, for
when he'd filled the tank over on Fourth Avenue his chatter with the
attendant had been manic even by his own standards.

"Why don't you just let me cut out? It's not worth it!" Flicka wailed
from the kitchen.

Walking in on this foofaraw confirmed his conviction that, Christ,
he'd earned doing one thing for himself, hadn't he? Just one?

"I don't want your stupid scrambled eggs!" Flicka was wheezing
when her father entered the room. "I don't want to spend all Saturday
afternoon with my speech therapist, and occupational therapist, and

physical therapist. I'm going to die anyway, so just let me watch TV! What does it matter?"

Carol had grabbed the girl's hair and was squeezing more Artificial Tears in her eyes. (One of the first signs of FD, that the baby couldn't cry, was something of a sick joke; any infant with a future like this had every reason to weep.) As Flicka was rasping, "Just leave me alone! Let me fall apart in peace!" she started to hyperventilate.

Granted, it wasn't always easy to distinguish the symptoms of FD from the side effects of the meds; nausea, dizziness, tinnitus, canker sores, backaches, headaches, fatigue, flatulence, rashes, and shortness of breath came with both territories. But the nature of this episode grew clearer when in the midst of her gasping Flicka started to retch. The dry heaving was excruciating to watch, somehow more so than before the fundoplication, when she'd have spewed what little she'd ingested of Carol's unwanted plate of scrambled eggs in a six-foot projectile plume. At least proper vomiting had seemed to offer relief. The retching was ceaseless and unavailing, as if an alien embryo in her guts were clawing its way out.

"It's a crisis," Carol told her husband grimly. Most wives would make such a statement in the spirit of hyperbolic melodrama; for Carol, the verdict was coolly clinical. "Thank God you're back. Hold her."

Jackson clutched his tiny writhing daughter to his chest. After wrestling with the button and zipper with some difficulty from behind, Carol pulled Flicka's jeans down, hastily coated her own middle finger with Vaseline, and slipped a tiny tablet the color of marshmallow peanuts as far as she could up her daughter's ass. Without taking a reading that they didn't have time for, it was always tricky to discern whether Flicka's blood pressure was soaring or plummeting, but Carol made an educated guess at low—the girl's skin was clammy, pale, and cold— and administered a pink tablet of ProAmatine in the same rude fashion. Flicka's whole digestive system would already have shut down, and even meds administered through her g-tube wouldn't absorb.

"Now, remember—" said Carol.

"Yeah, yeah, I know," Jackson interrupted. "We gotta keep her upright for the next three hours." Carol never gave him any credit. He knew perfectly well that lying down after ProAmatine could send Flicka's blood pressure from knee-high to through the roof.

All this time, Heather had been mooning on the sidelines looking envious, and envy in these circumstances made Jackson worry that she was far dumber than she tested.

For good measure, Carol inserted yet another tablet of diazepam, and within a few minutes the convulsive retches in his arms spasmed farther apart. Fortunately, Carol had crammed Flicka full of Valium fast enough to avert a full-blown crisis—the human equivalent of a hard-drive crash—which would have sent them straight to New York Methodist. However, the rescue did cost the cake, which was now filling the room with the sharp, not altogether unpleasant smell of charred chocolate.

I apologize for the store-bought cake," Carol said at the door. "We had a mishap with the home-baked one."

Carol never used Flicka as an excuse, a discipline Jackson admired. Nor would either of them mention how much they'd be out of pocket for the sitter. Flicka having been volatile, they'd called Wendy Porter, their usual registered nurse, who was FD au courant. Hell, they'd have cancelled altogether if it weren't for Flicka. "I *like* Glynis," she'd stressed while they hovered, making sure that she didn't lie down. "She never treats me like an idiot. She asks me about my cell phone collection, and not only about my stupid FD. She can be, like, sort of wicked, too, which I like tons better than all that goo-goo sweetness I get from those fawning therapists. And now she's sick. Sicker than I am, even if that seems totally impossible. She'll be looking forward to tonight, and if you suddenly don't show up she'll be crushed. So if you stay home on my account, I swear I'll swallow some milk the wrong way and give myself pneumonia." Blackmail, but it had worked; Flick didn't make empty threats.

Jackson bustled into the kitchen with an overkill of booze—two bottles of wine, two more of decent champagne—meant to impose festivity on an occasion that didn't easily pass for celebration. Marking the end of an era, this was the last gathering of their traditionally garrulous, fractious foursome that wouldn't be undermined by dietary restrictions, fatigue, pain, or disappointing blood test results, and the very end of any era was really the beginning of the next one.

Shep had taken the same obfuscating approach to the food. Enough appetizers crowded the table on their enclosed back porch to feed a party of twenty-five: hummus, grilled chili-shrimp on skewers, out-of-season asparagus, and scallops wrapped in bacon; the dim sum, which didn't quite fit in, had clearly been provided in order to employ Glynis's forged silver chopsticks. The windows were lined with tea lights. Glynis came downstairs draped in a floor-length black velvet number, which matched Carol's glittery jet cocktail dress; between the candlelight and the women's attire, the atmosphere on the porch was that of a séance or satanic ritual. When Jackson wrapped their hostess in a fervent embrace, his fingers sank alarmingly into the velvet; that was a lot of fabric and very little Glynis underneath. Her shoulder blades were sharp as chicken wings. That was no size in which to undergo major surgery, and now he got it about all that food.

"You look fantastic!" Jackson cried. She said thanks with girlish shyness, but he had lied. It was the first of many lies to come, thus another reminder that tonight marked more beginning than finale. Glynis had applied more makeup than usual; the blush and rich red lipstick were unconvincing. Aging anxiety was already etched into her face. Nevertheless, she was a tall, striking woman, and this was the best she was liable to look for a while. That it could well be the best she would look again, ever, was a thought he tried to block.

They settled into caned armchairs while Shep fetched champagne flutes. In the olden days, meaning six weeks ago, Glynis would have hung back on the sidelines conversationally. Wised up to the fact that sparse comment carried greater weight than garrulity, she was the sort who let everyone else argue forever over details, and then made the one sweeping pronouncement that brought the fracas to a close. But now her bearing was regal, as if she were holding court, Queen for a Day.

In turn, he and Carol were solicitous, careful to stop talking as soon as she opened her mouth. They let her lay out the procedure scheduled for Monday morning step by step, though they'd already got the whole lowdown from Shep. If Glynis was the center of attention tonight, it was the kind of attention that anyone of sound mind might gladly have skipped.

"At least I got contacting Glynis's family over with," said Shep. "Telling her mother was a trip."

"She's such a prima donna," said Glynis. "I could hear her bawling through the receiver from the other side of the kitchen. I knew she'd hijack my drama into her drama. You'd think she was the one who had cancer. She even managed to make me feel bad that I was making her feel bad, if you can believe that."

"Isn't it at least a relief," Carol said tentatively, "that she cares?"

"She cares about herself," said Glynis. "She'll milk this for all it's worth with her book club—you know, the terrible wrongness of a child falling ill before the parent, et cetera, et cetera. Meanwhile, my sisters are saying all the right things, vowing to visit, but they're mostly glad it's not them. Maybe I'll luck out and Ruth will send me some scented candle she got on a free offer from MasterCard."

There was a harshness about Glynis in the best of times, and Jackson wondered what reaction her family might have had that would have pleased her more.

"And how was telling your kids?" asked Carol.

Glynis visibly flinched.

"More difficult," Shep intervened gently. "Amelia cried. Zach didn't, and I wish he had. I think he took it harder. I hadn't imagined it was possible for that kid to get more closed up, more burrowed into his room. I'm afraid it's possible. He just—shut down. Didn't even ask any questions."

"He already knew," said Glynis. "At least that something awful was afoot. That I slept too much and my eyes were often red. That we whispered too much, and stopped talking when he walked in."

"I bet he thought you were getting a divorce," said Carol.

"No, I doubt that," said Glynis, taking her husband's hand and meeting his eyes. "Shepherd has been very tender. Very, obviously tender."

"Well, I hope a little affection isn't so rare that it's what set off Zach's alarm bells!" said Shep, looking grateful but abashed. "You know, this room thing the kid's got going . . . Nanako, our new receptionist, told me about these Japanese kids who never leave their rooms at all. What are they called, something like *haikumori*? The parents leave meals outside the door, collect the laundry, sometimes empty bedpans. The kids won't talk, and never cross their thresholds. Mostly hole up with their computers. It's a big phenom there. You should check it out, Jacks, right up your alley. A whole subculture of kids who say, fuck you, I'm not interested in your shit, leave me alone. We're not talking dysfunctional eight-year-olds, either; lot of these opt-outs are in their twenties. Nanako thought it was a reaction to Japan's hothouse competition. Rather than risk losing, they refuse to play. The indoor version of The Afterlife—without the airfare."

In widening the discussion to Japan, Shep implied that it was now all right to talk about something else besides disease. Even Glynis seemed relieved.

"Those *hiki-kimchi*, or whatever," said Jackson. "Precocious moochery is what that is. You gotta give these guys credit for figuring out so young that when you refuse to take care of yourself, someone else will come along and roll your sushi for you."

"But it's hardly an enviable life," said Carol. "Not what any of us would want for Zach."

His wife's persistent sincerity sometimes grew trying. "Hey, Shep, I been thinking about that problem of my titles not being sufficiently flattering to my would-be public." Jackson plunged a triangle of pita bread into the hummus with the pretense of an appetite. "So check this out: *Just Because You're a Quailing, Lily-Livered Twit Who Folks Smarter and Gutsier Than You Are Bleeding White Doesn't Mean You're Not Still a Nice Person.*"

It went over well.

"Speaking of being bled white," said Glynis, "Beryl came over the other night. Can you believe she expected us to put up the entire down payment on a Manhattan apartment?"

"Why not throw in a yacht while you're at it?" said Jackson. "Christ, that woman is Mega-Mooch. Ever notice how these arty bohemian types think we owe them a living? As if we're all supposed to feel so grateful that they're creating *meaning* and *beauty* for us poor uncultured Neanderthals. Meantime, they're always shaking a tin can in our faces—for another government grant, or a Midtown penthouse courtesy of Meany Capitalist Older Brother." He and Beryl had met once: oil and water. She thought he was a heartless right-wing kook, and he thought she was a soft-headed liberal pill. Whenever Shep's sister came up in conversation, Jackson couldn't contain himself.

"But, sweetheart," said Carol, "I thought Mooches were supposed to be 'smarter and gutsier.' I thought you admired them. In which case, you look up to Beryl, right?"

"I prefer folks getting away with murder who know they're getting away with murder. Instead Beryl has that attitude like she's the victim of some terrible injustice. As if the world needed another documentary. She should turn on the box. They're chockablock, and most of them bore the shit out of me, frankly."

When Jackson trailed their host to offer a hand in the kitchen, Shep remarked, "Say, you all right? You're walking funny."

"Aw, just overdid it in the gym. Pulled something." The line had worked on Carol.

Dinner was lavish, with a roast and a profusion of side dishes. Worried about interactions, Jackson made an initial effort to go easy on the wine, but it seemed that every time he reached for his glass it was empty again. At length he gave up and gave in. This was a special night, and not to enter into the spirit of the occasion would have been churlish. The evening had revved into high gear, albeit with a jittery underpinning, everyone laughing too readily, too hard, and too long. At least boisterousness beat moping.

"Been following the Michael Jackson trial?" Shep brought up.

The self-styled "King of Pop" was being charged one more time for messing with little boys at his sick-fuck fun-land ranch. "Yeah, the prosecution's making a mess of it," said Jackson. "He'll get off."

"I can't follow the details," said Carol. "I get too distracted by that face—all the plastic surgery. His face is always the real story for me. It exerts a warped, train-wreck fascination."

"You know, it used to be that when you had mental problems, they stayed in your head," said Shep. "Now we all have to look at them."

"I know what you mean," said Glynis. "It's like now everyone wears their neuroses on their sleeves. We used to be surrounded by a bunch of passably normal-seeming people who went home and peered miserably in the mirror. Now you walk down the street and women have breasts the size of Hindenburgs. Men in dresses on hormones are wearing push-up bras, and you can tell from the fold in their Lycra tights that they're all carved up with some grotesque gash of a vagina. It's like having to live in other people's dreamscapes."

"With Jackson—I mean, Michael Jackson," said Carol. "What breaks my heart is the shame. How somehow he's been made to feel that being black is humiliating, something to be effaced."

"At this point in time," said Glynis, "I have no understanding of going in for surgery, for anything, if you don't have to."

"The guy's got money," said Jackson. "If what he wants to buy is looking like Elizabeth Taylor, that's his business."

They all looked over at him as if he'd just grown three heads. He held up his hands. "I'm just saying, what's wrong with trying to make something you dream about real?"

"Because it doesn't work," said Shep.

"That's not how you felt about The Afterlife," said Jackson. "You wanted to make that real."

"We're talking about hacking up your body, not moving to a new house," said Carol. "It's obvious, for example, that every surgery and skin-blanching process that 'Wacko Jacko' has subjected himself to has only made the man more unhappy. Every disappointing nose job is one more reminder that he doesn't only hate his race, and his gender, but himself."

"It's like sexual fantasy," said Glynis. "I don't want to get into particulars—"

"Damn!" said Jackson.

"But have you ever tried acting them out? It's flat. It's messy or awkward and self-conscious. When you make it real, it doesn't get you off. Fantasy works better if it stays in your mind. Let it into the world, and it comes out like some gory, misshapen afterbirth. And Shepherd," Glynis paused, taking a forkful of green beans, "I *don't* think The Afterlife was any different."

Jackson worried they were getting into touchy territory, but Shep was used to taking gut punches with the smallest *hoof.* "Maybe," was all she got out of him, and he asked how she liked the almonds on the beans. At least Glynis was making an effort to eat, which clearly made the guy so ecstatic that he couldn't have cared less what she said.

It wasn't until they'd pushed back their chairs from the groaning board that someone brought up Terri Schiavo, the brain-damaged patient on life support in Florida whose bloated face had lolled on the lead story of virtually every TV newscast for weeks. Her husband wanted to withdraw her feeding tube, while her parents were determined to keep alive what was no longer a daughter, or even the family goldfish, but closer to an azalea bush.

"Man, am I sick of watching that same footage," said Jackson. He did an imitation, slackening his jaw and letting drool drizzle his chin, emitting a thin nasal bleat.

"Stop it," said Carol. "That's disrespectful."

He realized too late that the impersonation was a little too close for comfort to Flicka.

"What makes me mad is that this has nothing to do with Terri Schiavo anymore," said Glynis. "The husband and the in-laws hate each other, it's all about who wins, and that poor girl gets lost in the shuffle. They could as well be fighting over a scrap of meat."

"It's no longer all in the family," said Shep. "Whole country's at each other's throats over this one. But honestly, if you saw a movie in which some private medical face-off ended up involving the governor of Florida—the president's brother—the state legislature, the state Supreme Court, the federal Supreme Court, *and* the Congress of the United States, you'd think the plot was totally overdone and unbelievable."

"When you look at those video clips of Terri," said Carol, "it seems pretty clear that someone's home. Withdrawing the feeding tube would be murder."

"Oh, Christ," said Jackson. "Those are involuntary movements. Like when you poke at a sea anemone. Except that a sea anemone has more brains."

"What fascinates me," said Shep, "what with all the publicity, going on for months? I haven't heard a single shock jock speculate about how much keeping that woman plugged in for fifteen years has *cost*."

"Yeah," said Jackson, "and if you add in the lawyers' fees, court costs, and the time squandered in legislatures and the statehouse? That one human house plant in Florida must have cost millions, tens of millions—maybe even hundreds of millions."

"So?" said Glynis, looking back and forth at her husband and his best friend in horror. "What does that matter? What it costs?"

"We're talking about human life, Jim!" Jackson supplied, but Glynis didn't smile.

"Is that all that matters to you two? What someone's life *costs*?"

"It's not all that matters," said Shep. Jackson figured his friend was about to back down again, but surprisingly he held the line. "But it matters. It takes about five dollars a head to save the life of a kid in Africa with diarrhea. Something like two million kids on that continent basically shit themselves to death every year. If you took all the money spent on keeping Terri Schiavo alive—if you can call her alive—and spent it in Africa instead, I bet you could save every single one of those kids this year."

"But the money wouldn't be spent in Africa, would it?" Glynis glared. "Who else would you like to kill off, to save money?"

"No one, Glynis." To Shep's credit, he met his wife's eyes. "Like you said, the money wouldn't go to Africa anyway."

Jackson decided to come to the rescue. "Thing is, these gonzo evangelicals, who are so fired up to save Schiavo—who's reverted, at best, to a hundred-and-seventy-pound baby? They're the same folks who support capital punishment. They're gung ho on any military adventure abroad. If they had their say, they'd roll back the clock and you couldn't get birth control out of wedlock. They oppose stem-cell research because it uses a few microscopic specks from an embryo that's otherwise going to be tossed into medical waste. They may back national health insurance for children, but couldn't care less about health insurance for the kids' parents. They get hysterical about pedophiles like Michael Jackson, but they don't get excited about women being raped, who are supposed to bear the babies of their attackers. Add it all up? This type? They don't give a shit about *grown-ups*."

The diversion came at a price. Carol wasn't born-again, but he had still derogated a host of his wife's opinions. Her voice was frosty. "That's because adults can stick up for themselves."

"Not against these people!"

"*These people* stick up for the weak."

"Prefer the weak," Jackson countered. "No competition. And they *use* the weak to boss other grown-ups around."

Carol rolled her eyes. "The point is, we have no idea what kind of rich interior life Terri Schiavo might be enjoying. The dreams, the memories, how much she knows her family is there and feels them caring for her even if she can't communicate. Her husband has no right to make the high-handed decision that since he's tired of visiting and he's in love with someone else he's going to snuff her out."

"I have to agree with Carol," said Glynis. "You never know what kind of a life someone might still value even if you don't think you'd put up with it yourself. In fact, you might be wrong. You might put up with it. You never know what you'll put up with if the alternative is nothing."

Helping to clear the dishes, Jackson marveled at the last discussion's curious alignments. This foursome conventionally divided on issues of the day along the same axes. Shep and Carol were sentimental (they would say *compassionate*). Glynis was customarily on Jackson's side.

They were both practical (the other two would say *callous*). For *Glynis* to be arguing to continue artificial life support for a woman who, according to earlier photographs, used to be quite a looker, and who—were she to realize that the pics of her face running on front pages all over the nation were of a fat, vapid, floppy imbecile—would turn in her grave, if only she were allowed to have one . . . Well, Shep must have been wrong. Cancer did change people.

By the time they were picking at the bakery layer cake, the mood had sobered. They all seemed to remember the reason for this occasion; past midnight, Glynis's surgery was only a day and a half away. They shouldn't keep her up any later. She looked tired, and Jackson was rounding on an exit line when she rounded on him.

"Jackson, have you had a chance to think about what products you and Shep might have worked with in the early eighties that could have contained asbestos?"

"Well, I've really put my mind to it, but—"

"Jackson and I have already talked about this, and I told you we talked about it," said Shep, his tone uncharacteristically testy. "Maybe you should drop it."

"Hey, I don't mind—" said Jackson.

"I mind," said Shep.

"If some company had done this to you," Glynis charged her guests, "would you honestly be inclined to *drop it*?"

"Had this happened to any of us," said Shep, his voice flattened in a hyper-evenness that was obviously a substitute for shouting, "and if you're right about where the fibers might have come from, everyone at this table could have been exposed—I would hope we'd all concentrate first and foremost on getting well."

"It would be one thing if I fell and hit my head," said Glynis. "Or smoked my whole life when I knew it was bad for me and then got cancer. But this was done *to* me. By people who deliberately buried medical evidence. Who kept deadly products on the market because they wanted to make more money. Those people should pay the price."

Shep glanced at his guests with chagrin. They were close friends and went back decades, but he didn't commonly conduct marital spats in their presence. "I know it isn't fair," he said softly. "But you'll be the one who pays the price, Gnu, even if you do win a lawsuit."

"People who care that much about money can only be punished by losing it," said Glynis. For someone who was sick and at the waning end of a long evening, she marshaled a surprising vehemence, allowing Jackson to glimpse one appeal of her fixation: it gave her energy. "There's a whole specialty practice of 'mesothelioma lawyers' who advertise on the Internet. Asbestos is their entire practice, and they represent cases on a contingency basis. So it wouldn't cost us a dime, if *that's* what you're worried about."

Jackson rarely saw Shep have trouble with self-control. But the guy's jaw muscles were clenched, and he was holding his silverware like a pitchfork. "I repeat: the purchasing records for that era are no longer on file. I checked with Pogatchnik. I've done exhaustive searches on all the potentially suspect materials we might have worked with at Knack. Once in a while a brand name sounds vaguely familiar. But 'vaguely familiar' will never stand up to legal cross-examination. I do not—do not, Glynis—have any physical proof of having ever worked with a particular product whose manufacturer we could haul into court."

Jackson wondered how many times Shep had recited that same speech. Since this time, too, Glynis gave no sign of having heard it, his guess was several. "When you buy things, and especially when you work with them professionally, you rely on those manufacturers to have a conscience! You have to be able to trust that when you buy a loaf of bread it's not laced with arsenic! In metalsmithing, I have to be able to assume that if I subject a lump of solder to the torch, it is not going to give off poisonous fumes, or if I slip a piece of silver in the pickle it's not going to explode! I—"

And then she stopped. Her face suspended in an expression of intense concentration. She cocked her head and looked a little to the side, with her forehead creased.

"I don't know why it's taken me so long to think of this," she said. "In art school. The soldering blocks. The crucibles for casting, the lining we used. The heat-proof mitts. I'm almost sure they contained . . . asbestos."

"*Almost* sure," Shep said warily. If his wife was in the process of letting him off the hook for involuntary manslaughter, he didn't look too thrilled about it.

"Well, yes, pretty sure. In fact, very sure. When I think back, I remember one of my teachers mentioning the material in passing. But when you're a student, you work with what they order. You—trust."

"You can't sue the school," said Shep. "You told me that Saguaro Art School closed years ago."

"No, but virtually all our supplies were from the same company. I can visualize them perfectly, down to the elliptical logo printed on the bottom of the soldering blocks. The insulation lining for the crucibles was packaged in a cardboard canister with a metal top, like top-shelf whiskey comes in, only wider and shorter. The label was black and green. The mitts: they were cream-colored, printed with little purple flowers and green sprigs, and piped in pink. Those products have surely been discontinued or had the asbestos removed by now, but the company is still in business, because I ordered from them only last year." Glynis looked up with an expression of beatific revelation, like Mary after the appearance of the Archangel. "*Forge Craft.*"

That was weird," Jackson said on the way home. Having kept to soda water after one ceremonial glass of champagne, Carol was driving. She was the one who could really stand to cut loose once in a while, and he felt a little guilty that his own—call it *expansiveness*—rarely allowed for that.

"How so?" Her coolness derived from his having, in her view, drunk too much. So she had to take care of him, just as she took care of Flicka. Little wonder that at dinner parties her husband stuck up for the rights of grown-ups. Carol was the consummate grown-up, and he sometimes worried where she found any joy in her life.

"What took her so long to remember she worked with asbestos in art school? It's been weeks. Meanwhile, Shep's been raking himself over the coals about having been careless at Knack."

"Memory's fickle." Though there was hardly another car on I-87, Carol always drove the speed limit.

"I guess this asbestos thing has turned out to be a gold mine for a lot of people."

"I doubt Glynis cares about the money itself in the slightest," said Carol. "I'm glad if she's stopped blaming Shep. He's going to have his hands full in the coming months without feeling like, on top of everything else, her cancer is all his fault. Still, the asbestos thing—it gives her a sense of purpose. It makes cancer seem bigger than her small personal misfortune; it makes it seem more important than ordinary, pointless bad luck. It connects her to the world: to history, to politics, to justice. I can see why she'd cling to that. Because when you get sick, I think that's the hardest part: living in a separate universe from everyone else, like having been exiled to a foreign country."

Much like Shep, Carol wasn't given to speeches, but when she did say something it came out whole, considered. He knew what she meant, too. When they'd hugged goodbye at the door, the feeling was like being on the deck of an ocean liner with the horn sounding. It was time for the non-passengers to get ashore. When their car reversed out of the drive with their two friends waving on the porch, it was the house that seemed to be pulling away instead, released from its moorings to recede toward a horizon from which it was impossible to send postcards.

"Sort of like Flicka, and the Jewish thing," said Jackson.

"Yes, exactly." She seemed unnervingly pleased that they were conducting a successful conversation. "The members of our support group . . . The fact that FD only afflicts Ashkenazi kids, it makes them feel that gene handed down through the generations amounts to more persecution of the Chosen People, more of God's testing their faith. As if FD means something." Carol allowed herself a rare surge of speed. "Of course, it doesn't."

Though outsiders would never have guessed, Carol was much more of a nihilist than her husband. She sat for hours numbly at her computer doing sales outreach for IBM, filled the humidifier in Flicka's bedroom before fetching a new roll of Saran Wrap for their sadly plastic version of tucking their daughter in, and for years had risen wearily at 1:00 a.m. to pour the first of the night's two cans of Compleat into Flicka's feeding bag—all without any sense of mission. She just did it.

Paying Wendy in cash, Jackson reasoned that the nurse may have been worth it, since by some miracle both girls were asleep. As he and Carol got ready for bed, he waited for her to finish brushing her teeth before darting into their master bathroom himself, catching a startled expression as he closed the door in her face. "It's for your sake," he explained through the door. "Have to cut a wicked fart."

How many times a day was he going to have to fart? This was going to be trickier than he realized, and he wondered if he'd thought his strategy through. He took advantage of his privacy to inspect matters, since *matters* had begun to hurt. He'd been relieved at first that the "discomfort" was so minimal; the real story was that the local was only now wearing off.

By the time he emerged, Carol was in bed, her bare breasts curved over the top sheet. For her slender figure, they were unusually full, the kind of knockers that other women were always trying to buy and couldn't. That said, the lesson that you either had it or you didn't was not one he could accept on his own behalf.

"What's with the boxers?"

"Oh, I've been meaning to tell you." He had rehearsed this all day. "That appointment I had this morning. Seems I've got some kind of skin condition, probably from showering in the gym. The dermatologist warned me that it was microbial or something." He'd picked up the word from a pharmaceutical ad on the news the night before. "It's contagious, and you could pick it up if I'm not careful."

"Well, let me see it!"

"No way. It's kind of gross. I don't want to turn you off."

Carol slid down the pillows. "Since when do you ever turn me off?"

God, it was a waste, with those cherry nipples like the garnish on a two-scoop banana split. He loved her with her hair down, and had been wanting to pick the bobby pins out all night. Nevertheless, though most guys would consider him lucky, for Jackson desiring his wife was always accompanied by a gnawing little torture. He never felt quite up to her. Even after having been married these many years, he was never quite sure what she saw in him.

"That's the other thing," he said. "We can't—not for a while. This thing takes a long time to clear up, or that's what he told me."

"I still wish you'd let me take a look at it."

"You've nursed Flicka all day," he said, slipping in beside her with a discreet glance at his fly, which did indeed stay closed with the help of the safety pin. "You don't have to nurse me, too."

He didn't relish lying to her about the boxers, but she wouldn't have understood if he'd been straight—if he'd explained that when you give someone a present, especially a really big present, you had to wrap it first.

Chapter Seven

Shepherd Armstrong Knacker
Merrill Lynch Account Number 934-23F917
February 01, 2005 – February 28, 2005
Net Portfolio Value: $664,183.22

The Sunday before the surgery, Glynis wasn't supposed to eat any solids. Out of camaraderie, Shep felt he shouldn't eat anything, either. To his embarrassment, he got hungry. The fridge was packed with leftovers from the dinner with Jackson and Carol the night before. Fasting with so much food destined to go bad seemed perverse. So he would wait until she went to the bathroom, then stick a surreptitious finger in the hummus.

Zach came home from his overnight with a fellow *hikikomori*, hacked off a hunk of cold roast beef, and went straight to his room. Depleted and radiating an anxiety she wouldn't articulate, Glynis watched TV in the den. Whenever he checked on her, another pharmaceutical ad was reminding them of all the other ailments that lay in wait, and if they didn't slay you, the cures would:

. . . is not for everyone. Tell your doctor if you have an allergic reaction that causes swelling of the face, mouth, or throat, or affects your breathing or causes rash or hives. Side effects may include upper respiratory infection, stuffy or runny nose, and sore throat and headache . . . serious stomach ailments, such as bleeding, could get worse. Some people may experience fainting. Some people may have nausea, diarrhea, vomiting, bruising, or not sleep well. Some people may have muscle cramps or loss of appetite or feel tired . . . If you develop fever or unexplained weakness or confusion, tell your doctor, as this could be signs of a rare but potentially life-threatening condition called TTP . . . may have a higher chance of pneumonia . . . may increase your risk of osteoporosis and some eye problems . . . may increase the chance of heart attack or stroke, which can lead to death. All prescription NSAIDs increase the chances of serious skin reactions or stomach and intestinal problems, such as bleeding and ulcers, which can occur without warning, and can cause death.

Accompanied by the strumming guitar and uplifting flute cadenzas that in his boyhood typified alternative folk services in his father's church, these warnings were all delivered with a lilting, lobotomized pleasantness—the tone of voice in which one might read bedtime stories to small children about mischievous bears and over-curious kittens. Meantime, ads for high blood pressure medicine alternated with ads for salt-and-vinegar potato chips, ads for high cholesterol medicine with ads for two-for-one pizza, ads for acid reflux medicine with ads for a chain restaurant's baby-back ribs. Averse to inferring conspiracy, he perceived only an odd sort of balance.

He kept trying to come up with comforting things to say. He repeatedly fought the impulse to assure her that she'd come through surgery with flying colors, because he obviously had no idea. Yet absent sham clairvoyance, he could do little but ferry Glynis more apple juice than she wanted. Last night's voluble dinner now seemed improbable. Today Shep and his wife had barely spoken. Only a warm hand on her neck seemed to make a difference. This was a time of the body. To communicate was to communicate with the body.

He didn't want to tell her what he was thinking. His thoughts were selfish, but there was too much time. Too much empty space and suffocating quiet. So he couldn't stop himself from wondering if there was anything, any single prospect no matter how small, to which he was looking forward.

He hated his work. He hated hating it, too; to despise the company he had brought into the world seemed a parental betrayal. He feared his son's getting older almost as much as Zach did—since lately that's all the boy appeared to do, just get older, not wiser or clearer, no more determined or firm in himself. He dreaded suing Forge Craft for damages, when the damage was done; civil jurisprudence would entail more forms, procedures, and postponements, in which Glynis's medical circumstances were drowning him already. And he was hardly relishing the imminent arrival of Glynis's family from Arizona. He would put them up while Glynis recovered. Feed them, ferry them to the hospital, keep them entertained. The controlled neutrality he had maintained in relation to his in-laws for years now was bound to slide to impatience.

He tried to think conventionally, to anticipate the joyful day of his daughter's marriage. But Amelia was at that age when she'd doubtless marry the wrong boy, whom she'd rapidly outgrow. He would know this, despoilingly, on the day. At her wedding reception, he pictured his toast to the happy couple as forced, himself already mournful over their pending divorce. He pictured all the other guests speculating wanly about how long this one was likely to last, while making cynically good use of the open bar. Posing for group snapshots, he would envision the prints shoved ashamedly into a bottom drawer. The lavish flowers would wither in his mind's eye as in time-lapse photography. It would descend on the father of the bride like a divine vision that within a few years these two flushed and devoted young people would no longer possess each other's current email addresses.

Nevertheless, Amelia was the type who'd expect a wedding with all the bells and whistles. A modern woman who, over the course of her

life, would blithely recite "til death do us part" two or three times with
no sense of self-consciousness. She was a girl-girl. Clothes. As scathing
about violation of the rules of fashion as her mother felt above them.
Her hopped-up, hectic determination to have "fun" was a little tiring.
He worried that the intensity of her resolve to live it up in her twenties
betrayed a corresponding pessimism about her life thereafter. He worried, too, that she saw her own father as the embodiment of the very
party's-over adulthood that the girl was so desperate to forestall.

He was glad, he supposed, that she had earned a degree. Yet he
wondered whether the abundance of the information provided by a
$200K Dartmouth BA in "media studies" might have been available
through a free trial subscription to *The Atlantic Monthly* and a basic
cable package including Turner Classics for fifty dollars a month. His
daughter's dubious degree had alone decimated the savings he'd accrued previous to the sale of Knack. Shep may not have expected his
own father to send him through school, but it was customary now: a
child had a right to a university education. So he should not resent the
expense, and therefore he did not resent it. Yet after decades of single-
ply, turkey-burger stinting, actually to be punished for the frugality
had been, well—disconcerting. His cash assets had flat out disquali-
fied Amelia from financial aid.

He kept it to himself, of course, that he found Amelia's style of
dress—the bare midriff, the skimpy tops, the glitter on her breasts—not
so much risqué as obvious. Trying too hard to be a woman, and therefore childish. Consequently, in that vision of her wedding, he foresaw
her coming to loggerheads with her classically tasteful mother, who—

Who would not be there.

In relation to Glynis, there was nothing to look forward to. Nothing.
While friends would never have described Shep Knacker as irksomely
sunny, he was an optimist all the same. Yet he did not understand what
an optimist could contemplate when not a single cheerful advent plausibly awaited in his future.

Amelia called late afternoon. She surprised him. So demonstrably
upset by the news at first, she would surely have planned to visit before

the surgery. Her reason for demurring—having to work through the weekend on the next issue of the money-losing, negligible-circulation arts journal that she helped to edit—sounded generic. His daughter's pep talk with her mother was short. Of course, today he'd no right to complain that anyone else in the family had nothing to say.

Shep sneaked another skewer of cold shrimp, which he shielded ascending the stairs. He stood before his son's door. What a radical gesture it had come to seem, simply crossing this threshold. His first knock was soft, inaudibly deferential. He tried more loudly a second time. After formally opening the door, Zach stood blocking the entrance, as if his father were trying to sell him something.

"Mind if I come in?"

He did mind. But Zach was, on the surface, well behaved. He drew back to resume his seat at the computer. Feeling a little foolish still holding the bamboo skewer, Shep sat springily on the edge of the bed, ill at ease. It wasn't the posters of bands he'd never heard of, or the mess. It was the plain fact of not being welcome. Kids never seemed aware that "their" rooms were a generous conceit on the part of the parent who paid for the entire house. It was Shep's right, legally, morally, and financially, to walk into this room whenever he liked. Then again, some dim consciousness that in truth children had no territory may have explained why they defended their illusion of territory with such ferocity.

"I wanted to check if you had any questions," said Shep. "About what happens next."

"Happens?" Zach gave no indication that he had any idea what his father was talking about.

First Amelia, and now this. "To your *mother*," said Shep, as if reminding the boy that he had one.

"They're going to operate. And then she'll come home and take drugs and she'll lose her hair and shit." The boy's phrasing was crude, but uninflected.

"That's pretty much it."

"So why would I have any questions," said Zach, stating this very question in the declarative. "It's on TV all the time."

"Not—all of it," his father said lamely. Cancer in the world of entertainment was a neat one-word expedient for the disposal of characters who had served their purpose, and would vanish politely off-camera. It added gravitas to a series in danger of seeming trivial. It provided a plot twist from which primary players reliably recovered in an episode or two—never more than a season.

"So what part do they leave out?"

Agony, he wanted to say. Time, he wanted to say. Money, he did not even want to say, but that, too. "I guess we'll find out the hard way."

The boy was incurious. He should have had questions. Yet it was not as if Zach had no sense of mystery, as if he regarded the world as known. To the contrary, the appurtenances of his life were nothing but mystery. Take that computer. When Shep was fifteen, he did his homework on a typewriter. It was electric. He may not have completely understood the circuitry through which a tap on a key raised the arm of a letter. Still, he could watch the arm rise, inspect the three-dimensional backward *a* affixed to the metal. He could grasp the elementary process by which it struck an inky ribbon and stained a black *a*-shaped mark on a physical piece of paper. But when Zach typed an *a*, it was magic. His iPod was magic. His digital TV was magic. The Internet was magic. Even his father's car, the machine through which boys once achieved their first dominion over the physical world, was now controlled by a computer. Diagnosis of malfunction didn't involve tinkering with an engine and getting covered in oil. The car plugged into another impenetrable computer at the dealership. Were anything to go wrong with the technical furniture of Zach's life—and these days, machines didn't sputter on you, develop a funny hissing sound, or start to squeak; they either worked, or they stopped dead—the notion of fixing it himself would never enter his head. There were sorcerers for such things, although the concept of repair had itself grown arcane; one was far more likely to go out and buy another machine that magically worked, then magically didn't. Collectively, the human race was growing ever more authoritative about the mechanics of the universe. Individually, the experience of most people was of accelerating impotence and incomprehension. They lived in a world of superstition. They relied on voodoo—charms, fetishes, and crystal balls whose caprices they were helpless to govern, yet without which the conduct of daily life came to a standstill. Faith that the computer would switch on one more time and do as it was asked had more a religious than a rational cast. When the screen went black, the gods were angry.

At that moment, Shep had his first glimpse of why Zach might seem to be getting older in an exclusively temporal sense. Nothing the boy had been taught in school had supplied him the slightest jurisdiction over the forces that controlled his life. Second-year algebra failed even fractionally to inform him about what to do when their broadband service cut off besides call Verizon—the sorcerers; it failed to illuminate what "broadband service" really was, beyond merciful access to magic. This passive, unmastering relation to the material world permanently suspended his son in the powerless dependency of childhood. So it made perfect sense that Zach would be uninquisitive about his mother's treatment. Modern medicine's hocus-pocus was surely as supernatural as everything else.

Supernatural? Shep wanted to recall to his son the slick, membranous skin between the leaves of an onion. That, he would say, is like the onion's *mesothelium*. It will be tedious, but it won't be fancy: they will slice her like a vegetable. And then pick, bit by bit, the tiny shreds of that onion skin that look peculiar—too stiff or too slimy or the wrong color. Sewing her back up is not so different from the way we truss a turkey at Thanksgiving, to keep the stuffing in. This is the old world, he wanted to say. This is the world of typewriters and vegetables part spoiled, and what makes it so frightening to me and your mother isn't that it's inconceivable, but that we understand it.

"I think it would be nice if you helped keep your mother company today," said Shep. It was exactly the sort of near-order that his own father would have delivered.

"I don't know how," said Zach.

Shep almost rejoined, *I don't know how, either*, and could not fathom how they had all been reduced to such rudimentary social ineptitude.

Presumably people had been falling catastrophically ill since before the species walked upright. There ought to have been a protocol, perhaps a strict one.

"She's only watching TV," Zach added.

"Then go watch it with her."

"We don't like the same stuff."

"Go watch whatever she wants to watch, and at least seem to enjoy it."

His son sullenly closed out his computer. "She'll know you told me to."

She would know. And he could force his pliable son to sit vigil at his mother's side, but he could not make him want to. In general, Zach had inherited the worst from both his parents: his father's obedience, and his mother's resentment. The combination was deadly. At least rebellious resentment led somewhere—to defiance, to a sometimes flamboyant overthrow of the existing order. The obedient kind fostered only disgruntled inertia.

Shep put a hand on his son's arm. "The next few months are going to be difficult for all of us. Your mother won't be able to give you a ride to school; you'll have to take your bike. I may need you to chip in and do some cleaning, or make up beds for guests. You just have to remember that however hard it is for us, it's going to be a whole lot harder for your mother."

The speech was gratuitous. He was playing at being a good father rather than being one. Zach had sometimes been petulant about possessions, nagging for things that "everyone else" got—to Shep, costly gimmickry that would only fill the gap between the last and the next must-have. Zach found his father's constant budgeting for an "Afterlife" baffling if not deranged, and his campaign for that iPod had been so persistent that Shep had relented out of boredom. But in all other respects the boy asked for too little. So the one aspect of his mother's illness that he would have registered from the very start was that the importance of whatever he wanted or needed or was had just been demoted from slight to zero.

That night in bed, Glynis curled on her side away from him, assuming the same position that she had when she was pregnant. Shep drew up closely behind her, aware that he had become leery of touching her abdomen, yet sensing that this instinctive avoidance should be resisted. He felt distant from her. It wasn't Pemba; it wasn't Forge Craft. It was that what was about to happen to her was not about to happen to him. He pressed harder, since she would sense their distance. But when he laid a hand gently on her stomach, she moved it with equal gentleness away.

His experience of the night was of insomnia, though to remember the dream the next morning he must have slept. He was reroofing a closed-in porch, and the owners had wanted the original roofs removed before the shingles were replaced. It was an attractive house that seemed to have what they call "good bones." There were many layers of previous roofing jobs, and as he pulled them off each revealed patterns that he recognized as the sequence of wallpapers that he used to peel back from a tear beside the bed of his boyhood. When he pulled up the roof's last thin covering, expecting the blond timbers of this sturdy house, the cavity underneath the final tar paper was black and corrupt. The timbers were infected with mold. Beetles and grubs scuttled from the light. The wood of the frame was moist, and crumbled at his touch. Though seemingly sound from the outside, the roof had been leaking for years. As he stood to call down for his workmen, the beams would no longer support his weight, and the structure gave way.

Since Glynis couldn't have any, he skipped his own morning coffee, so mobilizing for their departure took too little time. He wondered if all along he had made coffee every morning not for the beverage itself, but for something to do.

It was still so early that the traffic toward northern Manhattan was light. The sun had not yet risen. Shep associated driving in morning darkness with excitement, a flight to India with a three-hour advance check-in. He was excited now as well, but it was the excitement of fire alarms, of blizzards, of 9/11.

"This is going to sound crazy," Glynis volunteered; he was grateful that she was talking. "But what frightens me most is the needles."

Glynis had a life-long aversion to shots. Like so many aversions, in the absence of her overcoming it this one had grown only worse. When they watched movies in which heroin addicts injected themselves, she turned her head away, and he had to tell her when it was safe to look back at the screen. During news reports about new drug discoveries or vaccination programs, she left the room. She was ashamed of it, but she could never bring herself to donate during blood drives, and traveling to countries that required inoculations for cholera or boosters for typhus had always been an issue. It had taken him years to appreciate the enormity of the gesture, the scale of her earlier determination to cooperate with her husband's aspiration, in her submission to hypodermics for his sake.

"I thought of that," he said. "The contrast medium for the scans . . . How did you do it?"

"With great difficulty. Before the MRI, I almost fainted."

"But you've also needed blood tests—"

"I know." She shuddered. "And there will be more. The chemo . . . You sit there with an IV in your arm for hours. When I think about it, I get woozy."

"But in relation to other stuff, you're such a stoic! Remember when you sliced your middle finger in the studio?"

"It's not the sort of thing you forget. I was using that flex-shaft burr shaped like a miniature buzz saw. It grabbed the silver and kicked. I was lucky I didn't lop off half the finger. I still don't have any feeling in the tip."

"Yeah, but you came downstairs all matter-of-fact, and announced quietly, like, *It is my clinical opinion that I may need a few stitches, Shepherd, and I'm a little concerned that I shouldn't drive with only one hand.* In the same tone of voice that you'd have asked me to run to the A-and-P because unfortunately we were out of chives. Which is why it took me too long to notice that the rag around your left hand had turned crimson and was starting to drip. What a hard-ass!"

She chuckled. "I bet if you looked closely I was a tad pale. And I've never used that buzz-saw burr again. It's still in my kit, with the grooves stained brown."

"But this needle phobia. Won't it probably ease up? With having to keep getting past it?"

"It hasn't let up so far. But it's so irrational, Shepherd. I'm about to be gutted like a fish, and all I can think about is a pinprick."

"Maybe," he proposed tentatively, "you focus on the irrational fear to distract you from the rational ones."

She slipped a hand on his thigh, the touch so welcome it gave him chills. "You may not have a college education, my dear. But sometimes you're very smart."

Merging onto the Saw Mill River Parkway, Shep wondered at how yesterday there seemed nothing to say, and now there seemed too much and too little time to say it. With foreboding, he could see how this vacant, wasted leisure followed by a desperate, too-late cramming-in could easily prove a paradigm for their future.

"I don't think I ever told you this," he said. "I can't remember what I was watching—maybe one of those forensic shows, like *CSI*. A medical team was doing an autopsy. The coroner said he could tell from her corpse that the victim had done a lot of sit-ups. I've no idea if the scene was realistic, but it's stuck in my mind ever since. This idea that even after you're dead they can tell if you went to the gym. Sometimes when I'm working out, I have a vision of having been in an accident, and the doctors are admiring my abdominal muscles in the morgue. I want credit for doing my crunches, even as a stiff."

Glynis laughed. "That's hilarious. Most people worry about clean underwear."

"I guess that's all by way of saying—well, these surgeons must have to operate on all kinds of people who look like shit. Old saggy people, fat people, patients who are totally out of shape. I've no idea if it bothers them, or repulses them, or if it's all the same to them. But your body is so slender. Perfectly proportioned and well toned."

"Lately I've missed a few step aerobics classes at the Y," she said dryly.

"No, a lifetime of self-respect—it doesn't go away. The point is, I'm a little jealous, someone touching you like that. Looking at you, even looking at parts of you that I'll never see. But I'm proud, too. If it does matter to them, those surgeons are operating on a beautiful woman, and they'll feel privileged."

While keeping his eyes on the road, he could feel her smiling beside him, and she took his hand. "I don't think they look at bodies the way we do. And I don't know if internal organs are ever 'beautiful.' But that's really sweet of you to say."

He parked, and saw her to Reception, touched and relieved that Glynis seemed to want him with her for as long as possible. She wasn't a woman who easily admitted to need. He filled out the forms, pleased to have finally memorized her Social Security number. She signed the release. They waited together. Their silence was no longer empty, impotent. It was thick silence, deep and velvety silence, the air between them like warm water.

He rose with her in the elevator, introduced himself to the nurses, folded her clothes as she changed, and helped to tie the gown. He wasn't very useful in tugging up the beige elastic stockings, but he tried. Then they waited, again. He was glad for the waiting; he could have waited forever. At last Dr. Hartness arrived. He was a wiry, efficient man who could easily have been mistaken for an accountant; even his hair was dry. Shep sat at her bedside while the surgeon explained the procedure again, employing the droning, unemotional tone of voice in which one might read aloud the complicated instructions for assembling flat-pack furniture. Now accustomed to the surgeon's slide-part-A-into-slot-B approach, Shep didn't take offense, since none was meant. In fact, despite all the disparaging things that people said about doctors, this one seemed personable and decent.

"Please?" Glynis pleaded once Dr. Hartness had left. "See me through the sedative?"

"Of course," he said, and turned her head. "Don't look over there. Don't think about it. Just look at me. Just look into my eyes really, really hard."

Shep kept a hand on her cheek, holding her gaze, careful to keep his own eyes from darting even briefly to the anesthetist as she filled the syringe. And then he told his wife that he loved her. The effect of the injection was almost immediate, and these would be the last words she heard.

He had infused the ritual with as much feeling as three words could bear. Yet he wished that by convention their invocation was rare. Between spouses, the declaration was too often tossed off in hasty, distracted partings, or parlayed lightly to round up banter on the phone. He might have preferred a custom that restricted such a radical avowal to perhaps thrice in a lifetime. Rationing would protect the claim from cheapening and keep it holy. For were he to have been doled out three I-love-yous like wishes, he would have spent one of them this morning.

After leaving his cell phone number at the nurses' station, Shep emerged from the lobby onto Broadway, blinking in the sharp, white winter sunlight. He'd given no thought to how he might occupy the rest of the day, aside from a vague ambition to get some coffee. Glynis wouldn't be wheeled in right away; after the sedative, she still had to be put under general anesthesia, and then for at least four hours she'd be in surgery. Thereafter, she'd be conked out on morphine for more than a day. Again he yearned for protocol. He couldn't see the utility of a civilization that had an etiquette for sending greeting cards in December or placing the fork to the left of a plate, but as for what to do while your wife was sliced open you were on your own.

Yet it took only one *café con leche* in Washington Heights to realize that there was a protocol. It was blessedly specific, and so iron-clad that it might have been chiseled into the Constitution: In America, if you had a job that provided even the most miserable health insurance and your wife was very ill. If you had been frequently absent from that employment, and were likely to miss more days still. If your employer was a dickhead. Then when your wife went under the knife, and at every other opportunity as well?

You went to work.

Jackson seemed surprised to see him, but only for a moment; Jackson was well versed in the unwritten Constitution, too. Within minutes of Shep's arrival, Mark, the Web designer who'd been especially caustic about Pemba, came up to his desk and squeezed his shoulder. "Be thinking of you today, bro," he said. Other co-workers smiled encouragingly, particularly those who'd worked under the old Knack regime—what few were left. Even Pogatchnik showed, for him, unusual sensitivity by at least making himself scarce. So: Jackson had told the staff. Shep might have been affronted—the guy had overstepped the mark, and for all Jackson knew his friend was experiencing a violent sense of privacy— but found himself grateful instead. For he felt anything but guarded: raw, unprotected, his very insides exposed to the air, as if he had no skin. Jackson would have meant the announcement as a kindness. Shep would receive it as a kindness.

Phoning disgruntled customers, Shep might have expected to be irascible, to chafe at the inconsequence of every grievance. To the contrary, each feebly glued tile of linoleum seemed to matter, because everything mattered. He'd been so thankful for the smallest act of consideration from total strangers this morning: a nurse's application of an ice chip to his wife's cracked lips. Consideration for other strangers seemed fitting repayment. He let the complainants go on at length, expressing his dismay that their workmen had failed to give satisfaction, and promising to redress the problem without delay. When a woman in Jackson Heights objected to Handy Randy's employment of Mexicans, insinuating that they were all illegals—which, let's face it, they probably were—he didn't impugn her illiberality, but explained patiently that while their Hispanic handymen were hardworking and competent, their English was often poor. They didn't always grasp what was required. He would ensure that a fluent native speaker was sent to fix her doorframe, until the screen door swung to with a graceful click.

Lonely, he was glad of the clients' companionship, glad for the contact, for the sound of the human voice. Customer relations as video game: focus, on anything but Columbia-Presbyterian. He was unusually

aware of his control over the quality of a few moments in these customers' lives—lives, after all, comprised of moments, and only of moments.
Single-handedly, he might redeem five minutes of their day. It was no
small matter. The redemption carried forward into the future, too, by
providing a remembered encounter with a helpful, receptive man who
had sympathized with their troubles, and endeavored to resolve them.
He could make jokes that were glorious for the very fact that he need
not have made them. How odd that at every point of contact with other
people, meaning dozens if not hundreds of times a day, he had always
wielded this power—to elevate the quotidian to the playful, the humor-
ous, the compassionate—and so rarely made use of it.

He worked through lunch and called at two. She was still in surgery.
He called at three. She was still in surgery. At four as well. He told
himself it was good that the doctors were being thorough. Yet that was
too long to lie with parts of you gaping open, the parts that you didn't
think about, that you didn't want to think about, that you took bliss-
fully for granted. By now customer complaints were failing to divert his
attention, and more than once he had to ask a householder to repeat the
problem, the address, the date of the job.

The fact that Glynis was in surgery for nearly twice as long as scheduled enabled Shep to put in a full workday—which, with his thin life-
line to insurance, was important even if it shouldn't have been. By the
time he got Dr. Hartness on the phone it was close to six. Jackson had
hung about, and was obviously listening in.

"Well, there's at least that . . . I see. And what's that exactly? . . . What
does that mean? . . . No, with me I'd rather you were frank. . . . Tonight,
would there be any point in my—? . . . No, I'll do it. Better it come from
me. . . . Dr. Hartness? You've worked very hard, and very long. You must
be exhausted. Thank you for trying so hard to save my wife."

When Shep hung up, he could tell from Jackson's stricken expression that his last sentence lent itself to misinterpretation. "Her vital signs
are good, and she's resting well," Shep assured his friend. "But, ah." He
remembered Glynis coming down the stairs with that hand wrapped in
red, the starkness of her message. This was another time to be factual.

"It was worse than they expected. They found what's called a 'bipha-sic' patch. Epithelioid cells, but with sarcomatoid mixed in. Like fudge marble ice cream, he said. The biopsy didn't detect it. These sarcoma-toid cells are evil fuckers, and—I guess the direct application of chemo doesn't work with them. They didn't install the ports. They got every-thing they could, which isn't the same as everything, I'm afraid, and sewed her back up."

"This is—bad," Jackson surmised.

"This is bad."

Shep would get plenty of practice repeating the same summation that eve-ning. He went home and told his son. Zach had only one question. His father dodged it: "That depends on how she responds to the chemo." Zach was having none of that. He demanded a number. So if the boy wanted to know, he should know. He took in the information like a pool swallowing a stone: after a little *bloop*, Shep watched it sink from view, and felt it settle on the bottom with a muffled clunk. It seemed to make sense. The boy did not seem shocked. His father anguished about what kind of a dreadful world Zach must have routinely inhabited where this sort of thing could seem nor-mal, or even expected.

At least from now on the two of them would be occupying the same universe. It was a universe that was falling apart. This was a purpose children serve that Shep hadn't appreciated before: when something terrible is happening to your wife, then something terrible is happen-ing to them also. You share the same terribleness, which for outsiders is mere misfortune. This mere-ness that he sometimes sensed in others had grown intolerable, which was why until today he'd avoided any discus-sion of Glynis's condition at work.

They ate together, which was unheard of. Zach offered to watch TV with his father, which was really unheard of. Shep apologized that he had to make phone calls. As they rinsed the dishes, he was pleased that, despite his good-natured permission, his son declined to disconnect the fountain over the sink.

He retired to his study. He compiled a list on the computer. He would need the list again, for other turning points, other news, and he did not want to admit but he did admit what news the list would finally be useful for delivering. He noted cell numbers as well as landlines, copying from his wife's address book. He separated the contacts into "Family," "Close Friends," and "Not So Close," thinking as he dropped this and that listing into the latter category how mortified some of these people would be by the designation. He was more inclined to put into the "Close Friends" list the few of her companions who had remembered to call on Sunday and wish her good luck.

He dialed methodically. The hardest, Amelia, he forced himself to call first. He was halting, unclear, and she kept interrupting: "But she's okay, right? She came through okay, right?" He remained on the line longer than he could quite afford to, making sure that she understood, and realizing at last that she had understood all too well to begin with and was waiting to be told something else. Getting his daughter off the phone was as painful as bedtimes of yore, when she'd wrap herself around his calf, and he'd have to prize his little girl's fingers from his trouser leg.

Yet soon his delivery of the details grew fluid: "'biphasic,' which means less aggressive epithelioid cells are mixed with the more . . ." His voice was calm. If the measured tone was misinterpreted as lack of proper feeling, he didn't care. When pressed for prognosis, he settled on the expression "a less optimistic outcome," which still had the word *optimistic* in it. They all had access to the Internet, if they really wanted to know.

This was part of his job now: disseminating information, orchestrating visits, protecting her from visits. He would be moonlighting from now on as a cross between an events planner and an executive secretary. He found himself instinctively distrusting the people he contacted who were the most lavish in their outpourings of sorrow, making nonspecific offerings to help "in any way they could." In his experience, the folks who were the most articulate about their feelings were the least apt to express them in any form other than more words. Beryl, for example, waxed especially eloquent, launching into reminiscence about marvelous times with the two of them that were either exaggerated or apocryphal, and extolling the character of a woman whom she did not like. In embarrassment, he'd cut her off, explaining that he had other calls to make. By contrast, his father said simply that he "would be praying for the whole family." While Shep might sometimes feel impatient with hackneyed Christian catchphrases, this time he was admiring of a religion that provided an idiom of well-wishing both sincere-sounding and succinct.

For more and more he was appreciating the limits of the verbal. The worse Glynis felt, the more what mattered wasn't solicitous conversation, but a hand on her shoulder, a plumped pillow, the television remote from the table, or a cup of chamomile. So he was far more moved on the phone by silence, by sighs, by palpable awkwardness. By people like their next-door neighbor Nancy, an Amway zealot with whom Glynis had almost nothing in common, or so you'd have thought. As for the dismal discovery in surgery, Nancy had honestly nothing to say and so didn't try to say it. Moreover, Nancy did not make a hazy offer of "help" that he could never call in. She asked when Glynis would be receiving visitors, when she would start taking solid food, and whether Glynis liked homemade buttermilk biscuits. She had brought over a cheese-and-broccoli casserole on the weekend, which is what he and Zach had polished off between them for supper. Shep was already getting the feeling that, in a crunch, the people you thought of as your "close friends" were not necessarily concomitant with the ones you could count on.

To his surprise, Shep slept deeply. To his shame, being in bed on his own was a relief. The simplicity of it, the undemanding expanse of empty sheet. He hadn't realized the strain of another body beside him, rotting a little more every minute from the inside out. The energy it sapped from him, not being able to protect her. You wouldn't think that something you couldn't do and were not doing would take any energy at all, but it did.

Two mornings later, Shep's trepidation about seeing his wife mirrored in some respects his dread of her return home the Night of Pemba, that distinctive horror of telling someone something that they did not want to hear. Nuttier was his nervousness that they might have changed her or exchanged her for someone else, removed something or inserted something in their knifing about that would make her unrecognizable to him.

But then, the anxiety was not entirely out of order. He did not know what character was, or under what degree of duress it broke down and adapted to a new form that bore no resemblance to the person "Family," "Close Friends," and even those "Not So Close" imagined they had known. It was even possible that "character" and its more superficial cousin "personality" were niceties, decorative indulgences of good health, elective amusements like bowling that the sick could not afford. Given his own robust constitution, he was forced to reference farcically minor ailments like colds or flu. He conjured the dullness of color, the irritating tinniness of birds and music, the unsettling pointlessness of all endeavor whenever he felt ill, as if he himself had remained the same and it was the world around him that had sickened. His spirits sagged, his appetites flagged, his jokes evaporated. Thus, by introducing a minimally toxic virus like adding a squeeze of lemon juice to a cup of milk, a lusty, upbeat, good-humored man was soured into a glum, indifferent pill. So much for the durability of "character." Multiply that effect by a thousand times, and it was little wonder that he feared for who, or what, lay in intensive care at Columbia-Presbyterian.

Shep was probably not alone in hating hospitals, in visiting someone he loved and still fighting an urge to flee. It wasn't just the smells, or a biologically instinctive impulse to avoid disease. If illness was the great leveler, the problem was to which level. Dressed in identical flapping gowns that gaped humiliatingly at the back, patients along the hallway were deprived of all that made them distinctive on the outside—accomplished, interesting, or useful. Sucking up fluids, drugs, and nutrients, producing nothing but effluvia in return, they were uniformly burdensome. Glimpses into wards at the sleeping lumps, the blank gazes at televisions, induced the impression not that all of these people were equally important, but that they were equally unimportant.

Nevertheless, he was moved by the fact that they were all admitted

for treatment, the Laundromat attendant and the Philharmonic con-
ductor alike. He had faith that the Laundromat attendant, no matter
how dim or surly or shiftless or readily replaced by another high-school
dropout, did not receive appreciably less diligent care than the maestro.
It must have been fifteen years ago when Shep was trimming a tree in
Sheepshead Bay, and the chain saw had kicked to the base of his neck—
much as that buzz-saw shaped burr had kicked to Glynis's finger, but
on a larger scale, and close to his jugular. The blood had been copious.
He still had the scar. What he remembered most of all was amazement.
Rapidly sinking into the early stages of shock, he could no longer trim
this customer's tree. He could not entertain the paramedics with interesting snippets from NPR. A man who had always measured his utility in the most tangible terms, he had rendered himself incapable of
fastening the bracket for aluminum blinds or installing a double-glazed
skylight. Yet total strangers had still hastened to press their clean towels
against his wound, and other strangers had tenderly loaded his leaking
body onto their stretcher. Some pragmatic side of him would have seen
it as perfectly reasonable that at the average hospital admissions desk
they would ask not only what drugs you were taking and were you allergic to penicillin, but what was your IQ and could you build a ten-story
condominium; how many languages do you speak and when was the
last time you did something nice: what good are you. Instead, astonish-
ingly, they pulled out all the stops to stanch your bleeding, even if you
were of no earthly use to anyone.

With multiple tubes extruding from under the sheet, Glynis took up
a childlike amount of space under her bedclothes. She looked like a sack,
like something discarded. According to Dr. Hartness, the night before
they had gradually reduced the morphine drip, and removed the tube
from her nose. The surgeon had warned that once she woke she would
still be groggy and disoriented. Ashen, she seemed to be dozing. For
once he gazed at his wife and failed to marvel that she was all of fifty
years old.

Shep pulled up a chair, careful to keep the legs from shrieking. He
sat on its edge. A mere elevator ride from the bustle of Broadway and

its oversized crullers on carts, this was an alien world of stasis, where minimal pleasures were nearly always more appealing in anticipation than in receipt—a sip of pineapple juice, the Tuesday blancmange with strawberry sauce, a visitor with flowers whose sweet, penetrating reek would end up unsettling a delicate stomach. A world where oblivion was nirvana, where one was never allowed the hope of no pain but only of less. He did not want to be here so badly that it was as if he were not here. He yearned to sever those tubes with a mighty sword as he would have hacked her chains in a dungeon, to scoop his beloved into his arms with her gown trailing, to sweep her back to the bright, clanging, frenetic world of taxis, of hotdogs, of crack addicts and Dominican pawnbrokers, where he would rest his damsel's pink bare feet to the cold concrete and she would once again become a person.

As he took the hand without the IV and warmed it with his own, her head lolled from the opposite side of the pillow to face him. Her eyelids fluttered. She licked her lips sluggishly, and swallowed. "*Shepheeerd.*"

Through the croak in a throat raw from intubation, she instilled his name with the deep erotic purr that had always stirred him, even when her intention was chiding. The eyes opened fully now and he recognized his wife.

It was she, though Glynis was not quite here. She had been on a long journey and had not, entirely, returned.

"How are you feeling?"

"Heavy . . . and light at the same time." She sounded a little drunk, and seemed to be having trouble moving her mouth. He wanted badly to give her a drink of water, but she was forbidden. Nothing by mouth until her bowels were functioning again. "Wondering," he thought she said, letting her eyes sweep the ceiling. "Everything amazing."

Well, she certainly didn't see the room as he did. "Don't try to talk too much."

"Dreams . . . So real. So long and complicated. Something about a silver tiara. It was stolen, and you helped me avenge—"

"Shh. You can tell me later." She wouldn't remember later. "Do you know where you are? Do you remember what just happened, and why you're here?"

Glynis took a deep breath, and in her exhalation was a collapsing. A sag into the mattress. "I didn't for the longest time." Now her voice was all croak and no purr. "It was lovely, like running time backward. But it came to me. You wouldn't think you could forget that you have cancer. You can, and that part is soft. But then there's the remembering, and that part is awful. Like having to go through it all over again."

"And by yourself, a second time," he said. "You should never have had to hear the diagnosis alone, Gnu. I should have been with you."

"No difference. Alone anyway."

"No, you're not." She was.

"Surgery. Don't worry, I understand, I'm not that out of it. That was the one consolation, when I remembered." Another hard swallow. "Since I also remembered that they scraped it out."

Not all of it, not by a long shot would not have made a therapeutic riposte. Still, she was more compos mentis than he had expected, just a little slurred, and he had promised the doctor that he would tell her. The surgeon was meant to stop by and speak to her later this morning. If Shep was going to break the news—*gently*, that was the conventional adverb, but there was nothing gentle about this news—he would have to do so during this visit.

"Gnu, the surgery was very successful. You're stabilized and recovering well. There were no complications. Or, rather, there's only one complication. That is, they—found something." He went through his patter, so practiced from the phone. *Less optimistic outcome.* The same phrase.

"No ports" was all she said when he finished. "Thank God. I didn't like the idea of them. I'd never say so to Flicka, but that plastic spout on her stomach has always given me the creeps. Like being half human and half . . . coffee creamer."

He blinked. It was as if she hadn't heard him. "Did you understand everything I just told you?"

"I heard you." She sounded annoyed. "Different cells, no ports, chemo. We were going to do chemo anyway."

Something had completely failed to register. Maybe the problem was the morphine.

Shep had taken the morning off, and stuck around to wait for the surgeon. Hartness was late, and Shep tried not to be angry at the man who had toiled so valiantly on his wife's behalf. Still, the extra two hours would cost him part of his afternoon's work. He could not afford many full days of absence. It was hard to keep up conversation, and as Glynis lapsed into a doze he got terrible coffee he did not want. Finally the surgeon strolled in, and Shep was able to watch the same drama from the outside, the same recitation about *biphasic* presentation, the same perfect absence of uptake from Glynis—no disappointment, no questions, no tears.

Dr. Hartness moved swiftly on to the bugle call. "But don't imagine we're throwing in the towel. We'll put you right on Alimta. It's a powerful drug. We'll give it everything we've got. We're planning to be very aggressive with this thing." *Aggressive* was a word that the medical profession often imputed to the cancer itself, and the cooptation of the same adjective for its adversary once again invoked battle—with weather. With a snowstorm, a gale wind.

Chapter Eight

Popping Tylenol like Tic Tacs, Jackson was growing concerned that the antibiotics weren't working. But this wasn't the time to focus on his comparatively petty medical concerns, and he was grateful for the sense of proportion. It was Glynis's second week in the hospital; out of intensive care and installed in a private room, she was now accepting visitors.

He'd racked his brains deciding what to bring. Shep said that her colon had finally kicked in again, and she was eating small amounts of solid food. Still, what did you bring someone recovering from major surgery, vanilla pudding? To protect her from infection, flowers were verboten. When Carol had run up earlier in the day, she'd brought a warm zippered fleece that Glynis could wear in bed, in a rich red that favored her coloring—an inspired gift of which he was envious. At last he'd hit on a quart of fresh passion fruit juice. If nothing else, it *sounded* life-giving, and for once he was glad Park Slope had gone all snooty, chichi, and ridiculous; the stuff was available in the first Seventh Avenue deli he checked. Hell, there was no telling how many more visits he would make before this nightmare was through, and he was already running dry on ideas for presents. The pattern was sure to develop that the more she deserved them the less she'd be able to find the food, the books, the clothing, or the music any use.

It was easy to identify Glynis's room; a hen party huddled outside the door. Bad timing. He hung back to collect himself, and to rearrange the drape of his trousers by sticking his hands in his pockets. These were the roomiest slacks he owned, from back when he'd weighed ten more pounds. He'd learned to walk while subtly poking the pockets forward from inside so that the fabric didn't touch anything.

He recognized the lady prattling to the two younger women. Surely over seventy by now but wearing a heavily accessorized floral getup that announced loudly, *I may be getting older but I still have my self-respect*: that was Hetty, the mother. He'd met her once before, up at Shep's, where Hetty had chattered at dinner with an exhausting vivacity. What had most impressed him in Elmsford was how she always had to be a-doing. Her host of involvements in Tucson ran from a campaign to keep illegals from getting driver's licenses to more neutral fare like an antique-finishing class and yoga for the over-sixty-five. She put him in mind of that perplexing variety of high-school classmate who had packed out his leisure time with "after-school activities" every weekday; Hetty might as well have been attending band practice and running for vice-president of the Debate Club. He'd been unable to discern whether this frantic bustle of hers was what it claimed to be—an ardent determination to live every remaining day to the fullest—or quite the opposite: an evasion. An equally ardent determination to distract herself, from what only she could know, and thus a complete failure to inhabit her life in the scarcest respect. In any event, she was the kind of lady who'd be learning Hindu on her death bed, and the fact that now she'd never make it to Delhi to try out "Where is the train station?" would never enter her head.

However long ago, that evening was easy to recall, since Glynis had got so mad. Hetty had made some, to Jackson, pretty harmless remark that Glynis construed as putting this basket-weaving-class nonsense of her mother's on a par with her own metalwork. Glynis had risen up and announced icily that she had a degree, thank you, citing the two museums that had added her pieces to their permanent collections and listing all the galleries that had shown her work, in *New York City* to boot—and not, by implication, in the no-account hinterlands of the Southwest. He remembered feeling uncomfortable. Glynis had been old enough to let the odd careless remark slide. Listing all those galleries one by one had turned her back into a little girl.

While he could see that over time that compulsive gushiness could grow wearing, Hetty Pike was nevertheless to the cold eye a rather ordinary person. Jackson was always amazed at the level of emotion that the commonplace shortcomings and piddling eccentricities of the most unremarkable character could rouse when that Jane Doe or Joe Sixpack just happened to be your parent. Granted Glynis and her mother were poles apart. A perfectionist, Glynis was reserved, hypercritical, and totally dark; Hetty was sunny, emotive, and not in the least concerned that the vase she pinched together in her pottery workshop came out misshapen and leaked. They didn't look anything alike; Hetty was short, with a round, beaming face and fluffy, permed gray hair, while Glynis's sharp, elongated features echoed the photos of her gaunt, lanky father. (Glynis had adored him. If nothing else, she may have held against her mother the fact that he, not Hetty, had tumbled off a mountain face in a rock-climbing accident some twenty years ago.)

Yet rather than shrug off the incongruity, Glynis let the fact that she and her mother were not the same, that she would never be known or understood or given the Good Housekeeping seal of approval, drive her insane. In middle age, she still wanted something from the dame, and he'd fought an urge at that dinner party to pull her aside and whisper in her ear to forget it. Hetty was a normal, limited woman who had probably been as good a mother as she knew how—meaning, your basic crummy one. So what? It was too late to be looking for something more. Besides, whatever Glynis craved—a host of trite abstractions like *validation*, *recognition*, and *acceptance* somehow failed to capture the nature of the lack—wasn't ultimately within the power of any parent to bestow.

After all, Jackson's own mom and pop were unpretentious folks who'd long run a secondhand furniture business from their garage. With his father's bad back, he might implore them to let him load the van when they'd finally sold one of the heavier white elephants, but he sure wouldn't head to Bay Ridge and eat reheated Marmitako—which sounded flashily ethnic, but was indistinguishable from tuna casserole when you made it with the canned shit—to feel better about himself. His sense of authority, of manliness, of forcefulness and surety was his responsibility, and *that* was why he'd taken action on his own account ten days ago. You didn't wait around for anyone else to give you what you wanted; you went out and got it for yourself. *That* was self-empowerment, and *that* conveyed self-respect.

"Jackson Burdina!" Hetty waved and put her decorative tin on the floor, the better to clasp Jackson's hand between both of hers, and she did not let go. A good memory for names probably came with the territory for a retired first-grade teacher, in which case his own had been added to a roster of thousands of six-year-olds. "It's lovely to see you, but I'm *so* sorry for the occasion. You have children, too, so I'm sure you understand . . ." Her eyes welled. "This is the worst thing that can happen to a mother."

"Yeah, it's rough," he concurred, wishing she'd let go of his hand.

Instead she pulled him over to the two women loitering on the sidelines. Presumably dragging them firmly by the hand was the way you introduced first-graders to their new little friends. "Now, I don't think you've met my other two daughters. Ruby? Deb? Say hello to Jackson. He and his wife are very dear to your sister."

He shook hands with both, marveling that Ruby, the middle sister, could so fantastically resemble Glynis and yet be so fantastically less pretty. Glynis was slim; Ruby was skinny. Glynis was stately; Ruby was gawky. The same set of virtually identical features were subtly repositioned in Ruby's face to the younger's disadvantage, and while you couldn't call the eldest well endowed, at least Glynis did have breasts. Glynis dressed simple-but-elegant; Ruby's straight-cut, overwashed black jeans and lank gray sweatshirt were simple-but-dingy. But the biggest difference may have been manner. Glynis had a sly aloofness that made her seem mysterious and almost regal. Ruby held herself at equal distance, but the effect was tight, stingy; she glanced too often at her watch, and tended to pace, as if this cancer thing had better get a move on because there was somewhere she had to be. Sure enough, they'd no sooner done the nice-to-meet-you when her cell phone rang. Frowning at the readout, she recited the credo of the contemporary busy bee: "I'm sorry, but I have to get this."

The hospital didn't allow cell phones, claiming that the signal interfered with equipment. (Total horseshit, according to Jackson's Web searches on Flicka's behalf. They just wanted to collect their whacking fees for bedside phones. But he'd never screwed up the wherewithal to thrust his research at a hospital authority. This manly-with-a-mouse but mousy-with-a-man habit was another thing that had to change.) So Ruby went down to return the call from the street, which left him with Deb, a plump, harmless-looking sort who radiated vacant good intentions. The clinging orange turtleneck and binding navy skirt of a matronly length weren't doing her any favors. "I've been praying for Glynis ever since I heard," she said. "Our whole church in Tucson is praying for her. You know they've done studies. It works."

Sure, it was unfair to discount all born-agains as automatons. But since when did he have to be fair?

"Now, we've discussed how to go about this, Jackson," said Hetty, placing a hand on his arm. "Glynis is going to be very tired, and we don't want to overwhelm her. I think we should go in one at a time, and try not to stay too long. Shep is visiting now, and if you can hold on, Jackson, we decided that Deb would go next, then Ruby, and then I can bring in her favorite cookies." She might as well have been lining up the class for the water fountain.

Shep slipped out the door and met Jackson's gaze with a private eye-roll. There's nothing quite so foreign as other people's families, and setting eyes on his old friend filled Jackson with that round, safe, grateful sensation of turning the corner and spotting his own house. "She's all yours," Shep told Deb and Hetty, and drew Jackson down the hall.

"Man, that wasn't easy," he mumbled. "Persuading Glynis to see family when they've flown all the way from Arizona. It was touch and go whether I'd just have to drive them back to Elmsford again. She feels like shit, and doesn't see why she's got to go out of her way to make other people feel better. This visiting thing . . . I mean, I'm sure she'll be glad to see *you*. But to Glynis it's an imposition. She gets pissed off."

"Well, how would she feel if nobody came to see her?"

Shep smiled. "Pissed off."

"Gotta love the bitch," Jackson said admiringly.

"You know, the word *patient*," said Shep, "isn't especially appropriate in Glynis's case."

"If she weren't being impossible, you'd be worried."

"Yeah. Though I'm still worried."

When they drifted back toward the room, whose door was half-open, the urge to listen in was irresistible. Even with Ruby's return, she and her mother's pretense of conversation was halfhearted. No one wanted to talk over the show.

"I can't believe you're using my being laid up after major surgery to play missionary." Glynis's voice was a little sloppy from low-level mor-phine, but Jackson was pleased to recognize its traditional edge. "Talk about kicking a girl when she's down."

"But what if I'm right?" Deb implored. "It's logical, Glyn. If you're right and all that awaits us is big black nothingness, then it doesn't mat-ter what you believe. But if I'm right—if Jesus is right—you need to accept Him as your savior to get into heaven. It makes sense to cover yourself, doesn't it? Just in case? It's almost like—math, you know? Your way you definitely get nada, and my way you have a chance at eternal life. Like, if a lottery is free, why not grab a ticket? All your teachers said you were so smart."

"*My* way I keep my dignity," Glynis croaked. "And I don't appreciate your coming all the way to New York to write me off. I don't want to go to heaven. I want to go home."

"It's never too early to prepare to meet God, and to ask Jesus into your heart."

"These days every family has one," Shep whispered. "It's usually the runt."

"That broad—*broad* being the word—is no runt," Jackson muttered back.

"Yeah, she's on Atkins. Knocks out pasta back at the ranch, which is a pain in the butt. But I meant runt like, bottom of the totem pole. Never had much going for her. No career, housewife, five kids. The Christianity thing, it gives her a leg up."

"It's cheating," said Jackson.

"Hey, whatever works. You've got two accomplished sisters you can't beat by their rules, you change the rules. Bingo, she has spiritual superiority, and she can finally condescend to all the folks who've condescended to her for most of her life."

"Do you vultures fly around the country swooping down on people too weak to put up a fight?" Glynis was saying. "You're like ambulance chasers. Christ, even Nancy didn't come in here trying to sell me Amway."

"You shouldn't take the Lord's name in vain," said Deb. "So many people like you who pretend not to believe still use *Jesus Lord* and *Christ almighty* and *good God* as exclamations. Our preacher did a whole sermon on that. He said you were calling out for God's love and redemption, even if you didn't know it. Something in you knows that His merciful hand is close by."

"Deb, I am damned if I can see what's so 'merciful' about this last three months."

"See, you did it again: 'I am damned.' You *are* damned if you don't open your heart to God. Who knows, maybe this sickness is God's way of getting you to see His light."

"So I'm being punished for my heathen ways? You can't possibly be claiming that your brain-dead born-again friends never get cancer."

". . . At least it's sure made you thin," Deb said wistfully.

"Yeah, right. The Mesothelioma Diet. The book's not out yet, but you could still get a head start by chewing on some old insulation."

"Shep said this has something to do with asbestos?"

"I was probably exposed at Saguaro Art. I'd 'smite' every stockholder of the school's supplier with peritoneal mesothelioma this instant if I could. Screwing them out of some money is going to have to do."

"You shouldn't think such evil thoughts."

"I think nothing but evil thoughts."

"I'd have expected," Deb said tentatively, "that mortal illness—"

"I love that expression. Ever heard of 'immortal illness'?" The chuckle stuttered to a cough. "Come to think about it, the illness is immortal. 'Mortal patient struck with immortal illness' is more like it."

"I thought that this situation would naturally bring out goodness and kindness and gratitude in a person." Deb sounded petulant.

"What *this situation* naturally brings out in me is bitterness and rage. When you get cancer, you can do it any way you want."

"But now you have the opportunity to realize how much your friends and family care for you. Shep says he's having an awful time managing your schedule, because so many people want to see you. This is a time to feel blessed."

"I feel cursed. If by nothing else than that kind of sad, impoverished homily from people like you who have no idea what they're talking about."

"You can be as spiteful as you like!" For some reason, Deb had started to wheeze.

"You bet I will," Glynis snarled.

"I still want you to know that I've always admired . . ." *Wheeze.* "And looked up to you. You're beautiful and talented and . . ." *Wheeze-wheeze.* "You've been a loving wife, and you've raised two . . . two . . . two beautiful children. Always remember . . ." *Wheeze-wheeze-wheeze.* "That I was proud to have you as my sister!"

Glynis flung, "Watch your fucking verb tense!" after Deb's back like a near-at-hand shoe, as her younger sibling fled through the door in tears, clutching an inhaler.

"This is like doing rounds in a cockfight," said Ruby as Hetty held and patted her sobbing youngest. "Champion bantam in Room 833 takes all comers. Wish me luck."

"Keep it short," said Shep.

"You can count on that, pal," said Ruby. "I plan to escape while I still have my tail feathers."

Perhaps mindful that it was boring in the hallway, Ruby left the door wide open. Shep having warned them off kissing, Ruby squeezed her sister's left foot before she drew up a chair, propping her long, scrawny legs on the bedrail. "Did you have to go for Deb like that? She's such easy pickings."

"I've only got the energy for cheap shots. Besides, using this occasion to try to convert me, again, is outrageous."

"She's trying to comfort you. The Jesus routine is all she's got."

"She's been brainwashed, and it's like being visited by Killer Zombie Cretins of the Living Dead."

Ruby cut a glance in their direction, and said quietly, "She can hear."

"I don't care."

"But she really believes that stuff. Just because we don't doesn't make her insincere."

"I loathe sincerity."

"Great. So I'll try to be as glib and false as possible."

"That would be swell."

"So—*how are you?*" asked Ruby. This prying, emphatic solicitation, that leaning into the words, must have been a regular tonal refrain during hospital visits, and probably backfired.

Glynis sighed. "What can I say? My whole body hurts. I can't sleep at night. Five minutes of lying here in the dark passes as fast as the Paleozoic era. Then during the day I'm groggy. I still have to make conversation with the likes of you when there's nothing to talk about. Because what's going to have happened? The TV is tiny, and only gets terrestrial channels with snow. In the afternoon, sunlight from the window wipes out the picture. Being moved to tears that I can't see *The Price is Right* is humiliating. But with the pain meds, I can't even concentrate through an article on this spring's eye shadow colors. The IV in my hand gives me the willies. I'm constantly convinced that the tape will come off, and then the needle will rip out sideways from the vein. I've trained myself never to look at it."

Jackson knew what she meant, although he himself vacillated between the same not-looking-at-all-costs and inspecting obsessively.

"Food is nauseating," Glynis continued after a sip of water. "When I keep it down it gets impacted, and they stick a hose up my ass. When Shepherd isn't here to help me to the toilet, half the time the nurses don't answer my call. So I struggle with the bedpan by myself. I pee on the sheets, and all over my thighs. Did you really want to know all that?"

"Sure I do."

"You're lying. Pretty soon people will ask, 'So—how *aaaare* you?' and I'll say, 'Fine.' Everyone will be happy."

"When are they going to let you out of here?"

She'd doubtless answered this question repeatedly. "Little less than a week, they think" was slurred with boredom.

"Mom and Deb are going to stay. But I'll probably have to fly back before you go home."

"You just got here, and the first thing you do is tell me that you have to leave." The guilt-tripping was pretty rich, given that Glynis hadn't wanted to see her family at all, but maybe the use of her illness to the hilt was a good sign. It meant she was still Glynis.

"It wasn't the first thing I said. But the Fourth Avenue Street Fair starts this weekend, and we have a table. Somebody's got to be back at the gallery minding the store."

"So never mind that your sister has cancer, if it's a matter of making more money."

"Glynis. Life goes on."

"For some people."

"Yes, Glyn, for some people," said Ruby. "Which isn't my fault."

"I thought your gallery was going great guns. Raking in the cash."

"It's doing okay," Ruby said moderately.

"Of course, some metalsmiths would find that a real opportunity, a sister who's joined the enemy. Too bad for me."

In the hallway, Shep groaned. "Not this again."

Ruby put a hand to her temple. "You didn't have a large enough body of work for a one-woman show."

"Because I'm so lazy. Because I loll around my nice house popping bonbons."

"Because you agonize over everything, Glynis. I've never understood why."

"You wouldn't."

"But life's too short for all that hand-wringing of yours. Maybe you can better appreciate that now. The other artisans I show just make stuff. And then they make other stuff. They don't give birth to it."

"I do. *I give birth to it*. Besides, after you'd regaled me with how urban and slick Tucson had become, and how your space wasn't some two-bit local storefront but a *respected institution* in a *major artistic hub*? I offered to contribute just a piece or two to a group show, and you still said no!"

"We've been through this! By then we'd changed the name to Going Native and specialized in Pueblo and Navaho work, along with showing other, mostly Southwestern craftspeople who exhibit those influences. Your work would have stood out like a sore thumb. It's too—severe, too—contemporary."

"God, I hate that ethnic shit," Glynis grumbled.

Ruby brought her feet to the floor and clapped her thighs. "Why go over this again? Doesn't this feud seem trivial now? Doesn't it seem stupid?"

"What do you want to talk about instead? Iraq? Terri Schiavo?"

"Maybe about how—we still love each other or something."

"Fine. We still love each other," said Glynis. "Got that over with. Next?"

She had a point. There proceeded an unwieldy pause during which they both seemed at a loss.

"Anyway, I don't care about Iraq anymore," Glynis muttered. "Or Terri Schiavo. I'm happy for them all to die. I'm happy about global warming, and nuclear proliferation, and shortage of fresh water. I'm big on earthquakes and floods and bird flu. I'd be thrilled for worldwide oil reserves to run out by 2007. I'd love to see the whole shebang go up in flames after being broadsided by an asteroid the size of Saturn."

"God, Glyn. I guess being sick doesn't always bring out the best in people, does it."

"Maybe it does," said Glynis, struggling up on the pillows. "But maybe the best in me, to me, isn't the best in me, to you. Maybe the best in me, to me, is hateful, vindictive, and ill-wishing. In fact, that's the perfect word. I wish everyone else were ill, too."

"I've been warned not to stay too long and tire you," said Ruby, though she was the one who sounded tuckered out. "Maybe tomorrow?"

"Great. And we can talk another half an hour about how much we *luuuv* each other."

"Whatever you want, Glynis."

"No, I get the picture. Not whatever I want. There's obviously some script here I'm meant to be following. I'll be sure and get Shepherd to download it from the Internet."

When Ruby came out, Shep suggested that the four of them go across the street to the Dominican coffee shop while Hetty made, as her son-in-law stressed, a *quick, low-key* visit. Schmoozing with only a portion of Glynis's clan appealed; whenever entire families convene, no one can bitch behind anyone else's back, and there's nothing to say.

They settled in a booth. It was a relief to sit down. Jackson had started to feel a little light-headed, and there was a hot, pounding sensation that he tried not to think about. This was not the time to dwell on his own problems; he didn't even have a problem, not really. It was a solution to a problem, and was simply taking longer to recover than he'd expected. That weird—lumpiness, the bulge. Only swelling, normal swelling that would come down. He fought an urge to go to the men's room and inspect it again, though he didn't see one; in this iffy a neighborhood, restrooms attracted bums. So he sat with his knees canted for air. One ran into Shep's leg, and when Jackson didn't move it his friend shot him a look.

"Honestly, all that bad blood over my not showing her work in my gallery," Ruby was putting to Shep. "Why can't she finally let that go?"

"You two always get into some ballyhoo over Going Native sooner or later," said Shep.

"Someday soon there could be no 'later.' That's the point. It's time to give it a rest. Also, under the circumstances, couldn't she cut Deb a little slack, too? At least say something like, *I have my own spirituality, and it may not be as different from yours as you think.* You know, try to meet her halfway."

"Well, has Glynis *ever* 'met you halfway,' Deb?" asked Shep.

"She's never been anything but contemptuous of my faith," said Deb.

Shep leaned back and swept the menu across the laminate. "You guys want everything to be different. To heal all the old sore points. I fight the same impulse. We all want to make sure that the relationship is put safely into, you know, what my dad would call 'a state of grace.' So if worse comes to worst we'll still be able to sleep at night. But think of it this way: maybe *Glynis* doesn't want everything to be different."

"Why wouldn't Glynis want our relationship to be left, like you said, in 'a state of grace'?" asked Ruby. "It's in her interests, too."

"On some level—deeper down than you have any idea—Glynis realizes that sometime soon she may not have any interests. So the only interests she has are right now."

"I don't get it," said Ruby.

"Well, haven't you three always bickered?"

"Yes! So let's draw a line, call it a day!"

"But Glynis is trying to hold on to what she has. And the relationship is—what it is."

Jackson guffawed. "I can't believe you said that." It was a running source of ridicule that Randy Pogatchnik loved the tautology ("It is what it is, man!" or "People are people, right?"), suffering under the illusion that he had said something profound instead of absolutely nothing.

"Yeah, I know, I must be tired," said Shep.

"I get what you're saying, though," said Jackson. "She's clinging to content. Even shitty content still means something. Besides, if she soft-focuses into a Hallmark card, Glynis like Glynis understands herself disappears. Almost like dying ahead of schedule."

"I still wish she'd think about us," said Deb. "After what you said about those cells, Shep." She teared up again. "The . . . *sarmacoide* or something. I mean, who knows . . . Like, whenever we visit, it could always turn out to be the last time . . . And then all we'd have to remember is a lot of bile and surliness and meanness!"

"Yeah, well," Shep said with a smile. "That just means you'd have to remember your real sister."

"So how do you figure those cookies are going down?" said Ruby after their coffees arrived.

Shep raised his eyebrows over the rim of his cup. "Badly."

"I was worried that all that chocolate, the Brazil nuts and butter . . . It's awfully rich for someone whose digestive system is barely functioning."

"You could say that," said Shep.

"Like, it's not thinking about what Glynis would really want."

"Yes." Shep's eyes shone. "I think that will be the issue."

"Mom's always been like that," said Deb. "She says you're supposed to give other people presents that you'd want yourself."

"That explains the dried flower arrangements and checkered aprons," said Shep. "They didn't go down too well with Glynis, either. And the potholder crafts kit was a disaster."

"Mom didn't want to give Glynis cookies; she wanted to make them," said Ruby. "And I'm really sorry about all the bother." She explained to Jackson, "Once she'd hit on this project, she sent Shep out to the store, and then for a second time because she forgot about the Brazil nuts. The A-and-P didn't have any, so we had to go all the way to the health food store in Scarsdale. She had to ask where every spoon and bowl in the kitchen was and how the oven works, and then she screwed up the fountain over the sink. She's not used to a hand mixer, and the dough spattered everywhere— on the appliances, the floor, and the walls. This is all to be *helpful*."

"Mom wants to be *seen* to be helpful," said Deb. "She wants credit. Notice that she only does the dishes when Shep is in the kitchen? When he's at work, she leaves them to us."

"If she really wanted to thrill your sister," said Shep, "she'd bring a few pieces from your father's old gem and mineral collection. Glynis has hankered after those specimens for ages. She's always hoped to incorporate them into her work."

"How's she going to do that now?" asked Ruby softly.

Shep pushed his *con leche* away. "There's the chemo . . . We don't know. Maybe it works. Otherwise, why would they do it?"

It was a sensible conclusion.

The group trudged back toward the hospital. As they waited at the light, Deb asked if she could log on to Shep's computer back in Elmsford. She was a member of a national prayer group holding an on-line vigil for Terri Schiavo, who was barely hanging on without life sup-port. "They unplugged her like a toaster!" Deb despaired.

"I guess this idea you've always had," said Ruby at Shep's side, "of moving abroad . . . It must have been put on hold."

"Well, your whole family has thought the notion was harebrained from the start," said Shep.

"I guess we never totally understood it," Ruby said cautiously.

"I didn't say you didn't understand it. I said you all thought it was *harebrained*."

"*Eccentric*, maybe. Although this idea that there's some other coun-try, some Valhalla out there—not always a different place, but a different job, or the perfect marriage, or if only I could get pregnant, something that's an answer . . . I can see the appeal, but I'm not sure there's ever an answer. Like, I saw a production of Chekov's *The Three Sisters* at the Temple last month. These women in the sticks pining away about how if only they could get to Moscow. And the audience knows full well that nothing would be any different for them in Moscow. So in a way, they're lucky not to go. Maybe you are, too. You get to keep the illusion, that somewhere there's a solution, a resort."

"But this is another country of sorts," Shep observed pleasantly as they entered through the hospital's double doors. "You know how in some economies you can live for a month on what it costs to buy a box of paper clips in the West? Well, you can work for a month to buy a box of paper clips in here."

Shep had picked up the tab at the coffee shop before Jackson could grab it, and though the amount was small the gesture was emblematic of a much larger assumption that all bills led to Shepherd Armstrong Knacker the way roads once led to Rome. Jackson knew for a fact that Shep had paid his mother-in-law's freight out, reasoning that her teacher's pension was pretty paltry, and that it was "hard enough" for a woman at her age to suddenly have a daughter she might survive. He'd paid for Deb's flight, too. The born-again had all those homeschooled kids, and a husband who worked fulltime for Raytheon Missile Systems—how was that for Christian?—so she had to pay for childcare while she was out East; buying her plane ticket was "the least he could do." Since this crowd had arrived, you could bet that he was covering the groceries, the gas, and the booze people suck up like lemonade at times like these. Once Glynis came home, he was planning to put her relatives up in a hotel (having eavesdropped on those family visits, now Jackson knew why). His hands full with Glynis, Shep hadn't been able to help Beryl move her crap out of her no-longer-practically-free apartment on West Nineteenth Street with the physical brawn he'd usually have volunteered, so he'd given her—even Beryl was starting to relinquish the pretense that the monies she took from her brother were loans—the couple of thou it took to have the stuff moved up to Berlin in a professional van. He was still subsidizing Amelia or she'd never have been able to afford to work for that circulation-ten-people journal of hers, and Zach's school fees were as high as sending him to a private college. Shep's father had no idea how high his winter fuel bills were running, since he hadn't paid one in years. *None* of this stuff was tax-deductible.

All that on top of the usual nonnegotiable expenses that would-be immigrants didn't take into account when viewing the United States with dollar signs in their eyes: the stiff rent (okay, Shep had been stupid, but if he'd bought in Westchester there'd be a mortgage, maintenance, and property taxes—aka renting your own house—so the difference was more negligible than you might think). The home insurance. The car insurance and rip-off repairs. Gas, electricity, and water charges, each escalating apace. The E-ZPass account, made seductively effortless so that you wouldn't notice every time you drove through the Holland Tunnel it was eight bucks a pop. The cell phone bills that could come in at hundreds a month when you had kids texting every citizen of China. The Social Security (ostensibly saving for your old age *for* you, but earning zero interest, and by the time he and Shep were sixty-five bound to be "means tested," ensuring they'd never see a dime of "their" retirement savings because the system was going broke). Not to mention nearly half of your earnings every year for *sidewalks*. So if in addition to all that the poor fuck was also getting reamed for forty percent of every three-hundred-dollar aspirin in this cathedral of health care, Jackson figured that once-untouchable Merrill Lynch account was starting to shrink.

When they returned to the eighth floor, Hetty was standing in the hall, still holding the tin she'd held carefully level all evening. Her eyes were puffy, and she looked bewildered.

With her free hand, Hetty clutched her son-in-law's arm. "Sheppy, you dear man, thank heavens you're back. Honestly, I know she doesn't feel well, and isn't quite herself. But I spent hours on those Chunky Chocolate Brazils. Shuttling the cookie sheets in and out of the oven, making sure each batch didn't burn, sliding them onto racks to cool, greasing the pan again . . . Just so my daughter could have something home-baked, a little reminder at her bedside of her mother's love and care. I could see if maybe she didn't want one right this minute. But why would she get so angry with me? Whatever did I do wrong? It's so hard for me to be strong for her when she's so terribly thin, and so terribly pale, and I just want to take her in my arms and cry . . ."

Shep put an arm around her shoulder and squeezed. "Trust me. Glynis got more pleasure out of having a problem with your cookies than she'd ever have got out of eating them."

"*Content*," said Jackson.

"Listen," said Shep, "I'm going to take these guys out for some chow." (And pay for it, Jackson thought reflexively.) "You want to say hello to Glynis? And keep it—"

"Don't worry."

Jackson's mind clamored with admonitions: *don't make her repeat details of her surgery when you know them already just to sound concerned, don't bring up the biphasic cell discovery unless she brings it up herself, try not to stare because she looks like death and equally don't avoid looking at her because she looks like death.* Yet the barrage of negatives was paralyzing. As he walked in, he remembered noticing how even her own sisters had kept a queer little distance; nothing drastic, but they'd both situated themselves subtly too far away. Though everyone knew that cancer wasn't contagious, avoidance of disease was born of a deep biological terror. He felt it himself and fought it, forgoing the chair and sitting on the edge of the bed by her knees. He expected nothing from her. Since the Tylenol was making as much difference as a handful of peppermint Altoids, he had a better appreciation than most of her visitors for the way pain wasn't just distracting; it exercised absolute veto power and, even at low levels, could so perfectly eliminate every other competitor for your attention that there was nothing else in your head to be distracted from.

"Hey." He worried that the fact she immediately closed her eyes meant she was too tired for this, although it might be a compliment; she felt sufficiently at her ease with him to do what she felt like. He rustled the passion-fruit juice from his pack and slid the carton onto her bedside table. He decided against calling her attention to it; he didn't want to seem like Hetty. The point was to give her something she might enjoy, not to get credit.

They stayed like that for three or four minutes. Jackson was manic enough by nature that keeping her still, wordless company was probably as good for him as it was for her. He took the time to study the bedside table's kooky homemade fountain; from the hallway, he'd unthinkingly mistaken that steady trickle for life support.

It was crude but cute. The basin was a bedpan. A pump pushed the water up a piece of manila rubber tubing and into an upright wide-bore syringe (so that's why Shep had asked for one of Flicka's old plungers from her g-tube equipment), to burble in a tiny plume peaceably out the top. All around the sides of the bedpan he'd glued latex surgical gloves stuffed with cardboard hands; the cardboard was curved, so the hands around the sides cupped the fountain protectively, somehow managing to convey safety, tenderness, and refuge. The workmanship was rougher than usual—it was obviously an epoxy job—and how the poor son of a bitch had found the time to knock this whacky thing together was anyone's guess. But if he were Glynis, Jackson would have found it comforting.

Glynis's eyes slit open. "I don't have the heart to tell him that it constantly makes me feel the need to pee."

"It's so—Shep."

She smiled, and closed her eyes again. "Shepherd as can be."

When you didn't know how to please, sometimes the best thing to do was ask. "What would you like, Glynis? I'm happy to just sit here. You don't have to talk. Or if you've had enough and would rather I beat it, I'd be glad to leave you in peace."

"No, stay a bit." Her head fell to the side, and she said dreamily, "Why don't you rant."

"Rant?"

"Yes, rant. You know, the way you do. About anything you want. Anything that makes you mad. That would be like music to me. Like playing a favorite song."

Jackson was not, for once, especially irate, and he felt the butterflies he associated with the rare occasions he got into bed with Carol and she was in the mood and he wasn't. Performance anxiety, they called it. "Well," he said, stalling. "I thought of a new title."

"Shoot."

"*SOAKED: How We Wet, Weak-kneed Wusses Are Taken to the Cleaners, and Why We Probably Deserve It*. I was putting in a load for Carol, so I was working on a laundry theme."

"Mmm. That's a start. Keep going."

"And, uh . . . I got a parking ticket yesterday."

Glynis tsked. "You can do better than that."

"It wasn't the usual losing track of the time, though. I was picking up some Häagen-Dazs for Heather at the Key Food just up from Knack, right? Flicka isn't allowed ice cream—no liquids, and it melts—so naturally Heather loves eating it in front of Flicka with a lot of *mmm*-ing sounds. Still, we keep it on hand so Heather knows we go to extra trouble for her, too."

Jackson rose from the bed. Ranging the room and gesticulating were wasted on Glynis with her eyes closed, but this was a package deal; antics came with the show.

"So I pull up to a meter and stuff in a quarter, enough for half an hour, okay? There's nobody in the express line at Key Food, and I guarantee you that I'm back in five. Only to find one of our local *public servants* writing me up. I say, hey, I'm here, I'll move it, and of course that doesn't make any difference, since this ticket shit's got nothing to do with fair and equal access to communal resources. It's a lucratative . . . like, money-making scam for the State, and it's a form of mugging. So I say, Look, I put in a quarter literally five minutes ago. Then this smug, officious twit points to the meter window, and he's right, it's showing a red flag. I'm so incredulous I put in another quarter to test it, and sure enough I turn the handle and the window keeps flashing red. So the fucking meter is broken. But get this: that is my personal fault. That is legally my fault, that I parked at a broken meter, even though by now I've paid for an hour's worth of parking and not even used ten minutes. The fucker finishes punching in the details and tears the ticket off his computer with a flourish and a sly little smile, and then I get it. That fucker knew the meter was broken. It's probably been broken for weeks. He hangs out by that meter, lying in wait for some sucker like me in a hurry who doesn't double-check that the damned thing is functional. I know it's pricey, but sixty-five bucks for a pint of Häagen-Dazs is pretty steep.

"Now, what is the logic of that?" Jackson glanced at Glynis to confirm that she still had that serene expression on her face; she could as well have been purring. "I pay taxes to have those meters maintained, since—the ultimate indignity—we're expected to finance the instruments of our own oppression. But if they can't get their act together, if they don't use the money I forfeit for that purpose, that's my fault, and I pay twice. The State rigs everything in its favor, and don't imagine reason or fairness or even common sense ever comes into it."

He had rounded up pretty well, he thought, but after a moment or two Glynis's eyes fluttered open again, and she scowled. "You piker. That's barely a start. Go on. Rev it up. Give it all you've got."

"All right," Jackson said with an uncomprehending shrug, figuring it wasn't his business to tell the *immortally ill* what she wanted to hear. "You know I play this game with Shep—Mr. Upstanding, Mr. We All Have to Do Our Part, aka Mr. Prize Chump—and he tries to come up with what, exactly, we personally get from our taxes. This bogus fees-for-services model supposedly keeps the exercise from being pure thievery, pure dogs licking their balls because they can. Me, I think they take our money because they can. They take more of it every year because they can. When you think about it, the absolute power is terrifying. With 'eminent domain' they can steal your house. They can pass any laws they want, and nothing actually stops them from changing the tax rate to 99.9 percent tomorrow. You realize that the IRS can reach in like the hand of God and simply clean out your bank account? Not only without asking, but without even *telling* you. One of the guys at Knack went to an ATM last year and the screen gave him this 'insufficient funds' error message. Checked the balance, and instead of several thou it said zero. He couldn't buy a single beer. Took days to track down it was the feds. Turned out his *ex-wife* owed back taxes. Though they'd been divorced for years, their having filed jointly for a single year, ever, way back when, meant that when she couldn't cough up the cash they went straight to him. And took it, just took everything. Can you believe it? When he didn't owe the assholes a dime! I'm telling you, the only thing that protects us from being robbed of every cent is that these fuckers are dependent on the slaves continuing to produce. If they take everything, they kill the golden goose. So fixing tax rates is all about figuring out how much they can thieve while still leaving us poor wretches enough to keep working so that there's more to thieve the next year. The government grows citizens like crops, and you have to leave a handful of seeds for the next planting.

"Anyway, a long time ago Shep named all the obvious supposed benefits of this, like, *industrial agriculture*, and one of the first ones he came up with was the police. They protect us from the scumbags, they keep us safe. Uh-huh. Sure, that traffic cop was preying on me to meet his ticket quota. But did my parking ticket make anyone *safe*? And just try to get any joy from our boys in blue if you tell them you were stuck up on the street or your house was burgled. They laugh in your face. That's just paperwork to them. They never catch those guys and they don't even try. They're way too busy going after drug dealers—who in a truly 'free society' would be your regular businessmen, retailing a product that didn't hurt anybody but your fully informed consumer. Selling heroin to junkies is no different from selling booze to drunks or butter to fatties or cigarettes to anybody. But no, we pay these guardians of pinky-raised propriety to enforce some moralistic, totally hypocritical 1950s bullshit, which takes up all their time, and meanwhile makes billions, *billions* for the criminals they're pretending to fight. It's symbolic . . . I mean, what's it called, *symbiotic*," he corrected himself, briefly flustered. "The cops and the drug barons are actually on the same side; they need each other. They both earn their dough from the same racket.

"I mean, think about it—what's your first reaction when you see a cop drive by? 'Gosh, I feel so well protected'? No! Anybody in their right mind is panicking, 'Am I doing anything wrong?' Or more like it, since chances are you're way too freaked out to be enjoying a moment of soul-searching, 'Could I be *perceived* to be doing anything wrong?' The police are just one more predatory species, another dangerous animal in the environment, and the fact that you are personally paying for their damn donuts and refueling their damn cars the better to stalk you and filch your wallet just adds insult to injury."

Jackson peered over at the pillow, and sure enough his lullaby had soothed her soundly to sleep. He pulled the covers to her chin. The red fleece was becoming, but he was no longer envious of Carol's flair for presents. He knew what Glynis wanted, and what to give her for many visits to come: *fury*.

Chapter Nine

B ack home after another visit to Glynis, now discharged but still abed in Elmsford, Jackson strode into his house on a roll. Some people might dread encounters with the gravely ill, but for his own part he'd begun to enjoy them. Now up to speed on what Glynis considered a proper convalescent present—perfectly distilled rage, which he pictured like crude oil: thick, viscous, and tarry, a substance that would stick to your fingers and stain your clothes and leave ineradicable prints on doorknobs—he stored up consternations from earlier in the day. Thus on arrival in Elmsford after work he had prepared a crescendo of acrimony that built like a stand-up comic's routine, save for the fact that as far as he was concerned none of this stuff was funny. Did Glynis realize that if you *win* a car on a game show, you have to pony up a percentage of its sticker price to the feds *in cash*? Did she know that so many Americans are now getting caught by the Alternative Minimum Tax that a flagrantly unscrupulous regime that levies, for example, taxes on *taxes*, is now *becoming* the tax code?

"In 1969, AMT applied to only two hundred families in the entire country!" he'd railed, pacing her bedroom. "Since they've barely moved the bracket to account for inflation, it now applies to nearly half the population. So it's like we have this really fair, decent, progressive system, although it happens to be a decoy—like one of those wooden ducks you put on the mantel. Looks nice, but you can't eat it. The *real* tax system is a scandal, but we don't take responsibility for that, since it's *alternative*. Ditto this bullshit 'mansion tax' in New York State. They haven't moved that bracket, either. So you've got all these one-family dumps all over Brooklyn, with weedy backyards the size of bath mats, thin cat-pee carpets, and mildewed basements. But because of this lunatic property boom, they're selling for a million bucks. At which point, abracadabra! It's a *mansion*, and the State takes three percent. This whole property thing, I swear the government itself could be behind it. You can't say it's in the larger social interest for your basic place to live to turn into a luxury way beyond the means of ordinary people—like glasses of water going for a hundred bucks apiece. But it *is* in the interests of the State. They're making a mint! It's so bad in New Jersey that you've got these old couples, own their home free and clear, been there for fifty years? They're having to move out. Can't afford the property taxes. Same poky three-bedroom they've always had, where they raised their kids, and suddenly these pensioners are supposed to fork over twenty-five K a year for the privilege of living in their own fucking house!"

Having gained an increment of strength, Glynis had sometimes coughed up her own sputum of spontaneous revulsion from the sidelines. He'd left the bedroom on a queer sort of high, apparently the kind of buzz you might get from chewing khat, the bitter leaves that Shep had explained underemployed slackers in East Africa ground between their molars all day long. Khat was a mild amphetamine, and Shep had tried it once. He said it left you edgy, jittery, annoyed for no especial reason, and primed for something that probably wasn't going to happen. He said it reminded him of Jackson.

Pausing at the entrance to the kitchen, Jackson assessed that Flicka was only medium miserable—meaning, as ever, that she couldn't walk properly or talk properly or breathe properly or even cry, aka business as usual—so he was not, for once, entering into the midst of a calamity, only into the slow-motion disaster of what they had learned to regard as normal life. Flicka's glower sufficed for hello. Other members of the FD support group described their disabled kids as all sweetness and light—as taking suffering in stride and lighting up whole households with gratitude for survival into each glorious new day—and he'd always suspected the parents were lying. Yet even if this gratingly chirpy, accepting type wasn't a myth, Jackson was relieved to have been awarded a sullen, aggrieved, precociously misanthropic kid instead.

Flicka was crooked at the kitchen table over her homework, a trickle of drool drizzling disdainfully onto the page. She could have wiped it away before it hit her algebra equations, but she let the saliva blot the numbers on purpose. "I wanna know why I have to learn factoring when I'm never gonna live long enough to use this junk," she grumbled.

"If it makes you feel any better," said Jackson, "your classmates who live to ninety-five won't ever use factoring either."

"Seems to me if I could drop dead at any time I should be able to do whatever I want. This is hardly making the best of a lifespan the length of a dog's."

"If we let you live like a dog—and not get an education—you wouldn't even know what you wanted to do."

"I'd rather watch *Friends*."

"You're a smart cookie. You'd get tired of *Friends*."

"It's all a farce," Flicka insisted. "And it's not for me, it's for you and Mom. I'm supposed to go through the motions of being a regular kid who goes to school. So you guys can pretend you have a regular family. So you can pretend I'm gonna graduate and go to college and get married and have kids, too. As if I'd want the little brats, which I don't. It's all a lie, and I'm sick of it. I'm warning you, too. I may stop playing along."

The trouble was that Jackson agreed with her. Maybe it would have been easier had they preserved Flicka's "innocence"—translation: ignorance—but you couldn't keep anything secret from kids these days, what with the Internet. He and Carol had signed up with their first dial-up service provider back in 1996, and the decision had been fatal. Flicka had readily figured out the drill, and her very first input into one of those early search engines—Northern Light or AltaVista—was the name of her disease. She'd stormed downstairs (which is to say, bounced down from wall to banister) and promptly vomited in a projectile spew of vengeful indignation. Their daughter hadn't been offended so much by the prognosis itself as by the fact that her parents had kept it to themselves. She'd been eight years old.

So tonight he resisted the prescribed theater. He was supposed to chime in that *new therapies for managing symptoms are being developed all the time* and that she had *no idea* how long she might live. He was supposed to remind her that most FD kids would have been dead by Flicka's age in the past—when she was born, her life expectancy was only about five years—*but many now lived to as old as thirty.* He'd heard this last figure touted out earnestly in meeting upon meeting of the support group, but Flicka knew full well that if you parsed this company line you figured out that just about all of them died *before* thirty. Flicka didn't want a cheerleader for a parent, and he didn't want to be one.

"Think of it this way," he said lightly. "If your days are numbered, you might as well be able to count them."

"Ha-ha. By the way, Mom left you some chorizo and chickpea mush on the stove."

"Is it any good?" he asked distractedly, poking a fork in the pan.

She snorted. "How would I know?"

Jackson scraped some of the red stew into a bowl and slipped it into the microwave. "Anyway, Flick, we have to send you to school. It's the law."

"I can't believe my dad is dragging out *the law.* 'Arbitrary tyranny,' I quote. Anyway, we could do homeschooling."

"Your mother has to work to cover your health insurance. She wouldn't have the time—"

"She wouldn't have to do squat. I could hang out and read—on the few days I can see anything and I'm not spending every minute wearing the Vest, grinding up meds, practicing my swallowing so I can eat food I don't want, doing those boring physical therapy exercises, and squitzering Artificial Tears."

"*Squitzering*? And you think you don't need an education."

"I don't. There's no point training me to be a *productive member of society* when I'll barely make it to being a grown-up. My having to go to school at all just exposes the whole thing as a big baby-sitting service. I don't need to learn about the causes of the Civil War, and you know it. What's gonna happen to all those facts? They'll be cremated. They'll literally go up in smoke."

Having successfully taught Flicka the proper meaning of *literally* gave Jackson a profound sense of achievement. Curious how most of the time he was able to keep her indeterminately terminal status at bay as an abstraction, or as material for easy father-daughter banter—as theoretical as his own death. For that matter, his personal mortality had become a comfort. It kept them both in the same boat. "Don't you like being able to meet other kids and make friends?"

"Not really. I'm more like their mascot. Being nice to me makes them feel better about themselves. They can show off to their parents by dragging home this stunted, scrawny kid who walks like she's about to fall off a brick wall, and look all *tolerant*. Then when I drool all over the couch the parents think twice. They've done their bit. I don't get invited back."

The bell rang on the microwave, and he sat across from her with his dinner. He'd over-zapped it, and the chorizo on the edges had gone hard. "All your teachers and classmates seem to be in awe of you."

"The only reason everyone thinks I'm so smart is they assume when I first open my mouth that I'm an idiot. I sound like an idiot. If my voice wasn't all strangled and I was taller and had breasts—not that I give a shit about breasts, Dad. *Please* don't go out and buy a stuffed training bra or something, 'cause I'm never gonna have a boyfriend even if I liked some creep. Which I don't. The point is, everyone thinks it's amazing I can string a sentence together. And I cash in on Stephen Hawking. I can't tell you, Dad, how many times I've been told I sound just like him. As if that's a compliment! He sounds like a dork."

"You could do worse," said Jackson, blowing on his fork and mentally apologizing for having drawn the parallel himself. Of course, this line about not being exceptionally smart was a load of hooey. She was showing off how really, really smart she had to be in order to realize that in the grand scheme of things she wasn't really so smart.

"I get better grades than I deserve. My papers suck. I can't type. But none of my teachers have the nerve to fail me. They think they'll be arrested. It'll seem like *discrimination*."

Since her papers tended, if in cryptic and sometimes unsettlingly parodic form, to reiterate her father's ebullient anarchism, Jackson took offense. "Your papers may be short, but they're more original than most of your classmates' work, I guarantee."

"Maybe," she admitted. "Not that any of those retards know the difference. They'd ooh and ah if I turned in copy from a box of cornflakes. The whole faculty at Henry Howe is scared of me. They've all been warned I can't be 'upset.' You know, like Mom. Her calm, quiet, happy thing when really she wants to belt me. If they've ever seen me have a crisis, they're *really* terrified. Like that *Twilight Zone* episode, when the creepy little boy turns anyone who talks back into a jack-in-the-box, or sends them to the cornfield. So nobody will tell me to shut up or give me a hard time for not doing the reading. If I don't do this homework, nobody will say a fucking thing." Flicka scrunched her worksheet into a feeble ball and tossed it toward the bin.

She missed.

"So much for your career in basketball," said Jackson, retrieving the wad from the floor. He considered smoothing it back out and returning it to the table, but what was the use? He tossed it in the trash. Because she was right, on every score; she was already brilliant at factoring the variables of her life that mattered. He was supposed to be stern, to insist that like every other kid she had to master the basics. He was supposed to admonish her not to use bad language, too, but he hated parental priggishness, and she was only using the same language he did. On the other hand, letting her get away with not doing her math and saying "fucking" to her father's face was part and parcel of letting her get away with pretty much everything else. He loved her, but she was obnoxious.

He loved her for the very fact that she was obnoxious, which only encouraged her to be more obnoxious.

Nevertheless, Jackson did believe in education, because he hadn't believed in it when he was getting one. He'd had contempt for his teachers in high school, sure that he knew more than they did, and only years later did he speculate that they might have been able to pass on a thing or two when he was still young enough for the knowledge to stick. In adulthood, he'd tried to make up for that misguided sense of superiority by cramming whatever information he could get his hands on, but it tortured him that he lacked a framework; he couldn't sort this grab bag into neatly labeled cubbyholes but could only throw stray facts willy-nilly into a mental cardboard box. Much of what he gleaned online seemed tainted with dubiety, for the Net was like the Bible: you could find ironclad support for any old position if you snuffled around in it long enough. Forgoing college had seemed savvy at the time, when Knack of All Trades was inundated with more jobs than it could handle, and, hey, *Shep* didn't need a degree, right? A university education was probably full of shit anyway. Still, that was only an intuition, and if he'd got one, then he'd have *known* it was full of shit.

What may have bugged him the most was words. In his early thirties, Jackson had made a systematic effort to improve his vocabulary, earning himself no small amount of ridicule at Knack, where he was razzed for referring to the "happy homeowner" as an *oxymoron*: "*Oxy* my ass, professor; our customers are morons, pure and simple." (With the new wave of handymen, this was ridicule that he now rather missed. Practicing *imprimatur* on a wetback from Honduras would have been perverse.) But none of the words he'd learned as a grown man had ever taken the way they had when he was a kid. Their meanings stayed beside them, and he'd have to recite a little definition to himself of *hegemony* (and was that a hard or soft *g*?) before employing the term with any confidence, by which time often as not the opportunity had passed. Whereas *cow* was so perfectly synonymous with a big dumb farm animal that the word itself didn't really exist. If he'd known what was good for him, he'd have memorized the dictionary when he was ten.

"Daddy, I had a spell in Carbon Footprint Lab and had to go home early!" Heather had tromped into the kitchen and went straight to the freezer for a Dove Bar. In the last couple of months, Heather must have put on another five pounds. Nuts, you couldn't win. Let them loose on the larder, and they got fat. Try to regulate their diet, they got all neurotic about food and ate in secret, and they got fat. Maybe he and Carol were lucky that at least Heather didn't try to compete with her older sister over who could be skinnier, a contest she could die losing.

"But are you feeling okay now?" Jackson solicited.

"Not really." Heather moderated her boisterous demeanor, and put on a poorly face. "I'm still a little light-headed."

"If you're not feeling well, maybe you shouldn't be eating ice cream."

"I may have low blood sugar. Kimberly has to eat sweet things all the time or she faints. Daddy?" Heather crawled onto his lap. When the heft of her ass hit a certain area, the pain was so sharp that his eyes smarted. He tried to rearrange her unobtrusively. "I'm having trouble paying attention in class, and I fidget a lot. I was wondering if maybe I need a higher dose of cortomalaphrine."

Christ, she'd been fishing for the designation of learning disability for months. The cold truth was that Heather wasn't as bright as her older sister, and maybe having a plain mid-level IQ was a learning disability of a kind. Strange how if you were straight-out dumb it was meant to be obscurely your fault, but with "ADD" your intellectual shortcomings became blamelessly medical. It didn't really make much sense for the "learning disabled" to be given an unlimited amount of time to complete standardized tests, while the hopelessly stupid kids still had to finish by the bell, when both camps were victims of genetics. Hell, it was the flat-out dumb kids who should get the extra time, since they'd yet to invent a drug to make you clever.

"Maybe," said Jackson. "But don't you think the answer might be to pay more attention?"

"I don't get it."

"Paying attention isn't something that happens to you. It's something you do. Something you make yourself do. Like you could make yourself stop fidgeting, too."

"How?"

Jackson jittered the knee onto which he'd shifted her, and as she jiggled Heather went *uh-huh-uh-huh-uh-huh* and laughed. "Stop that!"

"I'm fidgeting! According to you, I can't stop!" He deliberately kept jiggling her to the point where she seemed to find it unpleasant before planting his foot on the floor. "See? And you can do the same thing with attention. The teacher is talking about a story the class just read, and you've started thinking about what flavor ice cream you feel like eating. Then you decide to think about the ice cream later and think about the story now."

"I don't think it works like that. I think I need more cortomalaphrine." Heather squirmed in her father's lap and twisted her head. "Pee-yew, something stinks!" she declared, and slid off his knee.

For once Flicka's poor sense of smell was fortunate.

"Tell you what, you two," said Jackson, fishing a folded sheaf of printouts from his jacket. "How'd you like to play a game?"

"We can't play a game," said Heather. "We don't have a computer in the kitchen."

"For this game you don't need a computer. This is a brain game. A friend of mine emailed me a copy of a public school test from 1895. Do you know how long ago that was?"

Heather's face fogged. "It was in the olden days?"

Even through thick glasses, it was obvious that Flicka was rolling her eyes. "You'd think a fifth-grader would be able to subtract 1895 from 2005 without a calculator."

"Okay, Flick, if you're going to be so hard on your sister, let's see how well you do on a test designed for two full grades below yours."

"Three grades," Flicka objected scornfully. "If it wasn't for all that time in the hospital, I'd be a junior."

"*Three* grades, then. See, in 1895, this is what every student had to pass in order to graduate from the eighth grade in Salina, Kansas.

Which is the boonies. Nowheresville. And we live in New York City, aka the center of the universe, which should make us more intelligent and sophisticated than the hicks in the Midwest, right?"

"Right!" said Heather.

"And we live in a time with technology and everything, and so if anything we should know more than they did over a hundred years ago, right?"

"Right!" said Heather. Flicka disdained group participation and didn't chime in. Besides, she sensed a trap, and peered at her father's printout with suspicion.

"Now, Heather, this is obviously going to be too hard for you, because it's meant for kids three years older. But Flicka should be able to ace it, since it's for a grade she graduated from ages ago. Let's start with the first question, which is a real softball. 'Give nine rules for the use of capital letters.'"

"My name, my name!" Heather clamored.

"Very good. That's one rule. What are the other eight?" He could see Flicka trying to decide whether to play along. Since most folks did indeed assume when they met her that she was "learning delayed," she rarely passed up an opportunity to prove otherwise.

She shrugged. "Countries. Cities. States."

"Good. But I bet our friends in Salina, Kansas, would probably argue that place names count as only one rule."

"Mr. and Ms. and stuff," said Flicka. ". . . The start of sentences."

"Great," said Jackson, feeling like a proper father for once. "We've got four rules. Five to go."

"When you're really mad in an email!" said Heather.

"True, but they didn't have email in 1895, so I don't think that one counts."

"Titles of books and movies," said Flicka. "Organizations, like the PTA."

"Excellent. Three rules left."

Silence. "I'm bored with this."

"You're not bored with this, Flicka, you're stumped."

Granted, she did have to put in Artificial Tears pretty much all the time, but choosing to do so at this juncture seemed calculated.

"Okay, let's do another one, then," said Jackson. "'Name the parts of speech and define those that have no modifications.'"

"What the fuck is a *modification*," said Flicka.

"Watch the mouth," he said, embracing his new role as Real Dad. "And don't ask me, I'm just the humble test-giver. Can you at least name the parts of speech?"

"Yelling and whispering?" said Heather.

Flicka scrunched her eyes. "Is that like *naming words* and *doing words*?"

"They're called *nouns* and *verbs*. You can't be telling me that in tenth grade they still call them *naming words* and *doing words*."

"Well, they do. And that's not my fault," said Flicka.

"No, it isn't. But I pay taxes up the wazoo so that you girls learn something, and I don't want to buy goofball, patronizing lingo like that."

"I told you when you came home, I shouldn't have to learn any of this shit. It's a waste of their time, and it's a waste of mine."

"The education system isn't aimed at students who are probably going to be dead before they're twenty," he snapped. He shouldn't have said that, but Flicka was so brutal about confronting her terminal status head on that he sometimes made the mistake of being brutal in return. More to the point, the pain in his groin was nearly constant now, which shortened his fuse and addled his judgment. He tried to get the game back in hand.

"Let's move on to the math section," he proposed. "'A wagon box is two feet deep, ten feet long, and three feet wide. How many bushels of wheat will it hold?'"

"Give me a break," said Flicka.

"Don't like that one? Try this: 'If a load of wheat weighs 3,942 pounds, what is its worth at fifty cents per bushel, deducting 1,050 pounds for tare?'"

"That's bullshit," said Flicka. "You can tell it's just a bunch of farm stuff, for the yokels. It's what you'd need to know in stupid Kansas."

"Okay, then, here's a problem you'd need to be able to solve in New York today: 'Find the interest on $512.60 for eight months and eighteen days at seven percent.' Go ahead. You can use your pencil. In fact, if you want, I'll even let you use a calculator."

Flicka folded her arms. "You know I stink at math."

"Then how about geography? 'Name all the republics of Europe and give the capital of each.'"

"All right, Dad, I get it. We're all morons, and in the 'olden days' they were geniuses."

But Jackson was so riveted with this test that he couldn't let it go. "'Name and describe the following: Monrovia, Odessa, Denver, Manitoba, Hecla, Yukon, St. Helena, Juan Fernandez, Aspinwall, and Orinoco.'"

Since he'd had trouble pronouncing *Orinoco*—wherever the fuck that was—Flicka caught him out. "*You* don't know these answers, either."

He laughed, and was about to admit that he couldn't answer more than two or three questions on the entire five-hour test when Carol clipped into the kitchen. "Why are you trying to make your own children feel dumb?"

"I'm not! I'm trying to make them feel uneducated, which isn't the same thing."

"I'm willing to bet the distinction is lost on them." Carol tore the sheaf from his hands. "What is this? 'District Number thirty-three has a valuation of $35,000. What is the necessary levy to carry on a school seven months at $50 per month, and have $104 for incidentals?' Please. In eighth grade? Somebody's been pulling your leg, Jacks. Heather, it's time to brush your teeth."

"It's not a joke. This was a real test."

"Oh, how do you know?" said Carol. "You believe everything that pops up in your AOL in-box that reinforces your bitter, dyspeptic attitude."

"We pay good money so these kids learn something. Instead they're so coddled that Heather doesn't even get proper grades. What do we get on her report card? 'Does consistently,' 'does usually,' or 'does with assistance.' There's no 'doesn't do,' 'won't do,' or 'does, but it's crap.' And you saw that newsletter: they won't let her teachers use *red pen* anymore. Red's too 'confrontational' and 'threatening,' so now her tests are marked in a 'soothing' green. They've chucked the bell between classes to make the environment more 'welcoming.' They keep this up, Heather'll grow up and get a job, and the first time her boss says, 'You're late,' or has a tiny bit of a problem paying her to do work she didn't do because she didn't *feel like it*? She'll jump off a bridge."

"Just because your own schooling was cruel and critical and pitted children against each other," said Carol, "doesn't mean that your daughters have to suffer the same regime of public humiliation."

"But this obsessive bolstering of self-esteem—well, I got no problem with self-regard so long as you think well of yourself for good reason. But now they're told they're all God's gift, whether or not they've learned to spell. I read a study that was not in my 'AOL in-box,' thank you, but in *The New York Times*, which you worship, so I assume you don't dismiss it as made up. They asked a bunch of Korean kids and a bunch of American kids whether they thought of themselves as good at math; thirty-nine percent of the Americans thought they were great at it. Only six percent of the Koreans thought they were any good, and the rest thought they sucked. But when you looked at their test scores, the Koreans were way ahead of the Americans in math. Students in this country are taught to be delusional."

"So your answer is to make our children ashamed of themselves, which doesn't improve their math skills one bit."

Carol's whisk-whisk motions were her only giveaway that she was furious. She didn't exactly slam the dishes into the dishwasher, but he could tell from the obscenely controlled firmness with which she placed the plates in their slots that she'd have preferred to smash them against the wall.

"Hey, that chorizo-chickpea thing was top notch."

"Please don't try to butter me up. Flicka, did you finish your math homework?"

Their elder daughter wasn't prone to try her I-don't-have-to-doschoolwork-because-I'm-going-to-die routine on her mother. "I . . . finished with it," she said obscurely. Fortunately for Flicka, her mother had other things on her mind.

"How's Glynis?" Carol asked curtly, as if she didn't really care.

"Faintly better. Little nervous she should have stayed in the hospital longer, but the insurance company wanted her out. Then, you must know that, since you saw her yesterday."

"She's still in a lot of pain. I do think they sent her home too soon. But I gather you've been pestering her with your retrograde, right-wing political opinions."

"My opinions are not right-wing. In this town, that's just a label for 'evil' anyway. And I'd be awful surprised if Glynis described me as 'pestering.' She's mad as hell, and she enjoys the company of someone else who's mad as hell, too."

"Jackson, you know perfectly well that it's inappropriate."

Jackson hated the word *inappropriate*, which rod-up-the-ass prisses threw around with abandon these days to make other people feel dirty and ashamed. It made you immediately want to check your underwear for stains. The word had a deliberate vagueness, too, as if what you'd done wrong was too disgusting to name. And it attributed moral qualities to the merely normative. The incessant modern-day resort to *inappropriate* put a thin progressive gloss on what was really a regressive conformism. The folks who wielded that chiding adjective were the same buttoned-up paranoids who spotted pedophiles under every bush, since lately you could be as uptight and sexually repressive as you liked, so long as you projected your prudish Victorian revulsion onto children. He was no more pleased that his own wife had picked up the term than he would have been had she returned from a public pool with communicable plantar warts.

Carol swished the sponge across the counters in a reproachful show of efficiency, as if instead of wasting his children's time with some obviously counterfeit eighth-grade test he might at least have cleaned up the kitchen. The resentment was disingenuous, too, since she was clearly fuming, and thus grateful to have something to do. Without laundry, bills to pay, one sweaty, adenoidal kid in constant need of hydrating or

Saran-Wrapping, another kid in constant need of compensatory praise and attention, Carol would go insane. As much as she might experience these domestic duties as impositions, she was utterly dependent on this feverish morning-to-night beaverishness, for she had long ago lost that vital capacity to do nothing. Carol's industry resembled the full-dance-card cha-cha of Glynis's mother, except that at least Hetty was in doomed pursuit of an elusive self-fulfillment; Carol's ado had always to be in the service of someone else. This compulsive altruism seemed like self-denial, but it was creepier than that. She no longer had the faintest idea what she might desire on her own account, so what was she sacrificing? It saddened him to note that over the years she had insidiously replaced pleasure with virtue.

Carol dispensed the usual clatter of pills. Once Heather was bullied into getting ready for bed, Flicka loitered at the table, taking deliberately too long to grind her meds. The girl was an incurable busybody, and sensed something was up. Her mother would gladly have frustrated Flicka's nosiness, but at length couldn't contain herself. Searching out stray chickpeas with a whisk broom, Carol muttered to Jackson flintily, "So, you must be happy."

"As it happens, I'm not in a bad mood," he said. Feet on an adjacent chair and sipping his second beer, he adjusted himself by discreetly shoving a hand in his pants pocket. "But I get the impression that's not what you mean."

"You've seen the news?"

"Oh, that." He was relieved. Of course, Carol wouldn't allude to certain other issues with Flicka in the room. Still, any subject they discussed these days had an ulterior quality, and he was grateful for even this tiresome a diversion, just as Carol was grateful for sweeping the floor. "Why would I be 'happy' that Terri Schiavo died?"

All the in-laws' avenues of legal appeal having been exhausted, at the husband's request the Floridian's feeding tube had been disconnected two weeks earlier. The poor woman had actually lasted longer than her doctors had expected.

"Well, all that unnecessary *expense*," said Carol. "You and Shep must be tickled pink. Now we can send her IV and a fresh set of bedding to Africa."

"I guess I'm relieved for her that's she's out of her misery," Jackson said cautiously.

"But according to you, she couldn't feel anything. She didn't even exist, in your view. So how could she experience any misery to end?"

"Honey, I have no idea why this story is so important to you. You didn't know her; she wasn't your best friend. There were only a few snapshots to suggest what she might have been like when she was a human being."

"She was still a human being; that's the point! And she was murdered. As surely as if someone had shot her between the eyes."

"But *I* didn't kill her. So why are you mad at me?"

"You did kill her. Your way of thinking killed her. Oh look, that woman isn't pretty and entertaining anymore, so let's just pull the plug! So who else would you like to dispose of while we're at it? Who else is too expensive or inconvenient? Old people? Or kids with Down's? Would you put them in a gas chamber because they couldn't pass your 'eighth-grade' test? It's a slippery slope!"

"Oh, spare me the 'slippery slope' routine!" Jackson cried. "We live on a slippery slope, like it or not. It's amazing any of us can stand up. We do kill people. We give serial killers lethal injections and we mow down the Taliban in Afghanistan—"

"Not if I had anything to say about it we wouldn't." Carol reined herself in, glancing at Flicka in dismay. It was now too late to shoo her from the room without implying that at sixteen she wasn't welcome to participate in discussions of the evening news with her parents.

"Well, *I'm* happy she's dead," said Flicka.

"Flicka, don't you dare say that. Ever. About anyone. It's ugly."

"What's so ugly about it? Terri Schiavo was brain dead and no use to anybody. She was all fat and couldn't talk, and just blobbed around in bed."

"So now we're killing off fat people, are we?"

"I bet if that lady knew she'd turned into a blimp, she'd of pulled the plug on herself. She was all into bulimia and stuff."

"It's not for us to judge what's 'good life' and 'bad life,'" said Carol, "or what someone would prefer when they can no longer speak for themselves. Human life is sacred, sweetheart. In any form. Don't ever forget that."

"I don't see what's so damn *sacred* about it," said Flicka stolidly. "Sometimes it's crummy and dumb. Getting all messed up about Terri Schiavo kicking the bucket is like bawling 'cause you stepped on a bug."

Flicka was deliberately winding her mother up, pushing her to cross a line; it was a point of unity between Flicka and her father that they were both dying to see Mom lose it. Carol would not lash out, lest her daughter become 'upset.' But the whole purpose of parental reprimand was to make your kids upset. If you didn't affect them, you'd failed. So how could Carol be a stern, responsible parent who set firm 'boundaries' without throwing the girl into the FD version of anaphylactic shock?

"And you?" Carol said coldly. "How would you feel if someone talked about you like a bug?"

Though she knew she wasn't supposed to, Flicka took off her glasses and rubbed an eye. "Sometimes I feel like a bug. I don't see why being alive is always supposed to be so great. I think it stinks. In fact, I can't stand it. You can have it. Terri Schiavo is lucky."

If Flicka didn't have FD, Carol might have slapped her. But Flicka did have FD.

"Being alive is pretty wonderful compared to the alternative," Jackson offered.

"How do you know?" said Flicka. "Me, I think 'the alternative' sounds great."

"Sweetie, you're tired," said Carol. "Let's get you to bed."

"Yeah, I'm tired," she slurred. "Of the whole thing. Sweaty sheets. Itchy eyes wrapped in Saran Wrap like leftovers in the fridge. Never being able to walk down the hall at school without that geeky health aide on my heels—"

"Now, we had to campaign long and hard with the Board of Ed—" said Carol.

"I *know* we were 'very fortunate' they agreed to pay for her, but how am I supposed to make friends? Laura's a goon, and she hovers. Never gives me any space. She's mostly scared if I trip or choke she'll get sued. Always calls me 'hon' and 'pumpkin,' and I hate that. *And* I'm tired of sleeping with that oximeter on my finger. Stupid beeping sound. The way the alarm wakes everybody up. When half the time there's nothing wrong with me, and the machine is just fucked up. Sleeping with that oxygen mask over my face. Not being able to turn over because of the feed to my g-tube. Setting my alarm for one and four a.m.—"

"Look," said Jackson, "we told you—"

"I *know* you're 'happy to fill the bag for me.' But I don't want you to! I want *somebody* to get some sleep! You did that for years. Stumbling up in the middle of the night because your kid needs another can of Compleat. Like running some junky car that's always leaking oil. The point is, I'm sick of it. It's all bullshit."

"Sure it is!" Jackson declared cheerfully, sweeping Flicka into the air by her underarms; she was so tiny and light that it was easy to forget she was sixteen years old. "But it's all we've got. And you and Heather are all we've got. So you hang in there just to be nice."

Sometimes Flicka herself forgot that she was sixteen years old, and she curled onto her father's shoulder as he carried her upstairs.

hate it when she talks like that," Carol said as they got ready for bed. "I know she doesn't mean it, and it's probably down to the Klonopin and Depakote. They both list 'suicidal ideation' as a side effect. So she doesn't really understand what she's saying, but it still disturbs me."

"She may have a better idea of what she's saying than you think."

"In that case, she's cruel. What about us? Reminding us all the time, as if we need reminding. She uses the FD thing to goad us."

"Sure, she does. You use what's handy, right?" When Carol unsnapped her bra, Jackson felt a stirring, followed by a sharp, throbbing twinge.

"What's that smell?"

Jackson sniffed. "I don't smell anything."

"It's been nagging me all night. In the kitchen, wafting in and out.

I thought maybe something had gone off in the pantry, but now it's up here."

"Oh," he said sheepishly. "I've been having trouble with my guts. Could be the chickpeas."

"I know what a fart smells like, Jackson. It's not methaney; it's rank. Like spoiled meat."

He shrugged. "You've always had the more sensitive nose. I'm not getting it."

"Do you think some animal might have died under the house? I don't think a rat would do it. A cat, or a raccoon. If this keeps up, I'm afraid you're going to have to look for it."

"Ought to be some advantage to living with a handyman. That's the sort of fun job gets called into Knack every day." Having thrown his shirt on the chair, Jackson sauntered into the master bath in slacks.

"You're doing that again," said Carol.

Jackson raised his voice over the splash of his urine; the choked stream shot in uneven bursts, and it stung. "Doing what?"

"Closing the door while you pee. You've done that for weeks. Since when are you so shy? I've seen you pee several thousand times."

Last week Carol had tried just walking in, and found the bathroom door locked. That hadn't gone down well—she thought he'd lost his mind—and he'd concocted some cockamamie explanation about how he was used to locking the bathroom door at work and just wasn't thinking; thankfully she'd not called him on the fact that urinals had no doors, nor questioned why he would now routinely take a leak in the men's room at Knack in the privacy of its single stall. Nevertheless, locking the bathroom door thereafter would have raised more suspicions than the extra security was worth. So tonight she was able to poke her head in unannounced. "Come on," she said teasingly. "You know I kind of like it."

Cutting the exercise short, he stuffed himself back into his pants before he could completely squeeze off, and dribbled inside the fly. "Too late! Thrill's going to have to wait for another night."

More than one thrill had waited for another night for some time. "I can think of a way you can make it up to me." Carol put her arms around him from behind, her bare breasts warm against his back. Christ, this was far later than he'd planned to schedule the unveiling, and the "contagious skin condition" was approaching its sell-by date; pretty soon, Carol wouldn't buy it.

Still, he figured he could eke it through one more evening or so, the way you can sometimes coax a surprising number of extra brushings from a toothpaste tube to all appearances shot. "I'd love to make it up to you, sunshine," he said, fumbling to fasten the safety pin on his boxers. "But you know what the doctor said about the skin thing. I guarantee you don't want this crud."

Carol stiffened, and dropped her arms. Grazing past her to the bedroom, Jackson's gut clenched. There did come a time when you had to concede that the Colgate was kaput.

"Skin conditions aren't usually contagious."

"Well, this one is. Like athlete's foot." He was a little insulted, as if he wouldn't have thought his pretext through.

"I Googled the name of this ailment of yours. No match."

"I told you," he took off his watch with his back to his wife, "it's very rare."

"It's virtually impossible that a medical problem you share with as few as five people isn't cited somewhere."

"Maybe you spelled it wrong."

"*Genital cortamachriasis*, right?" (Granted, the name of his apocryphal scrofula sounded uncomfortably close to Heather's *cortomalaphrine*, but he'd had to invent it under duress.) "There are only so many plausible ways to spell it. I tried them all."

"Sounds like IBM ain't getting its money's worth!"

She would not be jollied. "None of this explains why I can't see it. The rash can't be that bad. And if it is that bad, then I *really* need to see it. That part of your body is part mine."

"A man has his pride." Jackson slipped off his slacks, careful not to tug the boxers along with. They were at the tail end of the laundry cycle, and the elastic on these last-generation boxers was weak. "The cream seems to be working, but it's taking longer than I'd hoped."

"What cream?"

"The cream! Jesus, why this third degree when I'm only thinking of you?" Reasoning that the best defense was a good taking-offense—a meeting of consternation with umbrage in return—Jackson flailed his arms for effect. "I don't like sleeping beside your naked body in my underwear. I don't like going without sex. I'm just trying to protect your health, at some sacrifice to myself, too—"

The flailing came at a price. With his arms outstretched, Carol reached swiftly for both side seams of his boxers and yanked them to his knees. She reeled back a step, and then she screamed.

Carol was not a squeamish person; as for poking about an unfinished basement with a flashlight looking for a rotting raccoon, Carol's level-headed temperament suited her far better than her husband for the job. The truth was, he may never have heard her scream before. It frightened him. If nothing else, the horror on her face enabled him to see his penis with nauseous objectivity for the first time.

It was the wrong color. Red, but not the cheerful cherry red that it had sometimes turned in its athletic adolescence. It had the purplish undertone of raw liver.

The sutures above his balls were binding. The flesh bulged from their constraint. A glistening yellow ooze seeped from between the threads. Liberated from the swaddling of his boxers, the smell rose more sharply. Though the effluents of one's own body are generally less noxious than other people's, this stench made even Jackson a little woozy. The animal from the basement had crawled upstairs.

But worst of all was the shape. It did not look like a dick.

In truth, he had never been entirely won over to the phallic worship of his peers. When he was eight or so, a little girl at the playground had intruded on him peeing in the bushes, and had screamed in much the same spirit of reflexive horror as Carol had a moment ago. Presumably the girl had never seen a penis before, and she was unimpressed. "Oooh, gross, what is that thing, it's disgusting!" she'd cried as she ran away. And then there was the other time, in gym in junior high. He'd barely entered puberty; still wet from the showers, he'd been cold. Nevertheless, the jibe from a much bigger kid had smarted: *looks like you're pack-ing a baby carrot and a couple of lima beans.* Thereafter, the boys had tagged him "the Vegetarian," a term whose innocence to his teachers' ears protected his classmates from punishment for bullying. For that matter, the very word *penis* had always sounded like something silly, trivial, and measly. Ever since Jackson could remember, his fifth ap-pendage had seemed subtly alien to him, apart, and capable of betrayal. It was this very sense of the extrusion being not quite a part of his body that may have enabled him to experiment with it.

The experiment had failed. He may never have quite fathomed why women would find a *penis* attractive—with its shriveled, too-thin skin, the blobby, drooping testicles with straggles of hair, the little mushroom cap at the end somehow not a form that human flesh should assume. At rest it looked frightened and depressed; when alert, impertinent yet insecure, waving about and trying to attract attention like a loudmouth acting out. He'd never entirely trusted Carol's enthusiasm for the thing; her natural kindness made her unreliable. Yet there were limits to Car-ol's altruism, since she was currently making no effort to disguise her revulsion, as there were also limits to his own disaffection with the phal-lus of conventional proportions. The unimproved version had still been preferable to this.

The lumpy tuber between his legs now looked like one of those bal-loon animals that children's entertainers twisted hastily together at birth-day parties. Where before the shaft was thicker at the base, now it was narrowest there, for the collagen used for thickening had slurped down-ward, bulging over the rim to partially bury the head. His dick had love handles. The filler tissue had migrated asymmetrically, too, and the bulge was larger on the right. Overwhelmed by what now hung more like a third testicle, the head appeared smaller and pokier, no better than a gumdrop. And the shaft emerged from too low down. The snipping of the suspensory ligaments was supposed to have released a full inch of length otherwise wastefully tucked inside his pelvis; now his prick seemed to be growing out of the balls themselves. The descended derivation jarred the eye, like a dirty scrawl on a men's room wall by a kid who couldn't draw. Inflamed, bloated, and seeping, this was the kind of fatally festering extremity that battlefield medics in the Civil War sawed off on the spot.

"What have you done?" Carol said when she had caught her breath.

"Mom?" peeped from behind the bedroom door. "What's wrong?"

"Heather, sweetie, go back to bed. Mom—saw something that scared her, that's all. A mouse."

"But I'm afraid of mouses! It'll come and get me in my bed!"

"No, honey, this mouse isn't getting anybody, not you, and *definitely* not your mother. It wasn't even a mouse, it turns out. A sock. A balled-up, smelly sock that can't do anything, not anything at all. I'm sorry I frightened you. Go back to sleep."

The boxers around his knees had intensified his humiliation, so Jackson had taken advantage of Heather's knock to kick them off. He sat slump-shouldered on the side of the bed, hands folded across his crotch.

"I don't want to wake the kids again," Carol said in a strained whisper. "But I want you to understand that no matter how softly I say anything else tonight, I am still screaming."

When she grabbed her robe and belted it with a double knot, Jackson realized that he should have pulled the boxers back on when he had the chance. Now he was stuck with the disadvantage. He was fated to have this conversation stark naked, because she had found him out, and putting his clothes on would seem like hiding the evidence—like putting the candy bar back in your pocket when you'd already been caught red-handed for shoplifting. He couldn't remember the last time he felt this intensely like a little boy.

"I am correctly surmising that you did this to yourself? Had this done? That you did not have your penis caught in a mangle at work and fail to mention the accident."

Her word choice was icy: *surmising*. She would never in the past have called it a *penis*. She wasn't a prude, and liked the sound of *cock* and *dick*, their hard consonants, their monosyllabic thrust. But that's what he now had between his legs, a *penis*—with its peevish whine, its soft, low-lying *n*, its cringing, retracted hiss. "I thought—"

"You had one of those stupid surgeries, didn't you?"

"We get all this email spam, and . . ."

"Penis enlargement ads are why God invented the Delete key. You're not telling me you found some hack on the Internet?"

"No! I got a referral. Still, I figured they wouldn't send out so many ads if there weren't . . . Well, obviously lots of people do it."

"Lots of people get addicted to heroin. Lots of people commit suicide. Lots of people drive over the speed limit and run headlong into cement barriers. That doesn't mean you have to, too."

"Carol, if we're going to talk about this, it really doesn't help for you to go all Mommy on me. Obviously the surgery didn't go very well."

"That's the understatement of the century. How could you possibly have done such a thing without discussing it with me first?"

"I wanted to surprise you," he said miserably.

"Congratulations, then. I'm surprised. In fact, I am dumbfounded. You cast yourself as such a maverick. Your own man, so outspoken, not duped by impositions like *government* that the rest of us 'Mugs' take for granted. How could you be so . . . *trite?*"

"I didn't get this surgery because I thought it was original. Just because I have strong political views doesn't mean that I don't want to measure up as a man—literally." Tonight, being one of the handful of Americans who used the adverb correctly failed to flush him with the usual self-congratulation.

"Doesn't anything you do down there have implications for me?"

"Yeah, sure, I guess. But you'd have said no. You don't call it a discussion when it's just a veto. And you may say that my dick is 'part yours,' which is sort of sweet, but it isn't yours. I lend it out, and I love lending it out. But it's still fundamentally my dick."

"Oh, it is now! One hundred percent. Welcome to it."

"I thought you'd like it, even if you wouldn't necessarily think you'd like it before you saw the results. And you know, we used to get it on all the time . . . until Flicka."

"With my doing the one a.m. feeding, and you the four o'clock, every single night? It's just been a matter of exhaustion, not lack of appetite."

"Yeah, but when Flick started doing the feedings herself this last year, we didn't . . . The frequency didn't pick up, right? Not really."

"Sex is a habit, like anything else. A habit you can get out of. And not that much has changed; if it's not the feedings, it's something else, and we're still exhausted. But that's not the point. If you wanted to have sex more often, all you had to do was say so."

"I just figured I could give us a jump-start. I thought it would give you a kick—the way it looked. And it would feel better. For you."

"You did this for me? I don't believe that for a New York minute."

"Okay, sure, I thought I'd feel better, too. It's always seemed, you know—a little small, that's all. In comparison. I don't think women understand. It's like me not being able to understand your feeling fat around your period, when I can't see anything different."

She forced him to meet her eyes. "Small in comparison to *whom*?"

He glared. "Just—other people!"

"Uh-huh." She stared him down until he looked away, and by dropping his glance, he appeared to admit something. "Tell me," she hounded, "have I ever complained?"

"No, but you wouldn't. You're terminally nice."

"I wouldn't complain because I didn't have a problem. But we have one now."

"I'll get it fixed," he said staunchly, although the assertion had a familiar ring of improbability; like so many of the handymen at Knack, he got around to repairing jammed pull switches and dangling towel racks in his own home last of all, if ever.

"You know that's going to require plastic surgery, which isn't covered by our insurance. When we have a hard enough time covering deductibles and co-pays already, and we're out a thousand a month for Flicka's Compleat alone!"

"I'll find the money somewhere," he said morosely. "I can always grab jobs that come in at Knack and moonlight on the side."

"That's cheating Shep."

"No, it would be cheating Pogatchnik. I never skimmed jobs from Shep. Eating into Pogatchnik's bottom line would be a pleasure."

"But come to think of it, our insurance doesn't cover self-mutilation, either. How much did this cost?"

He shrugged. "A few grand."

"*How much?*"

Carol could always track down the going rate online, and if he lied that's exactly what she'd do, too. If she started nosing about, she'd also find out that you weren't really supposed to do length and girth at the same time; determined to have the surgeries done quickly in secret, he'd insisted on the whole schmear at once. Maybe he should have been suspicious when the doctor relented for a price. "Mmm . . . seven or eight."

"Eight thousand dollars! My God, where did you get the money?"

Normal men, real men, controlled their families' purse strings—which they didn't call *purse strings*—but in the Burdina household, Carol controlled every dime. Was it any wonder that he'd wanted a bigger dick? "The dogs," he said meekly.

"You *promised* me you'd stop gambling!"

"Look, the odds against that stinking gene making it through both our families' *distal long arm of chromosome nine* for every generation to Flicka must have been ten thousand to one! Might as well cash in on a natural talent for winning long shots."

"I can't believe I owe this calamity to some sorry greyhound feeling frisky. If I could turn back the clock, I'd brain the stupid animal with a two-by-four."

"I haven't placed a bet since. On my life."

Of course, this version of events was crap, but the dogs story was also admission against interest, which is why she believed it. The truth was that he'd finally set up his own checking account—was that so outrageous, that a forty-four-year-old man would have his own bank account?—where Jackson deposited cash tips and the proceeds from the far-better-than-hypothetical jobs he'd been skimming from Pogatchnik for years. He hadn't amassed enough funds on the side to pay more than the monthly minimums on the credit cards that Carol also didn't know about, like the Visa to which he'd actually charged that $8,700 bill for ruining his life. But she was a worrier, already uneasy about the negative balance on the cards she did know about, and anxious to pay off the home equity loan they'd taken out to pay for the extras around Flicka's scoliosis surgery. He took no pleasure in the fiscal secrecy, but regarded himself as nobly sacrificing to protect what little peace of mind his wife had left.

Eyes closed, Carol rubbed her face and breathed into her hands. As she collected herself, he wondered if he could now infer that she was no longer screaming.

"Does it hurt?" she asked at last. "It looks like it hurts."

"Yeah, it hurts."

"A lot?"

"A lot."

"You'd better let me look at it." She touched his thigh, and in the gentler cast of her face he concluded it was safe. He withdrew his hands and canted his knees. She crouched before his dick and reached cautiously for the shaft, as if trying to befriend a skittish stray in the pound whose previous owner had beaten the shit out of it. As she moved it to one side and then the other, he winced. "What kind of butcher did this?"

"I got his name from my cousin Larry when we had beers last summer. Larry said the doc was 'a real artist' and his girlfriend went wild for the results. Made him a lot bigger—or 'even bigger,' as he put it. Hell, Larry wasn't even sheepish about it, like it wasn't even a hush-hush secret. Said you 'owe it to yourself.' He was so keen on the guy that he was planning to go back, get the next size up."

She rolled her eyes. "As if you can order a penis like a pair of shoes. Did you ever see what his surgery looked like?"

"Of course not! You don't ask a guy to whip out his dick in a bar. It wasn't that sort of bar."

Carol placed her palm gingerly over the sutures. "It feels hot. Does it still work?"

"Sort of. I haven't—experimented much. It's too painful."

"It's so puffed up it's hard to tell what it'll look like when the swelling goes down. But this is badly infected. You could get sepsis. Have you been taking antibiotics?"

"One course, but it's finished. I've applied Bacitracin."

She touched his cheek, and he could smell the infection on her fingers. "We've got to get you to a hospital."

Jackson looked away. "I'm too embarrassed."

"Better embarrassment than blood poisoning. And if you let that get any worse, it's going to fall off. Honestly, I'd go to New York Methodist right this minute if it weren't for the kids. Once they're off to school tomorrow, you're taking a day off and we're heading straight to the emergency room. I'll go with you. Even if you don't deserve it."

"Carol, it's really important that this doesn't get out, okay? Don't tell anyone, please. If they find out at Knack, I'll never live it down."

"Does Shep know about this? What you did?"

"No! Especially don't tell Shep."

"Men's version of what it means to have a 'best friend' totally bewilders me. What's the point of having one?"

"Just promise me."

"The last thing I'm about to advertise is that I married a fool. Besides, you're the one who can't keep your mouth shut. You're the one who told everyone in the office about Glynis, when Shep told you not to."

"It was for his own good. They kept making fun of him about Pemba, and for a little while Pogatchnik's pretending to be sympathetic got the asshole off his back." He didn't care if she was castigating him; talking about anything else besides his *penis* was a relief. After they'd brushed their teeth, Carol removed her robe and slipped under the sheets naked.

"At least now that you know," he said, thinking that a bright side was hard to find, "I don't have to sleep with you wearing boxers."

Carol turned on her side, facing away, and switched off the light. "Actually, my dear, I'd really rather you put them back on."

Chapter Ten

Shepherd Armstrong Knacker
Merrill Lynch Account Number 934-23F917
April 01, 2005 – April 30, 2005
Net Portfolio Value: $571,264.91

He knew it was wrong. But all his life he'd kept an eye on the future—naïvely, on the assumption that there would always be one. So as stringently as he tried to forbid himself, to draw a line in the sand, his mind shuffled forward and past a certain advent, crossing blithely into no-go territory that should have been intolerable to contemplate. That sand metaphor was peculiar anyway; whatever dire consequences you may have been warned will follow, crossing a line in the sand is a cinch. Moreover, the sand he compulsively pictured was white, knotted intermittently with mangroves, dotted with beached hand-carved canoes, scored from the wheels of ox-drawn carts, and bright with variegated *kangas*. If Shep Knacker was drawing any line in the sand, it was on the coast of Pemba.

He was upstairs in his office writing checks. Though the room was really, really a home office and nothing but, his accountant had warned him off claiming it as a tax deduction. It was a red flag, said

Dave, and sent your chances of being audited sky high. Every April—last month being no exception—Jackson railed about the fact that the feds put that box "Did you deduct for a home office?" high up on the front page of the 1040, virtually the first thing they wanted to know after your name and address. "Do they ask specially on page one if you deducted for rubber bands?" he fumed. "Do they ask right after your fucking Social Security number whether you deducted for donating your old winter coat to the Salvation Army? No! With that *we-dare-you, just-try-it* tick box, they're bullying you into omitting the one legitimate deduction that might keep more than the cost of a jelly donut out of their hot, thieving little hands." Well, if it was intimidation, it worked.

Given the monies flying out of this room the last few months, a few grand more or less on his taxes had hardly mattered: dinners with that Arizona crowd on the nights he hadn't been able to concoct yet another meal without carbohydrates; astronomical fuel bills, because Glynis got cold easily and during an unusually frosty spring he'd been heating the house to seventy-eight, even higher when she got chills; lab bills for the blood tests whose needles still made her lightheaded; and of course, dwarfing the rest to spare change, the surgery, gouging a meaty chunk from Merrill Lynch as if to fiscally mirror the violence inflicted on his wife's abdomen, and then chemo, each administration of which was over forty thousand dollars a throw. Once such a niggler about buying store-brand mustard, these days Shep was growing careless about money, almost indifferent to it. Something in him would walk out on the street tomorrow and foist a wad into the hands of the first stranger he encountered. *Take it, take the works. Spare me the agony of parting with it drib by drab.* This was a kind of torture, really, a death by a thousand cuts, and he would rather a dagger in the gut—an overnight worldwide economic collapse that turned his dollars into neat rectangular sheets for wiping his ass.

He'd left the door ajar to keep an ear out for Glynis, and sure enough he could hear her beginning to prowl. It was after 1:00 a.m., but the insomnia that had plagued her in the hospital was also one of Alimta's side effects (or what Glynis had taken to calling *special effects*, a term that lent the fallout from chemo an element of the spectacular). Which seemed so unfair, given that another of the drug's *special effects* was fatigue. Soon he'd go keep her company, but not just yet. He first had to get a hold of himself, to rein in the awful recognition that though it had barely begun, he was already waiting for all this to be over.

One whole shelf over his desk was lined with notebooks, hardback Black n' Reds that for years he'd special-ordered from a stationer in London—a rare indulgence. The spines were neatly labeled in fine felt-tip: Goa, Laos, Puerto Escondido, Morocco . . . Each was full of handwritten notes: the price of staples—butter, bread, milk. Average prices for two- and three-bedroom homes. Laws on foreign acquisition of property, and in more restrictive countries the susceptibility of officials to persuasion. Reliability of telephone service, electricity, and the mail. For the reconnaissance missions of the last ten years, Internet access. Target towns and neighborhoods. Crime rates. Weather. Especially meticulous in the older notebooks, detailed checklists on the availability of metalsmithing supplies—silver, solder, rouge, flux—and on how far they'd need to travel to refill Glynis's acetylene tank for her torch. As her productivity back home had dwindled, these latter notes had grown less thorough, for they serviced an increasingly tenuous myth: that his wife would get only more serious about her craft in a foreign outpost, where her materials had to be imported and prized from the hands of corrupt customs officials, when she would rarely venture upstairs to her attic studio with all that she needed at her fingertips in the Jewelry District of Midtown Manhattan.

The handwriting was his own: the neat, rounded script of a diligent student, the tails of *g*'s and *y*'s looping loyally back to the line, the tops of *a*'s and *o*'s painstakingly closed. His cursive had never lost a schoolboy's desire to please, a nervous determination to copy correctly from the blackboard. In addition to logistical notes, those pages were pasted with photos: once modestly priced coastline bungalows in Cape Town, Glynis posing before a pile of fiery rambutans in an outdoor market in Vietnam. Cards from guesthouses, restaurant menus. The addresses of newly made friends, usually members of the small English-speaking communities of British and American expats whose existence they had agreed at the outset was a requirement. He and Glynis were, so the catechism had run, adventurous but realistic; they would crave the company of their own kind. Yet no matter how well met the acquaintance, they had lost touch with virtually all these local contacts, who no longer enticed with dinner invites, the shared smugness of having built a world apart, the inevitable shared wistfulness of having lost a world as well. Indeed, once Glynis had put the kibosh on the country, thus dooming the exercise to mere reminiscence, he hadn't opened its Black n' Red again. The tops of the volumes on the left had grown dusty.

Since they had never been there, the final notebook on the right marked "Pemba Island" was nearly blank. Against it leaned a folder of printouts. In the absence of his own notes and snapshots, the Pemba file on his hard drive was full of hyperlinks to travel sites and other people's holiday photos posted online. With little patience for research that wasn't three-dimensional, Shep had mastered just enough background to fill out a third-grade presentation to the class. Pemba was fifty miles north of Zanzibar. The island having been colonized by Portugal, locals still staged a bullfight every year. Plantations grew not only cloves, but rice, palms, coconut, and mangos. Local wildlife included flying foxes, the marsh mongoose, coconut crabs, and the red colobus monkey. Naturally, the cuisine was heavy on seafood: octopus, kingfish, prawns.

He had never eaten kingfish, and would like to try it.

The population was 300,000, though that census was dated. Mostly hoteliers, the number of resident expats numbered only a handful. Yet the longer The Afterlife had stewed in his mind, the fewer of his "own kind" Shep imagined he'd require; perhaps one crusty neighbor up the beach would do to help him remember the English word *carousel* without wracking his brain. Keeping the tourists to a mere smattering at any one time, the fact that the island was hard to get to had suited his purposes. If the island was hard to get to, it was hard to be got at there, and equally hard to leave.

He'd transcribed the names of towns, that he might try out the feel of them in his mouth: *Kigomasha, Kinyasini, Kisiwani. Chiwali* and *Chapaka. Piki, Tumbi, Wingi, Nyali, Mtambili,* and *Msuka.* Or *Bagamoyo,* a village whose name meant "keep your heart cool." He loved the notion of living in a place that his spellchecker didn't recognize—that leapt from the screen underscored by alarmed red squiggles. He loved the merry prospect of flying into an airport in *Chaka Chaka.* He had memorized a few phrases while getting up the nerve to announce his intentions to Glynis, and had already come to relish the bouncy jubilation of Swahili. He'd always been intimidated by foreign languages in the past. Of all the tasks that The Afterlife might present him, he'd been leeriest of having to learn Bulgarian, or worse, one of those subtle tonal tongues like Thai. Yet Swahili was a toy language, full of silly repetitions of the sort that toddlers invent: *polepole, hivi hivi, asante kushukuru.* The language didn't frighten him. It seemed like play.

With the surreptitiousness of loading Internet porn, Shep shoved aside his checkbook and narrowed the crack of the study door. He booted his computer and sought out the hyperlinks. The screen blued with water that looked clean. The sand was not only bright and fine but more marvelously deserted. He was not naïve about beaches. He did not idolize beaches, their blaring, unrelenting white. He was well aware of how hot they got, how monotonous; of the unpleasant crinkle of skin once saltwater had dried; of how the sand buried in your scalp, creviced into the spines of paperbacks, and followed you inside. He was aware of the flies. But nothing about living near one obliged you to park on a blanket in stupefaction from morning to night. At sundown the heat would die, the colors deepen. And however inured you might get to the view, the birds, the coconut crabs scuttling at low tide, none of the vistas in these photos could possibly grow as wearing as the strip malls in Elmsford, New York.

"Shepherd?"

Glynis was slumped against the doorframe with a tissue pressed to her face. Blood was running down her arm. In his distress, Shep took a beat too long to minimize the beach. Though her head was tipped back, her yellowed eyes were open. He would indeed have been less embarrassed had she glimpsed bare breasts or an open beaver.

"Another nosebleed," he said, stating the obvious to distract from what she might have seen. With a hand under her elbow, he hustled her to the bathroom down the hall. She had dripped down the beige carpet. He didn't notice the trail in a remonstrative way; it was just that he was responsible for running the household now, and he would need to scrub the stains before they set. "Keep it tipped up."

He grabbed a washcloth, moistened it, and drew it down her arm. Removing the streaks of blood, he revealed the pinprick red dots on her skin that would not rub off, like the halo around spray-painted graffiti. As if she'd been basking along that on-screen beach, her skin was dark for May, almost the color of a good tan but not quite—grayer, yellower, more sullen. The hue put him in mind of those wipe-on artificial tanning products that weren't fooling anybody. And he was sorry to note that, despite the dexamethasone, patches of red, scaly rash had returned. They were inflamed: she'd been scratching again.

"I would have to be wearing this sweater."

He helped her out of the floor-length cardigan of cream cashmere, a wrap of which she was inordinately fond. The luxurious sweater had the warmth and comfort of a bathrobe with none of the depressing I-can't-be-bothered-to-get-dressed connotations, and now it was drizzled with blood down the front. So for now her bathrobe would have to do, and he fetched it while promising to rinse every drop from the cardigan. Anything that roused affection in her, that infinitesimally increased her attachment to the flotsam and jetsam of this earth, would have to take precedence over the carpet.

Bringing a box of tissues, he settled her downstairs on the pillowed love seat he'd moved permanently into the kitchen, that she might bundle there while he prepared their meals. Or meals loosely speaking. He'd had better luck with multiple snacks than imposing spreads. Because she often hadn't the energy to get up and sit at the main table, beside the love seat he'd moved in a small coffee table, from which he also took his dinner, to keep her from feeling exiled. Shep arranged a fleece blanket around her shoulders. At least the nosebleed seemed to be subsiding.

"I'm sorry about the mess," she said as he took the cardigan to the sink. "I'd have caught it better, but this neurotic antipathy thing"—she meant, of course, peripheral neuropathy—"it's made me a klutz. I can't quite feel the Kleenex, so I think I'm holding it, but I'm not and I drop it. It's so weird. Almost like not having hands. Like being an amputee."

Rinsing and squeezing out and rinsing again, Shep tried both to be vigorous about removing the blood yet also to move casually, routinely, as if the task were no trouble. Of course it was no trouble, but there was an extra art to making it seem that way.

"They'd better be right about these symptoms going away after the course is through," she added. "If I can't feel my hands, I'm hardly going to be hacking away with a jewelry saw."

"As I understand it, the only *special effect* they're worried could be permanent is the hearing loss."

"I'm sorry, what did you say?"

He raised his voice. "That as I understand it—"

"Shepherd. I was joking."

Of course she was joking. He would usually have been able to tell. It took concentration to remember that Glynis was still Glynis—that tautology so beloved of Pogatchnik—and he shouldn't treat her too gently or like a child. Yet what he said next was indeed parental, and fostered a familiar discomfort, the same sense of conniving complicity he'd first experienced with Dr. Knox.

"You have to focus on the fact that all this is temporary," he said. "I know it seems like the longest nine months of your life. But out the other side, the rashes, the sores, and the neuropathy will all clear up once you flush the drugs from your system. Try to keep your mind on the finish line."

"All I can say is, if this is tolerating A Lift into Manhattan 'incredibly well,' I'd hate to learn what it felt like to tolerate it badly."

A Lift into Manhattan meant, of course, Alimta and cisplatin. Seditious rechristening provided his wife not only a running source of entertainment, but ownership, a fragile feeling of control. Pharmaceutical companies would not tyrannize her with their perky nonsense trade names, whose subliminal positivism about the corruptions of the body she mercilessly mocked: Emend (*Amen*), Ativan (*Attaboy*), Maxidex (*Maxipad*). Yet Glynis herself had a knack for hijacking the heavy, forbiddingly multisyllabic generics into deviations that were harmless or even pleasant: lorazepam sweetened to *marzipan*, domperidone fizzed into *Dom Pérignon*, and lansoprazole lilted into *lamzy divey*, from the chipper gibberish ditty of the 1940s. The abundance of these drugs were to counteract the *special effects* of the chemo; these drugs, too, had *special effects*, counteracted with still more drugs, with perhaps still more *special effects*, so that the number of pills and potions she downed was potentially infinite. Thus none of her lighthearted nicknames compensated for the fact that her body had become, as Glynis would say, "a toxic waste dump."

"At least the nausea in your case doesn't seem to last more than a couple of days," Shep pointed out. "A lot of folks puke their guts out for weeks."

"Yeah, lucky me."

Shep held the cardigan up to the light. There were still pale purple shadows. He would take it to the dry cleaner on his lunch hour tomorrow. He had to get "up" in three hours, although the preposition implied getting to bed first, which looked dubious. "Did you talk to your mother today, or abandon her to voice mail again?"

"No, I didn't talk to her. Why should I? What's there to say? Yes, I took my folic acid and pterodactyl?" (Even for Shep, it was now taking work to remember that the real supplement was called pyridoxine.) "Nothing ever happens to me anymore. I never do anything but watch TV. We can't even talk about the weather. If I never leave the house, there is no weather. We end up talking for half an hour about what I ate."

"I.e., not enough."

"Don't start."

"I never stopped." Shep left to search out a hanger, and draped the sweater carefully so that it wouldn't dry with extrusions poked in the sleeves. While upstairs, he rinsed out the washcloth and went at the drips on the carpet. He managed only to turn the discrete droplets into large pink patches. It was the kind of damage that in times past he would have tried to ameliorate with obsessive scrubbing and violent cleaning products. He'd have been anxious that their security deposit was at issue, that the landlord might dock them for the cost of the carpet. Now he thought, fuck it, I'll throw a little salt on it later. There was something to be wrested from this mortality business, something more illuminating than mere perspective: apathy. He did not care about his landlord's carpet. He did not care about their security deposit. Ergo, he did not care about the stains in the hallway, and he tossed the wet washcloth in the sink. He could see how this liberating condition could grow progressive. How in the face of an end game there was virtually no limit to what did not matter.

Returned to the kitchen, he resumed the subject they'd left dangling. "I know it's tedious to fill the time on the phone. But your mother just wants to check up on how you're feeling."

"I have cancer! I feel like shit! What's to feel?" Glynis's breathing had gone raspy. The anemia gave her trouble catching her breath.

"She's trying to be a good mother," said Shep.

"She's trying to *seem* like a good mother. It's theater, so she can tell all those biddies she hangs out with how attentive she's being, so they'll feel sorry for her. Not for me! For *her*. She calls every day to make herself feel better."

Shep almost said, well, what is wrong with that, but held his tongue. Glynis didn't want other people to feel better. "Jackson's been a little weird lately," he brought up, propping her feet on some pillows; elevation kept the swelling, if not down, under control.

"How so?"

"Hard to say. Distant?" He massaged her instep. The bloated toes stuck out individually, like tiny tied-off balloons. "Some days he makes himself scarce at lunch, and we've always spent the lunch 'hour' together. He seems distracted. Like when we do walk to Prospect Park, he runs out of stuff to say."

"That's a new one."

"Maybe he's having a hard time knowing how to be consoling, about you." Her ankles had been so slender! He wanted her to gain weight, but not in her feet. "He seemed to handle the situation okay when you were still in the hospital, but you said mostly with those set-piece diatribes—"

"They were merciful. They got me out of having a conversation— Shepherd, I don't want to seem ungrateful, but I can't feel that."

"He wasn't dealing with what was happening," said Shep, leaving off the foot massage with a pat that tried to disguise that he was hurt. It made no sense to feel hurt. "Emotionally."

"Jackson is the most cut-off person I know. I've no idea how Carol stands it. He's the kind of person who's highly entertaining in groups. One-on-one, with me at least, he can't communicate 'please pass the salt.' But for you two it must be different."

Shep could feel the weariness in her observations. Glynis was an astute analyst of character. No artistic hermit, she had an extensive network of friends, and one of their favorite marital pastimes had long been the luxurious, sometimes cruelly accurate parsing of, say, the way Eileen Vinzano overcompensated for feeling overshadowed by her husband's prominence as a roving foreign correspondent for *ABC News* by praising Paul in company to the skies. "Rings a little hollow, doesn't it?" Glynis would discern slyly once their dinner guests had left. But nowadays Glynis had to put so much energy into expressing any given view that there was little left for the opinion itself. Throughout the average day now she doubtless thought a host of things that she simply couldn't marshal the wherewithal to articulate—to go through the arduous process of selecting words and putting them in the right order; to open her mouth, force air through her throat, and vibrate her vocal cords. Shep was sympathetic, but also felt cheated. Within fearfully short order, his wife's musings might no longer be infinitely on offer, but could instead constitute a finite and rather paltry collection of quotes, like one of those slight, undersized volumes of wit sold at bookstore checkouts around Christmas.

"It used to be different, with Jackson and me," said Shep. "But lately, even the diatribes—"

"He's so angry, but I'm not sure about what."

"I don't know if it's called 'anger' when you're enjoying yourself so much." He poured her a glass of soda water she'd not asked for, spritzing it with a wedge of lime. He could not bear empty time, when he did nothing for her. "But these days there's an edge on him. He's not having fun."

"It's a barrage, a"—the words were hard to find and heavy to lift—"broadcast. A force field, to keep other people at bay."

"I keep going back to when I visited him in New York Methodist, when he had that 'infection' and had to be put on an antibiotic drip. 'An infection'—he never said of what. I thought that was weird. You usually have an 'infected something,' right?"

"I don't know; I've been in the hospital three times now with 'an infection.'"

"But that's because you're susceptible to every passing bug. Besides, don't you spend a lot of time with visitors talking about the details of your treatment? We didn't. I mean, we didn't talk about what was wrong with him *at all*. And he missed a day of work last week, then never explained why."

"I forgot to tell you, Petra came by today," Glynis grumbled. She had finished with Jackson.

"Oh? How'd that go?"

Emptying the dishwasher, Shep braced himself. Now living on the Upper West Side, Petra Carson had been Glynis's classmate at Saguaro Art, and was his wife's oldest friend. The relationship of the two metalsmiths was delicate at the best of times. Like his sister-in-law Ruby, whose sheer industry he had always admired although never to Glynis's face, Petra was a hard worker, and her output was prodigious. Diligence more than gift had probably explained her rise in the ranks: her frequent admission to touring national craft shows, her supportive New York gallery. That the make-or-break attribute in lofty creative fields might be no different than the single most vital ingredient that had lifted his own pedestrian small business off the ground—humdrum perseverance—was a tactless intuition he had kept to himself.

Glynis disparaged Petra's work as safe and cookie-cutter. Unlike Glynis, Petra did not press against the limits of "craft" and yearn to join the art world proper. She made jewelry, period, for people to wear. Another tactless observation? Shep liked that. He liked functionality. He was a handyman. He had always cherished the fact that his wife made objects not only attractive but utile, which should have made them *more* valuable, not less. Thus he'd no patience for the loopy distinction between *art* and *craft* that put the latter at a commercial disadvantage. If you made a clay pitcher that held water, it was virtually worthless. Bang a hole in the bottom and it was "art"; you could charge an arm and a leg. How fucked up was that?

One would think that life-threatening illness would have finally neutralized this friendship's ongoing tension over which metalsmith was the more talented. (Glynis thought the answer was obvious.) While neither contested who was more successful, they'd been engaged in a tacit running feud for decades over whether a certain someone deserved her acclaim. Surely in the face of cancer Glynis should have called a truce, or even, in a burst of enlightened generosity, at long last given her colleague a little credit. (Okay, Shep caught himself, don't be fanciful.) Yet as far as Glynis was concerned, the rivalry was as ferocious as ever. She was loath to demote her oldest-friend-cum-nemesis to one more bland benevolent who tended the sick.

"Would you please stop fiddling about?"

Mystified, Shep froze with a spatula poised in midair. "I'm only—"

"I spend all day doing nothing. It would comfort me to be with someone else doing nothing, too."

He shrugged, dropped the spatula in the drawer, and pulled a chair up to her love seat. It was strangely difficult to do as she requested. He never stopped these last few months, what with all the errands on top of work, as well as trying and usually failing to find time to look in on Zach, whose withdrawal made it all too easy to ignore him. Simply sitting made Shep restless, claustrophobic. Relentless occupation was a therapy of sorts. Aggressive helpfulness disguised the fact that in any important sense he was helpless.

"Petra did nothing but moan, if you can believe it." Glynis struggled up on the pillows, which sent her into a coughing fit. Obviously her friend had offended her, since rare was the visitor who didn't. Umbrage was her drug of choice. "Oh gosh," Glynis rasped, "she has to fly to LA this week to go to the opening of her show. Isn't flying just awful these days; she used to look forward to flights, and now she dreads them—the security and the lines. And show openings are so dreary, all the brown-nosing compliments and then nobody buys anything, so it's obviously empty flattery. That was just the beginning, too. No matter what she talked about, everything she had to do, the endless polishing, the shipping and insurance, the dinners with gallery owners—it was all terrible, terrible, one big burden of the put-upon, when I can't even cross the street! I mean, the nerve! By the end of it I could have punched her in the nose."

"But . . . don't you think it's hard for people to tell you about the good things in their lives, when your life is so difficult?"

"She has no idea how lucky she is! Everyone around me seems to be feeling sorry for themselves, over nothing!"

Tempting Glynis to put herself in anyone else's shoes these days was nigh impossible. To be fair, compassion took energy. Then again, so did rage. "She's embarrassed, Gnu," he pressed quietly. "She's going to instinctively cast everything she has to do as disagreeable, so it seems like something you wouldn't want to do, since you can't do it. That's not because she feels sorry for herself, but because she feels sorry for you."

"Oh, fuck you and all your understandingness. You could use a little understandingness on me!"

Glynis cried easily. He stooped by her blanket and wiped the tears with his forefinger. While he was at it, he dabbed a tissue around her nose, to remove the last crusts of blood. "Your friends love you and don't always know how to show it."

"I'm sick of it." She pushed his handkerchief away, and fought again to sit more upright. "This parade of visitors. The cousins, the aunts, the neighbors we hardly know. The friends from fifteen years ago crawling out of the woodwork—as if there weren't a reason we haven't got together in all that time: *we don't like each other much.* But no, they all want their audience. They've all prepared it ahead of time, their little presentation. The things they wanted to *be sure to remember to say.* Honestly, they clasp their hands as if they're in church, or giving a book report. I've heard how much other people *luuuuuuv* me until it's coming out of my ears! To tell you the truth, at this point I might actually appreciate somebody walking through that door and saying, 'You know, Glynis? Honestly, I've never really cared for your company. Honestly, we've never got on. I've never seen the point of you,' or even, 'I hate your guts.' That would be refreshing. Anything but these nauseating speeches. Glynis, you're so talented. Glynis, you've done such beautiful work. Glynis, you've raised two wonderful children. I don't even know what they're talking about. Yes, maybe they're wonderful children to me, but to other people Zach and Amelia aren't wonderful, they're just my kids. And the upchucking reminiscences. Glynis, do you remember when we went on that skiing trip to Aspen and you got lost. Glynis, do you remember when we were kids and you dressed up like a gold prospector from the Wild West. Half the time I have no recollection of this supposedly precious memory whatsoever. What am I supposed to say? What do these people want from me? Yeah, of course I remember, that sure was funny, or scary, or dumb? Ha-ha-ha? And I *luuuuuuv* you, too? I don't *love* most of the people who come by here. Half the time I don't love anybody, not anything or anybody, not even you!"

Shep knew better than to feel wounded, and he stroked her thinning hair. Glynis had an aversion to gushiness, which she associated with Hetty. But something else was exercising her tonight that he didn't quite understand. Whatever it was, she needed to get it out of her. Like the first couple of days after chemo, he would hold her over the toilet until the last dribble stringed to the bowl.

"All this—sentimentality!" she went on, waving her hands. "It's just like my mother. They're trying to make themselves feel better. They're just *making sure*. They're just *making sure*, so that later, they don't have to feel guilty. They did their duty. They said their little piece. They can go back to their happy dinners and happy holidays and happy kiddies and happy biking around Tucson's cycle paths. Back to their tennis and wine and movies with a clear conscience."

"You don't . . . want them to have a clear conscience?"

"I'm trying to get well. I'm not shooting up that poison every two weeks from sheer perversity, but to get well. And these people—they're reading me my own obituary, Shepherd! Some afternoons I don't even feel I'm still in the room. It's like they've come to view the body, like I'm lying in an open casket. Here I'm throwing up, and breaking out in these disgusting rashes, and last week I could hardly swallow because of those sores at the back of my mouth. It's true I *look* like a cadaver, but I'm still here and I'm going through all this shit to try and stay here. It doesn't help to have a line of assholes trailing through my bedroom throwing dirt on my grave!"

"Okay," he said, taking her head to his shoulder. "Now I see." In all these months, this was as close as she'd ever come to saying the *D*-word.

He coaxed her into eating something—mashed potatoes, he proposed, you can eat a little mashed potato, surely. Soothing, smooth. She acceded only because she knew he would keep badgering, and after getting all that bile out of her system she didn't have the energy to resist him. He peeled and boiled two large bakers, and then mashed them with half a cup of heavy cream and so much butter that it nearly broke the emulsion. He slipped out some leftover roast chicken that was optimistic, but there was no harm in trying. Not hungry himself, he still took out two plates, serving himself a generous helping in a simulation of a hearty appetite. She wouldn't eat on her own. He took care to add a sprig of parsley and wedge of tomato for inviting color. With his first forkful he made *mmm*-ing noises, just as he had when getting their kids to eat something new and suspicious when they were small. Alas, Glynis looked at her plate as if presented with a freshly swirled patty of bathtub caulking when she wasn't in the mood for home repair.

"Try a few mouthfuls," he encouraged. "Maybe a little piece of chicken."

The amount of potato she skimmed onto her fork would not have fed a hamster.

Shep himself used to have one of those garbage-can metabolisms, shoveling in two-inch stacks of pastrami for lunch with nary a care. But that was in the days he was out on the job, pounding nails, climbing ladders, and hefting fifty-pound bags of cement. Once he assumed a largely managerial role at Knack, he'd started laying on the pounds, and discovered his vanity. Since then, he had joined Glynis in watching the waistline, and in so doing managed to mollify her long-standing resentment that he could eat like a horse while to maintain her figure she had to eat like a sparrow. Thus they'd stocked one-percent milk and those nondairy spreads that tasted like motor oil. Like most of their set in middle age, for years they had both regarded the food in their refrigerator with the wary hostility of grudging hosts forced to billet enemy troops. Since he always felt he could stand to drop a pound or two, his every mouthful had long been subtly tainted with self-reproach, and as for Glynis—well, in this department women were worse. So he felt he could speak for the both of them in having more or less forgotten that food was not purely a temptation to defy. Yet overnight his fears had perfectly inverted. He was watching his wife evaporate before his eyes.

These days when he went shopping, he checked the calorie count on the label, and if it wasn't high enough he put the product back. He spurned "Healthy Choice" soups for chowders he could spike with half-and-half. The fridge was stuffed with sour cream, cheese (soft ones like brie, as greasy as possible), pâté, and happy discoveries from the bakery section like pecan or mud pie, which ran to six hundred calories a slice. The freezer was stuffed with ice cream—never frozen yogurt but the real thing: rocky road or banana split. The pantry was packed with shortbread and bottles of fudge sauce; it hadn't seen a rice cake or water biscuit in months. There was, in retrospect, an animal rationality to maximizing fuel per dollar, as through all the years previous their lavishing just as much money on bags of air—puffed corn, pillows of baked chips—had been contrastingly insane. Yet if the new permissiveness had a dream-like quality of fantasy come true—behold, you may now eat the richest, sweetest dishes that you please, and the more the better—the caloric carte blanche was tragically mistimed. Finally his wife could eat all the foods she had denied herself for decades, and they all repulsed her. Hell, if he were really a loyal husband, he'd be forcing these mashed potatoes through a hose into her mouth, as if plumping a duck for foie gras.

"You remember how on research trips we'd go on ten-mile walk-abouts all day, taking notes and photographs, all on two cups of coffee?" Shep recalled. "Resisting the pad Thai or the samosas from street vendors, turning a blind eye to all those pastries in Portugal? Man, what a waste. If I have a single regret, it's ever having let you skip lunch. You'd have had a few more weeks' leeway this spring, and at least in those days you might have enjoyed the stuff going down."

"You wouldn't have wanted a fat wife, would you?"

"Yes. Right now? I would love a fat wife. I wish you were a blubber ball. I wish you were *enormous*. In fact, from what I know now, I don't understand why doctors don't advise everybody to lay on twenty extra pounds while they've got the chance. I might not advocate outright obesity. But there's a reason for fat. It's a resource."

She nibbled a few fluffs off of the tips of the tines, and put down the fork. "It is ironic. I guess I've put a fair bit of effort into staying slim. And now I'm punished for it. There's a lesson in there somewhere, though I'm not sure what it is."

"You've got to stop eating only as much as you feel like."

"I don't really *feel like* any."

"That's the point. It's a job. Now, you can do better than that." There was a hint of menace in his voice, a surprising undercurrent of pending physical violence. He could see it coming to that, too. Unfortunately, Petra and Ruby's perseverance had never been Glynis's strong suit, but defiance was. The harder he pressed her to choke down those potatoes, the more forcefully she'd push them away. But he was getting desperate. Most of the time, he didn't notice what she looked like; he was used to it, much as through his childhood he was largely unaware of the pong of paper mills that fugged his hometown. Yet once in a while he would catch a glimpse of her out of the corner of his eye, apprehending his wife as he might a stranger. Her cadaverousness—the sunken sockets, the striated breastplate, the wrists he could loop with his thumb and forefinger—would suddenly hit him like the piercing reek of Berlin, New Hampshire, after his family had been on vacation in the mountains.

Glynis took one more smear of potato, and set the fork down with resolution. Displaying a childlike deviousness, she had mounded the remainder, reducing its perimeter to make it look as depleted as possible. She had tucked the shred of chicken breast under the rim of the plate. He gave up, and cleared their settings; while enticing her to eat more of hers, he had somehow dispatched his own portion. As for putting on twenty pounds as insurance against disease, he was well on his way to taking his own advice. He ate the same butter-fortified meals that she did, and had always that Presbyterian aversion to throwing anything away. Glynis would eat two tablespoons of couscous soaked in half a cup of olive oil, and he'd polish off the bowl. The time he once spent at the gym he now spent at the A&P. Despite his own lauding of "leeway," he'd worked out one way or another his whole life, and the soft, slackening spread of his midsection was the one personal sacrifice he felt most keenly. Still, Shep had decided not to worry about it. There was plenty of time to take the weight off—plenty of time after. Given his natural pragmatism, it took effort to keep from forming in his mind too clearly after what.

Shep had lured her back to bed, but Glynis was still wakeful. He lay beside her, and left the light on. She trailed a finger pensively over the chain-saw scar at the base of his neck. Following on a long silence that suggested an uncertainty over how to bring the subject up, at last she announced, "The Afterlife."

The topic hadn't arisen in weeks. So she had seen the beach on his screen.

"I know we've talked about this ad nauseam," she continued, "but after all these years I still don't quite get it. What it was you needed so badly to get away from. What it was you hoped to find."

To his surprise, Shep reacted badly to her use of the past tense. Since they *had* talked about this ad nauseam, he fought an irritation that she could conceivably still not "get it." But expressing irritation to

Glynis—or anger, exasperation, even a mild negative like dismay—was now against the rules. Battling to remain serene, he tried one more time to put it into words.

"What would I like to get away from? Complexity. Anxiety. A feeling I've had my whole life that at any given time there's something I'm forgetting, some detail or chore, something that I'm supposed to be doing or should have already done. That nagging sensation—I get up with it, I go through the day with it, I go to sleep with it. When I was a kid, I had a habit of coming home from school on Friday afternoons and immediately doing my homework. So I'd wake up on Saturday morning with this wonderful sensation, a clean, open feeling of relief and possibility and calm. There'd be nothing I had to do. Those Saturday mornings, they were a taste of real freedom that I've hardly ever experienced as an adult. I never wake up in Elmsford with the feeling that I've done my homework."

"But you're accustomed to homework. With nothing to do you'd be climbing the walls. How would you have filled your day, making fountains?"

"I would make fountains," he said temperately, closing his eyes, "if I wanted to make fountains."

"But coming to any understanding of what you 'want' is the hardest job in the world. It seems to me that what you were always designing for yourself was a massive existential crisis."

Again that past tense, pricking his neck like a sharp-cornered care label, and Shep had never quite got his head around that word, *existential*. "Maybe it would turn out that I don't especially want anything."

"So, what, you'd lie around and nap? Take it from me, that's nothing to get excited about."

To the contrary, it sounded fantastic. The alarm would ring in an hour and twenty minutes.

"You can't take pleasure in your leisure, because it's been forced on you," he said. "And because you feel like shit. So it's the time we have while feeling *well* that's precious. I'm not just squandering my 'life' on botched Sheetrock jobs in Queens. I'm squandering my *healthy life*. You of all people should appreciate how raw the deal is. We slave away during the few years that we're capable of enjoyment. Then what's left are the years we're old and sick. We get sick on our own time. We only get leisure when it weighs on us. When it's useless to us. When it's no longer an opportunity but a burden."

In truth, he had given this matter of how to fill The Afterlife more thought than she realized. He did not venerate lassitude, or lassitude alone. He might learn to dive; the marine life around Pemba was spectacular, and several outfits rented gear. Snorkeling presented an appealingly low-tech alternative. They played a game on the island called *bao*, involving the distribution of sixty-four seed pods over thirty-two carved-out bowls, an agreeably unfathomable pastime that put much emphasis on grace and finesse. Or *keram*, which looked to be a hilarious cross between checkers, hockey, and pool; shuttling pucks against each other on an uneven homemade wooden table would surely prove a diversion one was in little danger of taking too seriously. Otherwise, he had always found his greatest satisfactions—which is to say, the feeling you got from doing something rather than having already done it—undertaking discrete, utterly elective physical projects: painting a porch that would easily make it another season, knocking together a spice cabinet whose shelves were tailor-spaced to fit the stainless-steel canisters from Zabar's, and—yes, Glynis, even if you find it comical—building fountains. So he might learn to carve a canoe. There were plenty of these crude boats called *mtumbwis* on the island, and chipping a trough from a log with dull hand-tools might take a fabulously long time.

"But Shepherd," Glynis interrupted his reverie. "It seems obvious that what you were really trying to get away from all those years was yourself."

Oh God, that old saw. The amount of effort it took to keep from getting annoyed was stupendous. "I have no problem with *myself*. What I would like to get away from is other people."

"Like me."

"Gnu?" He propped himself up on an elbow and turned her toward him. "I have never in all my life considered you *other people*."

He slipped his hand around her neck, noting mournfully how pronounced its tendons had grown, how prominent the veins. Nevertheless, it was still Glynis's neck. The breasts at the gape of her nightgown were smaller, though they'd never been large; the nipples had darkened and the skin was starting to crenulate, but they were still Glynis's breasts. He kissed her. She returned his kiss with all the hunger so little in evidence during their impromptu supper.

Shep had always felt a little guilty about the intensity with which he was attracted to his wife. Physically attracted—he did not confuse the desire with anything more ethereal or romantic. He loved the way she looked, not just well turned out but especially naked, and he worried that he loved the way she looked too much. He was addicted to the rim of her hipbone, to sliding his hand into its hollow, and down into the darkening crease. Because he'd begged her not to, she didn't shave her bikini line, allowing for the subtle shading and alluring gradation of lighter scrub thickening to a shadowy woods, into whose mysteries he had always ventured with the thrilled trepidation of a boy in a magic forest. She had long legs and sharp, shapely kneecaps. This attraction went back to the first time they met, and was excruciatingly specific to Glynis. It probably qualified as unhealthily obsessive. He would have been embarrassed to admit to his gruff, lewd co-workers at Knack that for the whole of his marriage he'd not been drawn to any woman other than his wife. They would never believe him, or if they did believe him they would pity him as somehow a lesser man with no imagination and no drive.

Perhaps this was true. Perhaps there was something wrong with him, something missing. Yet the fixation was exclusive, and not within his gift to relax. Its strength seemed to wax and wane somewhat, but within a narrow range. At any given time, he might be attracted to Glynis, incredibly attracted to Glynis, or overpoweringly attracted to Glynis.

Early on they'd experimented with the sort of improvisations that in those days had seemed obligatory. But not long into this variety-pack approach to sex, Glynis had arrested the slide of his head down her long, flat stomach and announced with a wicked glint in her eyes, "You know, I really like *fucking*." It was the most erotic declaration he'd ever heard, and on recollection it still made him hard. So that was what they did. They fucked. Sometimes often, sometimes less so, but he could honestly say that it had never bored him, never grown tired. Not that it was any-one else's business, but she liked it a little rough.

Which was giving him some problems these last few months. First there was the incision from the surgery, which he had to take care not to touch. Although she hadn't wanted him right after; too many hands and instruments had pried inside her, and she couldn't bear even so kindly a violation, sleeping in a tight, private ball. The scar wasn't as tender now, and she had gradually grown less protective of it; he was sure that at first she'd felt ashamed—fearful, that she was spoiled. True, he wouldn't call the red, now browning ridge exactly a turn-on, but it did something else to him, which did feel manly: it broke his heart. It drove him to shelter her, to press her torso against his own and thus place the whole of his mass between his wife and the knifing world.

Eventually it was Glynis who'd had to importune that he stop han-dling her like china. She had indeed come to seem breakable to him, and under the influence of Alimta she was literally bruisable, so that when he did as she requested she woke the next morning with thumb-shaped purple blotches down her thighs.

The thing was, he knew that he loved her in that finer way. But as much as he relished the mingling of the two, he knew also that this physical de-sire was separate—a distinct wanting that had to do with line and shape and color, with breasts and hair and smell. It did not have to do with her dry sense of humor, her slyness, the beguiling barbarity of her character. It did not have to do with her willfulness, her infuriating self-destructiveness, or her spiritual alliance with metal. It didn't even have to do with her sorely underexploited aesthetic talent. It had to do with the proportions of her legs, her long waist, her tiny, hard-muscled ass. It had to do with her dark, secret, forested cunt. For years he had privately anguished about her pending old age—the prospect of which was now a luxury. Inevitably, then, since January he had privately anguished about cancer. He was too attracted to his wife, but he was used to being too attracted, and if all that was left was the nice love, the warm appreciative admiring love without the gutter love, the unseemly, sordid animal love, he would feel lesser, and the love would feel lesser, in its very purity and high-mindedness and mere goodness smaller and less interesting and less addictive. He did not want to stop being attracted to his wife. It was not easy to face, but for twenty-six years he had not only loved a woman. He had loved a body.

Like the house of his dreams the night before her surgery, that body had good bones. But just as you want to be able to walk across a floor and feel a comforting solidity without necessarily envisioning the very joists that prop your feet, you did not especially want to bear witness to the good bones of your wife. As he ran his hand down the ladder of her rib cage, he could feel the underlying structure, the beams with which Glynis was built. He may have always savored the sharpness of her hip-bones, but now they were too sharp, the skin stretched across them like the very cheapest of carpets, so skimpy that you could discern not only cracks between the floorboards but the nails. These days he bedded a sketch of a body, a gesture toward it, a few strokes from which to infer the woman he had gleefully ravished for a quarter century. He fought a shiver. He did not want to find Glynis repellant, and he filled out her form from memory, as he might study an architectural drawing and mentally walk rooms that were mere lines on paper.

"Are you sure you're up for this?" he whispered.

In response, she reached for where his reluctance was most palpable; he arced in a shying sag. But a metalsmith has powerful hands, and the clasp of her fingers stirred him to remember that his wife was not a corpse. He needn't shrink from her body as if he might defile her, commit an indecency. Her grip brought a sharp, needy sensation to life, one he had forgotten altogether in the constant, more pressing needs for potatoes, fleece blankets, liquids spiked with cranberry cordial, soft, slow rides to chemo. Men were supposed to think about sex all the time, but he didn't anymore, and now the remembering was so keen that it hurt.

He was nervous of resting on top of her. Though she had always enjoyed the full weight of him, he didn't want to crush her, and propped his arms on either side. Easing onto an elbow, he reached for the lubricant on the bedside table, opening the cap with one hand and squeezing a dab of clear jelly onto a forefinger. When they'd first resorted to this small assistance she'd been wounded, as if her enthusiasm had been found wanting. But he had importuned that her body was under assault, and its failure to grease the skids was in no way a failure of heart. Indeed, when he slipped the finger between her legs the lips were dry; only the smear from the tube made her feel like his wife.

They could still do this. He kissed her, the taste with that metallic tang like sucking on a coin, as if she were no longer merely allied with metal, but were turning into metal from the inside. He looked into her eyes, saddened by their yellow tinge but still he found her there. The pupils were small and permanently frightened. It wasn't desire he read in them so much as desire for desire, which would have to do. Looking down, he felt sheepishly enormous, spreading and flabby in comparison. She gripped the barrel of his chest, the nails biting. He was sliding in with that diffident tenderness she hated. She took a buttock in each hand and shoved.

So he allowed himself to forget. He allowed himself to fuck her, as hard and as deeply as she had always liked, with that edge of abuse. Coming, he allowed himself to believe that this was the injection that would cure her, for once a mainline that wasn't full of poison but was full of life. The poison was forty thousand dollars. The elixir was free.

That should have been it. But before she drifted off in his arms, Glynis mumbled distinctly, "So. Do you think you'll have enough left?"

Shep felt his face burn. He stroked her hair silently (several strands came off in his hand), on the pretext that he didn't know what she was talking about. But it was nefarious, after you'd lived with a woman for this long, how well she knew you. How she could tell what you were thinking, even if you tried mightily not to think it, to hide the thinking from yourself. Enough of what left? Money, of course. *Only* money, Dad—on what else did the firstborn Knacker so famously dwell?

Should being capable of calculations like the one he'd made earlier this evening mark him as a sinful and selfish man, that was a truth about himself he would have to live with. An Afterlife for one would cost little more than half as much as an Afterlife for two. He would retain the funds for a solo escape, but only if Glynis died soon.

Chapter Eleven

Shepherd Armstrong Knacker
Merrill Lynch Account Number 934-23F917
June 01, 2005 – June 30, 2005
Net Portfolio Value: $452,198.43

Driving Glynis once more to Columbia-Presbyterian, Shep was hard pressed to contrive an analogy for his emotions that was anything short of ridiculous. Like opening the envelope that contained his SAT scores? He hadn't cared fractionally this much about going to college even in the days when he'd cared about going to college. Like opening the door to Dave's office the April after he'd sold Knack for a million bucks, and was about to find out how much he owed the feds? Sure, he'd felt a bit sick to his stomach then; The Afterlife was at stake. But he'd been familiar with capital gains rates, and had been prepared for the ballpark. For that matter, Shep's reputed concern for money was highly exaggerated. So he had never cared this much about any tax bill, even about the check he wrote to the U.S. Treasury in 1997 for close to three hundred thou.

No, for driving to get the results of Glynis's first CAT scan since beginning chemotherapy there was no parallel. They didn't talk. They had already talked. No amount of talk would affect the shrinking or expanding shadows on her slides. She was the same, she was better, or she was worse. The verdict was not on their efforts. That was one problem with a frivolous comparison to test results of the educational sort, whose scores rated having performed well or badly; they were outcomes you had ordained. However much Shep's father may have regarded his son as an alien philistine, the man had successfully inculcated in his firstborn a drive to be good, to do good, and to do well. Yet whether Glynis was *doing well* would not issue from either of them having *done well*. Having always strived for excellence even in humble endeavors like installing a new bathroom vanity, Shep was confounded by consequences at once so vital, yet determined solely by the heedless decree of fate. His anxiety was therefore akin to the way Jackson must feel when the greyhounds were off and running and he'd placed a sizeable bet on a dog.

Shep distracted himself by considering Dr. Goldman. Vigorous and aggressive, the internist was a roughly handsome man; at six-feet-who-knows, he was *large*. While you couldn't call him fat, a fleshy midsection did betray him as a man of appetites. Likely no stranger to a rack of ribs or a double Scotch, he displayed the very failure to take his own advice that Shep had missed in Dr. Knox—who, fit, trim, and younger by fifteen years, was by conventional measures far better looking. So why was Philip Goldman the more attractive man? Objectively his handsomeness was very "rough" indeed—which was to say that he wasn't handsome at all. His broad face was smashed flat, and his eyes were set too close together—small and almost piggy. Yet he moved with energy and self-conviction, swallowing hallways in the same hungry lunges with which he doubtless downed a meal. He *moved* like a man who was killingly handsome, and thus he swept you up in the illusion that he was. His appeal was kinetic, and would never translate to static photographs. A smitten girlfriend would proudly show his snapshot to a confidante, and the friend would privately shake her head, flummoxed by what on earth the poor woman saw in this homely lug.

Frankly, Shep was a little jealous. It wasn't only that the doctor was better educated, more successful, and rich. There was an intimacy between the doctor and his patient that Shep couldn't equal with twenty-six years of marriage. He didn't know what you called his wife's unquestioning devotion to her doctor if it wasn't love. She had merely trusted Dr. Knox, which was atypical enough; she *believed* in Dr. Goldman, and with a passion that felt erotic. When her husband admonished her to eat, she dug in her heels. But when toward the end of May *Dr. Goldman* urged her to eat, Glynis had made a proper project of gaining weight, cheerfully requesting her every favorite dish. Whatever had inspired her fuller cheeks shouldn't matter, but Shep was still bugged.

Shep's absenteeism was already teetering into the danger zone with Pogatchnik; at least Goldman's obliging this early evening appointment had enabled him to put in a full day at work.

In silence, Shep held hands with Glynis from the parking garage to the office on the seventh floor, using his free hand to hit the car's key fob and punch elevator buttons. Before knocking timidly on the door, he paused to lock eyes with his wife. It was the kind of glance that defendants and their spouses might share while the jury files in. Glynis was innocent, but this judiciary was capricious.

The door swept open. "Mr. and Mrs. Knacker, please come in!"

Shep took one look at Goldman's beaming face and thought: *Not guilty.*

"You're looking well!" Goldman cried, shaking Shep's hand and laying a second palm on the forearm for added warmth. (Shep was not looking well. After months of mopping up his wife's high-calorie leftovers, he looked more like Goldman every day, but several inches shorter and absent the poetry-in-motion magic trick.) When he shook hands with Glynis—"And you're looking *very* well!"—her wiry metacarpus was every bit a match for the big doctor's clasp. She may have underserved her talent, but even intermittent filing, sawing, and polishing had produced the fiercest grip of any woman Shep knew.

They sat before the desk. Shep was glad for the chair. He felt shaky. Asterisks were spinning in his visual field, as if the office swarmed with flies. He prayed that Goldman wasn't the round-up type, who would cast a merely middling outcome in glowing terms.

The doctor bombed to his seat, clasped his hands behind his head, and tipped rearward in his spring-backed chair with one cordovan on the edge of the desk. His lab coat was open, his shirt crumpled, his hair in disarray; he was a bit of a slouch. But then, any specialist with patients flying in from New Zealand and Korea could afford to look unkempt. "Well, boys and girls, I have fabulous news!"

Shep dropped his shoulders in relief. The internist was a man of science, not a car salesman, and by code of practice couldn't turn back the odometer on a last-legs clunker.

"The evil shrinketh before the mighty hand of righteousness," Goldman proceeded gleefully. "I know that Alimta is a bastard, Mrs. Knacker, and you've been a real trouper." (This much beloved term *real trouper* was apparently medical shorthand for *does not wake doctor in middle of night when suffering side effects hospital staff have already prepared her for.*) "But it's been worth it. I'll be honest: that one biphasic patch is being stubborn. But it hasn't got any larger either, so we've arrested its progress. The other two are significantly reduced in size. We're not seeing any metastasis, either."

Shep reached around Glynis's neck and kissed her forehead in blessing. They squeezed each other's hands while tumbling over one another to exclaim, "That's wonderful! That's terrific! We're so grateful!"

Goldman loaded a CD into his computer, showing them cross-sections of Glynis's organs, which looked like slices of a fancy game terrine in an upscale restaurant. Shep castigated himself for ever thinking critically about Philip Goldman. Maybe the guy really was handsome. Shep wasn't a female, so who was he to judge? And if Glynis "believed" in her doctor, the faith had been well placed.

By contrast, Shep felt traitorous, cynical, and shallow for having been a doubter, a religious skeptic. His sudden groundswell realignment in relation to his wife's disease was none too subtle, leaving him to wonder if all along he'd suffered from an attitude problem. He didn't buy into this New Age business of sending out "negative energy"—or he didn't think he bought it. Nonetheless, any atmospheric contribution he might have made to his wife's convalescence (might they dare now to call it "recovery"?) had been to her detriment. Since the internist produced more tangible redemption than either Gabe Knacker's traditional Presbyterianism or Deb's barmy born-again sect in Tucson, it was time to convert. To become a loyal, tithing parishioner of Philip Goldman's church.

Exercising his newfound faith, Shep regarded the doctor with fresh appreciation. You could tell from the assurance of his gestures that this was a man used to giving speeches to large audiences of rapt medical professionals. To having his articles published in *The Lancet*, and being sent lesser authors' research for review. To having dying people beg him to take their cases, perhaps in tears. Yet he did not seem self-important; that is, he didn't broadcast a compensatory bluster that would camouflage a private sensation of fraudulence. No, Goldman just seemed important.

The doctor pointed out the contrast between Glynis's last CAT scan and the latest. To the naked eye, the differences looked depressingly slight; it would take work, this conversion, spurning a natural agnosticism and getting with the program. Throughout, Goldman employed the inclusive first-person plural: *we've* shrunk this, *we've* shrunk that. But the pronoun was over-generous. *We* had done nothing, as Goldman knew very well.

The doctor's most conspicuous appetite was for accomplishment, and his drive for excellence put in the shade Shep's sorry aim to match roofing patches with original slates. Maybe Goldman liked Glynis; he liked being liked, so it was hard to tell. But his primary relationship was with her cancer. She was therefore a vehicle for his own beatification. In taming her malignancy, he was probably pleased on her behalf; he was unquestionably pleased on his own. More project than person, Glynis was an instrument for the furtherance of this doctor's galloping ambition, and not only to do good but to do *well*.

Her surrogacy was obscurely unsettling. Yet Shep couldn't identify what was wrong with it. He was ordinarily an advocate of healthy self-interest. For Goldman to have conflated his patient's survival and his personal conquest was in Glynis's interest, too. She didn't need another well-wisher, Shep told himself, another friend. She needed a competent, skillful technician who did the best job he knew how, and why the man made that maximum effort was his business. For that matter, maybe Shep should reverse who was using whom. He and Glynis were hijacking Goldman's ego to serve their own purposes, and looked at this way the scenario seemed perfectly cheerful.

"Since it's working," the doctor wrapped up, "and you seem to tolerate the drugs better than the average bear, for now we should keep hitting the cancer with Alimta and—with 'A Lift into Manhattan.'" As the doctor shot Glynis a conspiratorial smile, Shep tried valiantly not to feel wounded that she'd let Goldman in on their private joke. "I'm a little concerned about your blood count. But we have plenty of other options at our disposal if your tolerance slips, or your progress with Alimta flags." He rattled off a list of alternative drugs, and then asked about the current side effects. Glynis played them down.

It was summer. For the first time that season, it felt like summer, and the luscious weather was not a mockery. In the long light of early July, the sun was only now setting behind Hackensack, flashing tangerine sheets across the Hudson. Driving with thrust, Shep recalibrated the future. Maybe she'd pull through after all. Maybe he wouldn't have to go to Pemba by himself. Maybe there would still be sufficient funds in the Merrill Lynch, if not for the relaxed, luxurious second life he'd planned, enough to get by, to pick up a small house for a song and eat papayas. Maybe he would still have to prevail upon her to go, but maybe this experience will have changed her, given her a glimpse of how little time was left even for people who didn't have cancer. Maybe he would order up that kingfish, by candlelight, for two.

"How'd you like to eat out tonight?" he proposed. "I could give you a real 'Lift into Manhattan.'"

"It's a little risky, with other people's germs . . ." said Glynis. "But what the hell. Let's celebrate. I'd love to go to Japonica, but sushi is probably pushing it."

No matter how many restaurants he sampled, up against it like this

Shep often drew a blank, and they'd end up at some heavily advertised tourist joint like Fiorello's because it was the only name he could dredge up. But this evening was charmed. "City Crab?"

"Perfect!"

Bejeweled like a tiara, the George Washington Bridge had just switched on its lights. Undergoing maintenance, the span on the Manhattan side had been unlit for years now, leaving a single lit peak on the New Jersey end to dangle to darkness mid-river; the lopsided effect had been visually vexing. Tonight at long last the whole bridge was lit shore to shore. The renewed symmetry seemed to mean something. A rhythm and balance had been restored.

Being out in public was a novelty now. The evening got off to a rocky start when they noticed a patron coughing nearby, and insisted on being reseated. When the waitress acted miffed, Glynis played her trump card: "My immune system is compromised. I have cancer." After moving them swiftly upstairs, the waitress brought a complimentary amuse-bouche with the establishment's apologies. Once the girl left, Glynis muttered, "At least mesothelioma is good for something."

Glynis hadn't been strictly forbidden alcohol, and Shep scanned the wine list. He didn't much care about champagne, interchangeable with Mountain Dew in his view, and Glynis would likely sip a single flute. Still he chose a pricey Veuve Cliquot. He wasn't buying champagne. Like most people, he suspected, he was buying the *idea* of champagne.

"To your health," he toasted, pleased to note that in low lighting his wife's chemo-tinged skin color could pass for a tan. She looked fetching in her cream satin turban, which so suited her long, sharp face that onlookers might easily assume that she'd opted for the swaddling as a style statement.

"I've been meaning to tell you," said Glynis, tucking into her crab cakes. "I've been getting *loads* of ideas for new flatware projects. Like in the car just now. I got an image of a salad serving set, two nested spoons—one larger and thicker, the other thinner and more sinewy, both different but perfectly cupped. Forged, not cast, all on a slight curve . . . It's hard to explain."

The picture was romantic. "If you get back to work," he proposed shyly, "I wonder if you'd consider doing another fountain. With me. Not like the goofy ones I knock up, but classy, like the Wedding Fountain. We haven't collaborated since."

"Mmm . . . Maybe for the dining table? That could be fun. That's a great idea. Because I'm aching to make up for lost time."

In truth, her "lost time" in metalsmithing comprised not only the last six months, but most of her married life. The only sign Shep gave of this indiscreet observation was to rue, "I wish you'd never wasted whole afternoons making chocolate bunny rabbits."

"That was the point."

"You wasted your time on chocolate bunny rabbits to prove to me that you shouldn't be wasting your time on chocolate bunny rabbits."

"That's about the sum of it. Or to put it another way, I wanted you to see that your resentment over the fact that I didn't bring in much money was nothing in comparison to my resentment if you forced me to earn it."

"I never forced you to earn it, or resented that you didn't."

"Bullshit."

"Tell me some more. About your ideas for flatware."

"You're changing the subject."

"Yes." Dipping his jumbo shrimp into cocktail sauce, Shep hazarded the kind of thought from which he had protected her for months. Her delicacy was physical. Maybe he needn't treat her with kid gloves in every other regard. "If the situation were reversed, would you have worked to support me, and the whole family, while I stayed home pursuing my passion? Fountains, for example? Willingly. Without a word of protest."

"You'd never have been able to stand that."

"Dodge. The question was, could you?"

"Honestly? No. I wouldn't support you while you made fountains. Women . . . Well, we're not raised to expect that."

"Is that fair?"

"Fair?" She laughed. "Who said anything about fair? Of course it's not fair!"

Glynis was in such fine form that Shep could have wept. She finished the crab cakes; she finished her lemon sole. She ate the parsleyed potatoes and two slices of bread. She was kind enough not to mention that the chic seafood was lost on her dulled palate. Instead she quietly drowned both courses in Tabasco to get them to taste of anything but that tongue-curling taint of nickel, which contaminated everything from crab to kisses. Conversational strictures seeming to have loosened, they finally talked about the fact that Amelia had made herself so scarce. Their daughter had driven up to Elmsford only once this spring, excusing herself after a single hour lest her mother grow "too tired."

"I'm too close," Glynis speculated. "She looks at me and sees herself with cancer, and she can't bear it."

"But she isn't the one with cancer," said Shep.

"She's afraid."

"I don't mind her being afraid *for* you. I do mind her being afraid *of* you."

"She's young," countered Glynis, who'd not made such an effort to project herself into someone else's head since this whole awfulness began. "She's not in control of herself. I bet she's not even aware of what she's doing."

"Which is?"

"Avoiding me, of course. If you pointed out that she's only visited once, I bet she'd be shocked. I bet she imagines she's been up loads of times. I bet that when she finally makes herself call me on the phone? And she's thought time and again about phoning and then something mysteriously always comes up and she puts it off til tomorrow? I bet that happens so often, if not almost every day, that she thinks she's been calling all the time."

"I worry that Amelia could feel bad, later—" Shep stopped himself. That was the old thinking, based on the old assumptions. The ones from previous to seven o'clock this evening.

"About what?"

He curved the thought. "Once you're well again. She could look back and realize how inconsiderate she was. How uninvolved in such a big crisis in your life. She could feel guilty; you could justifiably bear her a grudge. I'd like her to get her act together, in the interests of your relationship out the other end. Maybe I should say something."

"Don't you dare. She should see me because she wants to, not because Dad gave her a hard time. Anyway," Glynis continued with a sip of champagne, "at least Amelia's shown up more often than *Beryl*. By threatening your sister with the specter of one person she has to feel more sorry for than herself, I may have single-handedly driven her to New Hampshire."

"You don't want to see Beryl anyway. And now, out of sheer cheapness, she's cornered herself into taking some responsibility for my father. Couldn't have worked out better. Might even build her character."

"With her raw materials, your sister building character is like you constructing a bookcase out of cardboard."

With disingenuous idleness, Shep raised over their cheesecake: "Now that the prognosis is looking bright, do you still want to go ahead with this asbestos suit?"

"Absolutely! I may be pulling through this, but I'll still have endured agony in the process. The people who did this to me should have to pay."

"Well, they'll not be the same people . . ." he said dubiously. "In the thirty years since you were in art school, the corporate higher-ups at Forge Craft would have turned over two or three generations."

"They're still drawing salaries from a company that's profited from *evil*. Best of all, now that I'm getting better I'll have the energy to give that deposition, and to stand up under cross-examination, too. I'll be able to take the heat if the suit goes to trial."

Shep's heart sank. He was desperate to escape the litigation. "Okay." He shrugged. "If you say so. I have another appointment with that attorney Rick Mystic next week."

He was careful to curl the conversation back to her metalwork over coffee and mint tea, thus ending the night on a high note. In the car, he suggested they schedule a dinner with Carol and Jackson to celebrate the scan. "A themed evening," she agreed. "We could serve CAT food."

Shep was pleased to catch Zach in the kitchen, whether or not his son was pleased to be caught. The boy was so intent on disappearing himself that for a moment he froze with no acknowledgment of his parents' entrance, as if they might walk right through him. His posture had further deteriorated. But Shep was relieved to come home and for once not start abjuring the boy that if he couldn't chip in by doing his laundry he could at least match his own socks, or chiding the kid to please turn down the music because his mother wasn't feeling well. ("What else is new?") Shep couldn't remember the last time he'd been able to deliver glad tidings, and the overpriced Mountain Dew at dinner had juiced his mood.

"Yo, I'm glad you're underfoot, sport," said Shep. Zach received the companionable clap on his shoulder grimly, as if withstanding a hard right punch. "We got some terrific news about your mother at Columbia-Presbyterian tonight."

Zach flinched. He didn't look like a boy about to receive good news. And he protected his turkey sandwich as if they'd caught him at something naughty. The boy was scrawny and still growing; why would he act guilty about a sandwich? "So what's up?" he asked glumly.

Shep detailed the CAT scan results, describing the diminutions of the two cowering patches of foulness; since he omitted mention of the "stubborn" biphasic presentation altogether, he might rightly have been accused of the very rounding up he had feared from Philip Goldman. But there was nothing wrong with emphasizing the positive, especially with a sixteen-year-old kid who'd had to weather plenty dire turns of the wheel with little help from his distracted, harried father.

"Uh-huh."

Shep kept waiting for the boy to have a reaction, until he resigned himself that this slumping, passive, unaltered will to vanish was his son's reaction. "Maybe you don't understand the full implications of this. It means your mother's getting better. That the chemo is working. That we're beating this thing."

"Uh-huh." Zach raised his gaze from his favorite middle distance and looked his father in the eye. Sorrowful and pitying, the boy's soft brown unbroken stare made Shep feel suddenly the younger of the two. Their son rotated toward Glynis, who was sitting at the table, and put a hand on his mother's shoulder to give it a squeeze; his motions were jagged and halting, as if he were operating his arm by remote control. "That's great, Mom," he said leadenly. "I'm real glad things are looking up." The gesture seemed to cost him, and he trailed exhaustedly upstairs.

Shep was about to mumble, "What was that about?" when the phone rang. It was late for a call. He had a queer premonition that he should let it go to voice mail. He and Glynis had not had such a fine night on the town together for the last year or more, and the interruption was unwelcome. He couldn't think of anyone to whom he wanted to speak right now besides his wife, now restored to him in all her former dryness, perception, and good humor, a miraculous resurrection courtesy of the Church of Philip Goldman. He didn't want to burst his own champagne bubble, and the night's magic felt fragile.

His "hello?" was wary.

As the call proceeded Shep said little, asking a few questions, ambling to the porch. It was still a beautiful evening—Elmsford was far enough from the city that you could see the stars—but it felt less idyllic now. He should have let the damn phone ring.

Driving up to Berlin on what was, catastrophically, the Fourth of July weekend, Shep thought about his father. With the man's professional devotion to more elevated matters, it had taken him years to notice that Gabriel Knacker was indeed concerned with money, which, when you kept track, consumed an astonishing proportion of the good reverend's conversation. He'd long preached about turning off lights, not because he wanted to save the planet but because he was cheap. Back when he'd run a parish, the minister had been every bit as grasping as any CEO, shamelessly squeezing his strapped parishioners for fatter fistfuls in the offering plate in order to refit the quaint clapboard church with somewhat less quaint plumbing. In fact, the budget clash between rising costs and a dwindling congregation had dominated the majority of Sunday dinners when Shep was a kid. His father would be mortified by the inference, but in the minister's scathing about wealthy mill owners, their second homes and sports cars, Shep had learned to detect a trace, just a trace, of ordinary envy.

In addition to some bashes and bruises, Dad had broken his left femur. He'd been buried in a Walter Mosley novel while walking downstairs. In point of fact, the accident was of a sort that any detective fiction fan might have suffered even at a younger age, and at least it wasn't his hip, but any broken bone at eighty was serious. Fortunately, Beryl had been around at the time. Unfortunately, her immediate ministrations had quickly drained her wading pool of Clara-Barton altruism; or, as Glynis might say, the cardboard bookcase of her character had already collapsed under the strain. Any further wrangling with paperwork, bills, and the logistics of a disabled elderly parent—dealing with whether Dad could go home, and if not where—was now Shep's problem. Honestly, talking to his sister last night, you'd think she was the taxi driver who'd dropped this geezer off at the hospital and wanted somebody to cover the fare.

He would have liked to wax sentimental. But like any sane modern-day American in the face of medical calamity, he could not afford to squander his energies on mere affection, mere concern. The costs of his father's immediate crisis would be picked up by Medicare, but only 80 percent; Shep kicked himself for not buying his dad a supplemental Medigap policy when he'd had the chance. The greater anxiety was after the crisis had passed. In the face of a home aide's salary or retirement community fees, it went without saying that Beryl would chip in her two cents solely in the figurative sense of the expression.

Rising on the river shore, the austere façade of St. Anne's hove into view, the severe vertical lines of red brick bespeaking rectitude and a stinting forbearance. With the elongated point of its left-hand steeple rising asymmetrically higher than the right, the signal Berlin landmark had always put him in mind of a prim, upright spinster brandishing her umbrella. In the context of the disheveled housing stock rising behind it, the cathedral's haughty grandeur looked out of place. For as the town's fortunes had foundered, the fact that it was located at the confluence of the Dead and Androscoggin rivers had grown more fitting. Berlin may not have been literally a dead end, but it was at the end of the Dead.

Opposite St. Anne's rose Berlin's last standing smokestacks. Rumor had it that Fraser Paper was doomed. (God help his hometown should its survival depend on the proposed park for all-terrain vehicles. Whiny kids on whiny carts that sounded collectively like a swarm of mosquitoes: it wasn't respectable adult salvation.) Sure, the soot-stained brick stacks of his childhood had pumped a hazy white stench into the atmosphere. Pulp workers had high rates of gut cancer and leukemia. In strictly environmental terms, maybe it was healthier for Berlin that most of the mills had closed. Still, he missed them. The poking skyline had been distinctive. During his boyhood, the fact that tourists heading for the White Mountains held their noses as they passed his hometown had been a perverse point of pride. The clattering, cavernous mills to which his classes had made awed pilgrimages in primary school had always been the real cathedrals of Berlin, New Hampshire. Besides, Shep had always appreciated coming from a place that made something tangible that you could hold and fold and write on. He didn't care for towns whose economies were based on ephemeral "services" or elusive ingenuity like software. Shep didn't really belong in this century, and he knew it.

When he'd first moved to New York, Shep had felt self-conscious about hailing from the boondocks, and had taught himself to say "tuna" instead of "tuner," "color" instead of "coluh." He'd practiced pronouncing the *r* in *start*, the *l* in *palm*, and had learned that *caught* was not strictly a homonym of *cot*. After only a few weeks, he was ordering "milkshakes" rather than "frappes," "sodas" rather than "tonics." But the shame had long ago worn off. It was interesting to be from somewhere so particular. Anyone who'd emigrated from a burg of only ten thousand souls was a scarce commodity; lots of people were from New York. He owed this bleak northerly outpost for a hardiness in cold weather. Slogging to school in three feet of snow, the driving sleet needling his cheeks and collecting in his lashes. The feeling in his feet already fading after the first two streets—how's *that* for peripheral neuropathy, Glynis? Keeping his head down, brow to the wind, concentrating only on the next step and then the next . . . Well, the same grit instilled in his boyhood had come to his aid these last six months: how to knuckle down in the face of hardship, refrain from complaint, and hunker into a small, core, preservative self when hostile forces lambasted from the outside.

Even at half-steam, Fraser Paper was still exuding its heady perfume. In the parking lot of Androscoggin Valley Hospital, Shep took a big lungful of acrid air: nostalgia. Faced in flat polished granite, this wasn't the grungy Victorian hospital of the same name in which he'd had his tonsils out at ten. With an atmosphere of suffering, stringency, and boiling sheets, the original Androscoggin Valley had seemed more honest, more like a real hospital. Constructed in the 1970s, the new one had a municipal innocence about it, less like a building where they'd cut off your leg than one where they'd renew your driver's license. Neater, cleaner, and brighter, it also seemed deceiving—like the blazing sunshine of winter mornings in New Hampshire that could look so inviting, until you stepped outdoors and were slapped in the face with a wind chill of thirty below.

By the time he was directed to the room where his father was still sleeping off the anesthesia from surgery that morning, Shep was no longer thinking about Medicare. They'd had their disagreements, but Gabriel Knacker had always been formidable. His resonant powers of oratory had been mismatched with his modest congregation, the minister's intense engagement with issues like world poverty and apartheid in South Africa out of sync with his parishioners' more immediate concerns with keeping their jobs at the mills. As a father, he had wielded his judgment with the same heavy-handedness with which other dads had slapped their kids' behinds, and the sting had lasted longer than any spanking. Shep's greatest dread as a boy was of his father's "disappointment." As a one-time handyman magnate who had demoted himself to functionary in his own company, no doubt he'd become a permanent disappointment. But then, Gabe Knacker wouldn't care if his son owned the company or worked for it. A corporate entity, if not outright wicked, was at best morally neutral, and good men doing nothing in the minister's view was tantamount to wickedness. Arguments about how if the entire population of the Western world joined the Peace Corps we would *all* starve went predictably nowhere, though Shep had won grudging acknowledgment for having at least provided employment for numerous hard-up Hispanic immigrants. Considering that he couldn't remember his father ever expressing sympathy for people of European extraction in his own country, it was a tribute that his white, American congregation had put up with the guy.

The moment must arrive for most grown children sooner or later: a startling apprehension that a parent is old. So abiding is the authoritative imprint from childhood that this realization might commonly descend years after said parent has appeared glaringly geriatric to everyone else. Yet however routine the epiphany, it did not feel routine. Washing his hands at the disinfectant dispenser outside his father's door presaged Shep Knacker's first belated reckoning with the stark, objective reality of paternal decline.

The looming figure of his boyhood took up an incongruously small amount of room on the narrow bed; maybe Shep should have tried to beef up his father's steady diet of grilled cheese sandwiches after all. His father's skin had a watery translucence that it had no doubt achieved years before and Shep had declined to notice; he did not enjoy noting it now. Well into his sixties, the Reverend had boasted a remarkably dark, full head of hair—which had somehow enabled his son to fail to observe that in the last decade the man had, finally, started to bald, and the wisps that remained had, finally, turned white. The hand that clutched the sheet was crinkled, spotted, and slight, and presumably this transformation of the broad, vaulting extremity once raised weekly in benediction had not happened overnight.

Shep and his father had fought plenty—over Shep's "spurning of higher education" and thus "wasting his fine mind," his selling out to Mammon, his tawdry pursuit of an apostasy of an "Afterlife." (Saving up to help the Third World poor would have been one thing; hoarding cash to kick back with pineapple drinks was quite another.) Yet the clash between generations was a battle that no self-respecting son would hope to win. Shep did not want his father to capitulate by dint of mere years on the planet, which converted stealthily from advantage to handicap while your back was turned; victory through youth alone was cheap. He did not want his father to stop being frightening, or intimidating, or infuriating, or insuperable. If he did not want his father to be old, that was only by way of saying that he did not want his father to stop being his father.

Shep kissed the sleeping patient's forehead lightly; against his lips, the thin skin was unnervingly mobile on the skull. He assumed a chair beside the bed. There he kept vigil for perhaps half an hour. He listened to the ragged breath, sometimes resting a hand on his father's atrophied arm. It was a short session of the simple being-ness that he had long coveted for The Afterlife. What Glynis had called "doing nothing," the smelling and seeing and hearing and small noticings of sheer animal presence in the world surely constituted activity of a sort, perhaps the most important kind. He wasn't sure if his father knew he was there, and that was all right. This was a form of companionship that he'd been especially cherishing with Glynis of late: devoid of conversation, but so surprising in its contrast to being by yourself.

Shep pulled in the drive on Mt. Forist Street; little wonder he'd felt like a hick when he first moved to New York, coming from a place that couldn't pronounce the capital of Germany or even spell *forest*. As ever, the sepia-shingled, two-story colonial with a wraparound porch was confusing. It fostered a warm, cozy sensation mixed ambiguously with depression, like a gallon of golden paint contaminated with few drips of greenish umber to become a queasy hue that didn't have a name. Hazily idealized pictures from memory clashed with the more hard-edged perception in the present that the place was growing dilapidated. The chipped cedar shingles could stand replacing. The porch railings were warped. Still, it was a solid building from 1912, with some architectural distinction in the quirky round turret that rose on the right to a third floor. His old bedroom was at the top. While it was impossible to arrange furniture properly in a small round room, that wasn't the sort of thing that bothered a boy. He'd treasured its spiral staircase and tree-house atmosphere, the sound of the brook down the slope trickling through the curved windows. Effortlessly convinced of occupying the center of the universe, as a kid you never seemed to notice that you lived in the back of beyond.

Beryl waved from the porch. The crochet weave of her misshapen chocolate-colored top was loose enough to expose her bra, an uncomfortably eye-catching pink. She no longer quite had the figure for those snug denim cut-offs. Then again, the days in northern New Hampshire when you could get away with shorts numbered a mere handful, and local gals were apt to drag on the hot pants the moment the thermometer edged above sixty degrees. Besides, he was in no condition himself to call the kettle fat.

"Shepardo! I'm so relieved you're here!" She gave him a bear hug. "You have no idea . . . I've felt so alone. God, I just keep reliving that sudden *boom-boom-boom* from the staircase. Didn't sleep a wink. And I can't stop thinking about what would have happened if I hadn't been home."

"Yes, that was lucky." Shep shouldered his bag inside while Beryl prattled about having done "everything she could" and being "frazzled" and "at her wit's end"—with a two-handed clutch of her thick, curly brown hair for effect—and "really needing some relief here." He couldn't imagine what had been required aside from calling for an ambulance and getting their father admitted, but he shouldn't be ungrateful.

Shep started up the stairs to drop his bag. "Oh, you should take my old room," Beryl called. "I'm in yours."

He stopped. "Why's that?"

"You know I always wanted your room. It was the coolest. And I'm living here; you're just visiting, right?"

He repressed an annoyance, one that resonated with an old twinge of resentment that at eighteen Beryl *had* to follow her big brother to New York City, like activating a touch of rheumatism when it rained.

Returned to the first floor, Shep took in the degree to which his sister had occupied their father's house. Her whacky antiques from the apartment on West Nineteenth Street were crammed into every corner, cluttering what had once been an airy expanse of hardwood flooring. Film magazines and photographic equipment piddled every surface like dog pee. Her laptop computer enjoyed pride of place on the dining table, strewn with printouts. A sagging bouquet of Queen Anne's lace in a mayonnaise jar was oblivious to the fact that their father suffered from hay fever.

"You saw Dad?"

"*Saw* is the word." Shep collapsed on the couch. "He was still asleep. But the nurses say he seems to have come out of surgery pretty well."

"I know, I know. I've been calling, like, every half hour."

Shep wondered if his sister called the hospital with the same imaginary frequency with which Amelia may have called her mother. "Hey, do you have anything to drink around here? I'm beat."

"Well, yeah . . . I guess I could find something." Beryl shuffled reluctantly to the kitchen, returning with a depleted bottle of Gallo rotgut. The glass she poured was about three sips' worth, so he got the message. In addition to having stopped by Nancy's next door to make sure Glynis could turn to her in an emergency, making breakfast for his wife who just happened to have cancer, boning up on New Hampshire retirement communities on the Internet in preparation for taking full responsibility for what came next, and driving the length of New England for eight hours in thick vacation traffic, he should have remembered to arrive with a couple of (unlike this one) drinkable bottles of wine, a six-pack of micro-brew, and a family-size bag of Doritos, preferably Beryl's favorite Cool Ranch.

"So where should we go for dinner?" said Beryl. "The Moonbeam Café? Eastern Depot?"

The Moonbeam was back down in Gorham, which he'd just driven through, and the trip back would constrain his booze intake to less than his mood required. The Eastern Depot was the swish place most folks reserved for anniversaries and birthdays, and Shep's natural generosity was under strain. "What's wrong with walking to the Black Bear?"

Beryl wrinkled her nose. "It's all meat. I've gone back to being a vegetarian."

"Since when?"

"Since that lasagna at your house. It made me, you know, totally ill."

What had made her ill was not getting her way. "Thanks."

"Don't take it personally."

"Why don't we eat in? I'll make a run to the state liquor store over on Pleasant Street, but that's all I'm up for."

As for not taking her out to eat, she would make him pay. One way or another, Shep ended up paying for everything.

'm starving," Shep announced, putting the bottles on the counter.

His sister raised an eyebrow at his waistline. "You don't look starved."

"I have to make Glynis the heaviest food possible. I end up eating it, too."

"Oh, I'm so sorry, with all this stuff about Dad, I forgot to ask!" Beryl turned from the stove and creased her forehead, assuming an expression of deep, worried solicitation. "How is she *doing*?"

It was a look that Shep had learned to recognize. The very music of her question—drawn out, searching, dropped in pitch—was identical in timbre to the queries he'd fielded from ancillary characters for months now. Beneath the perfunctory, brow-furrowed performance lurked the hope that the answer not be awkward, that it not ask anything of them, and that most of all it would be short.

"Seems we may beat this thing," he said, forcing himself to remember that he was a believer now, an evangelist, a zealot. "Chemo's working."

"Fantastic!" The cryptic, positive response had let her off the hook, and that was that.

Beryl cooked the way she dressed. Everything she prepared came out lumpy and brown. The concoction on the stove tonight was classic: a mash of soggy cashews, blobs of soy-stained tofu, and bloated pinto beans that were starting to disintegrate.

Abandoned on high heat, the gunk was clearly burning, but Beryl would never detect the singe in the air. Discreetly adding a little water, Shep reflected on the fact that his sister regarded her absence of a sense of smell as not a deficiency but a badge of honor. These days everything had got mysteriously turned around so that not being able to see, hear, learn, or walk made you superior. So he was bewildered by what to do with his sympathy. Wishing that his sister were able to savor the aroma of snapping pine logs was now apparently an insult.

Once they sat down, the serving on his plate looked like a meadow muffin from a cow with digestive problems. The Moonbeam Café served great homemade bread and fruit crumbles; maybe this sandy, sticky mass was what Beryl enjoyed, but he couldn't help but feel he was being taught a lesson. At least the dumpy dinner would not distract them from the main agenda, although the main agenda was no more appetizing.

"You know, about Dad," Beryl began. "I hate to say I told you so—"

"No, you don't. So go ahead. Smugness is one of life's pleasures."

"I just mean, like I was saying in Elmsford, this was bound to happen—"

"Okay, you finished? It did happen. Next."

"You don't have to be so snippy. This is hard for everybody."

"It's mostly hard for Dad."

"Well, of course," she backpedaled.

Stirring the crust from the bottom of the pan had been a mistake. Black flakes turned up on his fork in sheets.

"I'm horrified by the reason, naturally," Beryl continued. "But getting a break from Dad and me in close quarters will be a bit of a relief. He's grown so persnickety! His day is super-ritualized, and everything has to go just so."

Shep nodded at the computer at the end of the table. "He seems to have accommodated your stuff. That's pretty flexible."

"But I make him his grilled cheese, right? Trying to be nice? And it supposedly comes out too dark, and the cheese isn't melted enough. You have to keep the heat at exactly this little point on the dial, and put a pan lid over the sandwich, a particular lid that's exactly the right size for

Branola. And God forbid you should forget the two dill pickle chips, or come back from the store with a brand that isn't cut with ridges. I think of him as so frugal, but he actually threw the sandwich out and made another one!"

"Good for him," said Shep. "How many more grilled cheese sandwiches is a man his age going to eat?"

"Man, the other thing that drives me nuts," she continued, trying valiantly to draw him into filial cahoots, "is the paper. He still snips out all these articles—you know, about forgiveness of Third World debt, anything to do with Abu Ghraib, and obviously when anybody's starving he gets excited. So I get to the paper and it looks like one of those lace snowflakes we used to make in school. I've told him, you know, if he wants an article we can print it from the website, but, no, he has to have the newspaper version. You've seen his office upstairs. It's stacked with all these file folders full of ratty yellow articles. I don't know; it's a little sad. Like, what's he going to do with that stuff, really?"

"Seems like a good thing that he still takes such an interest in the world," Shep said staunchly. "Most folks at eighty wouldn't even read the paper, much less clip it."

Beryl didn't take the hint that he wasn't coming on board. "Do you realize he writes a letter to the editor practically every day? Sometimes to the *Sentinel*, but usually *The New York Times* or *The Washington Post*. They hardly ever see print. It's like, every time something happens the whole world is waiting to find out what Gabriel Knacker thinks. Now, *that* is sad. I picture all these letters editors getting another envelope postmarked Berlin, New Hampshire, rolling their eyes, and tossing it unopened in the trash."

Uneasy being apart from Glynis, Shep didn't plan to stay up here long; a prolonged cringe-fest about their remaining parent could wait for another time. "So what's the prognosis? Do you think he'll be able to come back here?"

"That would mean hiring a nurse or something, since he's likely to be bedridden for weeks. In fact, he could need round-the-clock care for, I don't know, forever."

"True . . ." Shep looked at his sister hard.

"And who knows what kind of person that would be. If she was some officious, bossy shrew, life around here could become unbearable."

"From what I've read, full-time, live-in medical assistance can come to about a hundred grand a year."

"I can't believe that we've only talked about this, like, a minute, and you're already talking about *money*." Her smile tried to cast the goad as a joke, without success.

"Since he's not here to tell us what he wants to do next, the only thing you and I can talk about is money."

"Whatever it costs," Beryl declared, "what matters is what's best for Dad."

"Don't you expect that he'd rather come back home?"

"But I don't think his living here is practical anymore," said Beryl. "It might even be dangerous; he could easily take another fall. Besides, it would just delay the inevitable. This is the perfect juncture to make a decisive move to some sort of facility, where he has doctors, and meals made for him, and the company of people his own age."

"Leaving you in this house. Is that what you picture?"

"*Maybe* I'd stay here a while longer. What's so terrible about that? Somebody's got to hold down the fort."

" 'The fort' is Dad's only asset. It's all he's got to help cover what's likely to cost a hundred K a year, whatever he opts for—whether that's home care, a nursing home, or assisted living."

"Are you saying you'd sell this place out from under me? Where the fuck would I go?"

"Wherever grown-ups go when they don't live with their parents."

"This is ridiculous! What's all that Medicare and Medi-whatsit for, then?"

"I tried to lay this out when my lasagna was making you ill." He shot a pointed look at his plate. "Medicare doesn't cover long-term care, period. You're thinking of Medicaid."

Beryl waved a bored hand. "I can never keep that stuff straight."

"Medicaid's requirements are stringent, and it would take a lot of paperwork just to get him on the rolls. It only covers the destitute. Dad will never qualify while he still owns this house and draws a regular pension. So we either sell off the property, use up the cash, and liquidate his pension fund, or we're"—he paused at the pronoun, but decided it was good for his sister's moral education to keep it—"or we're stuck with the bill."

"What about my inheritance?"

"What inheritance?"

"Half of this house will be mine, and I'm counting on the proceeds for a down payment on my own place!" she wailed. "How else will I ever have a home of my own?"

"I don't own a house, Beryl."

"That's your choice. You could buy whatever you want, and you know it." She crossed her arms, sulking. "Shit, there has to be a documentary in this. Dad working his whole life, and paying taxes, and then when he needs—"

"The depletion of assets for end-of-life care," Shep cut her off, "hasn't gone unobserved."

With evident discipline, Beryl unfolded her arms and placed her hands calmly on either side of her plate. "Look. We could do it this way. You cover Dad's nursing home, or assisted living, whatever. Give me two or three years here, and I can save up some capital. Then once Dad's passed away and we sell the house, your share of the inheritance would cover your outlay."

Shep sat back. He could only regard such audacity as rather magnificent. Nobody could claim that his sister wasn't entertaining. "My share goes to some nursing home. And you keep yours?"

"Sure, why not? And then I'm off your back. No more knocking on your door for cups of sugar. I could move back to New York."

"Leaving aside whether I'd buy your Brooklyn Bridge, just how much do you imagine this house is worth?"

"The property market has skyrocketed all over the country. Everything's, like, tripled in value in, like, ten years. Everybody but *me* has been making money hand over fist. Five bedrooms, three baths . . . This place must be worth a fortune!"

"I repeat: how much, exactly, do you think this house is worth?"

"What . . . five hundred? Seven-fifty? With that big backyard, I don't know, maybe even a million!"

Shep knew his sister loved this house, and to some degree for good reason. The dark interior woodwork was all original and had never been painted over. It was spacious, and it had funk. The place had further appreciated in her head for being where she grew up, and her memories were pleasant; she'd always been the favorite. He hated to burst her balloon, but Realtors were not so sentimental. "I did some nosing around on property websites. Houses this big in Berlin are going for under a hundred grand."

"That's impossible!"

"Fraser Paper is closing, and everybody knows it. Haven't you noticed how many vacant and derelict houses there are in this neighborhood? There's talk of building a big federal prison and an ATV park, but even if they happen you're talking a few hundred jobs tops. After making *Reducing Paperwork*, you of all people should know that everybody's moving out. Property values in this area are *falling*."

"They're not falling anywhere! This house is the best investment Dad ever made!"

"Beryl, think about it. Who wants to live here? Exiled New York documentary makers who lose their rent control. That's about it. And that's the real problem. Even if we put this place on the market tomorrow, it could sit there for months or even years, and meantime Medicaid won't touch Dad's nursing home fees with a barge pole. So don't worry about its being 'sold out from under you.' The worry is it won't be."

"Well . . . we don't know how long he's going to last, right? I mean, I've always heard that for a lot of old people a broken bone is the beginning of the end."

This was ugly stuff. "Yeah, if only he'd die right away, you could get your *inheritance*." He gave the last word a final hiss.

"I don't appreciate that insinuation! I was just saying—"

Shep collected the plates. He stood beside the stack, debating. He almost let the proposition go, but—maybe it was having Dad down for the count at Androscoggin Valley—he was starting to feel less like Ber-yl's brother than her father.

"The longer Dad is able to keep living at home," said Shep, "the better it is for him, and the better it is for us. But live-in help would be expensive and, as you pointed out, intrusive. So I'm curious. There's one possibility we haven't talked about. What if he came back here and *you* took care of him?"

"No way!" she exclaimed. Clearly this option had never entered her head.

"You suggested Amelia's old room in January—though that was be-fore we told you that Glynis was sick. Back then, his living with you in Manhattan was out of the question, since you were about to lose your apartment. But now you're ensconced here, and no one would be dislodged from their home, not you, and not Dad. You could make yourself useful."

"I don't have the qualifications! I'm no *nurse*."

"I'm sure the hospital could provide physical therapy. But the main requirements will be cooking and shopping and keeping the house clean. Changing his linen, doing his laundry, keeping him company. Giving him sponge baths and helping with his bed pan. For all of which you're qualified as anybody."

"Dad would never be comfortable having his daughter wipe his ass. It would be totally embarrassing for both of us."

"People change what they're willing to accept when you change what you're willing to give." Shep smiled. The homily sounded so much like their mother.

"I can't believe you're asking me this! I don't notice *you* volunteering to throw everything aside and take care of somebody else all day!"

"Oh, no? *Throw everything aside* and *take care of somebody else all day*—or all night—is exactly what I do for Glynis. While holding down a full-time job, which I loathe, and only keep to ensure that my wife has some kind of coverage."

Any discomfiture her gaffe occasioned was short-lived. "You're talk-ing about my putting my whole life on hold, possibly for years! Well, you only have a job, but I have a career! It happens to be a career that Dad himself believes in. He'd never want me to sacrifice my filmmaking about important social issues just for his fucking sponge baths! In fact, maybe I *will* do a documentary on end-of-life care. In which case I'd do a whole lot more old people a whole lot more good than I could ever do by hanging around here asking if a single elderly man needs a drink of water!"

"So that's it. No? End of story?"

"Better believe it. Not negotiable, a nonstarter. Absolutely, positively no, out of the question, forget it, period." She seemed frustrated to have run out of negatives.

When he sold Knack of All Trades, Shep had never expected to be treated with greater regard—to be provided preferential seating in restaurants, to have his small opinions accorded any extra weight—merely for having made some money. But damned if he'd expected to be punished for it.

"So that leaves me paying for the alternative—whether full-time home help or some sort of institution. As for your free ride in *my* old bedroom, you're lucky, since I'm not going to put this house on the market so long as Dad thinks there's a hope in hell he might come back home. But I'd like you to understand that covering the costs of his care is not going to be easy for me. I have huge costs associated with Glynis, and I'm no longer the moneybags you think."

"I don't understand," said Beryl with genuine bafflement. "You said you had health insurance."

Shep laughed. It wasn't a very nice laugh, but it beat crying.

Chapter Twelve

Plenty of couples stopped having sex and were probably fine. Big deal, their libidos ebbed. There was still that cozy thing, if you shared the same bed, which he and Carol continued to do, but only because she'd not have wanted to upset the girls with even a fanciful explanation of why Daddy had been exiled to the couch. Exile writ small, the foot-wide moat of cold sheet between them was arguably more painful. She couldn't bear the sight of him. Occasionally she turned toward him in sleep, but only from habit; stirring to find her cheek on his chest, she'd rebound with a harrumph to the far edge of the mattress. She reliably wrenched the bedding along with, leaving Jackson with nothing but boxers for cover. He'd come to detest sleeping in his underwear. The boxers had achieved the same shamefulness as his briefs in boyhood, when he'd been so mortified by the prospect of his mother spotting a brown smudge at the back that rather than toss them in the laundry he buried them in the trash.

Even if plenty of couples did cheerfully give up on sex, he had never expected Carol and Jackson Burdina to count among them. They may have got it on less often once Flicka was born, but ask Bobby Sands: there was a massive difference between a diet and a hunger strike. The loss created a sense of spoliation that spread far beyond sleep. For if he was not in bed, he was dreading when he would be. That floating, limb-tangled languor between snooze alarms used to be his favorite part of the day.

During the whole of his marriage, Jackson had chafed over a subtle inability to possess his wife. She was elusive; she held herself apart. Although Carol's repleteness had always awed him, he didn't covet the same blithe, needless wholeness for himself. However female the image, a little interior absence, that small soft bottomless hole that endlessly cried out for filling, made Jackson a more desirous and therefore a more desirable man. Why, were he suddenly to metamorphose into a kindred creature—a discrete, self-sufficient organism who puttered about his business as she puttered about hers, asking for and expecting nothing, efficiently and tirelessly doing what was required, well—Carol would be goddamned desolate.

For in the past, his frustration with his inability to . . . not own her, exactly . . . to *have* her had supplied Jackson an invigorating sense of purpose, and them both an inexhaustible source of entertainment. She enjoyed keeping herself teasingly just out of reach; he enjoyed playing the hunter who, since he never bagged it, would never run short of prey. But now Carol's tantalizing quality had hardened to flat-out unavailability, and it was no fun going on safari when there wasn't a single would-be quarry in the game park.

Since what had begun as his own whimsical, sexually freshening mischief-making had darkened to disaster, his folly came with inbuilt punishment, and Carol needn't have punished him twice over. Fair enough, he hadn't been *consultative*—which was merely by way of saying that he'd wanted to do something devilish, something unexpectedly impish and naughty and for once nothing to do with the kids, because, by God, the poor woman had little enough pop up in her life that wasn't just another bill or, surprise! a brand-new bacteria to invade Flicka's corneas. And sure, maybe he hadn't adhered to the general rule that in relation to any part of the body that's even halfway functional you leave well enough alone. But otherwise, he didn't see how the catastrophic fallout of this impetuous tomfoolery was his fault. Could he have predicted the infection, and hadn't he taken the full course of antibiotics? Hadn't he done plenty of research beforehand, and after his cousin Larry's rave testimonial how could he have known that the doctor was a hack? Was he to blame that the results of two exorbitant restorative plastic surgeries were disappointing, and his dick still looked like a lumpy, bun-crushed hotdog with a bite out of the middle? He was suffering plenty already, and Carol's coldness was undeservedly cruel. Yet she had never revisited the conviction that he had vandalized not his own person but his wife's. It turned out she really *did* think that his dick belonged to her—personally belonged to her, with the same simplicity and utterness with which she would own a spatula—and it was she who graciously lent it out from time to time, when he needed to piss.

Moreover, she pressed him into an introspection with which Jackson was impatient. It wasn't that he didn't "know himself" or some other claptrap; he just thought navel-gazing was girly and indulgent and pointless. What was done was done, right? So what was the use of an emotional autopsy? No matter how you cut it up, a corpse was a corpse.

Well, his dick was not exactly a corpse. It was worse than that. While deformed and slouching, it was still alive, which made it only more terrible. His dick reminded him of that story they'd read in Mrs. William's eighth-grade English class called "The Monkey's Paw"—the beloved son fatally mangled in an accident who was resurrected by evil magic and mooed, all cut to ribbons, behind the front door. Hell, at least in the story you were spared having to look at the thing with the merciful exercise of the please-God-make-it-go-away third wish. His dick was on its second wish—waving and mooing and wanting in.

A few weeks ago, Jackson had done his ever-loving best to try to explain why he did it, although as usual the elaboration seemed to make no difference, and he was left wondering why he'd bothered. "It was just for a kick," he'd started out. "One of those kooky, jaunty ideas you get, like when you've always given chocolates and this year you want to come up with a more outrageous birthday present that for once your wife will remember. We're surrounded by all these other folks getting piercings, or new noses, or liposuction—who treat their bodies like houses that you redecorate when you feel like it. I'm always fixing people's houses, right? So I was playing, right? One little gesture, for fun. Jesus, otherwise I'm not getting my stomach banded, I'm not getting 'man boob' reduction; I don't even have a tattoo."

"You don't mess around with that part of your body for 'fun,' " she'd insisted. "I don't buy it, Jackson. That the surgery was a ha-ha, a cutesy, off-the-cuff caprice."

"I've said I'm sorry until I'm blue. But I don't see the point in analyzing it to death. It's like I went on an expedition, like up some mountain, and the idea for the expedition was just for an adventure, to fill a Saturday afternoon. Then suddenly the weather goes funny and what was a lighthearted lark suddenly turns life-threatening, with gales about to blow you off the cliff and half your party getting hypothermia. It happens, right? But when the helicopters swoop in for the rescue, the medics don't give you the third degree about the deep, dark motivations behind your sick-fuck decision to go hiking on the weekend."

"You're making me tired, Jackson," said Carol, lids at half-mast. "I don't mind when you keep people at dinner parties at bay with a water cannon of crapola, but I don't expect you to spout nonsense at me."

He clapped his thighs, rose, and paced the bedroom—whose dimensions seemed to grow smaller by the day. He would have to throw her something meatier than the whimsy line. "Look. You want to know the truth?"

"That would be refreshing."

"It's awkward."

"I can't think of anything more awkward than present circumstances."

"I . . ." Nuts, this was definitely, totally awkward. He stuck his head out the door to make sure one of the girls wasn't up, pressed the knob until it clicked, pushed in the lock, and dropped his voice. "I came home once unexpectedly, since it turned out we had a job in the neighborhood. The girls were in school, so you must have felt . . . Well, you obviously figured you had the place to yourself. I came looking for you and you must not have heard me, 'cause you were . . . distracted. Turns out you were in here, and you'd left the door open." He stopped, and hoped she could infer the rest of it and instead she crossed her arms and said, "So?" He would have to spell it out.

"I wasn't spying on you, Carol. I was only going to ask if you wanted to have lunch together. But you were—well, you'd taken all your clothes off and it was the middle of the day, and that was a little weird. You were standing in front of the mirror, and your hands were covered in—I don't know, something greasy and creamy—"

She laughed. "Hair conditioner. Suave, the cheap stuff. It has the perfect texture."

"I'm sorry I violated your privacy, and I don't want you to think I was offended or anything—"

"Why would you be offended?"

"I take that back, actually. I was a little offended."

"I'm not allowed to masturbate? You should have told me that a long time ago."

"That's not what I mean. And *offended* is the wrong word. I was hurt."

"*Hurt*? Jackson, I work incredibly hard, the sales work for IBM is tedious, and sometimes I have to blow off a little steam."

"You're not getting it. The point is, you were high as a kite. You were doing something two-handed down there and obviously getting off on watching yourself, and this—so it was conditioner—well, it was all over the place. And you were gasping and talking dirty to yourself. Shit."

"I obviously made quite an impression. But why on earth didn't you join me?"

"I wasn't a part of it. And you're still not getting it. You were—you were getting off by yourself more than you do with me." He looked down. There. He'd said it.

She reached for his hand with the tenderness for which he was starved. "So you saw me on my own. It's a little different. Maybe it is a little more uninhibited without you there. I wish it weren't, but it's almost impossible to completely shed self-consciousness with another person, even if you love that person, and even if you are, more or less, relaxed with them. I still don't see why this little session you walked in on has anything whatsoever to do with your getting botched penis enlargement surgery."

He always winced when she had to say it plain like that. Since he had his own private rituals whose frequency—that is, previous frequency—he was loath to admit, Jackson was reluctant to get into the fact that for the last couple of years the "session" he'd walked in on had been his touchstone for getting high as a kite himself. Even talking about it now had given him a hard-on. (Or what passed for one. Supposedly he was to be grateful that it roused even to this spongy level of enthusiasm, to which he was alerted mostly because it hurt; the scar tissue from the infection bound the shaft in the middle, like a cock ring stuck halfway up.) Thinking about Carol clutching herself all covered in goo in front of the mirror got him off like nobody's business. But the home video also tormented him. God, you'd never know it to look at this woman, so composed, so . . . Well, other people probably thought of Carol as a little tight. He wasn't about to repeat to her some of the things he'd overheard her say that day—her running commentary of smut would be too embarrassing for both of them, and at once such a turn-on that it would send his dick into agony—but she was a fucking animal! That afternoon, he'd felt so cheated, that he'd lived for years with a wildcat, a wildcat with big bountiful breasts and one hand shoved halfway up her own cunt and her face a contortion of twisted, gory pleasure, and meanwhile for years he'd been having sedate, conventional, well-behaved sex with a domesticated tabby.

"I wanted you to feel that way with me," he said. "I wanted to introduce something that made you get as excited with me as you do by yourself. I didn't realize until I saw you by accident that you were—that you were capable of getting that off your head."

"Haven't I seemed to enjoy myself with you? We've had a lovely sex life. If we hadn't, why would I be so angry now that we don't have one?"

"See? *Enjoy yourself.* A *lovely* sex life. That's the kind of language you use when you go on a picnic. I don't want you to *enjoy yourself.* I want you to go insane."

"Congratulations, then. I am insane. Insanely disappointed and aggrieved. You could have talked about it with me, instead of carving yourself up like a rib roast. For pity's sake, if all you wanted was a little more kink, I'd have caught the two-for-one sale on conditioner at CVS."

In her humor he sensed a softening, and he sat beside her on the bed.

She'd started wearing a nightgown despite the close, thick summer air, but the door was already locked and nightgowns come off. He put a hand on her thigh. She looked at the hand, then in his eyes; her expression was skeptical but not, for once, hostile. It was a little early after the second plastic surgery—the scars were still red and sensitive—but like a job seeker during an economic downturn he would have to apply for the few openings that came along. When he kissed her she was passive, though she did not recoil. Yeah, as he got into the idea the Monkey's-Paw mangle mooed again, but nothing could be more painful than this months-long freeze-out.

As Jackson slid his hand up under the nightgown, they were miles from some breakthrough erotic melee with Suave. He was super gentle and super careful, implicitly asking permission with every caress, as if she were still a virgin and had to be broken in nice and slow, rather than his wife and the mother of his children. Still he did finally coax the boring white cotton sack over her head—heaven forbid she'd wear a negligee—and slipped his hands onto those twin scoops of vanilla ice cream. Carol didn't participate much, but she didn't stop him. There was only one stage to go, tearing off the damned boxers, an unveiling that now filled him with dread; he should have switched off the light on Carol's side of the bed when he'd had the chance. As he hastily dragged them off the elastic smarted; he could see her hating to look and yet having to look and so looking and then looking away. His erection was about as good as it got, meaning not very, and though this was hardly the time to entertain such thoughts he had to concede that if anything after all that snipping and pulling and chopping and patching the mutilated nubbin—which looked like some half-chewed chicken neck that had got stuck in a garbage disposal—was now even smaller than it had been to begin with.

When he eased on top of her, Carol's distorted, twitching face bore superficial resemblance to the expression she'd worn when he caught her slathering her pussy with Suave, but was probably closer to the wobbly grimace of a patient about to submit to a colonoscopy. Since Carol obviously wasn't going to help, he rose up on one hand and with the other tried to position his disabled ward for entry, wondering if you could organize wheelchair access to a vagina. Pushing at her, he cringed as his dick buckled. He tried one more time by keeping his middle finger underneath the shaft like a makeshift splint, but with one, he had to admit, graceful maneuver Carol was out from under him and standing beside the bed. "I can't." Shaking despite the muggy July, she reached for the nightgown scrunched behind her pillow. "I'm sorry. I tried, but even if you could get it in, Jackson, I can't do it. It's too repulsive."

Carol was not a theatrical person, and he didn't really believe that she rushed to the toilet to throw up. But she did flee to the bathroom and close the door, and she was gone for a long time.

Yes, Mr. Pogatchnik, it's just that—"
"You hear me? Not on my time. I've cut you plenty slack because of your wife, Knacker. But I'm not running a hospice here. A business is a business."

Jackson peeked around his partition. Spattered in freckles, Pogatchnik had short legs, a short neck, and short, Vienna-sausage fingers. In that red-and-white striped shirt, big-butt Bermudas, and a backward baseball cap that from this angle looked like a beanie, he needed only a large lollypop to complete the picture of an overgrown toddler. He was the only one in the office with enough natural padding to stay warm in summer togs; by contrast, in mid-August Shep was wearing a down vest, and he'd learned to type in gloves. Pogatchnik clearly took the Alpine gear as admonition, and since June the cycle had only accelerated: Shep arrived in a woolly scarf; Pogatchnik cranked the AC down two more degrees; Shep arrived in ear muffs.

"I'm afraid the phone lines at the World Wellness Group are only open during business hours," Shep was explaining in a calm, inhumanly even tone that sounded like Carol. "While I'm on hold, I do keep fielding calls for Randy Handy—"

"What did you just call my company?"

"I mean, Handy Randy, of course. That was just, you know, a slip of the tongue."

"You're on thin ice, Knacker. Under the circumstances, you figure it's smart to confuse the name of your only employer with jerking off?"

"No, Mr. Pogatchnik. I don't know why that came out of my mouth. You must be making me nervous, sir. On account of your—displeasure."

Fucking hell. It was like listening in on a pipsqueak draftee during basic training, quailing in front of his sergeant back in the days before the volunteer army began coddling the troops with Oreos. It made Jackson mad, and maybe it wasn't fair, but mad at Shep. The groveling in the next cubicle made him feel personally betrayed. What do you want to bet that "Randy Handy" slip really was a mistake, and not the sly, purposive subversion that it should have been? A recently installed office rule, the "Mr. Pogatchnik" routine was at least not Shep's ass-lick innovation. In an era when everyone from restaurant patrons to prime ministers went by first names, the absurd formality had gratifyingly warped to the tongue-in-cheek; though the fat red-haired toad was too stupid to notice, all over the office "Mr. Pogatchnik" rang with overt sarcasm.

"Personal calls are personal calls," said Pogatchnik. "Which you make at lunch, on your own cell."

While organizing work crews throughout the rest of the morning, Jackson chewed on a mystery that he'd never got his head around. The rest of the staff had always liked Jackson, or at least they put up with him—and tolerance, in such close-quartered, shoulder-to-shoulder work, believe it or not was something. But they'd always *respected* Knacker, even if back when Shep called the shots they hadn't always liked him. He'd run a tight ship. Caught you taking a slug from an open white wine bottle in a customer's fridge, and you were out on your ear. His lofty business principles may have been subject to mockery behind his back, but his workforce was still proud that stand-up practices brought in a host of repeat customers. When a licensed plumber had left behind a gaping hole in a living room ceiling, Shep would opt for a meticulously cut Sheetrock patch, which was cheaper for the customer, even though replacing the whole panel would've taken half the time and made Knack twice the money. He'd put in estimates on the low side when he sensed a homeowner was hard up. He'd stood by his price quotes, too, even when a job turned out more fiddly than they expected. It was their fault, claimed Shep, that a job took three times longer than it was supposed to; they should have seen the problems coming.

Of course, Jackson himself rarely ran over the allotted time, since he was fast—*slapdash*, Shep sometimes called it, and the word had stung. Jackson was fast but he was good, or good enough—and good enough was good enough. Polished workmanship was wasted on these outer-borough hovels. Most of the dumps they repaired were originally working-class housing stock, built for laundry workers or for that matter for tradesmen like themselves. Unless the place had been gutted and renovated from the ground up, the kind of la-di-da jobs that Shep had specialized in just made the rest of the house look worse. You know, he'd install a new closet door and frame, and it'd be the only door in the place that was parallel to the floor. The effect was to make the rest of the joint look like a funhouse, all out of kilter—as if he'd smeared "Clean me!" on the side of a dusty van.

Back in the Knack days, Jackson had enjoyed an elevated status for having the ear of the boss, almost like being an unofficial VP. But when Shep sold up, and Jackson's managerial job description did become official? His co-workers' deference flew right out the window. By contrast—this was the mystery, and Jackson had to admit that it griped him a bit—despite all the razzing about that "escape fantasy" and despite all the public groveling before "Mr. Pogatchnik" and despite having become an overnight nobody like a fairy-tale prince who'd turned himself into a frog, Shep still commanded a regard that never sank below a surprisingly high baseline level. Christ, the guy couldn't have humiliated himself more completely. Still, whenever a really sticky job came in—like the one this morning where knocking a hole for a pass-through window between the kitchen and the dining room entailed busting through a solid foot of concrete—to whom did the guys turn for advice? Helpful hint: it wasn't Burdina.

When lunch came around at last, Jackson forced himself to sidle up to Shep's station. He'd begged off lunch to do "errands" so many afternoons that his avoidance of his best friend was becoming too obvious.

The trouble was, he was now committed to omitting from his conversation everything he was going through with Carol; just as in boxing, none of his topics could target below the waist. While he could always resort to Mugs and Mooches, a tirade wasn't as satisfying when its purpose was purely diversionary. "You have to make some call, or can you grab a bite?"

"Forty minutes isn't enough time to get through to a human being at that switchboard," said Shep. "The thing is, I got sent a bill they totally refused. It's for fifty-eight K and change, too. The secretary at Goldman's office said it may have been some number entered wrong. One digit off, anywhere on the form, and they refuse to pay the whole thing."

"You realize what a fair whack of their 'administration costs' are, don't you?" said Jackson. "According to Carol, these companies hire scads of people whose whole job it is to find ways *not* to pay the medical expenses of people they're supposedly insuring. She says these fucks are so good at it that on average they manage to weasel out of thirty percent of the bills they get sent."

"Yeah, well, whenever they 'weasel out of it,' or some middleman transposes a number, the full bill goes straight to yours truly. I've got forty-five days to appeal this thing, and it's already been a month. After the forty-five days are up, I'm stuck with it. And this is just one glitch. These minions at Wellness query everything. Goldman says they even tell him which drugs he can prescribe. He wanted Glynis to use Dermovate along with a course of cetirizine for her skin rashes, but no—Wellness nixed them both. They said use *calamine lotion*. Which is a joke. No explanation, as usual. I guess they're not obliged to provide one. But these people aren't doctors. I don't understand how business graduates of two-year junior colleges are making decisions about what to prescribe my wife."

"Health insurance is health insurance," boomed from behind them. "You got any coverage whatsoever, and you're *complaining*?" It was *Mr.* Pogatchnik, who regarded eavesdropping as a privilege of high office. "That contract costs me a fortune, Knacker."

"Yes, I realize it's a major line item. In my day—"

"It's not your day. Haven't we got that straight yet? *It's not your day.* Repeat after me?"

"It's not my day."

"So don't imagine you have any idea. When you ran this joint, you were covering a fraction of the workforce I run now. I may have replaced that Cadillac plan you had for Knack with a serviceable little Ford Fiesta. Still, in just eight years, per head? The small-business employer premium has *doubled*."

"Hey, it costs what it costs, right?" said Shep, and Jackson was relieved to detect, for once, a seditious glitter in his friend's expression.

"What it costs is too damn much," said Pogatchnik, who would no more be aware of his reputation for the flabby, faux-profound tautology than he would understand the word itself. "I just renewed, too, and *your wife* was cited as one of the justifications for jacking the price. I sure hope you're sweet on the lady, 'cause she's costing me a mint."

"I am very fond of my wife, thank you."

"Anyway, all the new hires are on contract, no benefits. So count yourself lucky."

"I do count myself lucky," said Shep numbly. "But the new guys. If they get sick, or their kid does. What do they do?"

"Emergency room, or suck it up. Point is, it's not my problem. The way it oughta be, in my book. They want some fancy insurance package, they can buy it themselves."

"Private plans . . ." said Shep. "You don't pay them enough . . ."

"I pay them what I pay them. Pretty decent wages, too, since otherwise most of these wets would be packing pork or picking grapefruit."

"But this medical stuff can be—life and death," Shep submitted with a nauseating tentativeness. "Offering no benefits seems—a little harsh."

"I am what I am, right? I'm not handing out ice cream. I'm a businessman. If I don't turn a profit you're *all* out on the street. Besides, am I responsible for buying my employees groceries? Am I supposed to find them apartments? Aren't food and shelter matters of 'life and death,' too?"

"Fair enough," Shep conceded.

"Next thing you know I'm supposed to spring for their flat-screen TVs and premium cable fees. Which, by the way, would be a hell of a lot cheaper than fucking health insurance, even if I threw in a new dinette set and a book of all-you-can-eat coupons for Pizza Hut."

"Yeah, I been meaning to ask," said Jackson, "I wanted to swap my sausage for pepperoni."

"I hire people," Pogatchnik bullied on, not the least interested in banter that put his ingrate employees and management on the same side. "I don't adopt them. Least of all do I adopt their whole goddamned families. You two—for now—I'm stuck with. But I'm telling you, this shit, this big communist cradle-to-grave employment shit, is *over*. It doesn't make any earthly sense that just because I take on an employee to clear other people's hairy drains, suddenly I'm supposed to pay for his ingrown toenails. The insulin for his diabetes because he eats too many Krispy Kreme Bavarian custards. His hernia operation after he bangs his squeeze on the side with too much gusto. His ten-year-old's ADD medication, if only because nobody admits to having a kid any-more who's thick as pig shit. The five months his blind, harelipped, one-legged premature baby with the mind of an eggplant spends in intensive care, when it should have been thrown out with the bathwater. Not to mention the billions of dollars his wife's terminal cancer costs before she kicks the bucket anyway, since nobody in this country can die anymore without dragging the entire economy down with them."

Pogatchnik's pause baited Shep to take offense, but ever since "So long, asshole!" his self-demoted employee had been a paragon of restraint.

"Unless I quit being held ransom for health insurance, for this whole crowd?" Pogatchnik carried on. "Handy Randy would go under. Realize that's one of the main reasons American companies are moving over-seas, don't you? Health insurance. Hell, I'd move this outfit to China, too, if only my Mexicans could commute to Queens from Beijing. You guys came to me today, you could have a job. That's all. A job is a job. As for cancer, you'd die on your own dime. So you chumps don't like the World Wellness Group, you know where the door is. I'd replace you with a couple of Guatemalans at a fraction of the salary who'd be grateful for the paycheck, who wouldn't give me any lip, who wouldn't *misspeak* the name of the company kind enough to employ their sorry asses, and who wouldn't have an *attitude problem* because one of them is delusional and still thinks he's the boss."

"Just used up fifteen minutes of our lunch break," Jackson muttered once they'd escaped to Seventh Avenue. "Not enough time for the line at Brooklyn Bread. Guess we'll just walk. Bastard."

"He is who he is, right?" said Shep, and they launched toward Prospect Park.

I hate to admit it," Jackson said on Ninth Street, "but Pogatchnik has a point. I don't know what those new-hire sons of bitches are supposed to do when they get run over by a delivery truck. Still, plenty of those guys have big families. How's a little operation like Randy Handy going to cover all their medical expenses? I'm not sure why it should have to."

"Somebody's gotta pay for it."

They'd been so anxious to get away from Pogatchnik that Shep had forgotten to leave behind his down vest, which he now stuffed in his backpack. The sweltering sun had been a relief after the ice cave of the office, but only for a minute or two. Shep rolled up his sleeves; even after forgoing their joint weight-training sessions for months, he still had powerful arms. As for the poor fuck's steady weight gain since January, Jackson battled between an unattractive satisfaction and dismay.

"But the employer thing, it's just a historical fluke," Jackson said authoritatively; what the heck, he could probably fill out this entire walk with factual information. That was what real men traded with each other anyway. Properly edified, Shep would never be able to object that he'd been filibustered. "Until about the 1920s, there was no such thing as health insurance. You got a medical bill, you paid it. Even then, private plans were few and far between, really just meant to cover catastrophe. The employer-sponsored thing developed during World War Two, when labor was scarce. Big companies were making bids for the handful of guys left who weren't in the army, but they were hog-tied by government wage controls, so they couldn't offer higher salaries. To get around the laws, they added health cover as a come-hither. It was a little perk. Didn't cost much, since everybody in those days keeled over fast and young. You couldn't spend that much on people's medical care, because nobody had invented chemo, or heart transplants, or the MRI. Pogatchnik thinks he's being funny, but throwing in health benefits back then really wasn't so different from tossing the flunkies a coupon for pizza."

"Yeah, well now the pie comes with mushrooms, and anchovies, and extra cheese."

"The problem's not the pizza, it's the insurance companies, man! They're fucking evil, man! They're parasites, parasites on other people's suffering!"

"They're not *evil*, Jacks, they're just companies. Jesus, you sound like my father."

"Do they produce anything? Do they improve anything? Do they do anything for anybody, besides their own employees and shareholders? Even McDonalds makes hamburgers. Those cunts at Wellness, they just shuffle paper. All they accomplish is a little redistribution of wealth, mostly to themselves. They're Mooches pure and simple."

"They're private enterprises. They're supposed to turn a profit."

"That's the whole point, dickhead! That is the whole fucking point!"

They'd hit the park; maybe Jackson had grown a mite vociferous, since a lady nearby side-eyed him with recognizable urban alarm, shimmying her stroller rapidly in the opposite direction.

Jackson made an effort to moderate his tone to a level that didn't threaten the safety of small children. "You remember what you told me about gambling? How if most people didn't, on average, lose, there wouldn't be a gambling industry in the first place? For there to be money in it, the big picture has to be fixed."

"Yeah, sure," said Shep. "But you're not, still—?"

"Give me a break, I've sworn off the dogs completely," Jackson said hurriedly. So long as he was keeping his trap shut about everything else in his life, he might as well make it a clean sweep and lie about the works. "I just mean, health insurance works the same way, right? Any insurance. For these companies to run in the black, the majority of their customers have to lose. On average, you have to pay in more over your lifetime than you draw, or these companies wouldn't exist in the first place."

"Well, I guess the hard cases are subsidized by guys who live on rice milk and pay high premiums for forty years, and then drop dead in the street. You know, guys like that." Shep nodded toward an ostentatiously lean, shirtless runner showing off his gray-haired pecs and carrying a dumbbell in each hand. You didn't stay that taut and skinny past fifty without being a pain in the ass, and at a glance Jackson pitied the man's family. Puffing to overtake a female jogger up ahead in the midday heat, this geezer didn't simply run; he was "a runner." It was obvious that the pill's miserable circuit around Prospect Park was the most important thing in his life. Fucking pathetic.

"On the other hand," Shep went on, "Flicka, Glynis—they've both cost scads more than either of our families have paid in. We're the Mooches here. We've lucked out."

"Here we go, yet another improbably upbeat take on a national disaster. You seriously feeling *lucky*?"

"Good fortune is relative."

Jackson got a little tired of Shep's ceaseless *reasonableness*, his prissy, Sunday school sense of perspective. "My point stands. The very fact that these companies have to turn a profit means most people pay in more than they get out, period. So health insurance is, ipso facto, a scam."

"Ipso facto!" Shep chuckled. "Sounds like a fifties detergent slogan. 'Use Whiz, and, ipso facto! Stains vanish!' I don't know where you pick this stuff up."

"I read a lot. You should try it."

"Yeah, right. After I work all day, hit the A-and-P, make dinner, fetch Glynis her meds, and water, and skin cream . . . Give her a shot in the ass of Neupogen after drugging her out with lorazepam to keep her from getting hysterical about the needle . . . Keep her company because she can't sleep, do the laundry at two in the morning and pay the bills at three . . . Then I can put my feet up with a big, thick, educational tome before the alarm rings at five."

"What's the diff? Flicka, pal, is a full-time job by herself, and I fit in plenty of books."

"You've got Carol."

It was the very subject of recent reflection that indeed Jackson did not "have" Carol, now less than ever. "Yeah, well, this isn't a contest."

"A contest over which of us feels more sorry for themselves? Now, that could be vicious."

"I never said I felt sorry for myself," said Jackson.

"Well, I do."

"Why would you feel sorry for me?" Jackson snapped.

Shep shot his friend a look. "I meant I feel sorry for myself, dick-head. Feeling sorry for you, too, would be a tall order."

"Well, skip it then."

They strode on in stiff silence.

Jackson had noticed that whenever he bought a new pair of shoes, he went through a period thereafter when he couldn't stop looking at other people's shoes—wondering why they might have chosen that particular pair, appraising them as handsome or hideous. The same phenom now pertained to other men's dicks. With every jogger and dog walker they passed, he found himself compulsively checking out the mound under the fly, bitterly eying the well-endowed. Cyclists in their tight Lycra attracted his gaze to the groin, where they surely packed smooth, straight, functional equipment that they foolishly took for granted. Now a whole park full of jocks probably thought he was a fag.

"Glynis went in for another blood transfusion yesterday," Shep said after a bit, making a stab at convivial conversation. "Her white blood cell count was knee-high. They had to cancel her chemo. She's not strong enough."

"At least she gets a break," Jackson grunted.

"Yeah, but the cancer gets a break, too. Goldman's decided she can't tolerate the Alimta and cisplatin anymore, and when she does go back to chemo they'll change the cocktail. How do you like that word, huh? *Cocktail.*" Jackson had to hand it to him, Shep was really trying—either to pretend everything was fine between them, or to make it fine.

Jackson made a grudging effort in return. "Yeah, I picture this gorgeous Tiffany martini glass, gleaming with sweat and toothpicked with a stuffed olive—only what's shimmering inside isn't Bombay gin and a splash of vermouth, but strychnine."

Yet Jackson had no sooner congratulated himself for being so *supportive* than it grew hard to pay attention, because he was tortured by a memory from about ten years before. He'd been replacing the rickety risers of some schmuck's staircase, and though a one-man job it stretched over three or four days; by happenstance, the landing was right outside this loser's study. Jackson had always prided himself on being a lively presence in other people's homes, not just your average tight-lipped hired brawn. So long as a customer seemed obviously glad to lend an ear, he kept up a running patter—sometimes about the job itself, but more often about your basic issues of the day. Sort of like whistling while you work, but less annoying. Given Jackson's status as a well-rounded autodidact—like, he had taught himself the meaning of *autodidact*—edifying narration gave these homeowners a chance to learn something. The soundtrack provided free stimulation, free information, and they should have been grateful that he didn't charge extra for it.

But when Jackson was heading out on the third day of the riser job, Shep had pulled him aside and said, "This guy in Clinton, he wants you to, well . . . He wants you to shut up." Apparently the riser guy was some kind of fiction writer—and Jackson had the measure of the twit, so he was unquestionably some posturing amateur—and couldn't "concentrate" with all the commentary from the staircase. The customer was completely full of shit, since he'd eaten up everything Jackson had said, and was doubtless already planning to use this improbably intelligent, verbally agile, larger-than-life "character" from the world of home repair in one of his otherwise dull, unpublishable short stories.

Yeah, Jackson had dispatched the rest of the job keeping his mouth shut—or when he remembered to keep his mouth shut—but he'd have appreciated a little more solidarity from Shep. Instead, when Jackson had objected that you know what these pompous *writer* types are like: horrified by the blank screen and just dying for any distraction, any excuse to escape the impoverished confines of their pygmy imaginations, and "I'm telling you that customer was rapt, like he was practically taking notes," Shep didn't agree, *Yeah, I bet he was, too*, but interrupted and said, "Look, keep a lid on it, right? Just this once? We got work to do, they got work to do. You're not a talk show host, you're a handyman." That was really putting the boot in, since Shep knew full well that Jackson detested the word *handyman*, which he'd lobbied hard to replace on their business cards with something more dignified, something less low rent—you know, like *domestic construction consultant*. But no, the cards had to say *handyman*, because that's the word that customers "understood." Worse, Shep had pretty much implied that Jackson's running commentary got on everyone's nerves, and that this was merely the first guy to lodge a formal complaint. Well, Jackson had been supportive as all get-out through the sale of Knack and the deep-sixing of Pemba and now with Glynis, and frankly that support hadn't always worked the other direction.

"These blood transfusions take, like, *five hours*," Shep was explaining. "And Glynis still gets faint when they put in the cannula. Still, this neighbor of ours, Nancy, has been incredible. Comes with Glynis whenever I can't go. Holds her hand and distracts her with recipes and shit—so Glynis comes home yesterday able to recite every ingredient in a complicated cottage-cheese-and-pineapple dip that sounds disgusting. The idea is to keep her from watching the needle. That's not a small job, either. Lately they're having a hard time finding a vein, and have to jab her several times. Nancy's unbelievably boring, but nice. I'm starting to not care about boring. All I care about is nice."

Jackson wasn't sure if this compliment to some broad he'd never met was meant as a veiled reproof. Faithful at first, he hadn't gone to see Glynis for several weeks. Entertaining customers was one thing; keeping up the packaged rant with a friend going through hell had admittedly grown artificial. But he didn't know what to talk to her about otherwise, and he had his own problems.

"Meanwhile, they've moved my father out of Androscoggin Valley," Shep continued, "and into a private nursing home nearby. It's meant to be only temporary, while he recuperates. But he doesn't believe it. He's convinced he's been dumped there for the rest of his life, like a sack of old clothes tossed in a Goodwill drop-off. So he gives Beryl a lot of grief. My sister's solution is just not to visit him."

"Neat," said Jackson, with a guilty recognition that he'd arrived at the same solution to the Glynis problem.

"That means I'll have to keep taking trips to New Hampshire. Which is tricky, since I can't leave Glynis alone for long. I can't take any more vacation or personal days than I absolutely have to. Still, I don't want him to feel abandoned. Oh, and the Medicare people have cut him off, since they've now covered his 'crisis care.' So this Twilight Glens place is all on my dime. Eight grand a month, believe it or not, and a three-month deposit up front. With every aspirin extra."

Ordinarily Jackson would have sympathized, even though after selling Knack Shep had more in the bank than he himself would ever see in one place. But none of his ostensibly *restorative* operations had been covered by either World Wellness or IBM's outfit, since technically they constituted elective plastic surgery. So he'd been forced to charge all his medical bills to credit cards, at 22 percent interest; he was still paying off the original surgery as well, and those were just the debts that Carol knew about. Barely managing the minimums, he wasn't the usual soft touch for Shep's batty benevolence.

"As ever," Shep was droning on, "I've got to pay Zach's tuition, and keep topping up Amelia's rent—"

"*Why* are you such a pushover?" Jackson exploded. "With your dad, just *don't* go up to Berlin, right? You can't. Your wife has cancer. Period. And when the next bill from that nursing home arrives, *just don't pay it*. Fuck, you have the power! What do you think will happen, they'll toss him on the street? It's bad, but it's not that bad. You've told me he's got that house, which disqualifies him from Medicaid. Well, fine, when you don't pay the bill, this private shit hole will just transfer him to a public shit hole, right? I bet there's not much difference, when you're pissed off anyway and flat on your back. Then Medicaid will step in, and maybe they'll commandeer the house. Let 'em have it! Let 'em kick your self-centered, asshole sister out on her butt. Just walk away, bro! And while you're at it, pull Zach out of that overpriced sports club and resign yourself that he's an average fuck-off student who might as well be average and fucking off in a public school that you already pay for! Tell Amelia she's a grown-up now, and if her salary doesn't cover her rent and her own goddamned health insurance then she gets another job that does, whether or not it fulfills her tender creative urges! Why are you the only one who has to be responsible? Why can't you throw people on their own devices the way you've always been thrown on yours? Why can't you start to treat other people the way, for years, they've been treating *you*?"

"I am who I am." Shep's delivery was so robotic that it was impossible to tell if he was joking.

They about-faced, and marched back in silence. Jackson didn't know if he was supposed to apologize, but he was disinclined to. He realized that he was being irrational, but it kept sneaking back all the same: this conviction that the "whimsical" notion that had vaporized his sex life and still made it hard to take a leak was in some measure Shep Knacker's fault. Hey, that explanation he'd delivered Carol was genuine enough. He had almost walked in on her, and he had found the exhibition simultaneously exciting and disturbing. But there was a little more to it than that, not that he would ever let on to Carol, because, to add insult to injury, the additional explanation was clichéd. If she knew, she'd have contempt for him—that is, even more contempt for him, assuming that was possible. The whole nightmare would never have gone down in the first place if it hadn't been for Shep.

Moreover, despite the guy's earlier assertion that the scale of their respective travails "wasn't a contest," Jackson wondered if, all kidding aside, there wasn't a subtle element of competition in Shep's catalogue of woes after all. Shep always had to cast himself as the hero, the stoic who could bear up under all manner of impositions, the Atlas on whose shoulders the fates of nations rested. Jackson tired of his friend's infeasible virtue—the empathy, the bending over backward to see the other side, that numb-sucker-taking-it thing—and maybe he'd let fly just now to show this patsy how it was done: See? You don't sigh and take out the checkbook again; you get mad.

Besides, Flicka was more of a handful than Shep had any idea, and now Jackson was supposed to bow down and defer to Shep's terrible situation with Glynis's terrible illness. Well, Shep wasn't the only one dealing with the fact that someone he loved was probably going to die. In fact, Jackson sometimes wanted to grab and shake the guy. *Now* do you understand what's it's been like for me, ever since Flicka was diagnosed in her crib because she couldn't, of all things, cry? Never knowing when the one person you count on to make life seem worth living will suddenly make a rude, unannounced exit and then it turns out, gosh, you were right—actually, now life really isn't worth living? Shep did realize, didn't he, that even though Flicka now set an alarm to pour in her own cans of Compleat, her father still got up at his old shift of 4:00 a.m. most nights, pretending to get a glass of water, but really just to glide by Flicka's room and make sure she was still alive? Because that's how most of these kids disappeared on you: just went to sleep and never woke up. Nuts, according to that last CAT scan, Glynis seemed to have a hope in hell. But no test result was ever going to come in for Flicka that would suddenly open up a future with a career and a family of her own. Busy playing the supportive friend this afternoon, Jackson had yet to mention that Flick had been readmitted to New York Methodist the day before. The chest infections were recurring with greater frequency, and they were getting worse. The antibiotics were growing less effective, and a host of predatory microscopic crud was thriving out there that was immune to the drugs altogether. Simple family hangs like the one this spring, when he gave his kids that eighth-grade test from 1895, well, he couldn't remember having engaged in the same rambunctious after-dinner teasing since. Carol had to piss all over it, but they'd been having a good time.

There was even something showily turn-the-other-cheek about Shep's bringing up graciously as they neared Handy Randy, "I wondered if you'd found a hole in your schedule yet," after having been berated as a moron and a sap.

"Yeah, right," said Jackson. "That celebration, about Glynis's CAT scan. Sure thing, I'll check my diary soon as we get back."

In having repeatedly shied from the invitation, Jackson had no idea whether he was envious of their good news about the upbeat CAT scan, or if he just didn't trust it.

Chapter Thirteen

Shepherd Armstrong Knacker
Merrill Lynch Account Number 934-23F917
August 01, 2005 – August 31, 2005
Net Portfolio Value: $274,530.68

Shep had bustled down his to-do list all day. Lay in groceries. Buy charcoal. Cut up raw vegetables—which no one ever ended up eating. Whip up dip—to which he had, despite his own revulsion, added Nancy's canned pineapple because he couldn't think of anything else. Wrap potatoes in tin foil. Set table—with a sense of dismay that the menu could not plausibly sponsor Glynis's fish slice.

But their guests were late. Every item on the list was crossed off. Shep had nothing to do. Lending his wife's skepticism about his idyllically idle Afterlife some credence, the absence of an agenda was the one thing these days that Shep couldn't bear. In some comically microcosmic manner, this chasm of post-dinner-prep inactivity foreshadowed a more frightening abyss. As of yesterday afternoon, Shep had resumed residence on a world that was flat. He would soldier across the map only to plummet vertiginously off its hard edge. Thus, big picture, the evening's pattern of frenzy to freefall would repeat itself. Shep would feverishly meet every need—fill every prescription, arrange transport and company for every appointment, fetch liquids, plump pillows, and elevate feet. Then suddenly, there would be nothing—there would be nothing—there would be nothing to do.

He double-checked that Glynis was situated comfortably on the screened-in back porch. Too comfortably; she was slumped and asleep. Dressing for the evening had worn her out. He shouldn't be forcing her to socialize. The timing was terrible. But it had taken two and a half months to get their best friends to dinner. He wasn't about to withdraw the invitation and go through the same diary-shuffling folderol with Jackson again. He stirred the coals on the barbecue. He'd started the fire too early, and it would be too hot for the steaks. They'd been eighteen dollars a pound. It didn't matter. But if overcooking them didn't matter, then he shouldn't have sprung for New York strips in the first place. He was beginning to lose a grip on why they were having those two for dinner. He was losing a grip on why anyone had anyone to dinner. Why anyone talked to anyone. Or maybe he was mostly uncertain about why he himself would talk to Jackson.

Finally Shep grabbed the hose and went around the backyard topping up his whacky fountains: the festive, kinetic one with the pinwheels, paddles, and overflowing plastic Snoopy lunchbox that hadn't especially delighted Zach for his birthday even when the kid was nine; the more industrial structure with a handyman theme that sluiced the water around shovel blades, trowels, and spare lengths of drainage pipe. The fountains' sheer gratuitousness used to cheer him, but lately the contraptions seemed silly, and he'd taken to disparaging the lot, with sour sarcasm, as "water features." In a life ruled by grim necessity, gratuitousness itself was one more thing that he could live without.

Nearly an hour after the agreed time, Jackson hustled in from their car with an armload of booze—not only wine and beer, but all the makings for margaritas, as if the game plan for the evening were for everyone to get plastered. Maybe Shep should have phoned to forewarn them that the nature of the occasion had changed.

"You know, it slays me," Jackson started up right away, and that was assuming he'd ever stopped, "at all these major intersections in Brooklyn? They put traffic cops in the middle, and all they do—*all they do*—is wave through cars perfectly in sync with the traffic lights. Like, they are just human traffic lights. Do we really need some self-important fuck to point left when the Left Turn Only signal turns green? Do we need to *pay* this asshole to stand there like an urban scarecrow, when the lights are working for once, and easier to see? You know the only time you *don't* see some officious *public servant* out there is when the signal fails. The lights go black and it's pandemonium? Not a cop in sight."

It was going to be a long night.

"Oh, and guess what's the latest on the Net," he continued, slicing limes.

There was no purpose to interrupting. Jackson was like the topped-up fountains in the backyard, which would burble through the evening and tirelessly recycle the same few gallons of bilge.

"Know how, like, downtown," Jackson carried on, "around City Hall, it's totally impossible to find a place to park? Turns out there's a reason, and it's not just that it's New York and you got to share. It's the Mooches in government. The city's issued *142,000* permits that say the rules don't apply to them. These parasitic pricks put this little card on the dashboard, and bingo, they can park their butts in Authorized Vehicles Only zones and even where it says outright No Parking. In Lower Manhattan, they got over 11,000 spaces to choose from for free. Know how many parking spots the sad-ass general public's got to choose from down there? Six hundred and sixty-five. That's not democracy, friend. That's tyranny. We pay for the paving, the curbing, the pothole repair, the very signs that tell us to fuck off, and they park wherever they want, for no money, and for as long as they damn well please."

Shep knew better than to ever try parking in Lower Manhattan, and he didn't care. He shared a glance with Carol, who looked embarrassed. "That's just Jackson's ham-handed way of apologizing for being late," she said. "He insisted on stopping at Astor Liquors on Lafayette, where the tequila would be cheaper, and we spent forty-five minutes looking for a place to park. But since that's not quite 'Lower Manhattan,' I'm afraid we can't pin our rudeness on City Hall."

Naturally Carol asked if she could help, while Jackson proceeded to squirt lime juice all over the counters that Shep had just wiped down. And naturally she wanted to go say hello to Glynis. Shep hurried ahead to the back porch to wake her, although their guests finding his wife in a state of catatonic collapse would have been a more edifying introduction to life in Elmsford these days than any bear-hugging glad-to-see-you. Unfortunately, he didn't arrive in time to restore her turban, which had fallen to the floor. She had always been prideful about her appearance, if Shep shied from the word *vain*, and she was still prideful.

Carol had been up to her neck in nursing Flicka, whose pneumonia from August had proven tenacious, so Shep couldn't blame her for not having visited Westchester for six weeks or more. She did a good job of disguising it, but he could read the shock in her face. As far as Carol was concerned, they were still "celebrating" the wonderful news from Glynis's early July CAT scan that her cancer was in retreat. So she'd have every reason to expect her friend to look, if not robust, at least human-colored and three-dimensional.

But Jackson's multiple poor excuses and reschedulings had pushed this gathering to mid-September. Its ambiance had grown autumnal in more than a seasonal respect. Shep didn't usually notice himself. But seeing Glynis through Carol's eyes, he recognized that his wife's lush summer foliage had turned. The brown tinge to her skin had grayed, the way a beach vacation tan wanes to a dingy inland mottle that just looks dirty; its off-orange undertone was reminiscent of rancid tea. With the new chemo, Adriamycin (or, in Glynis-speak, "An Aging Mike Tyson," which lent the drug a pugilistic punch), she'd finally lost most of her hair; when she'd kept a good bit of it with Alimta, they'd hoped that she'd be one of those lucky chemo patients whose locks were spared. There was something horribly naked about the scalp showing through, especially noticeable with the darkness of the few remaining strands. More than the cleavage of a gaping blouse, those bald patches were un-nervingly intimate, like something others truly weren't meant to see. She'd grown thin again, of course, but damned if she didn't also seem shorter.

Carol's forced exclamation, "Glynis, that dress is gorgeous!" at least beat *Glynis, you look like shit!*

Groggy, Glynis looked confused why other people were in the house. The bowl of corn chips on the table seemed to clue her in. "Oh, Carol, thanks. I hope you don't mind if I don't get up. You look lovely, too. You work so hard, but no one would ever know it. Always so fresh and—vital."

It may not have been politic for Shep to notice, but Carol did indeed look lovely. Perhaps uneasy about outshining the hostess—Carol was like that; she would have considered the matter—she had clearly dressed down for the evening. Yet the just-threw-any-old-thing-on gambit had backfired. You could hardly blame the poor woman for looking her best at her simplest. The solid aqua shift only emphasized her willowy figure, and bound a bit across the breasts in a way that called attention to them. That was surely an accident, of course. The flimsy little sundress may have been a back-of-the-closet thing—it draped in those anatomically incorrect pleats distinctive to having wilted for months if not years on a hanger—and didn't fit that well. But as a consequence the nipples poked noticeably behind the material, and it was hard not to stare. Glynis didn't really have breasts anymore. The implicit contrast might have made any once equally handsome woman feel a little bitter. If so, his wife seemed to get the better of that bitterness with some success. In fact, no one but Shep could appreciate what an effort Glynis was making, though her voice was frail.

Jackson roistered in with a tray, the pitcher of margaritas brimming, the tumblers encrusted with too much salt. He had a careless side that had sometimes brought the friends to loggerheads when Jackson was still a jobbing handyman in Shep's employ, and it was probably best for everyone, customers included, that he'd moved up to a managerial post. Everything Jackson did ran to excess.

"Shep tells me you've been prescribed a new *cocktail*," he said, pouring Glynis a large measure. "Thought I'd oblige."

Glynis did not appear to get the allusion. (Shep had been disappointed to discover that on a Darwinian level Nature regards a sense of humor as dispensable.) As Jackson poured the rest of the round, she looked at her glass as if at a photograph from better times. Glynis wasn't supposed to drink much on An Aging Mike Tyson, which Jackson could have known had he asked. The glass did make a cheerful prop, though the fact that it was just that helped to underscore the theatrical quality of this whole event. They would execute the stage directions of *Another Boisterous Dinner with Jackson and Carol*, because no one had scripted whatever this was instead.

"You folks been following the schemozzle with Katrina?" Jackson introduced.

For once Shep was glad for current events, a formal Topic that would get them through the corn chips.

"Yeah, we've been keeping CNN on pretty much all day," said Glynis.

She might have added that she was relishing Katrina. Glynis had always harbored a mischievous, dark aspect, but now it was no longer a mere *aspect*. She loved watching destruction—the big bountiful houses of the sort she and her husband had never bought for themselves filled with acrid, oily water to the second floor. The stranded black matriarchs waving fruitlessly on rooftops for rescue that would never come, who now knew they were alone in the world and no one cared. *Well*, he could sense Glynis responding coolly, *welcome to the club*. Other people's suffering did not disquiet her. Glynis did nothing but suffer, and if others suffered too that was only fair. She seemed gratified by the prospect of one whole city that would not survive her. Had she her way, she might have clutched at others too, New York signally among them, to drag down with her to the bowels of the earth, like the end of *Carrie*. In a fell swoop of self-liberation, Glynis had relinquished her empathy for other people, defiantly reflecting back the very apathy about her own fate that she increasingly perceived in would-be well-wishers. She could tell, you know, however dutifully a few friends still attended her bedside, that they were relieved to leave.

"It's been so awful, seeing all those people in New Orleans lose everything," said Carol, her sympathy laudable but boring. "It pinched the budget a little, but I absolutely had to send a check to the Red Cross."

"You're kidding," Jackson said sharply.

"Think of it as from my earnings if you have to," said Carol. "I wouldn't have been able to live with myself if I didn't do something."

"But we've already *paid* to 'do something'!" her husband exclaimed.

"How do you figure that? It's the whole point of having a country, isn't it? To rally around, to lend each other a hand in hard times."

"The whole point of having a *government* is to lend people a hand in hard times!" said Jackson, who had already powered through his first margarita. "That's what taxes *ought* to be for. Sidewalks. And hurricanes!"

"And health insurance," said Shep. "For a guy who claims he doesn't believe in big government, you sure expect them to take care of a lot of shit."

"No, I don't. Like, I don't expect to pour *three billion dollars a week* into a sandbox in the Middle East, or to carry half the fucking loafers in my own country on my back. But, yeah, if my pocket's gonna be picked through legalized larceny, I want some pittance of a service in return. I don't want my wife working a job she hates just so my kid can go to the hospital. And I expect if a whole city drowns because of *more* incompetent civic management of its levees, somebody from D.C. will give the poor fuckers a bottle of water, a fistful of crackers, and a lift to dry ground! It's just one more example of the *tiny handful* of tasks that this monster of a government might be good for, and here they can't even be bothered to hand those guys a towel."

Shep might have been heartened by Jackson's compassion for their hapless compatriots in Louisiana, save for the little gladness that palpably energized the tirade. The poorly concealed delight reminded him of Glynis. Their friend was all too grateful for any turn of events, no matter how dire, that serviced his beloved construct: those wily, rapacious Mooches leeching off the pea-brained, pushover Mugs. Whenever someone else's misfortune validated your personal view of the world, maybe it was commonplace to feel more satisfaction than sorrow. But if Jackson's was a standard weakness, it was a weakness still: a glorying in having been right all along, regardless of how many other people's happiness had been sacrificed to prove it.

"It's because they're black," said Carol. "They're Democrats, if they vote at all."

"Yeah, I know you think that, and everybody thinks that," said Jackson. He dunked a celery stick in the dubious dip, took one bite, and slipped the remainder of the celery onto the table. "But I think it's simpler than that, and creepier than that. You've got a government that's really just a giant corporation, whose driving purpose is its own self-perpetuation and infinite enlargement. So it never occurs to them to help people. That's not their business, helping people. Their business is helping themselves and their little contractor friends, period. In fact, mark my words, the clean-up will end up lining more crony contractor pockets, and when it's over the contractors will be rich and the place will still look like a mud flat. Millions if not billions of dollars later, those poor bastards will still be living with shorted-out freezers reeking from rotting shrimp. Thomas Jefferson is rolling over in his grave, man. This country is a parody of what it was meant to be. A travesty."

"Is there any place you think is better?" asked Shep.

"No," Jackson said readily. "Of course not. They're all the same. It's human nature, man. You give anybody the power to take other people's money, as much as they want, you think over time they'll start taking *less*? Or work *more* for it, when they can get away with doing practically nothing? Governments are all the same, man. They eat their own countries until there's nothing left. They're cannibals."

Carol rolled her eyes. "Right. So we shouldn't have one. And we'd have no army to protect us, no one to defend our borders."

You would think, being married to the man, Carol would have known better.

"A million Mexicans and Central Americans a year wading across the Rio Grande, and you think our borders are *protected?*" Jackson cried. "And that army of ours, this whole superpower shtick, makes us *targets*. Two guys walking down the street in Riyadh, one from the States and one from Lithuania. Who's going to get kidnapped? The American! Which hotel in the Philippines is going to get suicide-bombed, the one that puts up locals, the one that caters to the Chinese, or the one renowned for drawing Americans? You think the towelheads are hot to blow up the Finns, or the Argentines, or the natives of New Guinea?

The Japanese haven't had an army since World War Two, and they're snug as bugs."

Shep was about to point out, "That's because they've had the U.S. to back them up," or to object that he'd seen somewhere that the Japanese had reversed all that and now maintained the fifth largest army in the world. But he stopped himself. He didn't want to fuel this conversation, which didn't seem headed anywhere he wanted to go. Kissing his wife on the forehead as an opportunity to straighten her hastily donned turban—she shot him a look of gratitude—he slipped off to turn the potatoes, and to lay the steaks on the grill.

The solitude of the backyard was a relief, the fountains' trickle lending the plain crabgrass landscape the tranquility of a rock garden. It didn't make much sense to invite folks over only to seize on an excuse to escape them. Still, Jackson's railing at the heavens had changed. The words were the same, but the spirit was no longer jubilant, or playfully seditious; it was plain angry. None of that badinage altered the way the world worked an iota, so if it didn't amount to genuine entertainment there wasn't much point.

When Shep filtered back up to the porch, intending to poke his head in to ask how everyone wanted their steaks, Jackson had routed some printout from his pocket, which was always ominous. "A hundred years ago, we were the most prosperous country on earth, right? We had the largest middle class on earth, right? *And* we had no national debt. We *also* had none of the following taxes."

Jackson smoothed out his sheaf, which was crumpled and creased, as if he'd given this performance more than once. Each time he reached the word *tax* he hit the table, turning the recitation into something between a poetry reading and a hip-hop concert. "Accounts receivable *tax*, building permit *tax*, commercial driver's license *tax*, cigarette *tax*, corporate income *tax*, dog license *tax*, not to mention the big daddy of them all: federal income *tax*—"

As Jackson paused briefly to draw a breath, Shep registered that the list was alphabetical, and they'd barely made it through *F*.

"Federal unemployment *tax*, fishing license *tax*, food license *tax*, fuel permit *tax*, gasoline *tax*, hunting license *tax*, inheritance *tax*, inventory *tax*, IRS interest charges *tax* (that's *tax* on *tax*), IRS penalties *tax* (more *tax* on *tax*), liquor *tax*, luxury *tax*—"

"Honey, that's enough," said Carol.

"Marriage license *tax*, Medicare *tax*, property *tax*—"

"Sweetie, we get the picture. Would you please give it a rest?"

"Road usage *tax*, recreational vehicle *tax*, sales *tax*, *state* income *tax*—"

"If you don't shut up right now—!"

"School *tax*, service charge *tax*, Social Security *tax*—"

"—I swear I will drive right out of here without you!"

"Look, pumpkin, hang on one minute, would you? State unemployment *tax*, telephone federal excise *tax*—"

This time it was Carol who hit the table, with the full flat of her hand, and it was loud. "*What* are you so mad about, Jackson? Really? *What* is so terrible about your life?"

"Telephone federal, state, and local surcharge tax," Jackson muttered quickly, absent the percussive theatrics.

"That's it!" Carol stood up.

"Whoa, sit back down. We can skip the rest, then. I'm finished."

"You bet you are," she said, and remained standing, towering over her round-shouldered spouse. "So you can answer my question. You have a decent house. Your daughter has a genetic condition, but she's at least still alive, isn't she? You eat well," she nodded at her husband's gut, "a little too well. What do you want that you don't have? Why do you feel so put-upon, so taken advantage of, so weak and sniveling and resentful? Who are all these other people you think are controlling your life, and why are they always winning? Why *don't* you ever feel in control, why *do* you always feel defeated and impotent, and as your wife, do you expect me to find that attractive? Why don't you feel like a man, Jackson? Why do you feel so—*small*?"

Jackson glared. Sloshing another margarita into his tumbler, he washed most of the remaining salt into the glass. Glynis and Shep looked away, embarrassed. Carol might sometimes plunge into the political fray, but she was usually the voice of reason, not to mention of kindness, and her tone erred merely on the side of the firm. For her to air dirty emotional laundry in front of friends was unprecedented.

The other three may have imagined that Shep streaked out the screen door because he refused to participate in hanging his best friend out to dry. But the truth was he'd been dying to read the same riot act to Jackson himself for years, and Carol's what's-your-problem was overdue. He'd never understood what fired Jackson from the inside, where the heat was from.

No, he'd just remembered the abandoned grill. When he reached the steaks, now less worthy for their table than for resurfacing a patio, he flooded with guilty remorse. The New York strips had trusted him. When he brought the platter of shrunken meat and charred potatoes back to the porch, Jackson was grumbling, "Nobody likes to be had. To be taken. It's universal. You remember when that kid came to the door, offering to wash the windows for twenty bucks? You gave it to him, and he ran off on his bike. Never saw him again. You were hacked off. It wasn't the twenty bucks, you admitted it yourself. It was being swindled."

"I was angry at myself," said Carol, who'd at least sat back down. "I'd been foolish."

"Right, well that's the way I feel. Made a fool of."

"No, I didn't feel *made a fool of.* I had been foolish. I deserved it."

"Maybe I feel that way, too." The couple shared a look.

After Shep fetched the salad from the fridge and opened the wine, Carol announced, "Jackson would like to apologize."

"For what?" her husband protested.

"It's okay, Carol," said Glynis, pulling herself up in the caned armchair. "If he weren't going on about taxes, he'd just be going on about something else."

"But this is supposed to be a celebration," Carol insisted. "Jackson seems to have forgotten why we're here. But I haven't. Both of us are so, so relieved you're getting better, Glynis. I swear, when Shep told me about that CAT scan, I cried. So I'd like to propose a toast." Carol raised her glass. "To recovery. To the miracle of modern medicine. To getting together like this for steaks and margaritas when Glynis is totally well again, and then *maybe* I'll let Jackson bitch about taxes!"

It was a brave stab at reversing the fractious tone of this gathering, but neither Glynis nor Shep lifted a glass.

"Sorry, Carol," said Shep. "We may have to drink to something a little more modest. To hopes for a raised white blood cell count or something."

Carol looked from Shep to Glynis, and put her glass back down. "What's wrong?"

"We got the results of another scan yesterday," said Shep. "Last time, Goldman invited us to his office. So I guess I should have known that the news was . . ." He reconsidered *terrible*, then *pretty terrible*, as well as *lousy* and *unsatisfactory*, and finally discarded even *bad*. "That the news was *less encouraging* than last time when he preferred to tell us over the phone. I guess we're lucky we didn't get an email."

"Which would have said?" asked Carol.

"That . . ." From the beginning, Shep had shunned euphemisms by policy, but under the circumstances he didn't have the heart to use the word *cancer* one more time. "That the situation has advanced. In retrospect, I regret that we didn't get to toast the last scan when we had the chance. This one—well, the results just aren't so great."

"It's only a setback," said Glynis staunchly.

"Yes," said Shep. "That's what I meant. We've had a setback."

"It simply means that I may be on chemo a little bit longer," said Glynis.

"Yes," Shep recited. "It may mean that Glynis is on chemo a little bit longer."

"Shit, that's a drag," said Jackson.

"I'm so sorry, that's . . ." Carol seemed to be rifling her own mental thesaurus. "That's disappointing. How dis—how much *less encouraging* is it?"

Shep tried to catch Carol's eye, but she had directed the question to Glynis.

"It's not as good as we'd hoped, that's all," Glynis said irritably. "But my tolerance of the An Aging—Adriamycin seems to be holding"—the cough, for illustrative purposes, was inopportune—"and there's a whole slew of other drugs we haven't tried yet, too." She met Carol's eyes with a challenge, until Carol lowered her gaze.

"Yes, the therapies available these days are amazing," Carol conceded, eyes darting to her plate. "Everything I read says that cancer of every kind gets more survivable by the day. That more and more it's just a disease that you have to manage, like lots of other chronic conditions that people live with: herpes, bad backs. I—I'm sure they can turn this thing around. Sometimes they have to find just the right drug, right? Experiment until they hit it." Looking back up, she managed a smile. Carol was a great deal more astute than she seemed at first meeting. Within a minute or two, she'd got with the program.

Yet whenever there's something you're not talking about—Shep was damned if he understood how this worked—it became mysteriously impossible to talk about anything else, either. In no time as they chewed laboriously through their overcooked beef—Glynis didn't touch hers—the foursome was at a loss for conversation.

"Glynis, can you not eat something?" Carol said tentatively after a maw of silverware clink. "It must be important to keep your strength up. And the beef may be on the well-done side, but it's obviously of very high quality."

Glynis poked at her steak. "I don't want to get into the particulars at dinner. But I can't look at anything like this without imagining how difficult it'll be to . . . to get it out the other end."

"Ah," said Carol.

The steak knives made an unpleasant screeching sound when they sawed down to china. By now Shep wished that Jackson would bring up something usefully enraging, like the Alternative Minimum Tax. After another ten minutes during which, in a single desperate interjection, Carol admired the bottled salad dressing, he was tempted to bring up the AMT himself.

Chapter Fourteen

Shepherd Armstrong Knacker
Merrill Lynch Account Number 934-23F917
October 01, 2005 – October 31, 2005
Net Portfolio Value: $152,093.29

Throughout his adulthood, Shep had tried very hard not to sour on people. People he knew; people in general. But he was running out of excuses—for their network of friends who he'd hitherto blithely assumed were decent, generous, and thoughtful; for the halfhearted human race. Though it might not have been a great night, at least Jackson and Carol had finally shown up. That was more than Shep could say for most of the others. In fact, the people in Glynis's life were proving so consistently disappointing that a choking misanthropy sometimes overcame him late at night, like a miasma from a broken sewer.

Back in March, Deb had been determined that Glynis should find salvation before it was too late. Ruby was committed to getting beyond old rivalries and advancing her relationship with her older sister to a "state of grace." So Shep had anticipated at the time that his tolerance for his sisters-in-law might, over many months of repeated visits, be put to the test. He'd been prepared for Deb's piety to wear thin, not to mention her latest fad diet. He knew she'd never stop trying to enlist his secular family in prayer for God's mercy, or cease badgering his private, inward son to join her in thanksgiving for every extra day that God had granted the boy's ailing mother. On frequent returns to Elmsford, Ruby's rigidity might wear as well. He had envisioned getting a shade irked with the way she had to go for a run every single evening, when everyone else was ready to sit down to supper, and he'd sacrificed his own workout yet one more night to prepare it.

Should their visits coincide, he'd foreseen growing weary of watching the sisters vie with each other over who ate less. He was bound to grow impatient with Ruby's always showing up her plump younger sister by taking only one scrawny drumstick if Deb took two. With Deb's persistent wistfulness in regard to his wife's poor appetite, Shep could see himself finally losing his temper—snapping that Glynis's miserable portions weren't any mark of superiority, but entailed an inadequate intake of calories, aka starvation, that could eventually kill her if the cancer didn't. Broadly, he'd been a little worried that, after stays of increasing duration, his sisters-in-law would get on his nerves.

Never in a million years had he expected to be contending with quite the opposite problem: that following that initial rush to his wife's bedside after her surgery, neither of her sisters would visit again.

All right, both siblings still phoned, but less and less often, and the frequency of these occasional calls had taken an especially sharp nosedive at precisely the point that their sister's short-lived "recovery" gave way to a resumed deterioration. Meanwhile, at least Hetty continued to call every day, and so reliably at the same witching hour of 10:00 a.m. that you could set your watch by the phone.

In late September, after one call had limped through its fifteen-minute paces with Glynis even more cryptic and sullen than usual, she handed the phone to Shep. "My mother wants to talk to you. Be my guest."

"Sheppy?" said Hetty, and he cringed. His mother-in-law's voice had that injured, pouty inflection that Glynis despised, since it sounded more like one of Hetty's own first-graders unjustly deprived of her lollypop than a retired teacher of seventy-two. In person she was prone to clutch his arm or drape his shoulders, and this puling intonation was the audio equivalent. The fact that she adored "Sheppy" the ideal son-in-law (i.e., that wonderful man who paid for everything) had long driven a wedge between him and Glynis.

"I try *so* hard to let Glynis know that throughout this time of tribulation I'm there for her. But she can be so—snippy! I know she's very ill, and I try to take that into account, but . . ." Hetty began to sniffle. "Just now, she was terribly cruel!"

"You know she doesn't mean it, Hetty." Of course Glynis meant it. Whatever she'd said, she meant it and more.

"I'm sorry to have to ask . . ." He could hear her blowing her nose, could picture one of the ragged reused tissues that populated her housecoats. "But does Glynis *want* me to call? Does she want to talk to me at all? Because she certainly doesn't act like it! I don't want to intrude if my reaching out isn't welcome."

Once he'd got his mother-in-law off the phone, Glynis had flown into a fit whose script he knew by heart. "This constant tugging on my sleeve . . . She's always trying to get something from me, and I don't have it! I've never had it, and now of all times I really don't have it! She doesn't call for me; she calls for herself! I'm supposed to reassure her what a wonderful mother she was, over and over, but she wasn't, and I won't and I can't! I'm supposed to entertain her and comfort her and come up with something to fill all that dead air time day after day after day, and the imposition is outrageous! For pity's sake, she's a black hole! Now that for one of the first times in my life, I could actually use a mother! Not another dependent, another problem, another demand, another drain, but a real mother!"

Fortunately flying into a rage had so worn Glynis out that she collapsed on the kitchen love seat and got some sleep. He was glad that she hadn't pressed him about what Hetty had asked, since he'd not have enjoyed taking the heat for his reply.

Walking with the phone to the back porch, he'd urged Hetty to keep calling. Every day. To not get discouraged, to attribute her daughter's frequent lashings out to the illness, to absorb all manner of insults and cross remarks and to decline to react. Implicitly, to rise to a level of maturity that she hadn't a hope in hell of attaining if she was still this far shy at seventy-two. Just who needed whom in that embattled relationship was forever a bone of contention. But the simplest answer was that they needed each other. Glynis hated those phone calls, and actively dreaded them. But if 10:00 a.m. ever came and went without a call from her mother, she would be devastated.

That said? Hetty may have been "there for" her daughter, but she wasn't *here* for her daughter. Since that first trip in March, *even Glynis's own mother* hadn't returned to Elmsford. Not once. Shep was incredulous. Moreover, a systematic withdrawal from his wife and her icky might-give-me-cooties cancer was hardly exclusive to her immediate family. It was universal.

Glynis's cousins, nieces and nephews, neighbors (save the indefatigable Nancy), and most shockingly of all her friends had rung up less and less frequently, speaking more and more briefly. They had all spaced their visits more and more widely, and withstood his wife's company a steadily shorter period of time.

Shep knew all the standard lines. About not wanting to tax her, or bother her, or interrupt her sleep. About never knowing whether she might be in the hospital, or undergoing chemo, or knocked out from a recent dose. Warned that Glynis was not to be exposed to infections, some friends broke multiple appointments in succession with nagging colds. They were only being *considerate*. Other excuses were so impressively creative that it would have taken far less effort to skip the arcane explanations to her husband after months of silence than to give the poor woman a buzz.

According to Zach, the Eigers—parents of one of Zach's regular "hangs," and Fourth of July barbeque/Christmas Party friends for many years—were so caught up in coaching their older son for the SATs that the exhausting trip from Irvington six miles away was out of the question, though that was a distance Zach regularly traversed on his bike. It went without saying—or at least nobody said it—that these rigorous tutoring sessions by both parents during every available hour of the day must also have precluded so time-consuming and debilitating a gesture as a phone call.

Marion Lott, the owner of Living in Sin with whom Glynis had grown quite chummy while gossiping through her ridiculous employment, had been attentive for a while. Apologizing that Glynis probably wasn't up for chocolate herself, at first Marion had shown up at the door with a bag of misshapen truffles for Zach and Shep, along with a fruit basket for the patient. But the care packages, and the visits that delivered them, had entirely dribbled off by May. So when in early October Shep ran into Marion at CVS—he was looking for more enema capsules for Glynis—the chocolatier launched into a nervous burble about how busy the shop had become and how they were getting orders now from as far away as Chicago, and then one of her employees got pregnant and had terrible morning sickness, and you know how unpleasant it would be in that case to be around the smell of chocolate, so now she was shorthanded . . . Oh, and Shep should know the replacement mold-maker had not proven nearly as skillful as Glynis, nor did she have the same sense of line or sense of humor, so he should please tell his marvelous wife how much she was missed . . . He might have taken pity on the woman and tried to stop her, but pity toward these people didn't come easily now. With conscious sadism, he let her go on for what must have been a good five minutes. It was a certain style of excuse, the kitchen-sink style, a messy and exhausting approach generally taken by people who weren't very good at lying. The verbal incontinence was at least a giveaway that she felt guilty.

By contrast, the Vinzanos opted for the big, clean, sweeping excuse that was at least efficient. Glynis had met Eileen Vinzano back when they were both teaching courses in the Fine Arts Department at Parsons, which dated their friendship with Eileen and her husband Paul back more than twenty years. But Shep couldn't remember having heard from either of them since he'd phoned to deliver the lowdown on the surgery. Not long after he ran into Marion, Eileen finally placed a hasty call, claiming that she and Paul had been out of the country since June.

The tone in which she asked after his wife's health was uneasy. She was afraid that she'd called too late. Clearly she was braced for something delicately put like, "I'm so sorry to have to tell you this, Eileen, but Glynis passed in September." (*Passed*, that's the idiom she'd expect. As if his wife hadn't died in agony but had simply walked in front of the house.) He told her instead that Glynis was hanging in there, and explained that they were now on their third cocktail of chemo. But when he offered to put Glynis herself on the phone, Eileen panicked. "No, no, do let her rest!" she'd urged with something close to terror—and what were these people afraid of? "Just please give her my best."

If one transitive five-minute call since March amounted to Eileen's "best," he would hate to see her worst. After all, even for a roving foreign correspondent, five months was a long time to be "out of the country"; Paul was based at ABC in New York. This wasn't the only dubiously vague explanation Shep was repeatedly offered by "good" friends who had virtually disappeared. Flatly, late on Halloween night he booted his computer solely to copy his medical-update notification list of "Close Friends" and paste it into "Not So Close." The "Close Friends" file he deleted.

In his more charitable daytime incarnation, Shep conceded that any number of these people had already given emotive testimonies to how important Glynis had been to them. How enormously they admired her work. How much her whole life had been characterized by an elegance and sense of flair. How fondly they remembered this and that event . . . By delivering impassioned, grandiloquent orations that, as Glynis had noted with such outrage, could have doubled as eulogies, previous visitors had painted themselves into a dramatic corner. It was theatrically unnatural to go from grand proclamations of love and admiration to chitchat about how it looks as if they're finally going to repave Walnut Street. Multiplied by a factor of ten, the subsequent awkwardness resembled the poor stagecraft of having said florid farewells after a dinner party—flashy, stylish farewells of the kind on which you rather congratulate yourself in the car—only to realize that you've left a sweater behind. You have to sheepishly ring the doorbell while your hosts are loading the dishwasher. Voilà, all the stylishness and waggishness and lavish gratitude of your original parting is replaced with a hangdog shuffle in the foyer while they wipe greasy hands on a dish towel and search for your wrap. It was, he supposed, always difficult with the mortally ill to arrange to leave the relationship on a high note. The only gambit that guaranteed a movingly climactic parting was to deliver your tender, tearful, well-rehearsed little speech and then never come back.

Besides, what *did* you say to Glynis, once medical inquiries were exhausted? She didn't want to hear about how great your life was, and she was wildly intolerant of complaint. The events of her own life had contracted to the events of the body: inflammations on her arms where the chemo leaked from the cannula and burned her skin; chest drains to suck up the pleural fluid that made it hard for her to breathe; fatigue that got slightly better or paralyzingly worse but never lifted altogether; rashes and swellings and the curious striations in her darkened nails. These were the stories she had to tell, and they were depressing and monotonous to Glynis herself.

Visitors seemed to sense accurately as well that mooting current events—the president's dubious nomination of his own lawyer to the Supreme Court, the haughty, long-winded speeches that Saddam Hussein was allowed to deliver at his war crimes trial in Iraq—was like bringing up the fascinating configurations of rocks on the moon. Aside from casual schadenfreude in relation to folks who'd also been rained on by a cloud of doom, like the dispossessed in New Orleans, Glynis did not evidence any awareness of the world beyond the confines of their modest house. After all, the average Issue of the Day derived its urgency from the fact that it was really an Issue of Tomorrow: climate change, the degradation of American infrastructure, a rising deficit. You only cared about any of this stuff if you also cared that someday San Francisco could slide into the Pacific, that dozens of cars might before long plummet off a collapsing bridge on I-95, or that your country might soon be owned entirely by China. But Glynis wasn't troubled by any of these advents. The first two struck her as cheerful. As for the latter stoop sale for the entire United States, well, as far as she was concerned the Chinese could have it.

For the biggest tipoff that she was not in as much denial as she feigned was that Glynis had no interest in the future. That left everyone pretty much stumped. When you weren't interested in the future you weren't interested in the present, either. Which left the past, and she really wasn't interested in that. (The sole exception to this overarching apathy was anything regarding their ongoing case against Forge Craft. The suit always stirred a look in her eyes that Shep recognized from nature shows—when, jaws open and gaze fixed, a panther is poised to pounce on live prey. But Shep avoided raising the subject. His wife's driving motivator made him queasy: vengeance, and of the most indiscriminate sort.)

Lastly, to be fair—Shep did not feel like being fair, but seeing things from other people's perspective was a lifelong habit—Glynis was difficult. A variety of subjects was no-go. One subject in particular was circumscribed by heavy red lines, with Do Not Enter signs bristling at every approach. The problem was that under the circumstances this was a big subject, arguably the main subject or even the only subject. As he'd noted at the end of that somewhere between plain failed and outright awful dinner with Carol and Jackson, whenever there was something you weren't talking about, you couldn't talk about anything else, either. Thus these visits seemed to skate along on artifice; they did not seem real; they had a pandering quality, a patronizing quality, and, well, a lying quality that was all Glynis's fault.

But that was as far as his sympathy could extend. Once it stretched this distance it always bungee-corded back to the bleak impression that the duration of his wife's illness had simply exceeded their compatriots' famously short attention spans. Mesothelioma having lost its novelty value, she had become one big enough-already. Just as most of them couldn't run two circuits around a football field without collapsing to the bleachers, their friends and family alike had poor emotional endurance.

Shep was born to a country whose culture had produced the telephone, the flying machine, the assembly line, the Interstate highway, the air-conditioner, and the fiber-optic cable. His people were brilliant with the inanimate—with ions and prions, with titanium and uranium, with plastic that would survive a thousand years. With sentient matter—the kind that can't help but notice when a confidant suddenly drops off the map the moment the friendship becomes inconvenient, disagreeable, demanding, and incidentally also useful for something at last—his countrymen were inept. It was as if no one had ever sickened before. Ever languished before, ever confronted you-know-what. As if mortality were one of those silly superstitions, like the conviction that one must always drink eight glasses of water a day, that had now been summarily debunked in the Health section of Tuesday's *Science Times*.

Because there was *no protocol*. The bravest face he could put on this baffling social attrition was that these people had never been taught how to behave in relation to a whole side of life—the far side—that had been staring them in the face since they had a face. Maybe their mothers had taught them not to eat with their elbows on the table or never to chew with their mouths open. But no parent had ever sat them down to explain that this is what you do and say when someone you at least claim to care about is deathly ill. It wasn't in the curriculum. Grim solace, many of these shabby specimens of the species would confront the same oops-just-remembered-there's-somewhere-I-gotta-be when they got sick. But by then they would feel too wretched themselves to spare feeling badly in retrospect about having turned their backs on Glynis Knacker in 2005.

With an acrid taste in his mouth, Shep sometimes recalled the fulsome offers of assistance with which friends and family had met the initial bad news. The Eigers had encouraged him to let them know *anything* they could do to lighten his load, but had never made an unsolicited gesture of any kind; surely they realized that he would never *ask* them to escort Glynis to her chemotherapy, to sit with her by the padded armchair for hours. Eileen Vinzano had gone on at length about how she could help Shep keep the house clean. Nothing would be too lowly, she swore, not even toilets or kitchen floors. But that was before the Vinzanos went "out of the country." Meantime, he'd been obliged to hire a Hispanic girl to come in once a week to do the cleaning he couldn't keep up with, and Eileen had yet to break a nail on a toilet brush. A former neighbor in Brooklyn, Barbara Richmond, had proposed a regular regime of dropping by whole prepared dinners that had only to be popped into the microwave, a virtually full-time catering service that had reduced in the end to one pie. Glynis's first cousin Lavinia had declared that she'd be glad to move in for weeks at a time! Just so they had someone on hand to run errands and keep Glynis company. Naturally she had never ensconced herself in Amelia's room, and she'd been MIA since April. Did these people remember having made those extravagant offers in the first flush of rash compassion? If they did remember, did they imagine that Shep himself had forgotten? He was not by nature a grudge bearer, but he had not forgotten.

Of course, as letdowns went, *Beryl* was in a class by herself. An additional $8,300 per month for their father's nursing home was accelerating the ravagement of Shep's resources. Even assuming that he was hardhearted enough to contemplate such a prospect, the Merrill Lynch account was now much too depleted to finance a solo retirement to Pemba or anywhere else. The issue was now covering the co-pays, co-insurance, and prescription charges for Glynis's treatment, period. So on the phone with Beryl in early November he hazarded the notion that they might have to start thinking about transferring their father from Twilight Glens to a public home. He might as well have suggested sending the man to Auschwitz.

"Those public homes are cesspools!" Beryl shrieked. "They let you lie for days in your own shit, and then you get bedsores. Public homes are always understaffed, and the nurses are sadistic. The food is awful, if you're lucky enough to get any, since some of these biddies are so neglected that they starve to death. You can forget any facilities like at Twilight—no rec rooms, no physical therapy machines. They don't have any events—no classes, no sing-alongs. Maybe a few magazines, and that's about it."

"Well, besides a steady supply of detective novels, about all Dad really requires is a stack of newspapers and a pair of scissors."

"But these public places are like Dumpsters for the elderly! Old ladies in wheelchairs slumped in hallways with their mouths open, drooling on their nighties and mumbling about how tonight they're going to the prom with Danny because they think it's still 1943. You'd do that to your own father? He'd never forgive you, and neither would I."

Personally Shep suspected that the difference between public and private care was exaggerated. He'd seen plenty of dementia at Twilight, and plenty of drool there, too. Unless he was leading the congregation in a rendition of the Doxology, Gabriel Knacker would never participate in any "sing-along" in the most palatial of institutions. Nevertheless, Beryl's grim image had popular currency. So he'd not have minded that she conjured the stereotype had it truly been fear for their father's misery that had brought the picture to life. Nor would he have minded her insisting so strenuously on continuing private care if Beryl were helping to pay for it.

He did mind that her righteous defense of their father's comfort hailed from somewhere else. The sole purpose of the transfer he'd suggested was to shift the fiscal burden to the public purse. It was his own fault that she knew the sequence of events that would accomplish this modern financial miracle, because he'd told her himself in July. To qualify Dad for Medicaid, first and foremost they'd have to sell the house. Or, as she surely alluded to the structure out of his hearing, *her* house. (Maybe Jackson's idea was technically feasible: simply refusing to pay Twilight and letting the cogs of bureaucracy creak along until the government seized the property. After all, to his quiet amazement, Shep and Beryl had no legal obligation to care for their father or to pay his bills. Yet that wasn't the way Shep Knacker had ever conducted his affairs. Walking out on his obligations and expecting someone else to clean up the mess seemed sloppy, disrespectful, negligent, and irresponsible. He was, Shep thought wryly, who he was.) The proceeds of the property sale would go to nursing home fees until their father was officially indigent. Bye-bye free digs, bye-bye inheritance—and *that* was the source of the outrage piping through the telephone.

Still, Shep lacked the resolve to fight her. He had his own misgivings about public nursing homes, and a strong sense of filial duty. Twilight was probably nicer. Dad might not have liked it there much, but he was at least getting used to it. Besides, were Shep to keep hemorrhaging $99,600 per annum a juncture would rapidly arrive at which he would not pay for Twilight not because he was a bad son but because he did not have the money. Obviously, it was wasteful to spend down his own last remaining dime before ending up in the exact same place: shifting Dad out of Twilight, liquidating the pension fund, selling the house. Yet in its simplicity, perfect helplessness might prove a blessing. Jackson was surely right, that in a country that confiscated up to half of your earnings, and that demanded an additional backhander every time you did anything from buy a screwdriver to go fishing, you were not truly free. But in that case, there was a genuine liberty to be found in going broke.

Meanwhile, Shep tried to talk to his father roughly twice a week. The broken femur seemed to be mending, slowly. But for the first half of November the phone at his father's bedside rang unanswered. Rather than talk directly to Twilight staff, he made the mistake of getting the medical lowdown from Beryl. All she said was that he seemed to be losing weight. Or that's what the staff must have said, since that was the same phone call in which Beryl had announced that she was "on strike."

"You can't expect me to keep visiting him all the time. It's not fair. Just because I'm nearby I shouldn't have to take on that whole burden. Really, Shep, I'm starting to feel used. I can't take it. Visiting is too depressing. I have a film to edit, and I have to protect my, you know, chi."

"How often do you regard as 'visiting all the time'?"

"I'm just not into it, Shepardo. All I hear about when I do go is why I haven't been to see him in so long, when it seems like I just saw him, like, that morning. If you think it's so important for him to enjoy the constant attentions of family, you're going to have to come up here once in a while yourself."

Shep sighed. "Do you have any idea what I'm dealing with here?"

"We're both dealing with stuff. And he's your father, too."

He reluctantly promised to try to make it back up to New Hampshire soon. As they wrapped up the call, Beryl raised, "Before I forget, what's the deal with the heating? I just got some, I don't know, eviction notice type thing from the gas company."

"I transferred the bill to your name. I'm sure I mentioned that."

"Well, to my *name*, fine, but you don't expect me to pay it?"

He took a deep breath. "Yes, I do."

"Do you know how much it costs to heat this place during the winter?"

"Of course I do. I've been paying the fuel bills for years."

"Look, I'm doing the house-sitting. House-sitters aren't expected to cover utilities. Sometimes they're even *paid* to take care of places."

"You want me to put you on salary?" Shep asked incredulously. Beryl had nimbly inverted her co-optation of the family home into a big favor. It was just the kind of ingenuity in his sister that had always wowed him.

"I don't have the money for the gas bill, period. So unless you want me sitting here with icicles in my nose while I burn the furniture to keep from perishing, you're going to have to send them a check."

Beryl had discovered the giddy liberation of penury years ago. He was envious.

Shep headed up to Berlin Thanksgiving weekend, planning only one Saturday overnight. The traffic coming home would be horrific, but at least an evening visit and another Sunday morning during a season of traditional family get-togethers might temporarily alleviate his father's sense of abandonment.

Twilight Glens was no country club, but it looked clean; perhaps the slight fecal whiff penetrating the astringent disinfectant was inevitable in any facility caring for the old and sick. For that matter, like the blackened Victorian hospital of his childhood, the institution might have benefitted from a few streaks of grime, which would have provided the plain square building a little character. As it was, Twilight had been given an architectural lobotomy. In fact, Shep was impressed. Surely such a perfect dearth of identity constituted as much of an achievement in the physical world as it would have in the social sphere, were an individual to succeed in generating no personality whatsoever. The lobby and hallways were decorated with potted plants and anodyne prints. The linoleum was bright and beige. Private rooms were trimmed in blond polished maple. The effect was dreamscape. After all, some nights your mind simply wasn't up to contriving one more backdrop with satisfying symbolism, and Twilight was the kind of non-place where your brain sets forgettable, second-rate adventures: those aimless confabulations with poor logic, distortions of passing acquaintances who don't matter to you, and frustrated searches for a bathroom.

At least when Shep spotted his father from the hallway, the old man wasn't catatonic or burbling about his upcoming high school prom, but was propped in bed wearing his reading glasses, intently underscoring a passage in *The New York Times*. Terrific: business as usual. But when Shep went in and kissed his father's cheek, he was unnerved. The weight loss was more dramatic than he'd been prepared for. Shep had had enough of living in the fattest country in the world while watching the people he most cared about evaporate.

"What's the article about?" asked Shep, pulling up a chair. The bedside table was layered with clippings, just as he'd imagined.

"About how much these blasted CEOs are getting paid. Millions, tens of millions a year! It's obscene. While the rest of the world is starving." *Stahving.* Unlike his son, Gabe Knacker had clung gladly to his Hampster accent.

"Yeah, well, in case you're wondering, I didn't pay myself tens of millions of dollars a year when I ran Knack." This was as close as he would come to alluding to Twilight's price tag, about which his father had never inquired. The Reverend seemed under the convenient illusion that the government was still picking up the tab.

"In my view," his father growled, "no single human being can be so gosh-darned important" (*impahtent*) "that he's worth ten million a year. Not one soul, not even the president. Well—especially *this* president."

"But if you think there's a limit to how much you should pay any one person as a salary," Shep speculated, "is there also a limit to how much you should pay to keep any one person alive?"

His father grunted, the rivulets in his furrowed forehead deeper and more numerous than in July.

Shep laughed. "I'm sorry. I meant that abstractly. It's not like Beryl and I are trying to decide whether your existence is cost-effective."

"I didn't take it personally. It's a good question is all. What a life is worth, in dollars. When resources aren't infinite, which they never are. When money spent on one person isn't spent on another."

(*Pahsonally* . . . what a life was *wahth* . . . *resahses aunt* infinite . . . isn't spent on *anuthuh*—music to Shep's ears, in which a *N' Hampshah* accent was the very soundtrack of earthiness and probity.)

"It's not as neat as that," said Shep. "Like, if Twilight Glens saves five bucks by giving you generic ibuprofen instead of Advil, the money doesn't end up in Nairobi Hospital. But . . . the question still bothers me."

"Glynis."

"Yes."

"You don't have any choice. You have to do everything in your power to help your wife."

"That is the . . . expectation."

"But theoretically," said his father, sitting up straighter and putting on a display of vigor that Shep hoped was not an act, "how would you arrive at a number? You're allowed to spend a hundred thousand dollars on a single life, but not a hundred thousand and one?" (The Reverend's citation of this laughably small figure elicited a wan smile from his son.) "And the wealthy will always be able to circumvent any limits. You cap expenditure on health care, you really only cap it for poor people."

His father was still sharp, and Shep thought, this is the kind of conversation that I'll miss when he's gone.

"More importantly," Gabriel added, "how is Glynis?"

"The chemo is wearing her down. She's always angry, and at this point that's a good sign. It's when she stops being angry that I'm afraid of."

"There's nothing to fear." *Feeyuh.* "She'll have to make her peace:

with herself, with you, and with all her friends and family. I know it's hard to see it this way, but grave illness is an opportunity of sorts. An opportunity you don't get when you're run over by a bus. She has a chance to reflect. A chance to turn to God, though I'm not holding my breath for that. Certainly a chance to say all the things that she wouldn't want to go unsaid before she's gone. In the strangest way, she's fortunate. I hope for both your sakes that this is a time you're very close."

"I doubt Glynis thinks of cancer as 'an opportunity.' Although I'm damned if I know what she does think. She doesn't talk about it, Dad. As far as I can tell, she still believes she's undergoing chemo to get better. There's none of this—saying of last things. Is that normal?"

"In this area, there is no normal." *Nahmal.* "And what would it matter if she were abnormal, when that's the way she is? People hold onto life with more ferocity than you have any idea. Or maybe you do have an idea now."

"She's always been so honest. Scathingly so. Frighteningly so. And now, with the biggest thing she's ever had to be honest about . . ."

"Remember: you don't know what it's like. I may have broken my leg and had a scare," *scayuh*, "but I still don't know what it's like, either. Neither of us will until it happens to us. You have no idea how you might react. Maybe in the very same way. Withhold thy judgment." Gabriel's tone wryly mocked his own sermons, and Shep was glad of any inclination toward the withholding of judgment, with which his father had always cudgeled him in the past.

"There's one other thing I wanted to ask you," said Shep. "When you were a minister. You'd have had plenty of dealings with folks who were ill. In your day, were people . . . good about that? Attentive? Did they stick by each other? And I mean, to the end. The whole ugly, bitter end."

"Some did, some didn't. For me, it was my job to stick by them. One of the things the ministry is good for—even if you don't give it much credence yourself." The admonishment was almost welcome. It issued from the father he remembered, and in Twilight that was a relief. "Why do you ask?"

"People . . . her friends, even immediate family. They've—lots of them have deserted her. I'm embarrassed for them. And this disappearing act so many folks have pulled, well, it hurts her feelings, even if she pretends that she's glad to be left alone. I'm very discouraged. I wonder if people have always been so—weak. Disloyal. Spineless."

"Christians accept a duty to care for the sick. Most of my parishioners took that commitment seriously. Your secular friends only have their own consciences to prod them, and that's not always enough. There's no substitute for deeply held beliefs, son. They call you to your finest self. Tending the sick is hard work, and it's not always pretty; I don't need to tell you that now. When you're relying on some flimsy notion that coming by with a casserole would be *thoughtful*"—an odd spasm of concern crossed the old man's face, and he briefly closed his eyes—"that tuna bake may not . . . may not make it to the oven."

"Dad, are you okay?"

Reaching for a buzzer, his father said, "I'm sorry, son, I know you just got here. But you're going to have to leave me alone for a minute with the aide."

A few awkward minutes passed, while his father curled in acute concentration and couldn't talk. Bedpan in tow, a Filipino bustled in, wearing whites ill-suited to her purpose. Shep waited in the hall. She came out a while later with a ball of sheets. A watery brown stain betrayed that she hadn't arrived in time.

"Fifteen times a day if it's once," Gabriel grumbled in fresh pajamas when Shep returned. "You imagine a body gets used to this, think again. It's humiliating."

Shep stirred uneasily, and moved his chair a few extra inches from the bed. "You pick up some sort of bug?"

"You could say that. A bug the size of a small dog. *Clostridium difficile.* Or *c-diff*, as it's affectionately known around here."

"What's that?"

"One of those infections that take hold of whole hospitals. Half the patients in this institution have it. Nurses wash their hands here like Macbeth, which far as I can tell doesn't make a darned bit of difference. Notice, even in the hallway? It smells. They're pumping me full of antibiotics, but so far that's like trying to shoot an elephant with a pop gun. Gotta lick this thing, too, since it's the biggest obstacle to my going *home*."

The even bigger obstacle was Beryl, but Shep had other matters on his mind. He stood up, hands held from his side, fingers extended, trying to remember every surface he'd touched since he came in. "I can't apologize enough, Dad. But I have to go."

In the hallway men's room, Shep sudsed his hands for minutes, and on up the arm, turning the taps on and off with a paper towel whose dispenser he had cranked with the tail of his shirt. He used the same shirttail to open the restroom door.

You asked—I should say demanded—that I come up here to visit Dad," he charged Beryl after his twenty-minute shower back at the house. "Before I obliged, why didn't you *tell* me he had one of those hospital infections?"

"What does it matter?"

"These superbug strains are *antibiotic-resistant*. I can't be exposed to something like that!"

Beryl looked perplexed. "You're pretty healthy. It's mostly old people who are at risk. I can see being worried about Dad, but I don't understand why you're so worried on your own account. It's a small risk to take for the sake of your own father."

"Even if I didn't come down with it, I could become a carrier!"

"Well, that's not great I guess, but so . . . ?"

"Glynis. Remember her? *My wife*. Glynis's immune system is shattered. Something like *c-diff* could kill her."

"Christ, you're being awfully melodramatic."

"I'll show you melodramatic," said Shep, and stalked back out to his car.

He arrived back home at 5:00 a.m. on Sunday, and took another shower. He threw his clothes in the washer and turned both wash and rinse temperatures to the maximum. He felt badly about trying to expunge any remnant of his own father's person, but this was no time to be sentimental. He helped himself to a backup prescription for antibiotics that Glynis kept on hand for emergency infections, and popped two pills before curling on the couch downstairs for a couple of restless hours' sleep. He was at war with himself. His stool wasn't loose; in fact, he was constipated, and the bready fast food on the drive to New Hampshire should make matters worse. The idea of keeping a physical distance from Glynis was intolerable. But if there was any risk . . .

He couldn't afford for his wife to be afraid of him; he was her primary nurse. Thus once Glynis woke, surprised to find him home so soon, he explained that after a long, fruitful but, for his father, tiring visit, he'd headed back last night to avoid holiday traffic. When he neither kissed nor touched her she didn't seem to notice, though his standoffishness may have registered on an unconscious level. So he was especially pleased on her behalf that for once that afternoon she was expecting a visitor.

Petra Carson had stopped by more doggedly than most of his wife's friends, in spite of the fact that Glynis's old rival from Saguaro Art didn't have a car, and had to take the train from Grand Central. She always insisted on a taxi to and from the station, too, mortified by putting Shep to extra trouble.

He didn't mean to eavesdrop, but because of Thanksgiving Isabel hadn't given the house its regular Thursday once-over last week. So once he led Petra up to the bedroom where Glynis was resting, he went back to cleaning the bathroom down the hall. (Glynis's last enema had been messy.) Petra must have left the bedroom door ajar, since their conversation was audible even over the TV that Glynis kept on low now all day.

Shep had always liked Petra. Glynis might have found her colleague's work glib and conventional, but the woman herself had a seriousness and social rebelliousness that he admired. (Her second marriage at forty-seven was to a boy of twenty-five.) Thus it wouldn't come naturally to

Petra to observe her friend's implicit Do Not Enter signs; they were, she would shrug, only signs. She put him in mind of Jed, Shep's tear-away next-door neighbor in boyhood. They'd been exploring one afternoon, and came across a fenced field—what Hampsters called puckerbrush—with "No Trespassing" plastered all over it. "We can't go in there," Shep had said, and Jed said, "Why not?" Shep said, "It says, 'No Trespassing,'" and Jed said, "So?" And lifted the wire. That little moment had been a revelation: when he ducked under the wire and nothing happened. Apparently rules have only as much power as you accord them. Well, Petra was a lift-the-wire type. Having advanced to the perimeter of her friend's no-go area, she ducked right in.

"So what's it like?" he heard Petra ask. "How does it feel? What do you find yourself thinking?"

"What's *what* like?" Glynis was not going to help.

"I don't know . . . Facing the inevitable, I guess."

"The *inevitable*," Glynis repeated sourly. "Are you not facing it, too?"

"Abstractly."

"It's anything but abstract."

"Well, of course. And of course, yes, we're all in the same leaky boat, I suppose."

"Then you tell me *what it's like*."

"You sure don't make it any easier, do you?"

"It's not easy for me," Glynis snapped. "Why should I make it easy for you?"

"I just don't think we should spend this time—this limited time—talking about rivets."

"That's the way we spent the other time: on rivets. It was the same time—our time, our 'limited time,' all there is. If it's wasteful now, it was wasteful then. So according to you, we should have been getting together all those afternoons to talk about death."

"That might have been a different kind of waste."

"Well, go ahead then. If that's what you want. Talk about death. I'm all ears."

"I . . . Sorry, I don't know what to say." Petra sounded embarrassed.

"I didn't think so. Why should I know, then?"

When Glynis raised the volume of the TV Shep could no longer make out their conversation. He suspected that this pervasive belligerence, aggression, and at times overt hostility greeted many of his wife's remaining visitors, which would obviously run some of them off for good.

When Petra emerged twenty minutes later, he invited her downstairs for coffee. She declined the coffee, but said she could definitely use a "debrief," and collapsed onto the living room couch. He was glad she wasn't calling for a taxi right away. Jackson had become so dark and intermittently silent and then explosive that Shep had cut a wide berth since that dinner. He didn't have many people to talk to.

"God, it's hot in here," she said, flapping her shirt. "That's why coffee is the last thing I need. What is it, eighty, eighty-five?"

"Glynis gets cold. How about a beer, then?"

"That's the ticket, thanks. But Jesus, keeping the whole house this warm must cost you a fortune!"

"Yes, it does." He was always impressed when anyone acknowledged the side of this nightmare that was supposed to be incidental.

He fetched them each a Brooklyn Brown Ale. Petra wasn't a bad-looking woman for over fifty, even wearing a button-down burned with acid holes and baggy jeans splashed with flux: studio togs. Like so many metalsmiths who fashioned adornments, she never wore jewelry. Her hair was frazzled, her nails jagged and black. Her palms were creased in crimson, from the polishing compound called rouge—the closest thing she wore to makeup. Petra was one of those people who didn't seem to care about her appearance, or beyond that; who didn't seem aware of being seen. A rare quality, and refreshing.

"So—can she hear me down here?" Petra asked quietly.

"No. The chemo has done a number on her hearing."

"She's not looking good, Shep."

"It's getting pretty grim," he admitted.

"I guess I want to apologize. I should really apologize to Glynis, but

I don't think she'd let me. She won't let me talk about anything, really, and when I try, she gets mad."

"It's not only you. And if you think *that's* mad, try mentioning Forge Craft."

"What's up with that asbestos suit, anyway?"

"We've had lots of foot-dragging delay tactics from Forge Craft; only to be expected. But what's keeping the case from going forward right now is Glynis. She has to give a deposition, and then be subject to cross-examination from the company's lawyers. A couple of times the deposition has had to be rescheduled because it was too close to chemo and Glynis felt too sick. But a couple of other times she seemed well enough—or as well as she was going to get—and she still insisted on putting it off."

"I can understand procrastinating. It doesn't sound like a lot of fun. All that pressure on her to remember everything just so, to not get mixed up, when she's talking about thirty years ago. Funny, though, how clearly she seems to recall those products we worked with. I mean, we were in the same metal classes. To me, the tools, the supplies, and the materials are all a blur. I sure as hell don't remember any tiny printed purple flowers with green stems on the heat-proof mitts, that's for sure."

"I don't want to ruin your day, but theoretically you could have been exposed to asbestos at Saguaro, too."

"Yeah, that's occurred to me. Except that I have this weird memory . . ."

"Of what?"

"Oh, never mind. It can't be right. I must be confused. Glynis obviously has keener powers of recall than I do." Petra took a long slug of her beer, and slid the bottle in front of the Wedding Fountain. For a long, awkward beat only the trickle of its sluices filled the stifling, overheated air.

"Listen," she began. "I—I said I wanted to apologize. I meant for not coming up here more often. For not being in better touch."

He braced himself for the usual slew of justifications: it's been a terribly busy time for her, she had these demanding commissions that had to be produced on deadline . . .

"I have no excuse," she said instead. "This has been a slack year. I make my own schedule. I could come up any time, and all the time. And it would obviously be no skin off my nose to call all the time, too. I just don't."

"You've been in better touch than most of her friends."

"I'm sorry to hear that. I'm surprised to hear that. She's always inspired powerful loyalty. She's a weird one, your wife, but that ferocity she's got, that wickedness, that slashing fuck-you defiance—which she still has, even if lately it's making her a pain in the butt—well, a lot of people adore it. Feed off it, even."

"For a while," said Shep, "when the visits were subsiding, she still got a fair amount of email. You know, *how are you holding up, we're thinking of you.* Personally, I think it's a medium for cowards. But at least those two-liners were better than nothing. Now I retrieve her email for her, and it's all spam. Except for the daily call from her mother, the phone can go quiet for days."

Petra put a hand to her forehead. "I have a Post-it note on the lid of my computer. It says, 'CALL GLYNIS,' in caps. I pasted it there back in February. A couple of months later I added some exclamation marks. They didn't make any difference. I'm used to that note now. It was chartreuse, but it's faded now, and a little dirty. Part of the landscape. I know what it says, I know why it's there, and I think about calling Glynis all the time, but I don't. Instead of calling I feel terrible about not calling, as if my stupid feeling terrible is doing Glynis any favors.

"Yeah, sure," she went on after chugging half the beer. "I come up once in a while, and call once in a while, but when I do I have to put a gun to my head, and I don't understand that. I know she's sometimes been prickly with me . . . You know, she just hasn't produced very much, which I can't explain, either, since she's really talented. I guess I should have told her so to her face at some point, but she's a highly original designer, and her execution is actually better than mine—that is, even better, since I'm no slouch—because she's such a perfectionist. I know she resents how much I sell, and I know she thinks it's crap, too. Well, I don't think it's crap, so that's okay. I know my stuff is mainstream, and that's why it sells, too. So that's caused a little friction. But, hey, I've always enjoyed our friction. We've had an energy together. I've loved getting into it with her, over the whole craft-versus-art thing, or even, I don't know, whether roasted radicchio is disgusting (which it is; it turns a hideous shade of purple-brown). I've never avoided her company before. Why am I not a better friend? Now, when she needs me more than ever? I should be up here every week, or practically every day! She's *dying*, isn't she?"

Shep sat back with a jolt. He wasn't used to having that question put so squarely. "Probably. Don't tell Glynis."

"She has to know. She has to know better than anybody."

" 'Knowing' is a funny thing. She refuses to know it. When you refuse to know something do you have to know it first? Or can you unknow things? She never talks about it."

"Not even to you? I find that incredible."

"Maybe there's nothing to say."

"Don't be ridiculous. Doesn't she ask how you'll manage without her? Whether you'll stay in Westchester once Zach's out of the house? I know you hate it here. Or how you feel about getting married again? How she feels about that? Does she want a funeral, and what would she like it to be like? Does she want to be buried or cremated? Is there any paperwork to take care of while she's got the chance to leave things in order? Is there anyone she'd like to leave one of her pieces, or would she like me to try to get her body of work—such as it is—into a gallery or museum?"

"Glynis doesn't regard any of that as her problem. As for leaving things neat and tidy, I think she'd rather leave everything a big mess. As retaliation. She's spiteful, you know that. It's charming, actually. Besides, maybe she understands death better than we think. That is, if she's not here, I'm not here. Westchester isn't here. If Glynis dies, everything dies. Why should she care if I move or remarry when I no longer exist?"

"But she loves you."

"The love dies, too. Sometimes I think she's not being evasive, or lying to herself, or living in a fantasy world. Sometimes I think she's a spiritual genius."

Petra laughed. "You're a very generous man."

"Yeah, well. That's one more thing that Glynis could never stand about me."

"What's the prognosis, then?"

"Her doctor claims not to believe in prognoses. But according to my Web research . . . Well, I suspect she's right on schedule."

"Which means?"

"That you're right. That you should probably try to visit more often."

The next evening, while making Glynis another fat-max-out dinner in the usual optimistic quantities and taking care to keep washing his hands, Shep considered Amelia. Of the long list of neglectful characters in this drama, their own daughter may have been the most disappointing. It was a rare business for Glynis to be more forgiving than Shep, but he himself could not readily overlook Amelia's behavior, which Glynis called understandable and Shep called appalling.

Granted, Amelia had finally returned home again in August, with the backseat of her compact piled with groceries. She was technically present in the house for the better part of a day, but spent most of that time preparing an elaborate meal of cannelloni (she even made the pasta), a fancy Italian bread salad that demanded plenty of chopping, and chilled parfait glasses of zabaglione. Making the family a complicated dinner from scratch *seemed* like a generous gesture. But Glynis had recently started the Adriamycin, and her anti-nausea drugs were only so effective. So she couldn't manage much of the meal. The timing was bad; she'd been up most of the night before, and the preparations took so long that once they finally sat down to eat Glynis had trouble keeping her eyes open. Worse, something about the lavish exercise had seemed diversionary. Amelia intently stirred and diced and whisked the hours away, while Glynis faded in and out on the love seat, apologizing that she couldn't be much help. Surely his wife would have been far more pleased had Amelia instead shown up with a frozen creamed chicken from Swanson and spent the whole day propped on the other end of that love seat, talking with her mother.

By contrast, with no further prompting from his father, Zach had got into the habit after school of drifting into his parents' bedroom and stretching out next to his mother. Shep didn't think they talked much. She'd be watching the Food Channel, which bored Zach senseless. Nevertheless, that was once more how he'd found them when he came home from work tonight: Zach's eyes calmly trained on a recipe for "Everything-Bagel Coleslaw" while he lightly held his mother's hand. Shep was very proud of his son.

When Zach drifted into the kitchen for a sandwich, Shep asked, "So how was school?" ashamed of resorting to a question that he'd hated being asked as a kid himself.

"It sucked," said Zach, avoiding eye contact. "It sucked yesterday, and it'll suck tomorrow, so you can stop asking that."

"I'm sorry. I didn't have any choice."

"Yeah, you said that, too. So give it a rest."

Reluctantly, Shep had slipped into his son's room shortly before the fall term started to inform the boy that they would have to withdraw him from his private school. Sudden relocation for his junior year meant separation from his friends, more restrictive electives, larger classes, and less luxurious facilities. Getting it all over at once, Shep added that they wouldn't be able to finance a fancy private college, either; the boy should consider a state school, and even there he'd have to apply for financial aid and take out some student loans. At the time, Zach had allowed himself one outburst, never repeated. When his father explained that their remaining funds had to be reserved for his mother's medical bills, the boy exploded, "What's the point? She's going to die anyway. So what are you buying? At least with an education you get your money's worth."

Their sixteen-year-old hadn't meant to sound heartless. He was his father's son. His reasoning had been eminently sensible.

"By the way," said Zach, nodding at the rosemary chicken thighs that Shep had just pulled out of the toaster oven, "Mom says no chicken. She's sick of it."

Shep took a deep breath. He'd still not caught up on sleep, what with merely dozing yesterday morning, after fifteen hours of driving. He was tired. But among the many rights he had abdicated since January was the right to be tired.

He put the chicken aside to cool. What Glynis was and wasn't sick of changed on a dime, and by tomorrow the chicken might appeal. He found some ground sirloin patties in the freezer and carefully defrosted them in the microwave on 20 percent power, turning them after every sixty seconds. He fried the meat. She liked it rare.

He arranged Glynis's tray. Trying to make the spread more tantalizing, he picked some sprigs of ivy from the porch creeper and put them with some water in a hand-painted crystal vase from their trip to Bulgaria. He delivered the tray, then retrieved his own plate to eat in the chair beside her. He wondered idly if Petra was right, that he should be aggrieved that his wife didn't ever ask about his plans after—and then he stopped. After what? How could they ever talk about "after" when they never got to the "what"?

Glynis was once more glued to the Food Channel. It was what she kept on most of the time now. He might have found her fixation on cooking shows more encouraging had the amount of food she watched not been inversely proportional to the amount she ate.

"You know what floors me," she said, not yet touching the food, which would soon get cold, "is the way people expect me to have some kind of *answer*. As if I must have discovered the Big Secret, and I'm supposed to come across with a blinding vision, a cloud-parting revelation from on high. Shit, on top of chemo, and chest drains, and MRIs, I'm supposed to part the waters for everyone else. It's fucking unreasonable. It's outrageous, really. I mean, what a burden to dump on someone who already feels like cat puke: What's the meaning of life. How have you changed. How does everything look from there. Now that you've seen the light, tell us what's really important. Christ, I'm sick, I'm not running an ashram. Just like my mother, everybody wants something from me. And then when I don't come across, I'm a big disappointment. I'm made to feel inadequate just because I can't crawl to the bathroom for an enema, choke down fifty pills on the hour, and recite the Gutenberg Bible at the same time."

This was as close as she'd come to discussing her conversation with Petra. "I can see how it might seem like an imposition," he said. "But I can also see how people might think you could tell them something. About what it's like to face down . . . something they never have."

"Well, they'll have to get their fucking salvation somewhere else. The Church of Glynis Knacker is closed for refurbishment." Finally she took a bite. "What did you do to the rice?" she asked irritably, as a chirpy girl on TV cracked a raw egg onto a steak tartare and made a joke about salmonella.

"I cooked it in chicken broth," he said. "I thought that would make it more nutritious." Substituting broth for water was an idea he'd picked up from the Food Channel.

"Tastes awful. I don't like it." She pushed the plate to the edge of the tray. "I'd rather have plain."

"All right," he said patiently, picking up the tray. "I'll make some plain, then."

He left his own meal to get cold. Downstairs, he scraped the offending rice back into the pot. He boiled more rice. When the rice finished steaming, he allowed it to rest, the way it said to in *The Joy of Cooking*. He placed pats of butter over the top—half a stick or more—then fluffed the grains with a fork. He microwaved her plate, again at 20 percent power to keep from overcooking the beef, and returned to the bedroom.

She took one bite of the new rice and chewed for a long time. That would be all she ate of the rice. This was par for the course. Lately she was prone to make very specific and sometimes obscure requests for a dish that she was craving, and nothing else would do. He always fulfilled her wishes. The last request was for Chinese sesame noodles, which absolutely had to be from Empire Szechuan in Manhattan. Fetching the take-out on the way home from work had cost him two hours in rush-hour traffic. She'd eaten one bite of the noodles, too. He thought he understood. The idea of food grew ever more enticing as the reality of food grew ever more vile.

"You don't think I'm doing this right, do you?" said Glynis, once she'd shoved the barely touched plate to the far edge of the tray a second time.

"Doing what?"

"You know," she croaked. "I'm supposed to be gracious. Philosophical. Kind. Loving and magnanimous and brave. Think I don't know the drill? I'm supposed to be like that little girl in *Uncle Tom's Cabin*. What's her name. Nell. Selfless . . . schlock."

"Nobody's asking you to do anything or to be any particular way."

"Bullshit. You think I don't know, but I know. What you think. What Petra thinks. What everyone thinks, when they think about me at all, which is," she coughed, "hardly ever. On top of everything else, I'm supposed to have cancer *well*."

"Just getting through the day is having cancer *well*."

"Oh, what a load of crap. That's one of those—soft—blah—*lines*. I can't stand it. I feel as if I'm trapped in a Top Forty by the Carpenters. Look at Petra. She used to fight her corner. Now she comes over and it's like having a visit from a vanilla pudding. I can say anything. *Your work stinks. You're a hack.* She just takes it. What do you people think I've become?"

"Sick, that's all. That means it's not you but everyone else who's supposed to be kind. Gracious. Like you said."

"Kind? It's not 'kind' to treat me like some—evil queen who'll cut off your head if you don't always tell her she's the fairest in the land. And *you're* the worst. You never get mad at me anymore! You don't call me on anything! I can hurl any abuse I want, like Linda Blair spewing green pus. All I hear back is *that's lovely green pus Glynis, now why don't you wait while I wipe this off and then I'll plump your pillows.* You're so endlessly fucking nice. It makes me sick. All the niceness, it makes me *even sicker.* You've always been a pushover. But now you're well on your way from worm to *grub*."

In sloshing her hand across the tray on "grub," she upset the vase with the ivy. Its neck shattered against the plate. The water spilled into the food and over the sheet. Shep put his own plate aside. He nimbly picked the shards of glass from the bed and then from the carpet. "I'll get you some fresh sheets," he promised.

"Look at you! Now you're literally on your knees! What's wrong with you? Why don't you say, 'Glynis you stupid cunt'? Why don't you say, 'Glynis clean it up yourself'? I just called you a grub! What do I get in response? *I'll get you some fresh sheets.* You're not even a grub! A grub has more guts! You've turned into some kind of—amoeba!"

He stood and picked up the tray. "Glynis, you're tired, that's all."

"Tired, I'm always tired! So what?"

There was rice on the sheets. Though they were fresh from two days ago, drying them would not suffice. He would have to wash them. "I don't know what you want from me."

"That's what I mean! It's always what I want. Don't you want anything anymore? You've—disappeared! You're not even there. You're a service provider. You could be replaced with a good Japanese robot."

"Glynis. Why are you trying to hurt me."

"God, that was a relief. Just a tiny glimmer of self-defense. Just a smidgeon. A soupçon. A pinch." She flicked a grain of rice on the sheet with her thumb and forefinger but couldn't marshal any propulsive strength, and the grain stuck to her finger. "But to answer your question? I'll hurt you because you're the only person I can get my hands on. And maybe to check if you've *got* any feelings to hurt."

"I have lots of feelings, Glynis." Yet his delivery was stoic. With the many subjects she avoided—her future, not to mention her lack of future—he'd often felt deprived of all that she didn't tell him. So perhaps she might also sense and resent all that he didn't tell her.

"You ask me what I want?" she snarled. "I want someone who wants. You never even fuck me anymore."

He was surprised. "I've assumed you weren't up for it."

"Screw what you think I'm up for! Want something for yourself!"

"All right," he said. "I'll try."

"More of the same. Compliance. So you will 'try' to ravish me. You will 'try' to rape me, in the same spirit you will 'try' to get me more cranberry juice. Compliance, nothing but compliance! Do you think that's sexy? All this nauseating *goodness*. It's no sexier to me than Jackson's sniveling defeatism is to Carol."

He was not sure how to manage this. She was in a very volatile humor. He did not want to make everything worse. But if he tried too hard not to make everything worse he'd put his foot in it with his very carefulness and make everything worse. "I'm supposed to feel bad for being too good?"

Though the very tentativeness of his tone might have inflamed her further, she shook her turbaned head in what looked like pity. "Look, you're amazing. The tirelessness. The patience. The unflagging devotion. Never a harsh word. Never a complaint. Working at that shitty job and caring for me morning to night—or more like night to morning. Any day now I expect to see your photograph on the cover of *Time*. But I don't want a paragon, I want a husband. I miss you. I don't know where you went. I think you're the same man who announced a little less than a year ago that he was moving to East Africa with or without me. Where did that guy go, Shepherd? I want a human being! I want a man who has limits! Who's sometimes cranky, who sometimes feels resentful, if not homicidal. A real man who at least occasionally gets *pissed off*!"

He thought hard. "I got pissed off with Beryl."

"Twenty years too late, too. But I mean me. I want you to get pissed off with me! I refuse to believe that all this schlepping and fetching and schmoing is not driving you crazy!"

"All right." He was still standing, holding the tray—regrettably, a pose of servitude. "I didn't like it very much—" He would have to start again. Glynis was right. The very vocabulary of such discourse was vanishing from his head. "I was annoyed when you asked for different rice."

"Bravo," Glynis taunted.

It was hard to remember how people talked to each other, well people, spouses. How he used to talk to Glynis. "I was annoyed because I knew that if I went to the trouble of making another pot you wouldn't eat more than a mouthful."

"That's right." She did seem strangely gratified, and all he'd had to say was that he'd been put out. "And that's all I did eat, wasn't it?"

"Yes. And the rice made with broth—I'd noticed the preparation on TV. I'd remembered to buy the broth at the A-and-P. I was only trying to make the rice a little more interesting, and better for you. Instead of thanking me, you punished me. You said the chicken-broth rice tasted bad. That annoyed me, too. Because the real story is that everything tastes bad. The real story is that instead of making rice at all I could have mixed up a fresh batch of cement. It's all cement to you, and that isn't my fault. It would make a big difference to me if you were sometimes a little more appreciative of how hard I work to make you comfortable and to . . . to keep you alive."

"There now," said Glynis. "Was that so hard?"

Shep surprised himself. He started to cry. He had not cried since the night he read his wife's prognosis online.

He probably hadn't contracted *c-diff*, and sometimes the risk of doing something is exceeded by the risk of not doing it. So he put the tray on the floor. He crawled onto the bed, lying on the wet part of the sheet. He rested his head on his wife's shrunken chest. She stroked his hair. She was probably not feeling very well—and that would be, as ever, a gross understatement. But for the first time since their delusional dinner at City Crab, he had the impression that she was happy. It had never occurred to him: that one of the things a woman "made comfortable" day in and day out might most have missed was doing the comforting.

Chapter Fifteen

The New York Times sat once more crisp and unopened on the kitchen table. They had a prescription—*subscription*, Glynis corrected herself, as if it mattered. But no one read the paper these days, least of all Glynis herself. It sat every morning in front of the same chair, where Shep ritually placed it when he brought it in from the front porch. So its content was an emblem of change, "news," but the object itself was an emblem of nothing happening.

Blue. The plastic bag the paper came in was bright cobalt blue. The fact that *The New York Times* plastic bag was blue shared the same level of importance as the stories on its front page. That had been one revelation, insofar as there were any: everything was equal. There were no big things and little things anymore. Aside from pain, which had assumed an elevated position of awesome sanctity, all matters were of the same importance. So there was no longer any such thing as importance.

An experiment. Sitting in front of the paper. Like in the old days, when she'd also have sipped a cup of coffee. (*Ugh—how possible, ever? Ugh.*) Cannot retrieve old days. Thinking of step aerobics at the Y: *Worse than coffee. How possible, ever? Ugh.*

Hard to sit up. Hard to see print. Keeps sliding. Not problem with vision, really. Eyes still work—one of only parts of body that work.

Eyes *focus*, she commanded. For a moment the blurred print stood still. "Study Finds No Link Between Low-Fat Diet and Cancer or Heart Disease." Huh, she thought weakly. There would have been a time she'd have been annoyed; all that watery cottage cheese, the bluish skim milk that turned her coffee gray: a waste. "Curfew Quells Three Days of Sectarian Rioting . . ." Iraq. Or it could be somewhere else and who gave a shit. She might once have made distinctions, but now all wars were the same. Background noise. There were always wars and you couldn't stop them so you shouldn't bother to try. If one stopped another would start up somewhere else, so they might as well keep fighting where they were. It was a little mystifying to Glynis how people ever got so exercised about anything that it would actually merit leaving the house.

Incredibly, she had once sat in this chair without fail every morning and turned each page of the A section. Always looked at the Arts section, too, looking for reviews of shows by people she knew (in the hopes the reviews would be nasty—which presumably she should feel bad about, but she didn't). Clipped recipes from the Dining section on—Tuesdays? Wednesdays. By contrast, her husband had rarely given the paper more than a cursory flip. So over dinner (*Before Dinners, food-as-pleasure: data no longer available; pleasure: data no longer available*), she would regale Shepherd with the outrageous details from an article about . . .

What? What had Before Glynis once decried? Impressed with herself, she thought: the plans to rebuild the World Trade Center. How some committee was ruining the design by that guy . . . *Cannot remember architect's name. Rather, cannot care enough to remember architect's name.* (Another revelation: it had never been clear to her before that thinking was an effort. That thoughts required energy. It turned out that very few thoughts, once laboriously formulated, proved worthy of that energy. Even this one: she could have lived without it. And that was the standard for everything now: mere living, aliveness. Yet it was beginning to slip through her mental fingers what being alive was exactly. It was entirely possible, for example, that aliveness was primarily defined by the capacity to experience pain, in which case it was befuddling why the state was so highly prized.)

That's right; there had been a particular evening. She had grown animated. Previously, she and Shepherd had attended the public exhibit of competing designs for the twin towers' replacement. Of the seven models on display downtown, Shepherd had, typically, preferred a squared, conventional skyscraper affair. Glynis had adored this other one, by what's-his-name, some foreigner. She could almost conjure the image: a dynamic fractal assemblage—complex, crystalline, like exploding quartz. No minor civic miracle, at length her own favorite model had been selected as the one to be built.

That was why that night she'd got so upset. An article in the morning paper had reported that this daring, inspired creation had been steadily subjected to death by committee. One by one every element in the design that had made the model distinctive, uplifting, unusual, had been chipped away and blunted, made earth-bound, commonplace. The acute angles went perpendicular. All the style had been sapped from the winning design's original plans just as all the style had now been sapped from Glynis herself, until it was clunky, chunky—yes, what Petra had called the fish slice: *chunky*. With no joy, no exaltation, no playfulness, the new World Trade Center would be a monument to After Glynis.

The memory floated in and out again: of having been offended, indignant, about a building. Because in those days she had cared about the look of things, all things. The line of things, all things. Perhaps it had been marvelous to have such passions. But Glynis could not be sure. She could not remember having passions. She could not remember reading the newspaper and having feelings about the stories. She could not fathom, now, ever having sat down and read from beginning to end a story about Bulgaria. *Bulgaria*. It was astonishing that she could still call up the word.

Was it possible to truly remember anything that you could no longer experience in the present? The question itself started to slide, like the print on the front page, the moment she posed it. She forced herself to think clearly, *no. Not possible*. Before the tiny mental entertainment had skittered off the table and onto the floor, Glynis thought wanly, *that means that everything stored in my head has rotted*. It was as if she had kept her treasured heirlooms in a leaky attic, where they'd been nibbled by mice, softened by damp, corrupted by mold. Falling in love with Shepherd—his first visit as a handyman to her apartment, to build the anchored worktable—had gone mottled, blotchy, wet. She could not summon the sensation of desire. She could technically recall having been transfixed by his broad, veined forearms, but only as an inert fact, like the capital of Illinois. Her one-woman show in SoHo in 1983—the satisfaction of it, the hopefulness for the future it engendered, the driving ambition it betokened, the hilarious, drunken celebration in Little Italy after the opening . . . all turned to a monochromatic mush, like books stashed under the eaves in sagging cartons and no longer legible, the ink bleeding, the pages sticking together, the covers warped. Remembering was a more active experience than she had . . . remembered. You could reconstruct the past only with the building blocks of the present. To remember joy, you required joy at hand. Thus to resurrect the celebration in Little Italy after her show, she would need at her immediate disposal: satisfaction, hopefulness, ambition, hilarity, drunkenness. The warehouse was out of these commodities. All she had left were the words, like labels under empty shelves. The warehouse stored only malaise, dread, and—saved for special occasions—the odd box of unopened fury. Only one unopened box contained not fury but self-recrimination, sticky black self-accusation, and it was leaking, steadily spreading like hot, unset tar.

Maybe this was merciful, the inability to remember, really, anything. Because if she could remember, she suspected that the one loss she would most lament would be the caring. Before Glynis had been deeply invested in everything from the spiral layout of shrimp on a platter to the single persistent scratch in a would-be mirror finish. Discovering such a scratch, Before Glynis had taken an otherwise flawless, fix-your-make-up-in-the-reflection surface all the way from rouge back down to 100-grit sandpaper to expunge it, proceeding once again arduously through the sandpapers, 200, 300, 400, careful to sand each grade perpendicular to the one before, onto polishing compound, again to rouge, then a final blazing burnish with the rouge cloth. It would take hours and her hands would ache, the joints in her fingers swelling—just to eliminate one scratch. So she must have cared very much. She did not know what caring felt like anymore, and you cannot miss what you can't conceive. So the not-caring was okay, in its way. It was all she knew.

Before Glynis had become something of a mystery to After Glynis—like the kind of faintly exasperating relative with whom you have little in common and about whom you have opinions to begin with only because you happen to be related by blood. (Were they? Related by blood? Arguably, not anymore. The blood in her veins had been replaced several times. She was no longer related "by blood" to herself.) This Before Glynis was a woman, she gathered, who had enjoyed the luxury of vast tracts of time unfettered not only by the need to make money, as Shepherd was forever harping on about, but—all that really matters, it turned out—by the impositions of the body. This was a woman who was "well." (Perhaps more than any other quality, this theoretical state eluded the After-Glynis grasp. But only as an experience. As a concept, she understood being "well" better than anyone on the planet. For After Glynis had discovered a terrible secret: *There is only the body. There never was anything but the body. "Wellness" is the illusion of not having one. Wellness is escape from the body. But there is no escape. So wellness is delay.*) What had Before Glynis—Well Glynis, Pre-Inexorably-Going-to-Be-Sick-Any-Minute-Now Glynis, done with her free ride, her gift of the soon-to-be-revoked illusion that she was not, after all, a body—a body and only a body?

She had baked pneumatic lemon meringue pies that rose almost as tall as they were wide. Flecked with brown-crested wavelets, the white domes now loomed in her mind's eye as purely architectural achievements, like the models of . . . *Daniel Libeskind.* (She remembered. The new World Trade Center architect was named Daniel Libeskind. A triumph. One such moment of victorious mental lucidity differentiated a "good" day from the rest.) Fleeting, corruptible, fragile, and destined to be eaten alive, such culinary projects were now baffling, as if this grown woman had spent her time making Play-Doh horsies or building pyramids with alphabet blocks that she would knock down at the end of the afternoon. She had been working in the *wrong material.*

She had raised children, but After Glynis had surprisingly mild feelings about this, too. They were not like pies. She had not made them. It was the parents who thought that they had made their children of whom, in the days that she had opinions, she disapproved. Zach and Amelia were fine, she didn't have a problem with them, but in the nicest way they really had nothing to do with her.

She had cleaned things that only got dirty again. No one ever put on a gravestone "Here Lies, etc., She Swiffered the Kitchen Floor."

But beyond pies, children, and floors, it was difficult to come up with how exactly Before Glynis had filled her time. What had specifically *not* filled the average Before-Glynis day was metalsmithing.

This was the focus of the perplexity.

Before Glynis had gone to art school. Before Glynis was very skillful, and it had taken many years of precious wellness to become skillful.

Pushing the newspaper away—she had not even skimmed the front page—she lurched to the kitchen drawer reserved for her own flatware. Back at the table, she slowly unwrapped the implements from their protective felt. As she gazed dully at the pieces she wondered if it was possible to gaze "dully" at objects so shiny. The sensation they provided her you could not call pride, since that was one more commodity that was out of stock, as if she lived in one of those old Eastern Bloc countries where you queued for hours because a single shop was rumored to have light bulbs. Nevertheless, as she gazed on her bewilderingly sparse handiwork, something stirred. Perhaps you could call it wistfulness. She had loved her husband, or at least she was willing to accept having loved her husband as a capital-of-Illinois fact. But these gleaming silver artifacts were the center. They had always been the center. They were, she thought anemically, what I cared about. The caring was gone, but the results of the caring still glinted in the finish of the metal.

Before Glynis had cared most of all about metal. So After Glynis would have cared about metal if After Glynis could care about anything. She was not sure, but maybe that meant that she could still care, that she was at least still capable of caring about not caring.

It did not necessarily reflect well on her: to have become one with a material so hard and cold to the touch. You were supposed to care about people. That's right, you were supposed to watch your house burn down and grip the hands of your loved ones out on the sidewalk, perhaps feeling a twinge about the books and the clothes and the china, yet flushing with the realization that you had got the really important possessions out, that you still had your family. But Glynis would have braved the burning building to rescue the fish slice, while thinking twice about risking her life for a baby. That made her appalling. She was at peace with that. Glynis—both Before and After—was indifferent to looking well or badly. She had cared about form. She had never given two hoots about virtue. She had never been especially keen on other people, come to think of it, and now she didn't have to pretend otherwise. That was one good thing: the liberation. She could be any way she liked now. She could be a woman who would save a fish slice and leave a baby.

The metal was all she had to show.

Why was there not more of it? The odd thing, this was the odd thing: for years she had privately thought of herself as a dilettante. The others, the hacks like Petra, her own family that she wouldn't rescue from a burning building, they thought she didn't know that's what they called her behind her back: a hobbyist; at their most flattering, a has-been. Of course she knew. But what they didn't realize? This was also the way she'd thought of herself. With contempt. Yet here at this stark end place was the useless discovery that she had been serious—that she had been serious all along. That she didn't treasure the pies or the floor or the kids, or not like this. The writhing fish slice, the knurling sterling chopsticks, the slender forged ice tongs with their beguiling copper and titanium inlay, the matching salad servers with crimson glass set inside the handles, their gleaming red flame-work streaming down the silver as if you had cut your hand . . . These objects were, and always had been, the point of her existence.

Everyone wondered what got Glynis through the day, and she wasn't telling. She was crossing a desert without water, but on the other side lay the oasis of After-After Glynis, the woman she had always been and would be again, only better. What got her through was the vision of her final chemo, Goldman announcing triumphantly that she was done, that the vileness would wash from her veins just the way Shepherd yearly sluiced out the debris and sludge from his stupid outdoor fountains. Day by day her pee would lose that dead gray smell of wet concrete, its alarming wrong colors of whatever chemical was most recently destroying her, like cherry red, or periwinkle. No, finally her pee would return to sunny uric yellow and exude that loamy, stinging smell that others foolishly found offensive and she had never before realized was rich and beautiful. She would sleep the night through and dream well and rise early, earlier than Shepherd even, padding immediately to the attic studio. Where she would remain all day. The silver would obey. Her output would be staggering. Shepherd would worry that she was working too hard. Shepherd would want to take his "research trips," but she would say no, I have to work; go alone if you have to . . .

He'd been planning to go alone! The traitor, to Pemba, pin-in-a-map Pemba, some squalid island in flip-flops besting twenty-six years with his wife . . .

Stop. He is paying. He is paying his price for that. He will keep paying, and he should pay. Rest assured, too, that he will never finish paying, like those credit card debtors on the hook for so much principal that they can never do better than fork over the interest and the debt remains, unyielding, irreducible . . . Some sandpit, imagine. No one but Glynis understood that her husband was insane, and where did all that dissatisfaction hail from anyway? What was so wrong with his life that he had to flee it, to flee Glynis herself, to betray her? Really, he shambled around here these days so hangdog, so humble, but he could get outside, couldn't he, just drive away, go to the movies if he liked, or to the A&P, which he did not understand was a privilege—yes, the A&P of all things was one more privilege! She had caught him doing push-ups . . . Push-ups! He could still do push-ups! And he was complaining? Implicitly complaining, pretending not to complain, but she could hear it, the underground mumble of self-pity, of noble sacrifice, of prostrating subjugation and sneaky self-admiration and plotting. Plotting! He was plotting! He had a thoroughly different picture of After-After, *as if she didn't know.* When it would all be "over" but she knew what he meant by "over," she knew what, or rather who, he expected to be "over," and his plotting, his plans, did not include her, did not have her in the attic returned to her torch, her polisher, her powers . . .

Stop. Think After-After. There were six more chemos to go. It wasn't fair, of course. They had said nine months, nine months of chemo. The nine months had passed. She should have been finished by now, and out the other side. But all the transfusions, the low blood counts, the you're-not-strong-enough-to-do-it-this weeks, had dragged the grueling business out. It was February, she should have been finished! Calm down. *I should have been finished!* No. Quiet. Calming now. Stay the course. Get through the course. Six. Six more. Concentrate on the other side. Concentrate. On the other side—

For After-After Glynis would be "New and Improved!" like a re-packaged cleanser. Because she understood now. She would keep her understanding out the other side. They had all clamored for enlighten-ment and she had denied being privy to any enlightenment but there had been illumination of a kind and they could not have it because it was private. Because she had paid for it so dearly and it was hers.

See, there had never been anything to be afraid of. Making things, starting that initial saw cut by notching the triangular needle file into the edge of a fresh sheet of silver, had always been terrifying in the past. She had feared disappointing herself, fashioning a monument only to her own limitations, as she had also assessed her finished pieces as stunted, only as good as they were. Well, yes. Of course. But now she realized that their limitations were part of their beauty. That is, her tendency to design flatware subtly the same way every time, that little rut she had resisted, that despair at the end in recognizing that the salad servers still looked a bit too profoundly akin to the ice tongs despite the innova-tive inclusion of flame-worked glass, and even her tendency to make the same mistakes—it was all part and parcel of what made the work specific to Glynis Pike Knacker. The unlimited craftsman had no iden-tity. Could make anything and therefore nothing. So your limitations were also your strengths. Besides, now she also realized that if she made a thing and it wasn't right, she could make it right. There was no risk, and never had been. Rather, there was only one risk: making nothing. Giving into the seduction of the unformed, the airy mental construct that was therefore infinitely perfectible and, in theory, infinitely fine. At last she got it: concept is incidental; execution is all. And she had the eye. *She was a master of metal.* In comparison, the materials that others commanded—messy, pliant clay, nothing more than wet dirt, really; or wood, corpse parts from the slaughter of plants—it was all lesser, sad, timid, easy, and small. She had some respect for glass. But it was the rulers of metal who ruled the world.

She had long contemplated a knife handle, which could be riveted onto a good Sabatier blade with its dreary black grip removed—or perhaps she could have a narrow blade of high-grade steel commissioned, its edge dangerous, illegally sharp. For the handle, something delicious, voluptuous, a sensuous fabrication from heavy-gauge sterling with heft and undulation, perfectly weighted and subtly, infinitesimally not quite straight . . . A line trailed through her head, in and out like a basting thread.

After all, implements of violence appealed. She could see After-After Glynis designing nothing but scabbards, meat carving sets, maces, brass knuckles inlaid with fine glinting diamonds to do yet more damage, or even instruments of torture—not only finely wrought, filigreed flaying knives, but the instruments of her own torture. A brilliant silver replication of the bags of poison that had for months wafted overhead, hooked on a drip stand; its mirror-finished pleats of sterling would catch the light. Perhaps she could face down the very worst of her horrors, since for Glynis the route to control and possession of anything was to Midas it, to turn all that she touched to metal, what she was made of, what she had loved, and what she knew. So she could also fabricate a perfect, gleaming replica of a syringe, replete with working plunger, whose slick, sweet mechanics would wow the galleries, the terrifyingly attenuated needle rendered for the luxury market in white gold. Because there was a market. She had met the market, at Columbia-Presbyterian, all those "fellow" sufferers mainlining death in sinisterly comfortable recliners.

The ones who never shut up, who blathered on their cell phones for hours and were lucky that Glynis didn't own a gun. They were all eager for trinkets, distracting treats, and the illusion of meaning. She could fashion a whole line of metalware for cancer patients.

Like Shepherd she had plans, but they were respectable plans. Not the plans of a coward who was tired, or thought he was tired yet had no comprehension of tired. Not the plans of a weakling who just wanted out from under, who was just waiting, waiting it out, waiting for his release, plotting his release, digging silently at night when he thought no one was watching, like an Alcatraz con with a spoon.

No spoons; they were too warm and cupping, too round and breasty and safe. Still, Glynis's head was crowded again, with all that After-After Glynis would make. Sharp things, aggressive things, uncompromising things. She would start with the knife. She could start with the design of the knife right now, getting a head start on After-After. Because there was not a minute to lose. Her poor husband had misguidedly hoarded his pennies, when the only currency they spent that had ever counted was time.

Making what was really a spectacular effort that would have read to outsiders as an unremarkable getting-out-of-chair, Glynis retrieved the pencil and notepad from beside the telephone. Shuffled back to the kitchen table. Tried to turn to a clean page. It took ages to turn the page. She could not get the corner raised with her finger, and at last resorted to prizing it up with the eraser. The hands . . . (*The* hands, not *her* hands; if anything, they owned her. That was it, referring to "her" body was all wrong now, since the body had its Glynis, really; the body possessed you, not the other way around.) Well, the hands were so numb that she could have slammed them with the phone book without flinching. The nails were lifting off, too, popping, they felt as if they were popping off her fingers like tiddlywinks—striated, deformed, so dark they were almost purple. These looked like the fingers of a heavy smoker who was into home improvement, and prone to bringing down a hammer on the wrong kind of nail. (She picked at them when Shepherd wasn't looking. They bled. She shouldn't. But fiddling with the raised nails, peeking sickeningly underneath, could absorb her for hours.) Her toenails were even worse, because there weren't any; the nail beds stared soullessly up at her in bed, blindly, ten gouged sockets—*wee wee wee wee*, all the way home.

The pencil felt like a shovel. When she dragged its point across the paper, the wobbly graphite trail bore no relation to the clean line in her head—her undulating knife handle, like kitchenware by Henry Moore. So she abandoned drafting the handle to first portray the blade, but that came out wobbly, too—slight, trembling, and drooped, the beveled side concave.

She could draw better than this when she was three. In a last effort for the morning she pulled at the page, failed to tear it from the rubber binding, and settled for scratching out the embarrassing blob with a squiggle whose faintness scarcely captured her rage.

Glynis woke with her face smashed on the kitchen table. The scribbling on the pad did not make a lot of sense to her. Funny, the bit of mental flotsam that remained from the morning's cyclone of elusive reflections was one distinct thought: "stupid outdoor fountains." She took it back. That had been mean. In truth, she treasured Shepherd's fountains. They were a little crazy, but derived from the crazy side of her husband that she liked.

Beside the notepad sat a plate of pasta salad, brightened with bits of red sweet pepper and parsley, alongside half a tuna sandwich with too much mayonnaise. Nancy, who had a key. How merciful, to have missed the kindness. To skip being thankful for the kindness. Most of all, to have missed being forced to eat this crap.

It must be afternoon. Friday. She was to have a visitor today. Ordinarily an odious prospect, but this was a rare visitor whom she did not much mind. Flicka. They were alike. How odd that she should now have more in common with a seventeen-year-old than with the girl's vigorous, bounteous-breasted mother.

Glynis groped upstairs, hand-over-handing the banister; no one would ever know how much energy she put into wearing a fresh velour lounge suit. She was winded by mid-flight, and paused, leaning on the railing, to catch her breath. Breathing—somehow whenever she inhaled these days it was too late. The breath was too late; she had needed the air in this breath in the breath before. Her feet hurt; bulging in their pink fluffy slippers, the skin was stretched from the edema and starting to crack. She shouldn't have fallen asleep in that hard kitchen chair; the pressure on her backside had aggravated the sores on either side of her anus—for on the rare occasions that she eliminated feces in the normal fashion it burned holes in her ass. Toxic Poo. Sounded like a rock band, or some awful contemporary eco-sequel to A. A. Milne.

Socks, to hide ugly swollen ankles. Woolen watch cap. Mustn't upset visitors with bald head.

Back on the landing, she nudged the thermostat upward another two degrees, not looking at the numbers, not caring about the numbers. She was always cold.

Three thirty. Carol had said four. With nothing better to do, Glynis peeked out the foyer windows, looking for the car. What she saw instead flushed her with a familiar, helpless, Pavlovian loathing.

One of the neighbors, running. In his fancy sweat pants with their little stripes, in his fancy shoes with more little stripes. A jaunty head-band. Looking so proud of himself. Exuding the same covert self-pity layered up with self-congratulation that she detested in her husband. In his fancy matching sweatshirt and special sporty gloves, he was running around the golf course. Aglow with manly discipline. Not to be deterred by a whipping February wind with a hint of snow. Yeah, sure, run your heart out, you sanctimonious prick. Think I didn't used to run? Just you wait. You'll see. One day you'll get some, ha-ha, *routine* checkup and the doctor will bombast you with a lot of long-winded Latinate claptrap and there you go, you won't be running around any golf course; you'll thank your lucky stars if you can still get out of bed. So run, run, run. For now. Because don't kid yourself. It just hasn't happened *yet*.

Sometimes Glynis rued the fact that mesothelioma wasn't contagious.

Granted, Glynis herself had gone to fitness classes and installed a variety of exercise regimes to keep what she had now been robbed of through no flagging of discipline, no indulgence or sloth, no laziness, no lack of resolve. During those workouts, she, too, would have imagined that she was exerting her willpower, at times to its maximum strength. *Wrong*. And that was the central source of the scorn that her neighbor inspired as he rounded the hill at the top and loped down the far side. He thought he was "pushing himself," when this very afternoon she had required *fifty times that much strength of will just to walk up the stairs*. He thought he was "braving the elements," yet had no appreciation for how kind was a mere February gale in comparison to an ill wind ripping through your own body. He thought he was forcing himself to do something he didn't especially want to do, and didn't realize that he did want to run, that running, like the A&P, was a privilege. He thought that he was building endurance, but was in for a big surprise when his own plague ship came in, at which point he'd discover that he had not built one scrap of the kind of endurance that newly unpleasant circumstances demanded. He thought, hilariously, that he was overcoming pain.

Sure, Glynis could no longer run from the porch to the mailbox. But the last year-plus? Cancer had required real endurance, real discipline, real willpower, in comparison to which a little step aerobics, a mince around the golf course, was a joke.

The half hour of waiting passed like a century. How disconcerting to have discovered that time was so precious at the precise point at which every judder of the second hand became excruciating. What did you do when the same quantity that was precious was also hateful? It was sadistic, an epiphany coupled with the perfect incapacity to act upon it. When the likes of Petra clamored for their Truth from on high, that's really what she should have spit at them: Just you wait. You'll get your beloved revelation in due course. But only once it's *too late*.

At 4:00 p.m. precisely, the car pulled in the drive. Glynis dragged open the front door and tried to look welcoming. Since her worthless family and fair-weather friends had left her to fend for herself, she'd had little practice of late at any welcoming.

Carol waved from the car, then helped Flicka from the passenger seat. Extricating herself from the vehicle by leaning heavily on her mother's shoulder, the girl seemed visibly weaker and more ungainly than on her last visit. Skinny as ever, flat-chested, and wearing thick, sexless glasses, she looked closer to nine than seventeen. The girl had been almost adorable when she was little, but as she'd aged her face had grown more out of whack: her nose was flatter; her chin bulged. Bouts of ill-wishing notwithstanding, Glynis was not so hard—not so made of metal—that she took any pleasure in Flicka's decline. Rather, she felt a camaraderie that she was glad for. Compassion by its nature was meant to be directed outward, and with no other object worthy enough Glynis's sympathy too often circled back pointlessly to herself.

For her own part, Glynis had banished photography. (And it was amazing how crass people could be, always trying to stick an aperture in her face. Utterly oblivious to the morbid it's-now-or-never implications of their impulse, friends were eager to immortalize her image now she had mouth sores and no hair. How often had they arrived with cameras when she looked *great*?) Sporting neither eyebrows nor lashes, her countenance was undemarcated, incompletely drawn. Fair enough, the eerie smoothness of her legs obviated hot wax treatments. But hairless forearms on a grown woman were creepy. Carol wouldn't know it to look at her, of course, but the biggest loss in the hair department was lower down; Shepherd had always celebrated her exuberant furze. It was a disagreeable discovery what a fifty-one-year-old pudenda looked like bald: shriveled, wrinkled, flapping, and strangely purple. Aesthetics weren't meant to matter anymore, of course, and in truth Glynis had found in the degeneration of her body a perverse and obsessive fascination, a debauched thrill. Yet whenever she glimpsed earlier photographs—her wedding album, her formal portrait for gallery submissions, the few framed shots from travels abroad—she looked at that fuller, younger face, the regal figure she'd once cut, and felt jealous. Jealous of herself. So dressed this afternoon in shapeless velour and these ludicrous fluffy slippers that were all her feet would fit into, Glynis battled shame. For that matter, ever since her diagnosis she'd been nagged by a persistent sense of having done something wrong. The hospital had never differentiated itself in her mind from a prison, and whenever she was incarcerated there she had that Kafkaesque sensation of never being sure with what crime she'd been charged.

Carol, by contrast, looked terrific.

It wouldn't do to hate Carol.

"Hey, Glyn!" Flicka whined, and opened her arms. For Glynis, it was like embracing her own torso—all the little birdlike bones discernible in the girl's back. Birds of a feather. Flicka was shorter, but otherwise they were the same size.

"She's not really well enough to be making trips to Westchester," Carol said with a hug. "But she insisted."

"Want to come upstairs to my nest?" Glynis invited.

"Sure," Flicka slurred. "But only if you turn off the fucking Food Channel." Fortunately, Flicka's high nasal tonalities occupied a register that Glynis could still distinguish; Shepherd's deep drone often faded to the plow of a faraway lawn mower.

"Okay. But only for you." Glynis gripped the banister and pulled. "Everyone else has to learn to make curried egg salad."

"Yuck."

"Is there anything you like?"

"Ice cream." Dragging herself up behind Glynis and winded by the fourth stair, Flicka darted a glance down at her mother and muttered, "I'm not supposed to have it, but sometimes I sneak a bite of Heather's when Mom isn't looking."

"I think I want things. But then it turns out that I don't." They were not yet halfway up, and Glynis slumped onto a stair. "Let's stop here, shall we?"

Having been watching the crips from the foyer, Carol called up, "I'll leave you to visit for a while just the two of you, okay? Glynis, don't worry about me, I can read the paper."

"Glad somebody will," said Glynis, relieved that Carol wasn't going to hover. Flicka found her mother oppressive, and in her presence tended to clam up and scowl.

"At least we've finally found a brand of g-tube port we can change at home," Flicka rasped, having collapsed on a stair as well. "So I don't have to go to the damn hospital every time it breaks. Dad's right, stupid country can't make anything that lasts a week."

"But don't you notice, in the hospital, how you start to feel weirdly at home?"

"Sort of. You do get to know the drill. Like, which nurses come at you with a hypodermic like a hole punch. I can't feel it, but when they jab-jab-jab on my arm for half an hour trying to find a vein it gets incredibly boring. Hey, you still afraid of them? Needles?"

"Horrified. Shepherd expected the phobia to go away, but if anything it's worse. After every chemo, he has to give me five injections to boost my white blood cell count. I don't know how he stands it. I can't even set eyes on the needle. I make him get the thing ready behind my back, and beforehand I have to take lorazepam. Or 'marzipan,' as it's affectionately known around here. The first time, before I knew to take the marzipan, I fainted. I'm a total baby."

"You picked the wrong disease, then. Should have gone for something where they throw up their hands. Something incurable."

"Mesothelioma is incurable," said Glynis softly. She'd never said this out loud.

Flicka looked embarrassed. "Sorry. Guess the word I meant was *untreatable*."

"I don't mind what word you use. You don't have to be careful with me." They started up the stairs again: one foot up, the next foot to the same step, rest.

"Don't you get sick of that?" asked Flicka. "The carefulness. Like, *ooh, ooh*, mustn't 'upset' Flick! Mustn't say anything 'insensitive' to Glynis! They treat you like a retard."

"I don't think we're supposed to say *retard* anymore."

"Nah, that stuff doesn't apply to us. We can say," Flicka smiled craftily, "anything we want."

"Sometimes that bothers me, to tell the truth. I had a big fight with Shepherd around Thanksgiving. About the fact that he *does* let me get away with anything. It's not human. It's patronizing."

"Yeah . . . Once in a while Mom gets mad at me, even though she's trying not to, and I kind of like it. Like, she's being a regular mom. Not some fucking saint."

In the bedroom-cum-entire-universe, Glynis crawled onto the king-size bed and arranged her five pillows, while Flicka grabbed the remote from the mattress. "Sorry about the state of things," Glynis apologized. As ever, the room was littered with prescription bottles, dirty glasses, and the congealed breakfast that Shepherd should have known better than to bring her in bed this morning. The chairs were rumpled with cast-off fleeces and sweaters, while the bed swirled with coverlets of varying weights. *Nest* was the word.

Without asking, Flicka turned off the TV. She had that bossy quality of a kid whom adults were always trying to please. "That's better."

"It creates the illusion of activity."

"Nah, I've experimented in the hospital. Having the TV on all day makes for a gross atmosphere. Silence is better. It doesn't make you feel dirty." Losing her balance half on purpose, Flicka fell back into the bean-bag chair that she always had trouble getting out of. "So. You get tired of this? Having to talk to people when you don't have any stories?"

"I don't like it when people come here and expect *me* to entertain *them*."

"But if they tell you about all the cool shit they're doing, you get pissed off."

Glynis shrugged. "I don't know what I want. So no one can please me. Funny—except you."

"Of course," Flicka said casually. "Misery loves."

"You know, a few nights ago I had a—an episode."

"So you do have a story."

"Not much of one. I haven't told anyone else about it. That night Shepherd had given me—sorry, this isn't the sort of thing you're supposed to talk about—an enema."

"That's okay. Mom has to give them to me all the time. With FD, constipation comes with the territory. Me, I'd rather skip digesting anything to begin with, but that solution in my house isn't too popular."

"Well, with Shepherd . . . I'm not sure people were meant to be that intimate."

"But you're married, right? So you must be used to his sticking a sort-of finger into another hole. What's the diff?"

Glynis's laughter degenerated to a cough. "Sex is a little better than an enema."

"Not that I'll ever know."

"You can't be sure of that. Don't you sometimes like boys?"

"There was one guy last year who asked me to the end-of-term dance. But he was obviously trying to impress the other kids with what a mensch he was. Earn points with his parents and teachers for having such *fine character*. You wouldn't believe the look on his face when I turned him down. I loved it. I'm not about to hire myself out for other kids' college application essays." In the last year or so, Flicka's manner had grown not only sarcastic but flip. "But back to your story."

"Well, the enema wasn't very effective, and the—well, the shit was . . . badly compacted. Dry. Almost like dirt. He had to . . . dig it out. I've worked on not feeling embarrassed, but leaning over the side of the tub with my ass in the air—well, the embarrassment comes back. My husband used to think I was beautiful. He didn't used to touch me and get his fingers cakey with shit. He's sweet about it, tender and businesslike at the same time, but still. That was part of it. Just basically being disgusted, with myself, with what we've come to."

"That wasn't the 'episode'?"

"No, later. Three in the morning. I couldn't sleep. We got up, but I didn't want to be up. I didn't want—I didn't want to be there. Just be there. After the enema, I'd spent, what, at least an hour in the shower to tamp down the itching, but the rashes on my shins were raging again. The ulcers in my mouth made it hard to talk or swallow or even smile—not that I was doing a lot of that. I was weak and exhausted and with the fluid in my lungs . . . This not being able to breathe, it's like drowning . . ."

"Tell me about it. My scarring from pneumonia only gets worse, and it's permanent."

"I—I wanted out. I wanted out so badly I felt crazy. I guess I fell apart. I felt so trapped. It reminded me of the time my sisters ganged up on me when I was twelve. They lured me into a small cabinet in the basement with some kind of dare. And then they locked the hasp. They laughed and left. It's one of my sharpest memories from childhood. Shrieking. For some reason my parents weren't around, or they couldn't hear me. My throat got so raw I lost my voice. I bruised my elbows and knees, pressing against the wood. I guess the cracks around the door must have been big enough that I wasn't really in danger of suffocating. But at the time, I was convinced that I was running out of air. I was locked in that cabinet for a couple of hours. I still have dreams about it."

"So what did you want out of, that night?" asked Flicka, but as if she knew.

"My—myself. Everything. I'm embarrassed to say it, but I must have got hysterical. Shouting something like, 'I want out!' You know, 'Get me out, I want out!'"

Glynis's imitation of herself was deliberately feeble. Her recollection was better than she was pretending. Clawing at Shepherd while he tried to restrain her, she'd drawn blood. He still had the scabs; her fingernails were looser now. Though gasping, she'd still managed to hyperventilate, and had grown light-headed. Since Shepherd would have cleaned everything up it was hard to know, but it was possible she broke things.

"I scared the daylights out of Shepherd," she admitted. "He was afraid I'd hurt myself, flopping and flailing around the bedroom like that. He finally held me down and shoved some marzipan down my throat, on which I almost choked."

Flicka looked unfazed. "Add a lot of retching, and what you're describing is pretty close to an FD crisis. But as for 'wanting out'—there's only one way out, Glyn."

"That's not true," she returned hotly. "I have six more chemos, that's all. My CAT scans could have been a bit better"—the infinitesimal pause was to consider that she was lying; ever since the bad one in September, Glynis had directed her husband and doctor to keep further scan results to themselves—"but we can still beat this. There's the other end of this. Real remission. That's the point. Out the other end, that's the whole *point*."

Flicka raised her eyebrows, making Glynis envious of the girl's having them. Her expression was tolerant. "Uh-huh. And you believe that."

"There's nothing else *to* believe."

"The cleaner way out. I'm not sure it's that bad."

"You can't think like that."

"I can too," Flicka differed, "and I do."

"I can see having black moments. That's what I was describing to you. But you have to hang in there."

"That's what they tell you."

"What do you mean?"

"In one more year, I'm a legal adult. I can do what I want."

"Is that a threat?"

"More like a promise. I'm sick of sticking around as some kind of big favor."

"My sticking around isn't doing anyone any favors," Glynis said quietly. "I'm ruining my husband's life."

"I don't buy that. You're Shep's whole purpose now, the whole reason he gets up in the morning. It's obvious. Not so different from me and my dad."

"Shepherd would rather go live on some desert island."

"Pemba's not a desert. He showed me pictures once. They have a rain forest and everything. Pretty cool."

Glynis fought a burst of rage. What business had Shepherd showing this poor girl pictures of an island she'd never get to, like flashing dirty postcards?

"But I still think . . ." said Flicka. "Well, after a certain point, enough is enough."

"I'm not at that point."

Flicka shrugged. "Only you know."

"I can still get better. Some days I feel it—I feel better."

The girl's expression reminded Glynis of her father-in-law. It was *ministerial*.

"As for my story," said Flicka, abandoning their previous subject as hopeless. "I did this video, for a fund-raising film. For the foundation, for research on FD."

"That was upstanding."

Flicka guffawed, and a burble of saliva drooled down her chin. "Not especially, as it turned out. We were all invited for the *premiere*. I wasn't in it."

"Why didn't they use your video clip? Did they explain?"

"Sure. The head of the foundation said, you know all apologetic, that they weren't sure I had the right *positive attitude*." Flicka yuck-yucked.

"I'd think you'd take that as a compliment."

"Maybe. But that wasn't the real reason. At the reception after, I overheard the head guy talking to one of the board of directors. About how tricky it was to strike the 'right note' for donors. How the kids had to be both 'sick enough' and 'cute enough.' You figure it out. Since I'm definitely," she coughed, "sick enough."

"I think you're cute."

"Spare me. I may have trouble with my corneas, but I'm not blind." Without the aid of a cigarette, Flicka had an ash-flicking dryness. "Otherwise? Something's up with my parents. They don't touch each other anymore. They don't fight anymore, either, which believe it or not is a bad sign. I think they may get a divorce."

"Oh no! I can't believe that!"

"Doesn't matter what we believe. We'll see. Maybe they'll stay together for me. But this feeling—like they're just boarders in the same house, you know, who pass each other in the hall? I think it's one reason Heather's got incredibly fat."

"That's too bad. She's a pretty little girl."

"Pretty, maybe, but she sure isn't *little*. She's got these friends on antipsychotics and anticonvulsants and Ritalin and stuff, and they're all fat, too. So she's been claiming the weight is all caused by her 'cortomalaphrine.'"

"What's that for?"

"It's basically sugar pills, a 'drug' my parents made up to make her feel special. The scam's been going on for years, though I only got wise to it a few weeks ago. I overheard my dad grousing to Mom about how they shouldn't bother to get the 'prescription' filled at the pharmacy at ten bucks a throw, when they could just keep topping up the bottle with M&Ms. I asked him later what he meant, and he came clean. Cracked me up. But this line Heather was pushing about 'side effects' when the real 'side effects' were from Häagen-Dazs . . . Well, it started to piss me off. So I guess I was . . . a little bad." Flicka's smile was sly.

"You told her."

"Yeah. She didn't believe me at first, until I pulverized the whole bottle of 'cortomalaphrine' with my pill grinder and mixed it with water to pour it through my g-tube. Nothing happened. Like, nobody had to cart me to the hospital for an OD. Once she got the deal—boy, was she mad."

"That was a little wicked," said Glynis.

"Yeah," Flicka said lightly. "But you know, I don't get a lot of fun."

"So what did your parents do?"

"They had to put her on some for-real medication, an antidepressant—and with this stiff, like, really polite, you know, *Jackson, dear, would you please pass the salad* thing going on at home, maybe she does need Zoloft. But that has real weight-gain side effects. In the last couple of months she must have put on another five pounds."

"You should ask to borrow a few."

"Yeah, you, too."

"Hey, you get any new additions to your cell phone collection lately?" The very idea that anyone would "collect" ancient specimens of a technology that was still, in her mind, a very modern innovation made Glynis feel old.

"Got a real clunker from back in 2001," said Flicka with the pride of an antique dealer who'd snagged an original Louis XIV. "All square and geeky and ginormous. Show up at my school with that thing, and you'd be laughed out of town. And what about you, when's your next chemo?"

Ah, for the days when guests had asked, "What are you working on?" or "When's your next trip abroad?"

"Next week," said Glynis. "That's why I'm not nodding off on you. It's been a couple of weeks. But they only go ahead with it if my blood count is higher than negative zero."

"Chemo—you've never told me. What's it like?"

Surprisingly, few people ever seemed to ask that. "Chemo" had become such a standard thumbnail for people Glynis's age that everyone assumed they knew what it was like already. They didn't.

"Well, some folks come by themselves, and others have minders. Me, I don't tend to socialize—"

"Big surprise."

"Everyone thinks I'm aloof and snooty."

"Which you are."

It was amazing what Glynis could take from this stunted upstart seventeen-year-old that she wouldn't put up with from anyone else. "You could hardly blame me. Boasting at the top of their lungs about how much they're throwing up, or what colorful new rash they broke out in after their last treatment . . . I'd rather fall apart in private."

"I don't like being around other FD kids, either," said Flicka, ritually wiping another trail of drool from her chin with the sweatband on her wrist. "None of us do. The summer camp is okay, but in the support group it got so almost nobody came. The parents still get together. We freak shows have all cut out."

"I'm surprised at that, actually. There are so few of you. Wouldn't you want to compare notes?"

"If you were me, would you want to look in the mirror? When it's just me, I can sort of forget. You know, I manage. I don't walk too good, but I eventually get where I gotta go. Then I see these other kids and they look spastic. Then I realize I look spastic. I could skip it. I do skip it."

"In case you think I'm totally antisocial, I did have one conversation in the waiting room before my last chemo. I guess I talked to him because I overheard that he had mesothelioma, too, and it's like FD: there aren't many of us. Some contractor, probably worked with asbestos on the job. Turns out he's *still working*. I couldn't believe it. I can't sponge my own countertops on chemo, and he's laying brick. But he can't quit. He has to keep the job to keep the insurance."

"Aren't we lucky, then. Shep and my mom both working crappy jobs so you and me can be tortured in style."

Ever since this horror show began, Flicka had induced in Glynis a curious confessional outpouring. But there were limits. It would not do to explain to this teenager that Shep's "crappy job" was part of his punishment. For Pemba, for scheming about an After-After in which his wife would play no part, and for the fact that she had cancer.

"Anyway," Glynis returned to the subject at hand, "Nancy usually comes with me, this next-door neighbor who used to get on my nerves and now I adore. First we cool our heels in the waiting room checking out the head gear; most of the women wear head scarves like babushkas, so it's like a time warp, back to some shtetl. The men are more creative— pork pies, baseball caps, sometimes a classy fedora. There's one guy who shows up every time in a big Western Stetson studded in silver stars. I'll have taken aprepitant before we left, and I try to time the marzipan about half an hour before. Oh, and I'm sure to be popping more pills while we wait. You know, that leather case your mother got me for carrying all my prescriptions is great. Before, I lived out of a Ziploc. Other visitors show up with scented candles that make me gag. But your mom has a terrific touch with presents."

"Yeah, when it comes to medical stuff, she's pretty cool."

"Oh, and there's this hilarious competition over who gets the good chairs. There are all these comfy La-Z-Boy-type recliners with little partitions to give you pretend privacy. You want to arrive a little early, so you can snag one of the recliners pointed toward the windows, so you can see the Hudson. Though when he wrote *A Room with a View*, I doubt Columbia-Presbyterian was what E. M. Forster had in mind."

"Sorry. Lost me."

"Well, that's what I get for confiding in children." Flicka scowled. She didn't think of herself as a child. "So if I'm quick, I get my primo front-row seat. And they come around with a refreshment cart, believe it or not, just like at Yankee Stadium. They want you to keep drinking fluids, but I don't let them bully me. I get sick of having to drag the drip stand with me to the restroom to pee.

"So then they soak my right arm in warm water, which in my day was the way you got sleeping campers to wet their beds. By the time they put the tourniquet on my upper arm, I'm already feeling woozy, even with the marzipan. It's not that the needle hurts that much; it's the idea of it. So Nancy always holds my other hand and keeps me looking her in the eye while they palpate for a vein, and she tells me these awful recipes . . . like, with Jell-O and pudding mix and canned pears! I think by now she knows I find the idea of cooking with powdered mashed potatoes repulsive, and she tries to concoct the most hideous dishes she can think of. They're more distracting. Then after the glucose flush . . . Well, it's surreal."

"Why 'surreal'?"

"A nurse brings out the chemo in what looks like a kid's book bag— heavy vinyl in school-bus yellow. Except instead of a picture of Daffy Duck, it's got massive uppercase warnings printed on both sides saying, CYTOTOXIC, like, 'Do Not Come Within a Mile of This Shit Because It Will Kill You.' Which it will. And we all sit placidly and let them hook the bag to the drip stand. We page magazines or watch the little TV attached to the chair while this venomous dreck drizzles into our arms for hours. Nurses scurry from chair to chair cheerfully handing out drugs like sweets—all to counter side effects of the dreck. Meanwhile, the IV makes a quiet, regular, lulling sound: *cowakak, cowakak.* You're too young to get the reference, but it sounds like when the needle gets stuck at the end of an LP and won't reject. *Cowakak, cowakak . . .* It puts me to sleep. I mean, we're all obediently mainlining hemlock, docile as sheep, like Jews lining up for the showers. That isn't surreal? In fact, every time I go I flash on—I've never told anyone this; it's too nutty. But have you ever seen *Star Trek*?"

"Give me a break. I may not play records, but I've at least seen *Star Trek*. Dad and I love it, and Mom thinks it's dumb."

"It's supposed to be dumb! Your mother needs to lighten up."

"Don't hold your breath."

"Anyway, there's one episode, something about a planet that's done away with war by having scores of people on both sides of a cease-fire volunteer on a regular schedule to walk into a chamber and be euthanized. It's all very orderly; you know, that program loved alluding to the Nazis. And then Captain Kirk comes in and messes up their thing, giving one of his breathy, emphatic speeches about how they either have to go back to killing each other the old-fashioned way or make peace. So every time I go to Columbia-Presbyterian I picture Captain Kirk bursting into the oncology wing and getting a load of all these delusional lemmings on Planet Bonkers mainlining strychnine. I see him getting self-righteously horrified, and yanking the needles out in a frenzy. Delivering a strident, self-righteous speech about how barbaric it is, how you don't cure disease with poison. Because the whole routine is completely sick. I really do think that years from now people will look back on chemotherapy the way we look back now on bloodletting and leeches."

The door tiddled, and Carol poked her head in. "I don't know who's being naughtier than who, but you're each wearing the other one out."

Glynis invited Carol in, though as a healthy person she was alien, extraneous, from another country whose customs were peculiar and whose citizens had cheating superhero powers; the dynamic quickly grew strained. Glynis considered trying to draw Carol aside and ask what was up with her marriage, until she realized that she didn't care. She was so suddenly, precipitously tired that spots blotched before her eyes and the perimeters of the bedroom closed in; she could not care about anything or anyone, not even Flicka. So instead she telescoped briefly that she was going to be trying yet another chemo cocktail next week, and Carol acted encouraged.

"That doesn't work," Flicka slurred on their way out, "there's always leeches."

Maybe it was the mention of leeches, but as she turned from the door once they were gone, Glynis remembered how shortly after she'd moved to New York, before Shepherd, the kitchen in her tiny Brooklyn walk-up had developed a roach problem. Of course she didn't like roaches, and rather than take them on, get into the nitty-gritty of extermination with Roach Motels and boric acid, she had *turned aside* from them. There was a gap between the standing cupboard and the wall where she stored paper bags from the supermarket, and before long the bags had begun to move. She knew, abstractly, that this was their nest, and couldn't help but detect a subtle rustling sound when she made her breakfast. But she had trained herself when she entered the room to keep her eyes fixed straight ahead, and to make her way around the sink and the refrigerator while carefully tilting her head so that the place where the bags were stored remained in the unattended blur of her peripheral vision. Eventually the nest grew so large that it constituted a dark patch on the wall, but so long as she did not look directly at the patch it did not reveal itself as a teeming mass of repulsive individual insects climbing over one another in a mound, but remained a mere shadow.

The sensation was identical now, a recurrent one that had visited ever since her diagnosis. There was a dark patch, a shadow, that she wouldn't look at directly, and in training her mental gaze resolutely elsewhere, anywhere but at this particular seething corner, most of the time she was able to dismiss it as a trick of the light. But much like the roaches, the longer she ignored it the bigger and blacker it became, and the wider a berth she was obliged to give it in her head. Some nights like this one it would make that same rustling sound, like thousands of tiny legs against brown paper.

Chapter Sixteen

Circumstances might rightly have taught that sex wasn't every-thing. On the loss of sight, for example, all one's other senses were meant to grow more acute, so that the blind developed superhu-man hearing and spine-tingling tactile sensitivity in compensation. By analogy, then, subtracting sex from the equation should have made the whole phantasmagoric cornucopia of life's many other pleasures only the more intense.

Yet sourly contriving the overwrought expression *phantasmagoric cor-nucopia of life's many other pleasures*, Jackson couldn't think of any. What pleasures? He hated his job. His alleged "best friend" was now the one man on earth whom he was driven most to avoid. His elder daughter's sense of balance had so drastically deteriorated that they would soon have to de-mote her to a wheelchair. He could hardly get at the younger kid through the defensive barrage of fat and fast food, though penetrating the vacu-ous bloat of his twelve-year-old's face would entail confronting her rage at having been implicitly ridiculed for years with "cortomalaphrine" and her staunch refusal to learn the word *placebo*. And his wife . . . So near at hand but glassed off, she might have been living in a parallel universe; he imagined that this sense he had of waving and shouting and jumping up and down while being obliviously unseen and unheard must be what it was like to be dead. He no longer lived with a wife; he merely haunted her. She seemed occasionally to discover that a sandwich had been gnawed or a pair of socks had been worn with the same unnerved quality of a confirmed rationalist forced to confront the invisible intrusions of the paranormal.

Furthermore, every subway poster for hair coloring, every television ad for chocolate, every steamy late-night movie and every snatch of bawdy banter at work bannered the fact that to the contrary sex *was* everything. With his vista abruptly switched to black and white, Jackson had never realized just how very important sex was until he lived without it. He wasn't forgoing only the literal activity of round-peg-round-hole, but the whole penumbral range of glances and brushes and touches, whispers and laughters and smiles, the girlish tuckings of a stray auburn wisp behind an ear or the two tender fingers on his forearm that had once electrified his day. So he missed not so much the thing itself but the energy, which powered every other purpose; sex wasn't the goal but the fuel. Flat out of juice, Jackson found no joy in food, which ensured that he ate more of it. Booze no longer induced elation but made him bilious; always hopeful that one more beer would tip him over into the ebullient loud-mouthery of yesteryear, he drank ever more alcohol, too. Indeed, it was only when Carol shot him a sharp, disapproving glance when he reached for another bottle in the fridge that he was persuaded that this sensible, unsuperstitious woman had come to believe in ghosts. Yet so harrowed and hollowed on his own account, Jackson considered too rarely that Carol's own vista had gone colorless, that Carol was running on empty, that through a fatal combination of his own foolishness and her obdurate refusal to forgive it, Carol was living without sex herself.

Meanwhile, the looming debts on his credit cards instilled the curious impression that he was being followed. Walking down the street, Jackson would catch a figure in the corner of his eye, or detect a rustle in the bushes behind him, feeling trailed by an elusive presence that when stared straight down would reveal itself as a wafting tree branch or the neighbor's dog. Yet the presence was always with him. The debts were much worse than Carol had any idea. In an ostensibly generous bid to pull his weight in paperwork, he'd taken over management of the household bills, since Carol handled all the claims for health insurance. To head off her alarm at the sheer profusion of his plastic, he had a couple of cards whose bills were sent to the office; another three were paperless, and he paid their minimums online. He wondered if the subsequent sense of corruption, of unwholesomeness and impending catastrophe, might mirror in some way Glynis's experience of having cancer. He didn't want to diminish what Glynis was going through, but there did seem to be a connection; Jackson had fiscal cancer. Thus even when he was thinking about other matters entirely, a wrongness-and-badness was eating away at him, in the same way that, while Glynis might occasionally be able to concentrate on one of the recipes she would never prepare on that confounded Food Channel of hers, a wrongness-and-badness was eating away at her, too. Terminal illness was insolvency of the body. Glynis and Jackson both lived in dread of that unnamed day around the corner when debt collectors would thump on the door to demand their pound of flesh.

Yet just as already having come down with the worst disease imaginable might drive you to take up smoking . . . Just as teenage girls might throw contraceptive caution to the winds because they were already pregnant . . . Just as the morbidly obese must so often say fuck it, I already weigh six hundred pounds that I'll never lose, so why not have another piece of coconut cake if I feel like it . . . Jackson was sunk so deeply in a financial hole that it didn't seem to matter at any given point if he dug the hole a teaspoon deeper still. Too, he seemed to be caught in a feedback loop: The debts made him feel bad. Larger debts would make him feel worse. In endangering his own future and his wife's future and his children's future he *should* feel worse, so to flagellate himself he made them larger. Some days it was dogs, others a magazine subscription or shirt from LLBean that he could have lived without; in fact, Jackson was fascinated to learn just how much money you could run through without appreciably improving your life or acquiring anything of value. This spending-in-place had become a game he played, a little entertainment in self-torture, and he took a freakish delight in the discovery that you could fritter all your money on utter trivia and nothingness and *nobody would stop you.* In a hallucinogenic fit of misguided piety, he could actually tap his account number and security code into a website to buy ten gross of deformed plastic menorahs for fourteen thousand dollars, and the charge would go right through.

Granted, he did not want to lose the house. Not only was the home equity loan outstanding; they'd still not paid off the original mortgage. But foreclosure was an abstraction. They lived in the house. He went home every day to the house. He had a key. His clothes hung in its closets; the food for their breakfast was stashed in its kitchen; his mail arrived daily at this address. Something about the sheer three-dimensionality of the place, the great big reach-out-and-touch-it, having-slept-here-most-of-his-married-lifeness of the place, made the prospect of repossession utterly incomprehensible, and if he did not understand it, it could not happen.

The habit wasn't charitable, but Jackson sometimes thought back bitterly to the early days at Knack, when he and Shep went out on jobs side by side—when the company was basically a two-man operation that occasionally had to contract with licensed plumbers or electricians but was otherwise a de facto partnership. So when he sold up, Shep should really have cut him in for half. Shep should have made him on paper what he was in practice. Then the company would have gone for that cool mil and he'd have five hundred K to float him painlessly through this ocean of bills. Better still, maybe he'd have put his foot down and refused to sign a rash deal drafted merely so that Shep could run off on a fool's errand to some Third World dung heap. Why, he could have pressed the guy to admit—and in those more credulous days pressed himself to admit—that Pemba, along with its many arbitrary antecedents, was a crackpot fantasy on which Shep would never act in real life. In that case they'd now still co-own a thriving Internet enterprise worth four times the 1996 sticker price, and Jackson Burdina, not Randy Fucking Pogatchnik, would be rich.

Slumped in his cubicle in February, Jackson registered rancorously that it was, of all things, Valentine's Day. It did occur to him briefly that he could go all out and make one more bid for Carol's clemency, like the many bids that had failed so spectacularly in the past. But he could see it: A dozen roses crammed perfunctorily into a pickle jar, with no effort made to arrange them in an attractive array. Chocolates slipped distractedly on a high shelf with a remark about making sure to keep them away from Heather. Not so much as a peck on the cheek, but a formal, "Why, thank you, Jackson, that's very sweet," delivered with the same impersonal coolness with which his wife declined telephone solicitations that were in violation of their household's listing on the Do Not Call Registry. Basically, his wife had put herself on a private Do Not Call Registry, a restraining order that applied explicitly to her own husband, which also knocked edible-crotch underwear totally out of the ballpark.

Did he not deserve a Valentine present himself? And in preference to another plaid flannel shirt, why not put himself further in hock to secure something that he genuinely needed?

Jackson had never done such a thing, but with Pogatchnik out, Shep AWOL on another personal day, and his workforce dispersed to the leaky faucets of three New York boroughs, he entered "escort service" and "brooklyn ny" into his search engine.

His pulse may have been pounding, but meeting his latest credit card purchase in a Fifth Avenue Starbucks was weirdly mundane. The girl in the picture he'd picked on the Web had long auburn hair, full breasts, and a remote expression that you'd think would have been a turnoff, but he missed the cat-and-mouse games that had once kept his wife just teasingly out of reach, and maybe he still wanted to have to work for it. He took a minute surveying the other patrons hammering at their laptops beside flat cappuccinos, only recognizing his Valentine's Day present to himself at last because she was bulging from the red leotard she'd described on the phone. In fact, giving a cheerful wave, she saw him first; doubtless the sudden-cold-feet look on his face—that darting glance at the door through which he might make a quick, skulking exit—was one that "Caprice" (or whatever her name was) confronted all the time.

"Sorry," said Jackson, pulling out a chair and immediately regretting that, since he just wanted to head out and get this over with. "You're not the girl in the picture."

"Oh, we never are, honey," she said with a laugh. "I don't know where they get those photos. Say, do you want a coffee?"

A double bourbon would have been more like it. Still, Jackson let her order a coffee for him so he could check her out, taking a beat to realize as she stood beside him that the arched eyebrows were for cash; all he had was a ten. While she stood in line, he confirmed that her figure wasn't bad, if a little heavy in the ass. He'd picked one of the pricier sites, so at least she wasn't tricked out in feathers, but wore a classy, form-fitting black suit. He might have been peeved about the switcheroo, but "Caprice" was at least—well—white. She was nominally blond—maybe the girls were color-coded—though he would have liked to return to the days when dying your hair was a disgraceful secret, and women wouldn't leave the house showing a millimeter of dark roots, of which his escort shamelessly sported a solid inch. The breasts, he noted on her return, were fake, too. Maybe in her late twenties, the woman was passably pretty, but the proportions of her face were askew. You got used to such anomalies in the likes of an actress like Julia Roberts, but on a hooker you couldn't help but envision how her mouth might have got that wide.

Sipping his grande coffee of the day—only a couple of bucks, and she'd kept the change—Jackson realized that this meeting-in-public ritual was mostly so she could check *him* out. The surest route to seeming normal was to be reassuringly dull. "So, how long you been at this—job?"

"Don't worry, I'm not a lifer," she said breezily, and Jackson had the unexpected impression (how was it that you could tell, with everybody, after under a minute? What fleck in the eye gave them away?) that she was smart. "I'm supporting myself through a course in Human Resourcing at Brooklyn Community College. You know, what they used to call Personnel Management. I figured, what could be a better way to get an on-the-ground education in *personnel management*?"

She'd probably aired the quip before, but it at least broke the ice. By the time they left, he'd shared his (reassuringly dull) job, adding that on his own time he was also writing a book. What was such an encounter good for if not a little rounding up? It wouldn't do to admit that he was still working on the title. He even tried out his latest on her: *The Myth of* the *"Law-Abiding Citizen": How We Gullible Goody-Goodies Are Brain-washed into Shit-Eating Compliance (or) You Have No Idea How Much You Could Get Away With If You Only Had Balls.*

"It's about how we're all manipulated into getting with the program," he explained with some of his old ebullience on their way out the door. "You know those cheesy TV shows like *World's Wildest Police Videos*? Some loser in a pickup streaks down the highway at a hundred miles per hour in the wrong direction, with our brave men in blue in hot pursuit. Does the villain ever successfully abscond into the sunset? Not on your life! The sucker's always cuffed in the dirt by the end of the clip. It's social engineering, and it ain't subtle, neither. *Crime doesn't pay. You can't get away.* Same as all those straight-ass cop shows, from *Dragnet* to *Law and Order*. Nobody ever gets away with jack. Pure mind-fuck propaganda."

He was standing out in the cold with a prostitute, and he was blathering about politics. She looked amused. "You know, there's no reason to be nervous."

"I'm not nervous," he said. "I talk this way all the time."

"No wonder you need an escort agency."

She was being droll. He should like that. After all, he couldn't do this impersonally; it wasn't in his nature. He wanted her to like him. He wanted to impress her, which was pathetic. "Gonorrhea isn't the problem," he said, and then as what he'd actually said echoed in his ears he kicked himself. "I mean, *logorrhea*. See, my wife is—what you'd call cold to my advances."

She kept her mouth shut, but couldn't control the little smile.

"Yeah, yeah, you've heard that before. *My wife is frigid.* Well, she's not frigid. And don't get the idea I'm stuck with some support-hose house-frowse. My wife is gorgeous." He kept himself from adding, *better looking than you are.*

"You don't need to apologize to me, 'Jonathan.' So, want to get a drink, bite to eat?"

"I don't have much time. Better skip to the main event, you know?" He'd rung Carol this afternoon to tell her he'd be a couple of hours late, because he was overseeing the repositioning of some kitchen cabinets whose installation had been botched, leaving a space for the fridge that was only two feet wide . . . He could have forgone the embellishments, since Carol wasn't even listening. What was odd about the conversation was that lying hadn't felt any different from all the other times he'd called and told the truth. Regardless of the details, these days the two of them were always lying to each other, really. That's why the literal lie had been almost a relief. It was honest lying.

Caprice led him to an innocent-looking hotel, a converted brownstone on Union Street that defied the seediness of his imagination. At check-in, they were brisk and blithe as he rifled his wallet for a Visa with paperless billing that had just, to his incredulity, further extended his credit limit. In the room upstairs, cloth lampshades danced with hokey tassels; the bedspread was a homey chenille, the print over the stead an exuberant color lithograph of the fireworks over the Brooklyn Bridge when it was first opened in 1883. The joint was, believe it or not, kinda cute.

Jackson studied the print while he undid the two top buttons of his shirt, but couldn't unbutton any further. "You know, a week after that bridge opened a rumor spread it was about to collapse. Stampede killed twelve people."

Caprice came up behind him and slid her hands into his trousers' front pockets. "You don't say."

"You're laughing at me."

She was obliged to deny it. "You're right."

Jackson turned around and slipped his hands around her hips, startled by their unfamiliar contour. Still, just the heat of her body through the fabric stirred him in the way that of course he'd been anxious about. He wasn't hot for the perfume; Carol rarely wore commercial scents, and what really turned him on was the musky waft off her skin when she'd been hauling Flicka in and out of the car all afternoon—a deep, loamy smell like rotting logs. If he'd really wanted to ensure rising to this occasion, he should have insisted that Caprice wear one of Carol's dirty T-shirts.

"You one of these girls doesn't kiss? I read you folks don't like to kiss."

"You've *read about it*." She kissed him lightly, no tongue. "I think your problem is too many books, buster."

Something about the *buster*. "You're still laughing at me."

"Did you also *read* this sort of thing has to be grim? You'd be surprised, but sometimes I have a great time. And you're a piece of work. You are—hilarious."

Jackson reclined on the bed as she shimmied out of the short pencil skirt and removed her jacket; her care to drape the suit smoothly over the chair was comfortingly domestic. The red leotard proved a teddy; how efficient. Carol's underwear tended to be simpler . . . He wasn't sure if he should be thinking about Carol, although he didn't seem to have a choice.

In retrospect, this is where he should have turned the light off.

Caprice slid next to him still wearing the red teddy. She had nice legs. Carol's thighs were just starting to . . . Whoa, this girl sure got right down to business. Carol didn't usually . . . That knee slipped between his legs was delish . . . Jackson flinched when she pressed a little too hard on his fly but managed to cover the wince, thinking, still a little sensitive, but maybe that was fine, because what was wrong with sensitive? She unbuckled and unzipped him, and he inhaled sharply at the sudden smack of cold air, the welcome release from his boxers, thinking maybe she could suck him first, go ahead baby, *suck it*—

Caprice had no sooner laid him open than she recoiled. "What's *that*?"

"Well, what do you think it is?"

Caprice took her knee back. "What the hell happened, were you born with some kind of defect?"

"I was born perfectly normal!" Or at least that's what Carol had been lecturing him for the last year.

"Look, I'm sorry, I can't do this." Caprice got up and started pulling her suit back on.

"Why not? My money's not good enough? You're supposed to fuck me, not fall in love."

"I just can't, it's too . . . Look, I'm not that hard up, okay? I'm afraid you're stuck with the hotel, but I can have the agency reverse the charges on the escort. There are some other outfits who cater to . . . You can look them up. Who specialize in—disabilities. Special needs."

Jackson fastened his fly furiously. "*Special needs?* I have some scar tissue, but I'm not an idiot!"

"Whatever you wanna call it, it's not my bag." When the zipper on her skirt snagged, this hitherto unflappable young woman seemed to panic, and when she finally got the zipper to budge she wore the expression of the sort of resourceful heroine in thrillers who barely manages to pick a lock with a hairpin before the serial killer busts in the window. "Good luck on the book!" she said, remembering her manners at the door. "I—I'll be sure to look out for it!"

The following morning Jackson was already at work when Shep arrived, because Shep was late—and not for the first time. Jackson would have liked to cover for him, but Pogatchnik was standing in his office doorway, lying in wait. Under his employer's scathing eye, Shep settled at his station, removing his sheepskin jacket to reveal a muscle T patterned in Hawaiian flowers; Jackson rued his friend's recent fleshiness, since otherwise the sleeveless T would have shown off a musculature that he himself had always envied. Shep wriggled out of snow pants, underneath which he was wearing the loud Bermuda shorts that Pogatchnik favored in summer, except that it was February. Lastly, he withdrew a miniature battery-powered fan that he propped atop his terminal. All part of the ongoing war over the thermostat (at only 10:00 a.m., it must already have been nearing ninety degrees in here), but if Shep was going to antagonize Pogatchnik with that getup, he should at least have been on time. Something was going on with the guy, something a little reckless and unhinged, but in a peculiarly quiet way; aside from the gear, Shep's demeanor was one, apropos of a certain pending bestseller, of *shit-eating compliance.* Meanwhile, the rest of the staff were silent, their eyes trained studiously on computer screens yet angled in such a way as to keep Shep and Pogatchnik within their peripheral vision.

"Nice of you to join us, Knacker," said Pogatchnik. "I'm, like, overcome by the honor of your presence. To what do we owe the royal visit? This extraordinary sighting of Lord Slacker, slumming among the teeming masses and deigning to come to work?"

"My wife was running a temperature of a hundred and three yester-day," Shep said evenly, booting up his computer and adjusting the fan. "Another infection. I was up all night in the hospital."

"You aware that chronic tardiness and absenteeism are grounds for dismissal—period, in any court you care to drag me into?"

"Yes, sir. And I can see how you might be driven to drastic measures if it were merely a matter of an employee who sleeps late. That being impossible when said employee has never got to bed."

"On top of looking the other way when you waltz in here whenever you please, you expect me to feel sorry for you?"

"No, sir. I expect you to take into consideration the exceptional med-ical circumstances in my family, as would any reasonable, fair-minded employer like yourself."

"Guess that makes me *un*reasonable, then. You're fired, Knacker."

Shep froze. His gaze burned straight at the screen. "Sir. Mr. Pogatch-nik. I sympathize with your frustration. And I promise to try and arrive on time and put in as many regular workdays as my current difficulties allow. With your permission, I would like to observe that I have contin-ued to keep up with my responsibilities. The many complaints about our substandard service"—here he paused, and Jackson could hear the im-politic inference, *our once-exemplary but now-substandard service*—"have not been piling up. As you're well aware, my wife's medical care is de-pendent on the insurance provided by this company. On her account and not my own I would beg you to reconsider."

"You're shit out of luck. I didn't hire your wife, and I don't run a hos-pice. You got problems with the system, write your congressman. Now, get your stuff, and get out."

Pogatchnik had made plenty of threats, but this time was different. Never mind the irony that in the olden days at Knack less-than-handy Randy had been a notoriously unpunctual sick-out artist himself; the game was up.

In recognizing that this fat, freckled erstwhile employee was not vul-nerable to persuasion, Shep dropped his shoulders. His back straight-ened, and his body realigned into such a relaxed, symmetrical pose that he might have passed for a yoga master. His mouth drifted into a fatalistic smile. He looked serene. Jackson thought he understood. When you've been afraid of something for long enough and then it comes to pass, the terrible thing is a release. You embrace it. You're glad of the badness. For in the belly of the badness there is no more fear. You cannot dread what has already happened.

As Shep logged off his terminal and crossed the room to retrieve an empty stationery carton, his bearing returned to that of the man whom Jackson used to revere and whom he'd made sometimes embarrassingly obvious efforts to emulate. At last the guy moved with smooth assurance and not like a groveling toady. Cool Hand Luke was back. Jackson hadn't realized how much he'd miss this man: powerful, competent, and stalwart. A man you could count on—who would never let your pets starve or your houseplants die while you were on vacation, who would never misplace the spare keys to your house. Who wouldn't bat an eye at extending a loan to a pal, be that five bucks or five thousand. Who wouldn't keep track. Who wouldn't expect it back. A reliable, generous man of the sort now an endangered species in this country, where everyone had a hand out, and therefore naturally prone to being taken advantage of by all and sundry. A man who pursued one eccentric hobby that most people considered ridiculous, but that it behooved Jackson to regard as endearing, for Shep Knacker's fruitcake fountains burbled a few wellsprings of whimsy into a life otherwise austerely pragmatic. A man who for all his kindness and hard work had asked for only one thing in the end, really: to be let go. Since, like it or not, he'd now got what he'd wished for, it was a goddamned shame that the timing was so piss-poor.

Glowering from his doorway, Pogatchnik looked strangely unsatisfied, having registered the corollary of a dread fulfilled: when you got a really fun thing over with, you could no longer look forward to it. Meanwhile, Shep strolled through the cubicles making good-humored remarks to his co-workers, shaking hands, gripping the odd shoulder, giving forearms a reassuring pat. Despite the zany beachcomber attire, any stranger scanning this room would immediately assume that the forceful, authoritative character in the Hawaiian print was the boss.

Well, he was. That's what Pogatchnik could never bear, and that's why Shep had been fired. Whatever the law, Shep was still the boss and he always had been, while Pogatchnik had the soul of a peon, and even sacking Knacker would never change that.

Thanks to Pogatchnik's ban on "personal paraphernalia," Shep didn't have to untape a collage of family snapshots, and the clearing off was brief. Coat over one arm, carton under the other, Shep surveyed the office at the door.

The website designer shouted, "Yo, Knacker, left something behind, didn't you?"

Shep raised his eyebrows.

"Your fucking company, man!"

Squelched at first, a seditious laugh rippled through the staff. The accountant cried, "Yeah, take me with you!"

Jackson had taken his exclusion from Shep's round of goodbyes as a compliment; he wouldn't have wanted to be one more co-worker. "Let me give you a hand with that," he said.

Though Shep could handle the single carton on his own, he said, "Thanks," and they left together.

They walked in silence to deposit the box in Shep's car. "I had to sell Glynis's Golf," Shep remarked mildly, closing the trunk. "Fortunately, she hasn't noticed yet."

"She still thinks she's going back to driving it?"

"Probably. Or I don't know what she thinks."

"Living in her own reality the way she's been," said Jackson. "Not facing the music. Must make it, for you—kind of lonely."

"Yeah," Shep said appreciatively. "You could say that. Listen, you'd better get back. Don't want to get sacked, too. You know he'd leap at the chance."

"Let him. You can't imagine that I'm gonna keep working there, with you gone."

"You might surprise yourself. Bills to pay. Don't think you have to do anything dramatic on my account."

"Don't worry," said Jackson. "If I do anything dramatic, it'll be on my own account."

Funny, the resolve didn't manifest itself all at once. No light went on—or out. Neither his mind nor his humor took a sharp turn south. But it was right around the point that Jackson could not picture toiling in that stultifying cubicle one more afternoon, and could not picture earnestly applying to toil in any other cubicle either, that what had for some months now been a resort—a theoretical island of respite in his head not so different from Shep's, his own private Pemba—began to solidify into a land mass to which he might actually travel. Because this blank he drew, it wasn't from a failure of imagination or even a refusal, à la Glynis, to face the music. It was not denial, but recognition: that he could not conjure an image of himself slogging once more through the paces of meaningless employ, numbly poking his head above the soil as one more perennial in the government's crops of citizenry, because he would not. That was not what was going to happen.

"I think," Jackson announced lightly, "this is a *personal day.*"

Shep shrugged. "How about a walk, then? Prospect Park, for old times' sake. Since from now on I don't seem to have anything but *personal days.*"

"Only if you put on that coat. Just looking at you makes me cold." Shep dutifully pulled on the sheepskin. "Pants, too," Jackson chided.

Shep looked down at his bare legs and grinned. "I don't think so. Something about this getup suits my mood."

"You look like a nut."

"That's what I mean."

So they launched down Seventh Avenue. That was the next moment, the juncture at which his hitherto hazy mental Pemba sharpened another increment, as if focused in the viewfinder of a point-and-shoot throw-away camera: when he realized with certainty that this was the last walk. That they were rounding onto Ninth Street together for the last time.

"So—how *are* you?" Shep asked, with the same emphatic inflection that Ruby had used in her sister's hospital room.

Jackson took a moment and did seriously consider spilling his guts— about the debts, about having already defaulted on the minimums for one Visa and a Discover card. About the surgery, the infection, the ham-handed reconstructions that just made everything worse. About the revelation on Union Street that apparently he could not even pay a woman to have sex with him. But it felt too late and it would take too long. More to the point, at the end of any confidential outpouring, nothing would have changed. Chances were, of course, that it would all come out in the end, but that was acceptable. It would give them all something to talk about, and they would need topics; they would need reasons. These weren't really the reasons, but the explanation would be tidy and they would cling to it. As for the real reason, Jackson couldn't be bothered to formulate it, since one of the many appetites of which he felt himself letting go was any desire to be understood; gloriously, today's Get Out of Therapy Free card also exempted him from any obligation to understand himself.

Nevertheless, he did not want to keep hurtfully shutting Shep out, so he confided out of kindness. "Flicka's falling apart. That being inevitable is no help. My marriage is falling apart, and that *not* being inevitable—does that make it *evitable*, is that a word? Well, the *evitability* is no help, either."

"I'm sorry to hear that. What's happened?"

Jackson tried to speak honestly but to keep it short. Shep was the one with the real problems right now, and he shouldn't be selfish. In fact, presented with the cheerful immanence of the very sort of permanent vacation that Shep had planned for years, and no longer gazing at his own private Pemba from a distance but coming to view the foreshortened present from the perspective of the island itself, Jackson felt truly and deeply unselfish for perhaps the first time in his life. "The truth is, I never felt I deserved her. She's so good-looking, and really capable at everything she turns her hand to, whether it's landscaping or IBM or adjusting to the curse of a kid with a condition so rare that only three hundred and fifty other people in the world have it, too. And she's so, well, *good*. But I guess she finally came around to my way of seeing things. Now she doesn't think I deserve her, either."

Maybe it was the calm, philosophical tone that Jackson had assumed, the uninvested flippancy of that last line, but Shep turned and looked hard at his friend and seemed disturbed by what he saw, or disturbed by what he could not discern, and he said nothing.

As they entered the park, Jackson was reminded of their conversation strolling this circuit about a year ago, a chill ramble during which Shep had vowed not to buy Glynis "turkey-burger medical care"; now the guy had gone and bought top-shelf, aged-Angus-crown-rib-roast medical care, and Glynis was still going to croak. Another happy advent that Jackson was now planning to skip. The opt-out didn't strike him as cowardly, but as sensible. Why, the miseries that he soon planned to escape were too numerous to list: Flicka checking out; maybe Carol getting cancer, too; Heather ballooning even bigger and not being able to find a boyfriend; the unpleasant scene in which he came clean to Carol about the debts because a For Sale by Lender sign was about to be planted outside their house; not to mention the hurricanes, crop failures, stock crashes, and civil wars that the rest of the world pissed down on you just for getting out of bed in the morning. Good fortune being mostly about dodging bad fortune, that made him presently one of the luckiest guys on the planet.

Jackson was waiting for Shep to raise the matter of his rudely cancelled health insurance. Instead he talked about his father.

"I've felt bad about not visiting him," he said. "Not being able to come near him with this *c-diff* thing because of Glynis. They can't seem to kill it off. Round and round of antibiotics. Afraid I lost my temper with one of the nurses on the phone a few weeks ago. But get this: when I groused about how their outfit obviously has some cleanliness issues, and if they'd only start washing their hands? She *laughed*. She told me that, in lab experiments? If you put *c-diff* bacteria in a Petri dish with this violent disinfectant they use, *it grows*."

"That shit multiplies in the stuff they use to kill it? Man, you gotta admire an organism that determined. Lotta people think someday the human race'll be replaced by some higher, more evolved life form. Me, I figure the future belongs to the tiny and mindless. Few thousand years from now, Earth's gonna be crusted solid with nothing but rhinoviruses, head lice, mildew, and streptococcus."

"You sound like you're looking forward to it."

"I am," said Jackson. "Immensely."

"Dad's lost more weight, they say, and he can't afford to. But the last two or three phone calls, what's knocked me out isn't just that he sounds so weak. He says he no longer believes in God."

"Not possible," said Jackson. "It's just a bad patch, or he's pulling your leg."

"He's totally serious. He says the closer he gets to the end the more he can see—that there's nothing to see. He says he doesn't know what took him so long, since it's so simple, but when you die, you die. And he says that after he's been a faithful Presbyterian minister for all these years and then he's allowed to suffer months of humiliation—lying in liquefied feces, having his privates roughed up by an irritable overweight nurse from Ghana with a cold wet sponge, well—there just can't be anyone out there. He says it's what a lot of his parishioners tried to tell him when a kid died or they came out the other side of an auto accident a drooling paraplegic and he wouldn't listen, but now he gets it."

"Wow. That's actually pretty sophisticated."

"I thought it was horrible."

Jackson stopped and turned. "I thought you didn't buy into that Christian malarkey."

"I don't especially. I mean, I don't. It's a pretty good story, but too fancy for me—all that son of God and virgin birth stuff. And any religion that claims our one species, on this one planet, circling this one star, just happens to be the whole purpose of the universe, the be-all and end-all—well, it's suspect, isn't it? When you look up at the sky, with everything else out there? It's self-serving and, on a statistical level, plain unlikely. Also, some of the things I've seen in these really poor, scraping countries that Glynis and I have traveled to: open sewers, running sores, little kids going blind from parasites in the water . . . It doesn't make you think there's anyone up there in control—or at least not anyone decent. Still, Dad's believing has always made it relaxing for me not to. If I think there's nothing and *he* thinks there's nothing, too . . . I don't know. Suddenly it's all a little chilling. In fact, I've found myself in a weird position. I feel like what I should really be doing, if I care about him? Is trying to talk him back into believing something I don't. Like I should be reading him scripture from the Book of Job. Belting out 'Bringing in the Sheaves' on the phone. Because I've found these conversations incredibly depressing. Christ, I thought people were supposed to *find* religion when they were afraid of dying."

"Glynis hasn't."

"She's too perverse. Even if she saw the light, she'd pretend she hadn't, if only to spite her sister. Besides, she's so convinced she isn't dying that she refuses to even be afraid of it."

"If willpower has anything to do with it, Glynis will live to a hundred."

"Do you believe in an afterlife? Other people's kind—small *A*."

"Nah," said Jackson. "Besides, I don't want one. I mean, who would want more of *this*?"

"I think the idea is there's no mesothelioma or Handiman-dot-com."

"Even so. I just get tired, man."

"Of what?"

"Everything, man. Fucking everything."

Shep shot him another one of those looks.

They passed the corral, where a young woman was walking a horse that looked cold. She side-eyed the guy in the sheepskin coat and Bermuda shorts, but may have been comforted that at least the stocky guy walking alongside looked halfway normal. Yet mostly Prospect was deserted, its branches bared claws, its gruel of a sky lumpy and congealed. The tarmac of the perimeter roadway was mottled with salt, while on the verge clumps of hard black ice were evaporating to gradually reveal their chunks of frozen dog shit. The city shouldn't even have parks in the winter, really. They were just wrong.

Shep's delivery was as gray and stark as the landscape: "I may have to declare bankruptcy."

Until now, Jackson had been sliding into a nice coasting elegiac apathy, such an anesthetic rising-above that he could see their two figures rounding the bend by the Fifteenth Street exit as if levitating from overhead. But Shep's revelation dropped him butt first on the pavement. "Whoa, you're kidding! After all that money you got for Knack?"

"Forty percent co-insurance. My dad. Amelia's premiums . . . Meanwhile, I've sold everything I can shed on eBay: Glynis's car, my fishing tackle, my record collection; came close to selling the Wedding Fountain, but I was afraid it would just get melted down for the silver, and in the end I couldn't do it. All that amounted to spare change, anyway; barely covered one blood test and a PET scan. Especially after capital gains, turns out you were right all along. I wasn't rich. A million dollars isn't that much money."

"Does it make any difference if—if Glynis . . . ?"

Gently, Shep took the thought from him, in a gesture of almost physical generosity, like lifting that carton of chattel from Handy Randy from Jackson's arms at the car. "If she dies sooner? Yeah, that might spare me. And, sure, I've thought of that. Couldn't help it. This practicality of mine, you know, it can be a curse. You can't imagine how awful that is, to think thoughts like that."

"But wouldn't it be better for her, too, at the end of the day?"

"What are you suggesting, I should smother her with a pillow? It's not my business to conclude that for her. She's hanging on. With a fistful of pills every hour, and tiny pureed meals whenever I can force them down her, she's hanging on. So I have to assume she wants to. Still, even one more month, with no insurance, and I'm wiped out. Worse than wiped out. Up to my neck in red ink, and now I don't even have a salary."

"You'll probably get severance."

"It'll just go to creditors."

"Well, maybe going broke is okay, then. See this thing with Glynis through, let the bills pile up, then file the papers. Draw a line. Start fresh. That's what bankruptcy is for." Whimsically, Jackson entertained the same solution to his own debts, then dismissed the idea. Not because of the ignominy. It was too much trouble.

"I've always kept up my end of things," said Shep. "You've ragged on me for letting people like Beryl take advantage, but I've never cared about that. I care about holding my head high, being someone other people can depend on. Now I'll be just another deadbeat, like everybody else."

Yet Jackson's initial burst of disgust on his friend's account had already sloughed to boredom. He would have called Shepherd Knacker's fiscal disgrace an injustice if he were still interested, but he wasn't. Funny, the high-octane mix of emotions that had fueled his whole adult life—outrage, consternation, and contempt—appeared to have abruptly run out like a tank of gas. He would have liked, of course, to foment on Shep's behalf, if only, like this ritual shuffle around Prospect Park, for old times' sake. But he couldn't have worked up a proper tirade with a gun to his head.

They walked the full four-mile circuit this time, during the last long rise keeping their own counsel. When they returned to Shep's car, Jackson wanted to impart something wise and memorable, but he couldn't think of anything besides "Take care of yourself," since somebody would have to. Still, though they'd never been big on clutching and pawing, after an awkward dawdle by the driver's door Jackson reached out and embraced his best friend hard and for a long time. Once they'd separated and Jackson waved before turning to hunch down the avenue he thought that a good hug had been the ticket, really. Better than being clever.

Heading home in the early afternoon of what would prove the ultimate *personal day*, Jackson strolled with an accelerating ease and lightness, possessed of the same serenity that had descended on Shep at Handy Randy when the worst had come to pass. He felt cleansed—as if Gabe Knacker were wrong, and some poor fuck really had died for his sins; as if he'd just stepped out of the shower in the days before he was immediately driven to bundle his groin out of view with a bath towel. Jackson wasn't worried about the credit card bills anymore; he did not feel followed. He was able to see yesterday's encounter with "Caprice" in a comical light, and rather regretted that he would not cash in over beers on this cracking good story. He was a little sad about Shep being broke and unemployed, but it was a soft, comforting sadness like the overcast sky. Shep's plight clearly illustrated that there was no point to anything and there was no relationship between virtue and reward and there never had been. But this perception was calm and straightforward and factual, and he was able to consider it evenly and placidly, as he might have reminded himself to buy paper napkins.

The sensation of being perfectly untroubled was a reminder of how contrastingly tortured he'd felt over the last year or so, if not for most of his life. In retrospect, he should have promised himself this island respite long ago. Shep was a psychological genius, really. Everyone should have a Pemba.

The mild, balming insouciance soothed him most of the way home. He felt tired, of course, but it was a nice weariness, like after weight training. Experimentally, he called up a host of topics over which he'd got exercised in the past: the Alternative Minimum Tax, lax education standards, and the public-servant parking fix in Lower Manhattan aroused nothing but amiable indifference. He didn't care about excessive building regulations, and he didn't care about Iraq. He didn't care if one of his crews let wet cement drizzle down a customer's patio drain, and he didn't care if they left gouges in drywall from a recoiling hydraulic nail gun. If he were totally honest, at this very moment he didn't care if someday soon Flicka just didn't wake up, since that was a good way to go and she was going to die anyway. He didn't care about leaving Carol in the financial lurch, because she was an attractive, resourceful woman who would find another husband in no time.

As for cheating the feds out of another twenty years' worth of pilfering his income, the sly little opt-out he had in mind was spitefully ingenious, the ultimate tax deduction. He would deduct himself. In fact, it would serve those assholes right if in an act of spontaneous civil defiance the entire working population of this country followed his lead overnight. Where would that leave the Mooches? High and fucking dry. *Oh shit, where did all the slaves go, where is my breakfast?*

Yet this brief sense of gratification immediately gave way to a deeper, sleepier weariness far more encompassing—like being a boy surrounded by toys he'd outgrown, when all the other kids were still enthralled with them. The sensation was probably commonplace for a man of ninety; if so, arriving there in half the time was at least efficient. It started on

Windsor Place, whose solid, palatial dwellings from the 1920s he had always envied. Suddenly the amount of work it must have taken to jigsaw the fiddly wooden filigree that trimmed the big, indolent brick porches seemed incomprehensible; it seemed more incomprehensible still that anyone would bother to repaint, repair, or replace this vain architectural detail, and rather than admire the geometric lacing one more time Jackson thought: *they can have it.* Then the same painless generosity spread to everything in a giddy hurtling rush, like that little threshold you cross when cleaning out closets, and suddenly, instead of agonizing over every heel-worn but still wearable pair of boots, parting with all the junk you'll never use anyway is no longer a sacrifice but a joy. *They can have it*: not just Sunday lunches in Bay Ridge trying fruitlessly to impress his parents with how their son wasn't some lowly slob—he was Shep Knacker's *right-hand man*, or later he was *in management*—but the very tradition of Sunday lunches, and the day of the week itself. Thank-you notes and surreptitious spongings of gravy stains; heat-crimped packaging that only opened with pruning shears, and incompatible software. Ramadan, Columbus Day, and picnics. National self-determination, recipes for banana bread, and Amazon.com. Bungee-cord jumping, suicide bombing, and falling in love. Space stations, purdah, and male pattern baldness. Right-to-life protests, self-defrosting refrigerators, and hemlines; Christmas-tree air-fresheners, presidential assassinations, and ten-year retrospectives on the fall of apartheid. Micro-lending, woodworm treatments, and anti-vivisection leagues. West Bank settlements and genetically modified corn; nuclear antiproliferation treaties, National Salt Awareness Week, and fluoridated water. Narco states, dust ruffles, and bus shelter vandalism; lucky numbers, favorite colors, and button collections. Tribal scarring and Polka Album of the Year awards; tea ceremonies, buzz cuts, and alternative energy. Feature films, the Fifth Amendment, and weather forecasts; Arctic exploration, affirmative action, and cell phone contracts. The South Beach Diet, elder abuse, and the Battle of Waterloo; burkhas, bedsteads, and the designated hitter rule; heirlooms, insoles, and the European Union. From IEDs, GDPs, and MP3s to Gore-Tex®, gas shortages, and gardening tips: he was just sick of it, man. Of people and their shit.

When Jackson reached his front door, its bolted top lock confirmed that no one was home. Heather had a Diversity Awareness Workshop after school, and Carol was taking Flicka to her food therapist.

He ambled down to the basement in no particular hurry. He dislodged the metal box concealed inside the pyramid of the three cartons of prefinished oak, the ample leftovers from reflooring Heather's room that the manufacturer hadn't allowed him to return. He'd wildly mismultiplied the small bedroom's square footage and ordered too much wood. Though the company really should have taken the unopened boxes back, he could no longer fathom why taking the fall for five hundred dollars' worth of excess tongue-and-groove had driven him to such a rage at the time; the arithmetic mistake was his own, after all. He'd wasted a lot of energy in his life, and if he'd only had the wit to plug his temper into the mains he might have lit the whole house for free.

Turning a key whose gentle jingle on his chain had buoyed him for a month or more, he released the metal box's padlock and removed the contents. Even Jackson had to admire any nation that so gamely enabled the procurement of this particular item—not to mention a nation perfectly happy to let him charge yet another $639.95 when he already owed more than the value of his house. What the hell, maybe the U.S. of A. was a free country after all.

Upstairs in the kitchen, he stirred the utensils drawer. The spike of fury when he couldn't find what he was looking for was a chemical surprise; in his frustration, he yanked the drawer from its track, and its contents spilled on the floor. The crash of spatulas, slotted spoons, and whisks jangled his nerves, although the inane dribble of the garlic press, egg cups, tea balls, and julienne slicer at his feet was a useful reminder of his new motto: *They can have it*. He was grateful for the return of his tranquil methodicalness when he located the implement in the next drawer down. There he also found the steel. Most people had no idea how to use one, and so ruined their knives. Executing a few uniformly angled sweeps, he remembered how many bevels he had shorn off altogether before he got the hang of this thing. But he was good at it now, and it was nice to have developed the expertise by the time the facility mattered.

Steel: what *Burdina* meant in Basque. A metal to test his own. When applied to the tool, a name he had always liked. Funny, while he couldn't conjure anything else under the sun that he could possibly miss, he thought he might miss a few words—*confiscatory*. Maybe it was a shame he'd never written that book. Though the titles! For his titles alone, Jackson Burdina would be legendary.

The logistics were a little awkward, and at length he achieved the best purchase (another word he liked, when it didn't mean another worthless acquisition) by placing the cutting board down on the breakfast table. Unbuckling his belt, Jackson considered dragging his trousers off altogether, to avoid the undignified rumpled-about the-ankles effect. But he wasn't much concerned with presentation. When he cooked, for example, his fare was manly, rough and ready, and he wasn't wont to serve a steak with a chilled melon ball of herb butter, to frond the fish with chives.

Pulling with one hand and raising the cleaver high with the other, he brought the blade down in a clean whack, long practiced on chicken legs to separate the drumsticks from the thighs. He hadn't meant to be melodramatic; the gesture was meant as insurance, a guarantee that there was no going back. Nevertheless, the vision of that gristly shrivel on the cutting board was strangely satisfying. *Vengeance*, he thought, then put the pistol in his mouth and pulled the trigger.

Chapter Seventeen

Shepherd Armstrong Knacker
Merrill Lynch Account Number 934-23F917
January 01, 2006 – January 31, 2006
Net Portfolio Value: $3,492.57

As he headed north on the West Side Highway, Shep reflected that he should get fired more often. Traffic was so much lighter in the middle of the day.

Calling their next-door neighbor on his cell while driving was technically against the law. But something inside had started to slide. Every other New Yorker ignored the ban, and Shep was no longer inclined to embrace his role as the sole exception to thinking one's self an exception.

Usually, he dreaded calling Nancy. All his life the man other people had asked for help, he was uneasy as a supplicant. Although she was always cheerful about doing favors, it was a relief to contact the poor woman for once to let her off the hook. Now pumped full of antibiotics—again—Glynis was free to go home, and he could pick her up on the way back to Elmsford. So grateful to be of service, when relieved of the need to drive down to Columbia-Presbyterian Nancy sounded disappointed. They didn't make people like that anymore. Christ, in return he'd never even ordered anything from Amway.

He had already resolved not to tell Glynis that he'd been sacked. Nancy had remarked on his sudden freedom in the middle of a workday. But Glynis had grown so oblivious to the fact that he still had a job that he might not have to fake a thing.

For Glynis had given over to such a perfect selfishness that she made Beryl seem like a full-time volunteer for Save the Children. She ordered him around, and he allowed himself to be ordered. Odd how illness conveyed an awesome power, of which Glynis availed herself with not only imperial self-righteousness, but a hint of vitriol. It was payback for something, his stillborn declaration of independence over Pemba merely a single line item on her long list of grievances. Times past, Shep had conceived of himself as a tad henpecked. Glynis had always ruled the roost, getting her way on everything from drapes to where Zach went to school. But that may not have been how she saw matters. He strained to see his wife's side of things: a brilliant but underappreciated artisan trapped in a conventionally paternalistic marriage, she'd slaved away at raising kids and preparing stylish suppers when she should have been crafting museum pieces. (Never mind that nothing had ever stopped her from doing so; never mind that her husband had himself slaved away at repairing other people's generally rather depressing and tastelessly decorated houses in order to ensure her freedom to create whatever and whenever she liked. Indulging his own perspective was not what this mental exercise was for.) So her husband having become the menial who vacuumed, shopped, cooked, and ran to the pharmacy must have seemed only just.

The grievance was larger than that, of course. Glynis was only fifty-one, this shouldn't be happening, she had been wronged, and she was owed. Exactly who paid down the astronomical debt was probably immaterial.

He took the Ninety-sixth Street exit onto Riverside. Weak winter sunlight strobed through the bare branches of the park, flickering off and then stabbing again like an unwanted memory. The scene he'd walked in on two nights before was still with him.

That evening when he'd got back from work, all the lights were on. He ambled upstairs, but Glynis wasn't nesting in her usual swirl of coverlets in the bedroom. He rapped on his son's door and asked Zach if he knew where his mother was. The boy shouted over the sound of rapid gunfire that he had no idea, but that she must be somewhere in the house. Shep searched the first and second floors again before heading to the basement. She wasn't messing with laundry, either, or rummaging in his workshop. He even hit the front and back yards with a flashlight. Before calling the police he decided to be perfectly thorough, and ducked up to the attic. There was nothing up there besides Glynis's studio, and as far as he knew no one had been up there in months.

He found her slumped over her workbench, the desk lamp providing the tableaux the golden glow of a Rembrandt: *Still Life with Illness and Silver*. She had managed to insert a blade into her jewelry saw. Strung with the requisite tautness, the slender blades broke easily; this one had broken. It was stuck in a square sheet of thick-gauge sterling that lay across her bench pin. A single saw line wobbled into the sheet from its perimeter perhaps an inch or so. There the snapped saw blade remained, the saw itself dangling from the cut, which held the blade captive. Beside his wife's limp hand lay a piece of paper scrawled with uncertain shapes and slashed with irritated arrows. He couldn't tell if she was asleep or unconscious, and for a moment he feared—worse than unconscious. So when he touched her brow, he was relieved to find it instead burning with fever. Before carrying her downstairs, he eased her arm aside and worked the broken saw blade from the metal. This square sheet with its minimalist incision was, he suspected, her last creation.

As anticipated, when she looked up from the hospital bed Glynis didn't act surprised to see him. Nor was Shep surprised to encounter a wife so frail, the tendons extruding from her neck like jewelry saw blades she had swallowed. Accustomed to her decline, lately he was in danger of believing that this was what his wife looked like. Only photographs shocked him into recollection of the woman he had desired for

twenty-seven years, so he understood why she might now forbid the taking of pictures. With no visual record, this sunken image would fade,
having been rapidly eclipsed by the regal woman he had wed, with her
fierce hands, her languid legs, that enchanted forest between them.

He helped her to dress. When he had trouble fitting her arms into
the sleeves of the cherry-red fleece from Carol, she snapped at him. "Get
away from me. This is harder than doing it myself!" The nurse delivered
another prescription, which he could fill on the way home.

"Goldman wants to try something new," Glynis said in the car,
propping her turban on the headrest with her eyes closed. "An experimental drug for colon cancer is getting great results in trials. It might
give this gunk in my guts a last knockout punch." She coughed; she
always coughed. "Though I'm sure it comes with another goody bag of
special effects."

He would have liked to ask whether it was worth going through yet
another drug, but he knew better. Glynis had not learned the results of
her CAT scans since September. "That's pretty exciting"—it was an effort, pushing an exuberance of air through his throat—"if this stuff is
getting such promising results in other patients."

"Oh, and Goldman told me a wonderful story! Some colleague told
his mesothelioma patient after the guy was diagnosed, 'Don't make
plans for Christmas.' I mean, talk about callous! So the patient bet this
asshole doc a hundred dollars that he'd be alive and kicking two years
later. The doc scoffed, and gave him odds of fifty-to-one. Well, that oncologist just had to pay up five grand! I loved it. Thank God I don't have
one of those cynical doctors who take pride in their 'realism'—who all
but hand you the spade to dig your own grave."

"Too bad Goldman *isn't* more cynical," said Shep, trying to sound
hearty, but privately a little exasperated that her internist didn't keep his
wonderful stories to himself. "At fifty-to-one, we might have made some
serious money."

The sun over the Hudson was anemic, as pale and unconvincing as
this conversation.

"Shepherd," she sighed, "to say I'm really looking forward to this being over doesn't begin to . . . Now I know what it's like for a marathoner, on the twenty-sixth mile. You'd think with the finish line in sight it would get easier. I thought the last few treatments would be practically cheerful—you know, almost through. Instead, it's harder, it's worse. Being over and being *almost* over seem nearly the same. But they're not. They're opposites. *Almost* over means it's still going on. You want to round up, to say basically that's it. But that's not it. Like having one more mile to run, but you're still running. You realize that however many miles you've come already doesn't make any difference, because a mile is still a long way. Sometimes I think even one more day is more than I can bear. A whole day. You have no idea how long it can seem, a whole day."

"I know it seems like forever, like it will never end. But it will end," he said firmly, and this time with feeling.

Glynis waited in the car while he ran into their local CVS. Presumably it was gratifying to have a bartender pour your usual without asking, but it was disheartening to have got on a chummy, first-name basis with your pharmacist. Once he'd pulled in their drive, Shep held his arm out for her to lean on, and they took each porch stair slowly, one at a time. Even the walk from the car had winded her, so he settled her in the living room to recuperate before tackling the flight to the bedroom. Besides, there was something he needed to raise with her, and the more formal nature of a living room seemed fitting.

He left to fetch her some cranberry juice, which he poured into a wine glass, though the bendable straw undercut the stemware's pretense of adulthood. She was weak enough that leaving her to lift the glass and sip and put it down again invited spilling. The couch was white, and there was always the possibility that she would care.

He set the glass on the side table at her elbow, turned the straw toward her, and shook two tablets from the vial of antibiotics, placing one, then the other, on her tongue. All the while he was nagged by something wrong. Something missing. It was the silence. He looked to the Wedding Fountain on the glass coffee table. He was distressed to note that the silver of those sluicing, intertwining swans' necks had jaundiced, now turned the same off-yellow of the afternoon's sickly sun. Hitherto in the worst of all this he had still managed to find a moment to polish the sterling. Worse, the steady, lilting trickle that had formed the aural backdrop to many a happier pre-dinner drink had ceased. He must have forgotten to top up the water for at least a week.

Shep filled a pitcher in the kitchen. When he returned to pour the water into the basin, it sat stagnant. Predictably, once the fountain ran dry, the pump had burnt out. Not for the first time, and there was no reason to be alarmed by the small impending repair. Nevertheless, the omen unsettled him.

This clearly wasn't the moment, but it took discipline not to fix the fountain then and there; he had some spare pumps in the basement. That was what he did, he fixed things. He fixed things, or had until this morning, for a living. As he stared down at the still water, the strain of not remedying this minor mechanical malfunction right away reflected back at him the greater strain of more than a year: he couldn't fix things.

Abandoning the pitcher on the floor, he eased beside his wife on the sofa and took her hand. "I'm not sure if you're keeping track of the date. Are you remembering that tomorrow morning you're supposed to give your deposition about Forge Craft?"

She took a ragged breath and coughed. "I remember."

"I'm concerned that you may not be up to it."

"Well, the timing isn't great. I'm over the fever, but the infection isn't . . . So I guess we could always . . ."

"I know we could reschedule, but I'm concerned about that, too. We've moved this appointment several times now. It's become embarrassing, and too many delays may count against us in the suit. You know that I've never been that big on the whole business. But there's no point in pursuing it at all if we lose. I wish you'd got this over with when you were stronger. It's not only delivering a statement on video. Forge Craft's lawyers will be there. Rick has warned me that it takes hours, and the cross-examination can be grueling. But I'm not going to ask for another delay. You either go through with it tomorrow, or we withdraw the suit."

"I don't want to withdraw it," she said sulkily. "Someone has to pay."

"Then you have to testify tomorrow."

"I feel terrible, Shepherd! Why can't you reschedule? Even by next week, I'm sure to—"

"No." The sensation of laying down the law was strangely exhilarating. She would not have heard a refusal from her husband for many months. "If you feel so strongly about 'making someone pay,' then I don't understand why you keep putting it off. Get the deposition over with. Tomorrow. Or we're calling the whole thing quits."

Glynis was sitting upright, palms flat on her thighs, eyes closed, the turban lending her figure a droll hint of the swami. In such a composed position she would have radiated a meditative repose, save that she had begun to shake. When he touched her hand, it was trembling like one of their electric toothbrushes.

"Glynis?" he said gently. "What is it you're afraid of? I'll be with you, and we can take lots of breaks."

Deep in her diaphragm came a lurch, rising to her throat, where she tried to keep it swallowed. Successive shudders shook her body as if someone were pounding on her chest with a sledgehammer, trying to knock down a door.

"Gnu, what's wrong? If it's too stressful, we can just withdraw the suit—"

Though the shudders that rocked her were seismic, the lone vowel that emitted from her mouth was timorous, something like *ih*.

"Sh-sh." He stroked her hand. "Take it easy, we can hash this out later."

"It's," she said more clearly now, fighting with the words, wrestling with them in her throat as if they were trying to take over.

"Take some deep breaths, and don't try to talk."

Yet when he made a bid to embrace her, with strength he'd not have imagined she still possessed she shoved him away. Although Shep had become adept at not taking anything that Glynis did these days personally, the violent physical rejection was unexpectedly wounding. He withdrew to the opposite arm of the sofa and folded his arms.

"It's," she squeezed out again, and then finally threw the words at him, getting them out of her with the twinned revulsion and relief of vomit: "*It's—all—my—fault.*"

"What's all your fault, Glynis." The coldness in his voice was an indulgence. "I can't think of anything that's your fault."

"This!" she spat, sweeping a hand over her concave midsection. "All of it!"

"All of what?"

"The cancer, the chemo!" she got out through her weeping. "I asked for it! I did this to myself!"

"You're talking crazy. You're just exhausted—"

"Shut up!" she cried, slamming her hands to her thighs. "*Shut up, shut up, shut up!*"

She waited for him to demonstrate his obedience. As he sat mutely apart from her, she seemed to regain a measure of self-control.

"At Saguaro," she said. "The millboard blocks, the mitts, the lining for the crucibles—sure, in the mid-seventies putting asbestos in products like that wasn't against the law. But it had become an issue, okay? I knew about it, and my teachers did, too. In fact, my metalsmithing professor was really concerned about it, right? I mean, how did you think I knew these things contained asbestos to begin with?"

He wanted to say that just because she knew didn't make it her fault, but he could tell the edict to "shut up" was still in force, and her question was rhetorical.

"Anyway, that professor, I still remember her name, Frieda Luten. She'd read up on all this stuff. So at the beginning of my first term she'd collected all the blocks and mitts, absolutely anything that might be a 'health and safety' issue, and put them in the storage closet. The shelves were marked 'Do Not Use and Do Not Touch.' She'd ordered replacement supplies, but didn't want to throw the old stuff out. Forge Craft's salespeople had told her that the company was probably going to announce a recall, when the school could trade the old supplies in for their new, safer products. The company did issue a recall, too, though not until the next year. That's the recall that Rick Mystic said would help to hang them in our suit."

He couldn't contain himself. "So are you telling me that you never used those products after all? In that case, how would you—"

"*I'm not finished.*"

Shep contained himself.

"You have to understand," she said, training her gaze dully forward toward the Wedding Fountain; defunct and tarnished, it now looked disturbingly junky, like a gaudy thrift-store knickknack. "Or remember. What it was like to be young. That feeling that older people's neurotic little worries don't apply to you. The asbestos thing, it was abstract. I thought everyone was making a big deal over nothing, the same way they made a big deal over red dye number two when I'd eaten all the maraschino cherries off my Dairy Queen hot fudge sundaes as a kid and lived to tell the tale. And you know, they're always changing their minds about what's good for you and what's going to kill you—like all that hoo-ha over saccharine, and then they bring in aspartame, which is probably just as bad . . . Well, who can take any of the toxic this and toxic that seriously after a while? And there wasn't any Internet in those days; I couldn't Google *asbestos* and get fifteen million hits. So I didn't know anything about the cover-up that had been going on for over a hundred years, or about all those miners dying back in the 1930s. And I was pretty fucking broke."

She turned and glared. He felt he was meant to say something. "So . . . ?"

"Oh don't be an idiot! *I stole that stuff, Shepherd!* I knew I was going to need to set up my own studio once I was out of school, and you should know—metalsmithing materials cost a fortune! I figured if those supplies were out of commission, nobody would miss them. For God's sake, why do you think I remember the exact label on the bottom of the soldering blocks, or the exact little purple flower pattern on the heat-proof mitts? Because I stole a whole boxful of stuff from those 'Do Not Use and Do Not Touch' shelves, because I packed it all with me when I moved to New York, and because I worked with it in Brooklyn *for years*! It's no different than if I'd smoked two packs a day for decades and then act all surprised when I get lung cancer, since I knew that stuff was contaminated and I used it anyway, because I was too—fucking—cheap!"

Ah. On his own account, Shep was relieved. The original alert having come from Forge Craft's own sales force, they would have to withdraw the suit. Even if there was no record of the upstanding heads-up, to pursue their claim for opportunistic financial gain wouldn't be right. To protect her, perhaps he could explain to Mystic that she no longer had the strength to make it through a deposition. Now he would escape a tedious legal process that had made him queasy from the start.

At last she did not resist when he slipped to her side of the sofa and slid his arm around her shoulders. "That's ironic," he murmured. "One of the things I took a shine to when we met was how frugal you were. You sure drove a hard bargain for that worktable I built you in Brooklyn." He chuckled. "What you were willing to part with barely covered the materials. Accepting peanuts, well—that's how I first knew I must have had it bad for this woman. I'd never have worked for next to nothing for anyone else. But I wanted to fuck you," he said softly into her ear, and even saying that he started to get hard. "I really, really, really wanted to fuck you."

"I don't know how you can bring yourself to still speak to me," said Glynis, her voice muffled in his shirt. She'd noticed his erection, and reached for it, held it lightly through his slacks. Stroked it in sync with his stroking of her shoulder, as if caressing a beloved albeit increasingly elderly family pet. "After I blamed you. I can't quite understand what drove me to that. Except that it was so hard to take . . . the diagnosis . . . what was going to happen to me, the surgery, the treatments . . . I just couldn't handle the blame, too. It was too much. It wasn't as if I didn't remember about swiping those supplies from that closet at Saguaro, exactly. I just didn't . . . . *turn to it*. But turning against you instead, putting it on you instead—because you were there—because you were strong and I thought you could bear what I couldn't—because it made a better, a plausible story that I could stand to tell to other people . . . Well, it wasn't fair, and I don't know how you can ever forgive me."

"I'm more than still speaking to you," he whispered, kissing the smooth top of her head. "Eventually you pointed the finger elsewhere, and that was nice. It was easier for me after that, not thinking I'd made you sick, just from . . ." indeed, it was hard to say it aloud without his throat catching, "hugging you hello when I got home."

Shep was debating doing something with this hard-on versus simply enjoying the state, those insistent, pumping twinges that made him feel young again, and married again, when the phone rang. He might have let it go, but it sometimes behooved him to remember that he had a son, now late coming home from school. The poor kid's parents having been inaccessible in every other sense for over a year, they might at least deign to answer the phone.

It wasn't Zach. Recognizing the voice on the other end, he raised a forefinger to Glynis with an apologetic arch of his eyebrows. She looked suddenly so spent that a few minutes to rest might be welcome. He slipped off to the foyer. As the voice carried on, he feared its penetrating wail was audibly escaping the receiver, and he slid out to the front porch. It was cold outside, but he had gone so cold inside that he might as well match the temperature of the air and his blood, like a reptile.

It would be fair to say that Shepherd Armstrong Knacker re-entered the living room a changed man. For the benefit of what little remained to him of his married life, he would have wished that his immediate resolution to shelter his shattered wife from a certain piece of news was central to his transformation. But ever since he had read her prognosis on the Web and kept it to himself like his own private cancer, ever since he had concealed from her the results of her CAT scans at her own perplexing behest, shielding Glynis from vital information had become habitual. If by only dint of omission, he was, and had now long been, dishonest at home.

Yet until that phone call, he had never been dishonest in public. He had always filed painstakingly accurate tax returns, declaring remits from jobs paid, with a wink, in cash. Unlike his tragically light-fingered wife, he had never stolen a single screwdriver from Pogatchnik. He had signed a contract with Twilight Glens; bound by his word, he had never seriously entertained that notion of cancelling the monthly payments, and leaving the institution or the government to sort out the messy business of selling the house in Berlin out from under his sister to cover the outstanding bill.

For decades now, he had listened to his best friend regale him with what a "Mug" he was—alternatively, what a Patsy, Fall Guy, Sap, Slave, Jackass, or Lackey he was, depending on the man's cockeyed terminological vogue. While Shep might sometimes have conceded that his taxes were not always devoted to purposes that he personally might have endorsed, for the most part Jackson's purple rants about the real class divide being between the takers and the taken had fallen on deaf ears. Shep had found the man's tirades merely entertaining, an amusing diversion for passing the time while circling Prospect Park.

But now they were his best friend's legacy. Aside from one sick kid and one fat one, and a wife whose preternatural composure had finally cracked in half, the memory of those diatribes was all that he had left behind. To honor them was to act on them. For once in Shep Knacker's life, he'd make Jackson proud.

Glynis was curled in a ball at the end of the couch. Shep knelt before her and gently prized her open, like spreading a tight bloom without snapping the petals. "Gnu," he said levelly, taking her hands. "Sit up, would you? That's right. Now, I want you to listen to me. Look me in the eye, okay? It's all right, I'm not angry with you. I understand how hard it's been, carrying this secret for so long. But I've been carrying secrets, too. They're not much easier."

He waited until she met his gaze squarely.

"You know that with the sale of Knack of All Trades, and our investments finally recovering after the tech-stock crash and then 9/11, we were pretty well off, right? That's what made it possible for me to announce I was going to Pemba, with or without you. We had the money. Fine, my timing was bad, and that's an understatement. But Glynis, your treatments have been very expensive. Those two specialists at Columbia-Presbyterian are out of network. I've tried to spare you this side of things, so you could concentrate on getting better. But I think it's time I put you in the picture.

"We're going broke, Glynis. From the age of eighteen, I—Jackson and I—worked sixty-plus hours a week, building up that company from scratch. Ever since its sale, I—Jackson and I—have been step-and-fetching for some fat, feckless former employee with a chip on his shoulder who hates our guts. Meanwhile, you and I have never lived high on the hog, and now I'm sorry that I hardly ever took you out to dinner while you still had an appetite. But everything I earned and everything we saved—it's gone, Glynis. My account at Merrill Lynch has been savaged. It's touch and go whether I can make next month's rent, much less another bill for chemo.

"And here's another thing I didn't tell you: I was fired today, Glynis. I don't have a job. I don't have a salary anymore, but more to the point we have no more health insurance. I could buy into COBRA, but we can't afford that, either. So the next bill for chemo is one hundred percent mine, and once you're out of the system they double the price. We're headed for bankruptcy. You may think you have some idea of how I feel about that. You probably assume that I feel embarrassed. But I'm not embarrassed. *I'm angry.*"

Their financial plight didn't seem to be making much of an impression, but his fury did. "My, my," she marveled. "Well, it's about time."

"Jackson"—Shep stopped to collect himself. He did not want to cry, or he did, but he did not want to have to explain why. He was having a hard time saying the name, though it seemed important to say it. "Jackson lets the unfairness of it all get him down. It eats him up. And that's a shame. But the way he thinks about the world isn't completely crazy. When you play by the rules and other people don't, you're a fool. When you hold up your end of things, other people figure that while you're at it you might as well hold up *their* end of things, too. Jackson's been explaining till he's blue in the face that people like him and me, we're taken advantage of. We're punished. For the sale of Knack alone I paid two hundred and eighty thousand dollars to the federal government in capital gains. Add up all I've shoveled those sons of bitches since high school, and it has to be somewhere between one and two million bucks. And that's the same government, when my wife has cancer, won't buy her a single Tylenol. They won't take care of my elderly father, either, though he's paid into the system his whole life, too—just because he's led his life responsibly, like I have, and he isn't destitute. Jackson's right. It's not fair. And I don't think he'd want us to roll over and take it. Maybe the best tribute to a really good friend is to listen to the guy for once, to—to take him seriously for once, in a way, I'm ashamed to say, I may never have done before."

Shep's use of the present tense was an anachronism, but *Jackson lets* and *Jackson thinks* came readily enough; the verbs weren't merely for concealment. It had taken his father years to remember to say that Shep's mother *was* a good cook, that she *worked* tirelessly for his congregation. For the living, with no conception of any other state, the use of the past tense in relation to the bewilderingly disappeared was a discipline, a learned grammar and an unnatural one.

"My father would say it's *only* money, of course," Shep continued. "Maybe you think the same thing, when the only currency in your life right now is your health. But I can't keep this roof over your head without money, or heat this place to ninety degrees in February, or drive you to the hospital in a car. Besides, I don't want to be 'cynical,' but— whatever happens to you? I have to survive afterward, if only to take care of our son. I've tried to take care of you, too, the best I could, but now I'm asking something in return."

"You want me to go back to making molds for chocolate bunny rabbits?"

He smiled. They gave Pulitzers for lesser achievements than a sense of humor at times like these. "In a way," he said. "Back when you took that part-time job to spite me, I'd dared to suggest that it was too bad you hadn't made at least a small contribution to our income. But right now you can make a big contribution. In fact, you can save the day. You can lay a chocolate egg. A big chocolate nest egg."

"I don't get it."

"I understand what you just told me. That in fact you'd been forewarned about those products in art school, which were withdrawn from use before you ever started your coursework. That you knew perfectly well that they contained asbestos. That you knew perfectly well that asbestos was supposed to be deadly. That you stole those supplies in defiance of warnings from your teacher, who was alerted to an upcoming recall by Forge Craft's own salespeople. I think you're right, that if you were to testify to all that, our case would be compromised, and our chances of a big payoff would go way down.

"But Saguaro closed years ago. Even if she went on to teach somewhere else, Frieda Luten has probably retired, and who knows where. None of your former classmates has cropped up in this case. Petra may remember something, but she's your friend and she'll keep her mouth shut. No one knows what really happened but you and me. So I want you to give that deposition tomorrow and really put your heart into it. And *I want you to lie.*"

Starting promptly at 9:00 a.m., the deposition in a sterile conference room in Lower Manhattan the next morning took four hours. Shep assumed one of the chairs along the wall, while Glynis took the hot seat at the head of the oval table; other than be present and occasionally insist on a break, he couldn't help her. The camera to her left stared her down on its tripod, destined to record every hesitation, every broken eye contact, every nose-scratching tell. Forge Craft brought a team of four lawyers, all men, all studiedly supercilious. Once Glynis was finished describing the products she remembered, giving a detailed account of how they were used in which processes, their lawyer conducted his Q&A.

Located with a lackluster Web search, Rick Mystic was only in his thirties, and Shep had learned to discount his own alarm that this was just a kid; if he kept mistrusting anyone younger than himself, he'd soon trust no one. Mystic had the well-proportioned, square-cut good looks that would have come across well on TV; a leading lady in flats would have helped disguise the fact that he was short. Belying the classic ambulance-chaser tag, the lawyer claimed to have had a favorite uncle die from asbestosis, which gave his specialty a sense of personal mission. Although with that flash suit and designer haircut the young man couldn't have been motivated by philanthropy alone, Shep figured that they could harness Rick Mystic's avarice to their own purposes, just as they had co-opted Philip Goldman's ego. After all, altruism trailed near the bottom of the list of effective human drivers.

Thus aside from generational prejudice, Shep's primary misgiving about their lawyer was ridiculously decorative: Mystic's insertion of "sort of" or "kind of" two or three times a sentence. Sure, the verbal tic was commonplace. But this modern proclivity for incessant qualification leant all assertions an exasperating vagueness, an evasion, a suspicious shilly-shallying uneasiness with being pinned down. That table would never be "brown"; it would be "sort of brown," and what color was that? In a lawyer, too, the tic provided discourse an imprecision at odds with the profession, and in the case of Glynis's deposition a surreal understatement: since her illness, hadn't she been "sort of unable to work?" With these qualifying types, Shep wondered what terrible thing they thought would happen if they landed on a noun or adjective and stuck, committing to a quality or an object that was exactly this or exactly that, and not slightly something else.

"No, I can't work," Glynis replied. Though her sentences were cogent, every other phrase was punctuated with a cough and a raspy pause to catch her breath. "And I've tried, too. I can't concentrate enough to follow the plot of *Everybody Loves Raymond*. So I tune into the Food Channel. My attention span is about as long as a recipe for goat-cheese brochettes."

"And would you describe yourself," said Mystic, "as kind of in pain?"

"I often feel nauseated," she said, "and have trouble breathing. Honestly, it's harder to go get my own glass of water than it used to be to complete an hour of step aerobics at the Y. And in the deepest sense, I have no privacy. Other people are constantly poking needles in my arms. Shoving tubes down my throat and capsules up my colon. My life is one big violation. I used to love my body. Only a year ago at fifty, I was still beautiful. Now I hate my body. It is wholly a house of horrors. I should have a life expectancy of over eighty. Now I believe that number is . . . greatly reduced."

Of those gathered, only Shep recognized what a concession she'd made.

Thereafter, the defending lawyers took turns trying to poke holes in her testimony. They cited a host of other suspect materials in everyday life with which she might have come in contact since art school, but she batted the queries away like a pinch hitter: did she look like the kind of woman who would install her own insulation?

Citing the same theory about clinging fibers that their first oncologist had floated, one lawyer brought up her husband's handyman business, in which he must also have worked with, say, asbestos-enhanced cement. In addition to observing that during most of their married life Shep's duties were managerial, Glynis asserted archly that she was never given to embracing her grubby husband in the days he still made house calls "before he'd had a shower." Moreover, she said, that route to contamination was too complicated. "Remember Occam's Razor? The simplest explanation is usually the best one. In fact, I looked up the definition on the Web." Glynis read from her notes, " 'When multiple competing theories are equal in other respects, the principle recommends selecting the theory that introduces the fewest assumptions.' So there's no need to construct an elaborate scenario of my husband—who has *not* come down with an asbestos-related cancer—working with asbestos, getting it on his clothes, embracing me, and leaving fibers on my own clothes that I inadvertently ingest, when I flat out worked with asbestos myself."

Surely, another lawyer sneered, her schooling was so long ago that she could not possibly remember the individual products with which she had worked, including the brand of the manufacturer.

"To the contrary," said Glynis, affecting the same imperious manner that had always both infuriated and beguiled her husband. "I was just learning my craft, getting my first inspirations. That was a vivid time in my life"—she stopped to cough again—"as opposed, I'm afraid, to this one. So my recollection is quite sharp, just as you might remember with unusual clarity when you first fell in love. And I had fallen in love. Those were the years when I first fell in love with metal."

Shep had more than once encountered the glib aphorism that "you always kill the thing you love"; he had never come across its inverse: that the thing you love would kill you.

"Also," Glynis continued, "the studio kept catalogues from Forge Craft along with other reference books and trade magazines on the shelves beside the drill press. I used to flip through those catalogues, since I was hoping to set up my own studio once out of school. I remember being horrified by how much everything cost. Being worried whether I'd ever be able to afford my own polishing machine, my own set of hammers, my own centrifugal casting apparatus. Because at that time, Forge Craft had a virtual monopoly on metalsmithing supplies nationwide. That's why the company was able to get away with pricing its products sky-high. So Saguaro wouldn't have stocked tools and materials from anywhere *but* Forge Craft, which had knocked out the commercial competition. So maybe right now you're a victim of your own success."

Yet what most impressed Shep was her coolness during a line of questioning intended to achieve, in the popular imagination, the impossible: putting a dollar value on human life. To this end, they grilled her on exactly how much money her metalsmithing work had netted per annum, and Glynis managed to quote the meager figure without apparent embarrassment. More insultingly, they wanted to know whether before falling ill she did the shopping, what proportion of childcare responsibilities she'd assumed with Zach, how many meals she'd prepared in the average week, and even *how often she'd done the laundry*. They were measuring the value of his wife's life in wash loads of lights and darks. Glynis's blithely factual answers to these degrading questions were the product of far greater self-control than Shep could ever have marshaled in her place. From the reflex of decades, Shep thought, *I can't wait to tell Jackson about this circus*, before he caught himself.

Glynis was magnificent. She never faltered or let them trip her up, meeting the gaze of her tormentors straight on. On Mystic's advice she'd worn no makeup, and the accusatory specter of her sunken cheeks, her glaucous lips, the sheen of her bald hairline when her turban slipped, was a more piercing indictment of their company's products from the 1970s than anything she said.

Only when the procedure had drawn formally to a close and the opposition's lawyers had cleared off did Glynis's posture collapse, and she slid onto the slick polished table like a pool of spilled tea. She was so depleted that Shep half-carried her to the car.

"You were a star," he whispered, wishing that bearing nearly all of her weight were harder than it was.

"I did it for you," she slurred. "And the lying? I *enjoyed it.*"

Yet once they got home, the dignity she'd assumed for hours had left a residue, and she refused to let him carry her upstairs. Instead she crawled the flight on all fours. With a recuperative sag on both landings, the fifteen steps took her half an hour.

Shep had left multiple messages on Carol's cell on breaks during the deposition; she wasn't picking up. Once Glynis had dropped to sleep upstairs, he tried again, and finally Carol answered. While during her initial call the night before Carol had been hysterical, now she was catatonic. At least the dead monotone allowed for the exchange of information. She had walked into the kitchen with Flicka. "I will never forgive him for that," Carol added flatly. "It was child abuse. I don't use the term lightly." Unsurprisingly, the girl had immediately plunged into a dysautonomic crisis; "that surly, offhand thing she's got going," said Carol, "it's all an act. Compensation. She can't take stress. Taking any old test in school, she falls apart. So you can imagine . . . I hate to admit it, but dealing with Flicka yesterday, the blood pressure, the retching—and I almost joined her—well, it was a relief. Concentrating on my daughter's immediate medical needs, whose urgency trumped even what Jackson had done. I guess we've always used her like that . . . At the beginning, as a point of unity, a mutual project, but later as a distraction . . . We'd focus on Flicka to avoid each other."

Bundling Flicka off to New York Methodist, Carol had called Heather, still at school, from the car. She'd insisted the younger girl come straight to the hospital, where they'd all three spent the night. Flicka had stabilized, and by this evening would probably be discharged; Carol was planning to decamp with the girls to a neighbor's. Meanwhile, according to the neighbor, the police had come, an ambulance. It came as no surprise that Carol did not, under any circumstances, wish to re-enter that house. Shep promised at his first opportunity to go there for her, to retrieve any clothes they might need, Flicka's medications, perhaps Carol's computer. Of the many favors he had offered to do his friends over the years, this one seemed costlier than most.

When she conceded that the neighbor was good-hearted enough but that they were not very close—it was a relationship of pie exchanges and kindly reminders to move your car for alternate-side parking—he begged her to bring the remains of her family to Elmsford instead. There was Amelia's room, and the couch downstairs. He admitted that he had not yet told Glynis. He said they would deal with that, though he was not sure how.

"You will deal with it," said Carol, her voice the color of ash, "by telling her. She's ill, but she's still with us. Being sick isn't the same thing as being stupid or a small child. Ask Flicka. Glynis was Jackson's friend, too, and she deserves to know. If I can tell a twelve-year-old," the pause was heavy, "you can tell your wife."

"I guess telling her," he said, "makes it . . . more real."

"It was real," Carol said wearily. "It was very, very real."

"Jackson and I took a long walk yesterday. I should have noticed something. But I was too wrapped up in my own problems. Actually, all I noticed was he seemed unusually at peace. Philosophical. In fact, it's the only time in recent memory that he *didn't* seem pissed off. Maybe that was the giveaway, if I'd been paying attention."

"This is what people do," said Carol. "Comb back through the past, take it on themselves. But Jackson himself was always going on about 'personal responsibility.' So if it's anyone's fault, it's Jackson's. His, and . . ." She sighed. "I don't want to get into it now, but mine, too."

"Now you're doing the same thing."

"I told you. It's compulsive."

He implored her to come up to Elmsford once more, and she relented. They arranged that she would arrive with the girls around nine o'clock that night. Meanwhile, for later this afternoon Shep had made an appointment with Philip Goldman, to whom it was about time he spoke without the encumbrance of his magnificent but delusional wife.

So what's this," said Shep in Goldman's office, "about an experimental drug?"

The internist usually communicated a rambunctious quality; a small room had trouble containing him, and he was wont to prop his foot on the edge of his desk and spring his chair back, to bounce up to draw illustrations of some medical procedure on scraps of paper, to punctuate his points with generous sweeps of his large hands. But now that boundless energy was more cramped, his restiveness reduced to fidget. In the tinier, more circumscribed tap of a pencil and jiggle of a knee, the doctor was deprived of the grand kinetic theater on which his illusion of attractiveness depended. The fact that his eyes were too close together, or that his middle was paunchy, became more pronounced. Losing, Philip Goldman was not as handsome.

"It's called peritoxamil," said Goldman, "also known as—"

"Cortomalaphrine," Shep said sourly.

"Come again?"

"Never mind. In-joke."

"It's in phase-three trials, and is showing a lot of promise. Not for mesothelioma, but there could be some crossover effect from therapy for colon cancer. Now, I'm afraid that your wife is—isn't qualified right now to participate in the clinical trials themselves, but—"

"You mean she's too sick," Shep interrupted again. "Since she's a goner anyway, she'd drag down the cheerful statistics."

"That's a harsh way of putting it, but—"

"I like a harsh way of putting it. Let's put it that way, then."

Goldman eyed his patient's husband with a nervous side glance. Shep Knacker had always been so docile, so cooperative. But the doctor would have seen all manner of reactions to extreme medical circumstances, and maybe belligerence was a standard variation.

"The point is," said Goldman, "we can appeal for the drug's release for compassionate use. Explain that we've depleted the traditional arsenal at our disposal. I grant it's a long shot, but it's all we've got. Frankly, at this juncture there's not much to lose. One small downside, however."

"It makes your head fall off."

Goldman's half smile was unamused. "Not a side effect—except for you. Since peritoxamil isn't FDA-approved, it's not going to be covered by your insurer."

"Uh-huh. And how much does this new snake oil cost?"

"For a course? In the area of a hundred thousand dollars. Fortunately, it's in capsule form, so Mrs. Knacker wouldn't have to come in for treatments."

"A hundred grand. There's 'not much to lose'? I guess I'm not in your income bracket. Since that strikes me as losing a whole lot."

Goldman seemed taken aback. "We're talking about your wife's life here—"

"*Jim!*"

The doctor shot him a worried look. "I have to assume that money is a secondary issue at best, if it's an issue at all."

"So if I say it *is* an issue, I'm an animal, right? But even if I fall in line and say, by all means, doctor, do anything you can, throw the kitchen sink at that cancer—a gold-plated kitchen sink—because I love my wife and *money is no object*. Why do you assume I've *got* a hundred grand?"

"It's often possible to take out a personal loan in such cases. Mr. Knacker, I know you're under stress, but I'm concerned about your combative tone. You don't seem to appreciate that we're on the same side here. You, Mrs. Knacker, and everyone in this hospital are united in a common cause."

"Are we? So what are you trying to achieve?"

"Obviously, I'm trying to extend your wife's life for as long as possible."

"Then we're not on the same side."

"Oh? What's your objective, then?"

"To end her suffering as soon as possible."

"It's really Mrs. Knacker's decision, when she wants to call off further treatments. But when I spoke to her about peritoxamil, she sounded keen to try it. Obviously, we'll make every effort to keep her comfortable. But to talk about . . . Well, simply planning to 'end her suffering' once and for all is defeatist."

"Fine. I am defeatist," Shep announced. "I have been defeated. I admit it: mesothelioma is too big for me. If this really has been a battle," *with weather,* he thought, "maybe it's time to lay down our arms. As for that being my wife's decision, I realize she'll try anything. But it is not my wife's decision if she's not the one who's going to pay for it."

Goldman was overtly discomfited by this kind of talk. He kept averting his gaze, working his face without concealing his disapproval, and edgily hitting his keyboard's space bar. Shep got the impression that making a medical decision of any magnitude in consideration of how much a treatment *cost*, in mere money—"only money," as his father would say—was crude, foreign, and offensive. "I want to be very clear, Mr. Knacker. This drug is our last hope."

"I was fired yesterday, Dr. Goldman. I just lost my job."

It was interesting, the subtle but discernible change in the internist's demeanor, once he registered the implications. "I'm sorry to hear that."

"I bet you are. But I'd been repeatedly absent and late for work. My wife's illness alone has substantially raised the health insurance premiums for my employer. As the former custodian of that company, I applaud my being dropped from its workforce as an astute business decision."

"That's an awfully understanding spin to put on your own misfortune."

"I am known," said Shep, "for my *understanding.* But as a result of my early retirement, the World Wellness Group will not only neglect to pay a hundred K for pterodactyl, or whatever it's called, but it won't be paying your bills, either."

"I see," said Goldman. "And I infer that your personal resources are somewhat depleted."

"*Somewhat*? You could say that."

"With what you just informed me, I can see why you might be feeling a little angry."

"No, you do not see. Getting fired was the nicest thing that's happened to me in over a year. But you're right that I'm 'a little' angry. I realize this is just what you people do. It's the way you're programmed. You just keep plowing through the drugs, working down the list, keeping everyone's chin up, looking on the bright side, *never saying die*. My wife, for example, never says die. Honestly, I can't remember the last time I heard her use the *d*-word. Nobody in this biz is ever supposed to throw up their hands and call it quits, so long as there's any last teensy-weensy, teeny-tiny smidgeon of a chance that some new therapy will eke out a few extra days. So you've just been following the script. But can we, for once, with Glynis not here, drop the pretense? This 'experimental drug'—you don't *really* believe it would make any difference, do you?"

"I did say it was a long shot."

"What are the odds? Fifty-to-one? Willing to put any of your own money on that?"

"It's hard to put a number on. Let's just say the chances are *distant*."

"Me, I wouldn't put a hundred grand on 'distant' even if I were a betting man. Would you?"

Goldman declined to answer.

"Secondly, let's skip the 'I don't believe in making prognoses' thing. You've been around the block. You know more about mesothelioma than anyone in the country, you're an expert. So tell me: how long has she got?"

The expression on Goldman's face reminded Shep of wrestling as a boy in Berlin, when sitting on Jeb's chest and pinning each wrist to the ground he finally got his friend to cry *uncle!*

"Maybe a month? Possibly more like three weeks."

Shep crimped forward, as if from a gut punch.

"I realize that's difficult to hear," Goldman continued softly. "And I'm very, very sorry."

Three weeks was within the range that Shep had forecast himself, but it was different hearing the bleak estimate from a doctor. It wasn't possible to keep being pugnacious, aggressive, and hostile, although as the humor slipped he knew he would miss it. This appointment excepted, the amount of his life that Shep Knacker had spent being pugnacious, aggressive, and hostile probably totaled under five minutes.

As Shep recovered himself, the doctor filled the silence. "I think of all the patients I've ever had, your wife may have shown the most tremendous spirit. She's put up a remarkable, a truly admirable struggle."

"That's nice of you to say, and I realize you're trying to pay her a big compliment, but . . . this way of thinking . . ."

Shep stood up, and paced the small patch of carpet before the door. "*Struggle. Surmounting* the odds. Like, the online support group that Glynis joined for a while was always talking up *hanging tough. Refusing to let go. Not giving up. Going the last mile.* You'd think they were organizing a grammar-school sports day. Dr. Goldman, my wife is very competitive! She's a high achiever, a perfectionist—which is why, though it doesn't seem to make sense, she hasn't been as professionally productive as she would have been with lower standards. A striver like that—how's she not going to rise to this stuff? And then you guys jack up the stakes even more. It's not just a potato-sack race, it's a war. The *battle* against cancer. The *arsenal* at our disposal . . . You make her think that there's something she has to do, to be a *good soldier*, a *trooper.* So if she deteriorates anyway, then there's something she didn't do: she didn't show courage under fire. I know you mean well, but after all this military talk she now equates—dying—with dishonor. With failure. With personal failure." It was the first time that Shep had put it together for himself.

"The military language is just a metaphor," said Goldman. "A way of talking about medical issues that laymen understand. It's not meant to hold the patient accountable for a therapy's results."

"But for Glynis, when you 'admire her struggle' she thinks you blame her when it doesn't do any good, don't you see? That's why she won't quit. That's why she and I can't talk about . . . well, anything."

"I see no reason for her to 'quit.' Glynis—Mrs. Knacker takes heart from her tenacity. Since I've come to know her somewhat, I think I'd counsel you to keep my prognosis to yourself."

"What's one more secret?" Shep said morosely, plopping back in his chair. "Though that's a fucking big secret."

"I'm only thinking of preserving the quality of the time she has left. Keeping her upbeat."

"But won't she know? What's going on in her own body?"

"You'd be surprised. Not necessarily. Still, I'd advise you to contact her family and friends. Underscore that we're talking days or weeks but not months, and they mustn't delay a last visit. So they can say good-bye."

"What good is saying goodbye when you can't say goodbye?"

"Pardon?"

"If we're not telling Glynis, nobody can say goodbye. Not even I can say goodbye."

"Well, sometimes *hasta la vista* is just as warm, but it's easier to hear, isn't it? And we say, 'See you later,' to all kinds of people whom we'll never meet again, really."

"I guess," Shep said reluctantly. "Maybe you're right, Glynis doesn't want to hear it. She sure hasn't wanted to hear anything else."

"I suppose I can see why you might want to pass on the peritoxamil. But she was very eager to take it. If you want to keep her on an even keel I could prescribe a placebo."

Which really would entail treating Glynis like a twelve-year-old on "cortomalaphrine." His wife's final days being webbed in a skein of deceit depressed Shep more than he could say. "Maybe. I'll let you know."

"Meanwhile, keep me apprised of her condition, and contact me if you need any advice about how to keep her comfortable."

"There is something you can do," said Shep, looking at his lap. "I really don't want her to die in a hospital. But also I don't want her to experience any more pain than she has to. I'd like something to—ease the end."

"There's nothing easy about the end. It can be very unpleasant. Professionals have a better chance of keeping her comfortable."

Repeated at least three times now, the set phrase jarred. Shep suspected that the medical establishment's usage of *comfortable* strained the definition of the word.

"Are you sure you don't want to reconsider, about the hospital?" the doctor pressed. "You feel strongly about this?"

"I do. And I honestly think that if Glynis ever faces up to what's happening she'll feel the same way, too."

"Painkillers are controlled substances. We're closely watched by the FDA. I can't hand out capsules willy-nilly, because of the danger of addiction."

"The government is afraid that my wife will become a drug addict when she's *dying*?"

Goldman sighed. "I grant it's not all that rational . . ." He bit his lip. "This is a little risky . . . But I suppose I can give you a prescription for liquid morphine. It's not complicated. Just a few drops on her tongue when she seems—"

"*Uncomfortable*," said Shep, with a trace of his earlier sourness. He stood up. "Thank you. And what I said before, you know, my 'tone'—I didn't mean that I'm not grateful."

"I know you're grateful, Mr. Knacker. And I'm sorry I haven't been able to do more for your wife. We've tried everything we could—as you observed. But mesothelioma is a virulent, deadly disease. It's not for nothing that *asbestos* means 'inextinguishable' in Greek. And you're a repairman, so you understand: there are only so many tools in the toolbox."

After they'd shaken hands and he was leaving, Shep turned back in the doorway. "One last thing. The surgery, all the chemo. The blood transfusions, the chest drains, the MRIs? According to my calculations, Glynis's medical bills for all these treatments already come to over two million dollars. That sound about right to you?"

"It's plausible," the doctor conceded.

If in a moment of idle perversity Shep had worked out that so far they'd paid over $2,700 per day, he'd also estimated that Glynis would often have paid that much to skip one. Of course, he couldn't vouch for the comparative awfulness of her disease left alone to its evil devices, but as for whether the cure or the cancer had been worse it was at least a contest. "So what exactly did we buy? How much time?"

"Oh, I bet we've probably extended her life a good three months."

"No, I'm sorry, Dr. Goldman," Shep said on the way out. "They were not a good three months."

Back in Elmsford, Zach had left a message from Rick Mystic, leaving the lawyer's home number. Since Carol and the girls would be arriving in an hour or so, Shep returned the call in his study right away, closing the door.

Rick got straight to the point. "They want to settle."

They did not, for once, *sort of* want to settle. "That was quick."

"These kind of cases can drag out for years, but when they move they can change your life in an afternoon. I bet Forge Craft's people were kind of impressed by your wife's deposition. But they were also kind of impressed by her—condition."

"You mean they're afraid she's going to . . ."

"Yeah. In which case, the size of a jury award could sort of skyrocket. You've got them sort of scared."

"So what are they offering?"

"One-point-two million."

Since twelve divided evenly by three, calculating what would remain after the lawyer's one-third contingency fee was elementary arithmetic; Mystic's cut amounted to somewhat more than the U.S. government's *contingency fee* for his sale of Knack. "So what do you advise?"

"Well, if you take them to court, especially once you've suffered—a greater loss, I'm kind of certain you could double that. But I'd be kind of remiss if I didn't warn you what a jury trial would involve. It's kind of brutal. Once liability has been established, the process is all about assessing what your marriage was worth. In dollars. So it's kind of in their interest to prove that your marriage was sort of shitty. A sort of shitty marriage doesn't, legally, merit nearly as high a compensation as a good one."

"What business is it of theirs, what quality of marriage I had?" The past tense made him glad that the study door was closed. "You're telling me they, what, deduct ten grand for every time Glynis and I had a fight?"

"You may find that kind of ludicrous, but you're kind of right. I mean, they'd grill you on how often you had sex. They'd go after your friends and see if they could find anybody who described your marriage as kind of unhappy, or kind of fractious. I had one client who had a sort of iron-clad case on an evidential level; her husband had worked for twenty years in fireproofing with sprayed asbestos. But they dug up that she'd had a, sort of, lesbian affair during the marriage. She hated to let her family know, and withdrew the suit. It was a kind of blackmail, really. And in your case, what you told me about being sort of packed and ready to move to Africa? By yourself if necessary, right before you found out that Glynis had cancer? I promise you they'd find someone who knew that story, and it would look kind of bad."

"If I accept the settlement, how soon could they cut me the check?"

"You'd have to sign a nondisclosure agreement. But after that? They'd cut you a check in a heartbeat. Especially with Glynis in sort of rough shape. They wouldn't want to be, uh, overtaken by events—when you might have, you know, kind of a change of heart. The worst coming to worst could make you decide to sort of go for the jugular."

"I'll have to talk to Glynis. But if you get us that money ASAP—and I mean, like, *Monday*, not weeks from now, because we don't have weeks—then I say take it."

Once he hung up the phone, Shep once more thought mournfully about Jackson. It was criminal that his best friend never lived to witness this conversion: from Mug, to Mooch.

Chapter Eighteen

Shepherd Armstrong Knacker
Union Bancaire Privée Account Number 837-PO-4619
Date: 21 February 2006
Our reference: 948378
Funds transfer: $800,000.00

Shep packed with a surety born of rehearsal. Rather than select a few arbitrary implements, this time he would take his whole trusty toolkit, toted from job to job from the earliest days at Knack. After all, these ancient wrenches, awls, and pliers were of a sturdy quality that you couldn't buy anymore. Rolling the tools with pristine newsprint from an unread *New York Times*, he lodged the bundles snuggly inside the familiar two-tiered box. Most of the once-bright red paint had chipped off the metal, like a beloved childhood wagon. He nestled the tools so that they didn't rattle, then hooked the metal clasps. He bound the box in a blanket from among the many pieces of bedding that he planned cheerfully to abandon, then wrapped it tight with twine. The toolbox had survived intact for thirty years, and he didn't want it to dent in its dotage on baggage belts; this was the same care that he would soon apply to his animate cargo. The likelihood that the toolkit would incur overweight charges was a matter of supreme indifference.

Next he wrapped and boxed the Wedding Fountain, having installed a new pump. He retrieved Glynis's flatware from the kitchen drawer—the Bakelite-inlaid fish slice, the knurling sterling chopsticks, the copper and titanium ice tongs—already conveniently bundled for transit in loving layers of sea-green felt. He even trotted up to the attic to rescue the plain sheet of heavy-gauge silver, with its single wobbly saw cut of less than an inch. As before, of course, the StairMaster, the salad spinner, the burdensome furniture would stay mercifully behind, but every work of Glynis's hand was guaranteed a place in the ZanAir ark.

He had researched the weather, and a few pieces of light clothing would suffice for most of the year, although yesterday he'd also purchased top-shelf rain gear from Paragon for the monsoon season. Having emailed Fundu Lagoon's management, he was now up to speed on electrics. Prepared for European 220 current, he packed three Radio Shack converters that would connect with British-style three-prong sockets. After grabbing a fistful of spare brush heads, he unscrewed the Oral-B charger from the bathroom wall. Nothing about the Third World obviated oral hygiene, and he would take the electric toothbrushes.

It was a relief this time around to shed the sheepish skulking—to pound boisterously down the hallway with the floorboards squeaking beneath the carpet, still stained from Glynis's nosebleed last spring; to let the screwdrivers clatter unashamedly against one another as he rolled them in bunches with newsprint. Otherwise, the exercise was a faithful repetition, like having conducted conscientious fire drills when the house was truly ablaze: duct tape; a selection of screws, bolts, and washers; silicon lubricant; plastic sealant; rubber bands; a small roll of binding wire. A flashlight, for power cuts, and a stack of AAs. A stock of Malarone tablets, and a fresh tube of cortisone, for the skin condition on his ankle that had thrived under the stress of the last Jobian year. This time, a packet of enemas, an overkill of antibiotics, and, reverently nestled between rolls of socks, the liquid morphine.

Improving on his dry run last January, he had bought a thicker, more serious Swahili-English/English-Swahili dictionary in preference to a mere phrasebook. He had pulled the Arts sections from the last month's newspapers, and torn out the crosswords; it had been years since he'd had the leisure for this frivolous pastime. Shep had always been terrible at crosswords, and without practice he'd be worse, which was a fine thing; they'd last longer that way.

He had given much more careful consideration to reading material. A brush with what real guns did to real people had cured him of any desire to seek out casual depictions of bogus violence by people who'd no idea what they were talking about—so thrillers were out. Nor did alarmist tracts appeal, about climate change, or the rise of Islamic terrorism; if they were right, catastrophe would ensue of its own accord without his having to read about it. He had never been one for serious novels; he'd never had time. But he was buying time. Consequently, on yesterday's trip to Manhattan for provisions, he had consulted a bespectacled clerk at a Barnes and Noble who, unlike most of their staff, seemed to have learned how to read. Thus in the corner of the hard-shell Samsonite on the bed upstairs he stacked four fat new paperbacks: Ernest Hemingway's *For Whom the Bell Tolls*, whose brave, self-sacrificing protagonist described on the back had seemed comfortingly kindred. William Faulkner's *Absalom, Absalom*, since the grand, rolling sadness of the first few pages he'd read in the aisle now suited his mood. Fyodor Dostoevsky's *The Idiot*, a title that seemed to encapsulate all of Jackson Burdina's long-winded subtitles in just two words. Besides, the young man at B&N had explained that the novel was about goodness, and how goodness just made people hate you; that suited his mood, too. When Shep had mentioned Africa, the shop assistant steered him toward Paul Theroux's *The Mosquito Coast*. Given the plot synopsis, inclusion of the Theroux was a fine joke at his own expense. These novels wouldn't last forever, but thankfully he was a slow reader. Tourists would likely leave spent paperbacks behind, and who knows, maybe for a price Amazon would deliver to Pemba.

Of course, the abortive rehearsal of 2005 had been quiet, furtive, intensely concentrated. Given that the household was now a cross between

a hospice and a refugee camp, the repeat performance was eternally interrupted by Heather's clamoring for a second slice of Entenmann's crumb
cake, or Zach's sullen complaint that with a little more advance notice he
might have ordered *Mighty Mordlock and the Sword of Doom* in time for
UPS to deliver before Thursday. Shep couldn't help but be distracted by
snippets of conversation that he caught while whisking in and out of the
bedroom, where Glynis and Carol were huddled in sotto voce consultation
on the pillows: what really lay at the bottom of Jackson's misery, whether
he had acted out of sadness or out of spite. Shep was jealous. Jackson was
his best friend. If there were answers to those questions he would like to
hear them himself. The jealousy thickened when at heated junctures in
their conversation the women went silent when he walked in.

After getting off the phone with Rick Mystic last Thursday night,
he'd had one hour to prepare for the arrival of Carol and the girls at
nine, and that was not a matter of making up beds. He couldn't invite
Carol to stay here and then expect her to say nothing to Glynis about
why she was an exile from her own house and why her husband was
so conspicuously AWOL. Real hospitality entailed telling Glynis in advance. He liked to think of himself as courageous. But without such a
hard deadline, he probably would have put it off.

Shep's inclinations had been at war. The advice he'd been given that
same day was perfectly conflicting. *You deal with it by telling her*, Carol
had abjured. *Being sick is not the same thing as being stupid or a small
child.* Goldman had countered a mere two hours later, *I think I'd counsel
you to keep my prognosis to yourself . . . Preserve the quality of the time she
has left . . . Keep her upbeat.*

It was a hackneyed formulation, but this was not a time to worry
about originality:

"I have some good news and some bad news," he'd announced soberly
in their bedroom after delivering her dinner of canned split-pea soup—
all he could rustle up in five minutes. "Which do you want first?"

Blowing to cool a sip, Glynis eyed him over her spoon with gladiatorial wariness. "Since we get so little good news in this household lately, maybe you'd better start with that."

"Forge Craft wants to settle. They've offered us one-point-two million."

Given that the offer was an accolade for her spectacular performance that morning, he would have expected at least a limp high-five. Yet her reaction was bafflingly mild. "That's nice," she said, and took her sip of soup.

"Do you want to accept?"

"I seem to recall there was an issue, with the rent," she said, dabbing the corners of her mouth with her napkin. "So I suppose so, yes."

To the extent that he might have described her as "quietly pleased," he dreaded moving on to Part II. Although his "good news and bad news" cliché had about it a sense of equivalence, the bad news far outweighed the good. In point of fact, there was only one piece of good news, which was now over, and had fallen disappointingly flat. As for the bad news, the pieces were two. Torn between Carol's honesty as best policy and the doctor's let sleeping cancer patients lie, for now he would split the difference.

"The bad news," he stalled, "is very bad."

Her eyes charged at him. "Are you sure you want to tell me?"

"Of course I don't want to. But I have to."

"You *have to*."

"Not telling you doesn't change anything, doesn't—make it un-so."

She put her spoon down slowly. Sliding her hands on either side of the tray, she gripped its sides the way a trucker would steady his steering wheel with his foot on the gas. Were the bed a semi-trailer, she would have run him over.

"Jackson shot himself."

Apparently what he'd said was so far afield from what she'd expected that she almost didn't hear him. Her question was insensible. "Is—is he okay?"

Shep gave her a moment to rehear him. "No."

"Oh." She dropped her hands. Her face was full of complexity, and it took a tiny instant for deep and genuine sorrow—"Poor Carol!"—to get the better of her guilty relief.

Now six nights on, he wouldn't go so grotesquely far as to claim that the suicide of one of their oldest and closest friends had cheered his wife up. Nonetheless, Glynis seemed palpably thankful to throw herself into suffering other than her own. Pausing only for embraces, she and Carol had hardly stopped talking since the Burdinas' arrival. Finally feeling useful if only as a confidante, Glynis seemed to be experiencing a resurgence of physical energy whose timing was fortuitous. He planned to draw on all her strength for a demanding journey beginning tomorrow afternoon that would take more than a full day.

But then, nothing could be harder than the much shorter trip he had taken the Friday morning after Carol and the girls arrived. To be fair, Carol had given him ample opportunity to get out of it—they could buy new clothes, she said, get new prescriptions—but he had promised.

With a detailed list of the Burdinas' vital possessions and their locations in his hip pocket, Shep had sat in the driver's seat that morning for a solid twenty minutes without starting the car. He was not by nature a procrastinator. But he did not want to go. For most of that twenty minutes not wanting to go had translated into not being able to go: not going. He could not start the car. True, he had summarily forsaken a sense of duty in all other respects: to his company, his country, and—in bilking a management that, whatever their predecessors may have manufactured thirty years ago, had never themselves done his wife a speck of harm—his very conscience. Yet he could not forsake a sense of duty to his friends. He believed in little now, but he did still believe in that. If he broke down this onerous mission into tiny, achievable units—reverse down the drive, signal right, round the golf course, merge onto 287—it would soon be over, and in this mechanical spirit he turned the key.

At the front door in Windsor Terrace his heart thundered in his eardrums, and a rush of adrenaline made Shep feel light-headed and slightly sick. Despite the mantra of his mental reassurance, his inner organs did not believe that there was *nothing to be afraid of.* The feeling was quite otherwise: of being trapped in a horror film on the wrong side of the screen. Once he'd let himself into the enclosed front porch, he stood clutching the duffel for his plunder and stared ferociously at the floor. Beside his shoe, the aqua linoleum was stained with the slender footprint of a woman's shoe. The footprint was rust-brown. There was no escaping what had happened here, even by staring at the floor.

He raised his gaze and entered the living room. At the far end of the room, the entrance to the kitchen was feebly barred with yellow police tape. The stairs to the bedrooms and study, where most items on Carol's list would be found, rose on his left-hand side. So he needn't enter the kitchen, or even look into it. For a moment he blinked and squinted, so that the kitchen opposite remained a blur. But it was what you didn't look at that frightened you. He would do this job more competently if he faced the kitchen down. Moreover, loyalty to Jackson demanded that he take on the full splatter of his friend's unhappiness.

He walked to the tape. Sunlight poured derisively through the windows, ensuring he would miss nothing: a peculiar litter of spatulas, serving spoons, and metal skewers all over the Forbo marmoleum that Shep had helped Jackson to install ten years ago. A cabinet drawer as well on the floor; a second drawer gaping open. A steel and heavy Sabatier cleaver on the breakfast table, both discolored with the same reddish brown of the footprint—as if left to rust, and despite his slapdash side Jackson Burdina had always been respectful of tools. A thick wooden cutting board customarily positioned on the counter by the fridge, but moved to the table, and soaked in the same sullen hue. There was something that Carol hadn't told him.

Otherwise, it was what he had tried to prepare himself for, although some things were not subject to preparation, and having been braced was no help. When affixing the squares with Forbo glue, he could never have known that Jackson's choice of a parquet alternating "Lapis Lazuli" and "Blue Mood" would provide such stunning contrast for the heavily tracked splashes and coagulated puddles. Nor could Carol have anticipated when she sewed the cream curtains patterned with pale cornflowers that they would double as canvases for the Rorschach of her husband's despair. For it was everywhere—as if a boiling pot of marinara had been left to spit and bubble over on the stove. Surly pools of slurry had thickened under the table, from which one hardened drizzle snaked to that impossible-to-clean flooring beneath the fridge. The splay was dull and darkened; a brighter, more glistening vista would have greeted Carol on her return home. She had literally tackled Flicka in the doorway, she said, and dragged her daughter to the porch, but not in time.

It was a pilgrimage. There was nothing to learn here besides that what had happened had happened, but this was information that Shep had needed to absorb.

He took the duffel upstairs to load it with school books and clothes. He rifled the filing cabinet in Carol's study, locating the wills and insurance policies she had asked him to find; with an instinct that would impress him in retrospect, he also snagged a pocket file that she had not requested: the family's passports. He picked a few choice selections from Flicka's cell phone collection that she hadn't requested, either. All the while he felt stalked, eyed by a presence behind his back, and he jumped when a hanger clattered from a rail, or the transformer on Carol's computer cord smacked to the floorboards. At last at the front door again, he turned the key to lock not burglars out but something in. The sharp white February air was cleansing, and he took in thirsty lungfuls like gulps of water.

As a salutary gesture, Shep spurned the toll-free Brooklyn Bridge and took the less congested Battery Tunnel. Four bucks on E-ZPass, but after this next errand he could afford the toll. Trolling Lower Manhattan inevitably recalled Jackson, and his rant about the area's wholesale confiscation of parking spaces by their overlords. In tribute, he pulled into an "Authorized Vehicles Only" space to invite a ticket. He could afford that, too.

In Rick Mystic's office on Exchange Place, he signed the nondisclosure agreement. Incredibly, Mystic promised that he could indeed get Forge Craft to cut the check by Monday. These people were in such a hurry that they could as well have been eavesdropping on yesterday's shattering appointment with Philip Goldman. Meantime, even twenty-four hours of keeping "one more" secret from Glynis had been intolerable. Her prognosis sat undissolved in his gut like a kidney stone.

The notion had first entered his head during the phone call with Mystic the night before, when the lawyer delivered the settlement offer: his nest egg for The Afterlife, miraculously restored. With every sluggish homeward mile in horrific Friday traffic, idle whimsy had crystallized to solid game plan.

The scene he walked in on with the duffel slung over his shoulder made him sorry that Carol's family didn't have the privacy to lick its wounds—or open them—out of another family's earshot. Still, it would have been unnatural to have made a U-turn in the foyer when it was his house.

Flicka had long been impatient with her mother, intolerant of that smothering concern for her welfare, but ever since they'd got here the girl had been outright cold. Save for the odd logistical request, she hadn't been speaking to her mother at all, which, considering what she said when she did speak, may have made Carol lucky.

"All he wanted was a little admiration," Flicka was delivering in a hot nasal snarl. She was bunched in the corner of the living room sofa, while Carol was sitting stiffly in the farthest chair. "He went to all that trouble to learn stuff, and think about stuff, and not just be some lame-ass *handyman*. He *told* you he hated that word, too, and you still said it all the time: *handyman, handyman, handyman!*"

"Honey, I'm glad you're proud of your father, and you should be," Carol said with rigid self-control. "But if I sometimes called him a 'handyman,' that's only because there isn't any other word, and that's what he was. Which is nothing to be ashamed of."

"You never paid any attention to him! He'd start talking and you just *turned off*. Think he didn't notice? You listen more carefully to the radio! And I mean like, the ads!"

"Your father sometimes used talking as a substitute for saying something. I guarantee you that when he spoke to me about anything important, I did listen. Very carefully."

"You mean important *to you*, not to him. And nothing that was important to him was important to you! No wonder Daddy killed himself! Every day, you made him feel *useless*, and *boring*, and *stupid*!"

Carol bowed her head soundlessly, until tears ran off her chin and spattered her hands—the kind of slow, insistent leak that any handyman would recognize as difficult to stanch.

"Sweetie," she said at last, looking back up at Flicka. "You're not the only one who's lost your daddy. You're not the only one who feels bad. You might have a genetic disease. But that doesn't mean you can say whatever you want—when it doesn't help anyone or change anything and it's terribly hurtful. I'm sorry you have FD. But you still have to be kind."

It was the stern parenting of which, out of fear of the emergency room, Flicka had been too long deprived. Dovetailing the silence of her mother's weeping, Flicka began to sob, but without the tears. When emotionally demonstrative, her eyes didn't cry; they got infected.

"It's not your fault, it's mine," the girl got out between shudders. "I was the one kept saying sticking around wasn't worth the bother. I was the one kept saying that being here isn't so great. I think I talked him into it. I think he got the idea from me."

Carol crossed to the sofa and took Flicka in her arms. "Shush, now. It's an idea we all get from time to time. You didn't invent it. But I'll tell you this much: *I* think one of the biggest reasons he left us? He was afraid that something would happen to you, and he couldn't bear it, sweetheart. He couldn't bear the idea of this world without you. He loved you so much, honey, more than you may ever know now, and it wasn't very brave of him, or even very nice. But whenever people do something out of love, then you have to be extra forgiving. Because I think he couldn't face your getting worse, or something worse than getting worse. I think he wanted to go first."

The following Saturday morning, Shep threw some blankets in his backseat. Entrusting Glynis to Carol's care, he headed for Berlin.

He worried that he'd encounter resistance. He wasn't accustomed to telling his father what to do, and the elderly were famously averse to change. Driving north, Shep had to remind himself that a nursing home was not, technically, a penitentiary. Surely springing your own father from its clutches wasn't actually against the law. But it was surely in violation of some institutional rule or other to simply scoop up one of their charges absent a stack of paperwork. That said, to whatever degree he was breaking the rules he was beginning to enjoy it.

At reception, he informed the nurse that he was taking his father on "an excursion." She frowned. "He's pretty weak. And it's nasty out there. Looks like snow."

"Don't worry," said Shep. "Where I'm taking my dad it's very, very warm."

The painfully diminished patriarch was dozing. Shep consoled himself that at least a man that thin was easy to carry. He whispered in his father's ear, "Hey Dad, wake up."

Once the old man's eyes opened they widened further, and he wrapped his arms around his son with the same surprising strength with which Glynis had thrust him away three days before. "Shepherd!" he croaked. "I was afraid I'd never see you again!"

Shep gently pulled from his father's clasp. "Shh. Now, listen. We're going to have to play it cool. As far as the staff is concerned, I'm just taking you for a spin, right? But I want you to think about anything here that you have to have with you. Because you're about to be kidnapped."

"You mean—we're not coming back?"

"No. Can you live with that?"

"Live with that?" Gabe hugged him again. "Oh, son. Maybe there is a God!"

Quietly packing up a few clothes and sweeping up the bottles of tablets from the bureau, Shep mumbled that they were driving back to Elmsford "first."

His father ceased to ease his spindly legs over the side of the bed. "But what about Glynis? Your dad is the personification of one of the Ten Plagues of Egypt. You told me yourself. I mustn't come near my daughter-in-law. You warned me I could kill her."

"*C-diff*? If we're going biblical here, then Glynis has hit the Book of Revelation. She's in the end of days, Dad. Being around a little more germ warfare isn't going to make any c-difference."

"Are you sure?"

"I—I've never done this before. You've been through it countless times with your parishioners. We could use your company. I could use your advice."

"Advice? On what?"

Shep took a breath. "How to help my wife die."

When Shep informed his father on the long drive back to New York that they were all going to Africa, the old man took the news in stride—merely remarking with standard Knacker pragmatism that unfortunately his passport had expired. (Shep explained that It's Easy, Inc., in midtown could turn around an application overnight for a price, and when his dad asked how much, Shep said with a blissful smile, "I don't care.") The summer they'd spent together in Kenya may have made the "dark continent" seem less forbidding. For that matter, his father didn't seem bothered by any itinerary that took him away from Twilight Glens. The sing-alongs, apparently, had not been a big success.

Shep wondered if he should have said goodbye to Beryl. But she'd been incensed when he suggested transferring their father to a public nursing home a few miles away; on being informed that instead her father was being kidnapped to Africa, she'd have gone apoplectic. Besides, she'd made it all too plain just what she thought of her brother's aspirations to any so-called Afterlife. At least now that the nursing home would no longer ravage the family's finances like a necrotic disease, she could keep the house. If that seemed a generous reward for short-of-generous behavior, in Shep's experience the house of one's childhood was more curse than windfall. And even if the past failed to exert its commonly crippling influence, Beryl would find those tall three stories on Mt. Forist Street considerably less of a jackpot once she paid her own fuel bills.

The drive was interrupted more than once for pit stops. After half-carrying his father to a gas-station men's room, Shep would support the torso with one arm and work the pajama bottoms below the buttocks with his free hand—a move at which, from his wife's periods of similar incapacity, he had grown expert. He'd leave his father to get on with things with the stall door closed, though this pretense of privacy would never last. Dad's assurances that he could see to his own cleaning up proved exaggerated, and of course getting the pajama bottoms up again entailed more assistance. In the Middle East, it was considered the height of humiliation to glimpse your father's genitals, but for Shep it was merely another exercise in getting real. So they both had penises. Big deal.

Inevitably, during the last late-night leg in northern Connecticut, too many stations and diners were closed. His father didn't make it. A stinging brown smell infused the car, and his father started to cry.

"Dad," said Shep. "I've been up to my elbows in shit for months, and I'm not being figurative, either. I still love my wife, and I'm intimately acquainted with her body's every ooze and spew. I'm going to take care of you now, and instead of hiring some stranger to wipe your backside I'll wipe it myself. It's nothing to be embarrassed about. The only people who ought to be embarrassed are me and Beryl, for ever offloading the ass-wiping onto someone else."

They got back to Elmsford at 1:00 a.m. After fifteen hours of driving, Shep should have felt bone tired. But ever since Pemba had been resurrected from pitiful pipe dream to definitive destination, he'd been riding a curious high. There was still a spring in his step as he cleaned his father up and settled him on the couch in the den downstairs, close to the ground-floor bathroom.

While Glynis was still asleep Sunday morning, Shep tackled the Zach issue. Once his son allowed him reluctantly into the inner sanctum, he bounced onto the boy's bed and announced, "We're moving to Africa."

Twisting around from his computer screen, Zach looked at his father with a humoring deadpan. He no more believed in the guy's screwball "Afterlife" than Beryl did. "Uh-huh. When."

"I have to hit the BA website, but hopefully before the end of the week."

Zach inspected his father closely. Shep looked pleasantly back, satisfied to assess that, as expected, his son's features were squaring up, and at sixteen the young man was almost handsome. "You're not kidding."

"Nope. So you'd better start collecting a few things. Pack light. Even if we can't find everything we need on Pemba, I think Zanzibar is pretty well stocked, and we'll be a half-hour's flight from Stone Town."

"We're 'moving to Africa' for how long?"

"For me? Forever. For you? That's your decision. Once you turn eighteen, you're a free agent. But hey, you don't like that new school anyway."

"I thought . . ." Zach licked his lips. "I thought it was kids who were supposed to get these sudden ideas in their heads to do something crazy. And then it's the parents who sit them down and make them be, you know. *Realistic*."

"I've been 'realistic' for forty-nine years, sport. And when you make something real, then it is realistic. By the way, Pemba does have broadband. I knew you'd want to know."

"What if I don't want to go?"

"Well . . . You could go stay with your Aunt Beryl at your grandfather's in Berlin—though as you know it's a pretty small town. So you'd still be in the boonies, but without coconut palms or snorkeling on coral reefs. Gets pretty cold up there. Pretty soon, if I'm not mistaken, your grandfather's house is going to get a whole lot colder, too. Alternatively, you could stay with your Aunt Deb, though you'd better be ready to do plenty of babysitting and to at least pretend to become a born-again Christian. There's Aunt Ruby, but she's a workaholic who won't even make time for a boyfriend, much less a live-in nephew. Your grandma in Tucson would love to have you, although you always complain she treats you like a six-year-old. She's seventy-three. I bet she won't stop now."

"You're seriously planning to dump me on relatives?"

"No, I'm seriously planning to take you to a fascinating part of the world where you can learn to fish from a wooden canoe called an *mtum-bwi*. Go diving. Learn Swahili. Eat the best pineapples and mangos you've ever tasted. And help me build a house."

"You seem—a little weird. Like you're on something. Sure you haven't helped yourself to some of Mom's meds?"

"I guess if you really don't want to go, then you can throw yourself on the mercy of a social worker, because your father's become a drug addict."

"Z" had never been comfortable joking with his father, and looked pained. "How long do I have to think this over?"

"I made up my own mind in the time it took to drive from Lower Manhattan to Westchester. But that was a Friday, and the traffic was bad. So I'll give you half that."

"I'm supposed to decide whether to turn my whole life upside down and 'move to Africa' *today*?"

"Decisions take a split second. It's not deciding that takes all the time."

"But what about Mom? She's not, you know, looking so hot. In Africa—what about doctors?"

"We've had enough doctors."

"But I mean, how does she feel? Is she cool with this?"

"That," said Shep, rising, "is what I'm about to find out."

He slid onto the bed as Glynis stirred, and pulled her head to his lap. She nuzzled. "So how's your dad?" she mumbled.

"Ask him yourself. He's downstairs."

"You brought him home?" she asked sleepily. "What for? Is that advisable?"

"It is *advisable*. He's my father. I want to take him with me."

"With you?" she muttered, and sighed. Her hand on his thigh felt as delectable as it always had. "With you where?"

"Gnu?" He stroked her temple. "Remember last year, when I asked you to come to Pemba? Well, I'm asking again. And this time cancer's no excuse."

"Mmm?" She resettled her head. She kept it covered around others, but he had come to admire the strong, clean form of her crown without the hair.

"It's warm," he intoned. "The beaches are white. The trees are tall. The fish is fresh. And the breeze is spiced with cloves."

"Hold it," she said, opening her eyes. "I'm not dreaming."

"I'm not, either, and I never have been. I want to take you to Pemba. I want us to go this week."

She sat up. "Shepherd, are you mad? This is hardly the time to start talking about Africa again."

"This is the only time left to talk about Africa. And the only time left to go."

"Even if I don't start that experimental drug, I have five more chemos! I may be almost through, but I'm not through."

"No." He placed a palm on her cheek. "You're through." He had meant through with any more treatments, but the assertion came out more starkly than he'd planned.

She twisted from his hand. "What, are *you* writing me off now, too?"

"Gnu. What is happening to you? What do you think is happening to you?"

"I'm obviously very sick, but the last couple of days I've been feeling better—"

"You can hardly eat anymore. You can hardly shit anymore, or climb a flight of stairs anymore. *What do you think is happening to you?*"

"Stop it! You're being cruel! It's important to stay positive, to keep trying—!"

"I think it's cruel to keep trying."

She started to cry. "I'm telling you, I can beat this!"

"See? It's not your fault," he said. "You have such a will. And then all this talk, at the hospital, about 'fighting,' and 'beating,' and 'winning.' Of course you'd rise to that. Try to shine in the contest. But it's not a contest. Cancer is not a 'battle.' Getting sicker is not a sign of weakness. And dying," he said the word softly but distinctly, "is not defeat."

Glynis naturally thrived on enemies, and would readily replace the villain of disease with her husband. "What do *you* know about it?" she growled.

"What do I know?" He took a minute to consider. He had fought the urge to confide in Carol since Thursday night. He had resisted pouring his heart out to his father yesterday, despite the long drive, and had refrained earlier this morning from taking his son aside. He had neglected to make all the calls that the doctor expected—to Petra, to Arizona. For once his restraint did not derive, like breaking the news about Jackson, from dread of "making it real." For Shep to inform a single soul before Glynis herself was *insulting*.

"Goldman didn't want me to tell you," Shep plunged on. "In fact, he wanted me to tell everyone else but you. So your mother would immediately fly to New York, and your sisters. Your friends would suddenly show up here all at once to recite their little speeches again, those speeches you hate, and you wouldn't understand why. Goldman wanted them all to know, and to keep you in the dark. But you know what? I'd rather keep them in the dark. Fuck them. But not to tell you is disrespectful. And I respect you. I don't think I've been acting as if I do for the last few months, but I respect you."

She was on all fours in a crouch, as if about to scratch his eyes out. "Tell me what?"

"Goldman gives you three weeks."

She crumpled, but he would keep talking. He was tired of not talking.

"That's closer to two and a half now. Maybe I'm wrong and you'd really rather not know, but I don't think that's fair to me. All these things I'm supposed to keep to myself—like the CAT scans. They've been terrible, Glynis. Can I get that off my chest, too? The patches are spreading. Oh, and guess how long you were expected to live to begin with? One year. One year from diagnosis, that's the average with mesothelioma. Right, with only epithelioid cells, you might have had up to three years, on the outside, with chemo. But the moment Hartness found that *biphasic* crap, your life expectancy plummeted right back down to twelve months. You've made it almost two months past that, and we're supposed to be grateful. But I've had to live with that one-year death sentence all on my own; you made it clear in Knox's office that you didn't want to know. So Jackson offs himself, and my first instinct is: I can't tell my wife. Because I'm not supposed to tell you anything. But it makes me lonely. I don't want to be alone right now. I have less than three weeks for the rest of my life not to be alone. And we have less than three weeks to do whatever it is that we're going to do, ever, and that's why I want to go to Pemba. *Now.*"

He had told her that it was not a fight. That it had never been a fight. That if there was no fight there was no losing. He had let her off the hook. She could stop fighting. Lying on her side like a trophy he had bagged—like a *gnu*, gut-shot but still breathing—Glynis mumbled into the sheets, "Okay, I give up."

Yet when she lifted her head after officially *giving up*, she looked agreeably surprised to find herself still here, as if the only thing that had kept her from dying on the spot for months now was her determination not to. "So, fine," she assented brightly. "Let's go to Pemba."

As she crawled into his arms, Shep had the astonishing impression that she meant it. He held her.

"There were a lot of things I wanted to do, too, Shepherd," she said. "So many things I wanted to make, and now they're stuck in my head."

"It doesn't matter." He skipped the pro forma tribute to how exquisite were the few of her works that had made it into three dimensions. Time was short, and the compliments would bore her. "I don't have the eloquence to explain why, but I know it doesn't matter. Because maybe, if you take a step back . . . since you, and everyone, and everything, eventually, dies, and the whole world is all so, weirdly . . ."

She made a dismissive, rippling gesture with her fingers. "Fuff."

"Yeah, it's all *fuff.* So maybe—what you made, but only in your head? Is just as important, and just as real, and just as beautiful, as what you made with metal upstairs."

She kissed him. "Thank you."

"You know, these movies . . ." He was groping. "Remember how sometimes, in the middle, a movie seems to drag? I get restless, and take a leak, or go for popcorn. But sometimes, the last part, it heats up, and then right before the credits one of us starts to cry—well, then you forget about the crummy middle, don't you? You don't care about the fact that it started slow, or had some plot twist along the way that didn't scan. Because it moved you, because it finally pulled together, you think, when you walk out, that it was a good movie, and you're glad you went. See, Gnu?" he promised. "*We can still end well.*"

By the time he slipped from the bedroom they were actually laughing, although whether Glynis's renewed sense of humor was rooted in a release from denial or its immediate restoration was hard to say.

Before heading downstairs to mobilize breakfast for seven, he rapped on Zach's door. The leery visage that peered from the crack betokened a fervent hope that whatever mind-altering drug had infused his father's bloodstream had now worn off.

"Your mother's game. So what's it gonna be?" said Shep. "In or out?"

"It's only been an hour!"

"So? I have to buy the tickets after breakfast."

"This is completely nuts. But . . . I can't stand that vegetarian slop Aunt Beryl makes. I don't feel like asking *Jesus into my heart*, and Grandma is always hugging my face into her boobs, which is totally embarrassing. And I don't . . . Well, I don't want to leave Mom. So I guess I don't have any choice. But you're right, if I told your bizzaro plan to a social worker, I bet you'd be arrested."

"That's why we have to move quick," said Shep lightly. "We're *absconding.*" *Absconding* was just the sort of word that Jackson had loved.

Indeed, he'd delivered to Carol a similar sense of liberation when she'd confessed miserably that under the circumstances she dreaded organizing a funeral, and he'd pointed out that you didn't have to have one.

"So don't you have to contact my school and shit?" said Zach. "Get permission?"

"Probably," said Shep. "But I won't."

"Well, you can't just *leave*."

"Mooches do." Shep's beatifically off-kilter smile discouraged further inquiry.

Zach gestured downstairs, where Heather was throwing another fit about the crumb cake. "And what about those guys? Like, what are you planning to do, leave them behind in this house? 'Cause I don't get the impression they're heading back to Windsor Terrace anytime soon."

His son had been the only recipient of the news about Jackson who hadn't acted shocked. Perhaps understandably, the *hikikomori* the boy ran with considered suicide a perfectly reasonable alternative to a life of indefinite self-imprisonment in a small bedroom. Zach's casual revelation that he and his friends talked about "checking out" as commonly as teenagers in his father's day had withdrawn books from the library had further motivated Shep to haul the kid out of the country.

"I guess I haven't addressed that yet," Shep admitted. True, abandoning the furniture was an active pleasure. The landlords would be stuck with its disposal, but Shep was discovering that the process by which he had all his life assumed the burdens of other people could be accomplished in reverse. Abandoning the Burdinas was another matter.

Having learned the secret that decisions take no time, Shep had resolved the issue between his first step at the top of the stairs and his arrival on the ground floor.

Heather was running water at the sink purely to make the kinetic fountain work, and her poking at the twirling whisk was getting the floor wet. (Since she'd got here, the girl hadn't acted mournful but manic.

Hyperactivity and nonstop food tantrums were the sole indicators that she had registered that she no longer had a daddy. Shep wondered if there was such a thing as antidepressants working a bit too well.) Right now Heather was tunelessly belting out the theme song of Pogatchnik's television ad, "The handyman can, oh, the handyman can!" turning the faucet on and off in time with the monotonous song. It was annoying— worse than annoying really, it was excruciating—but he didn't have the heart to tell her to cut it out any more than he'd be able to deny her yet another slice of crumb cake.

Meantime, Flicka was propped disjointedly on the kitchen stool like last season's manikin. His father—predictably—was in the bathroom. Carol was gesturing toward breakfast more than making it. Ordinarily so effi- cient, she had put out a single box of cereal, but no bowls or spoons. Instead of getting out the milk, she'd got out the tonic water. When he walked in, she was standing in the middle of the room, frozen, as if about to do some- thing but no longer remembering what that was. Like several he'd had to replace in his digital camera, Carol's memory card was corrupted.

He led her to the table and sat her down; she was pliant. Since cards corrupt in discrete sectors, her brain started up again and proceeded to output what Carol Burdina was supposed to say. "We've really appreci- ated your hospitality the last few nights. But we can't continue to im- pose . . . Maybe a hotel . . . The girls . . . They should go back to school." But her heart wasn't in it, and she sounded like a robot.

So he ignored her. "Glynis, Zach, my father, and I are leaving for the island of Pemba as soon as I can get flights out. You and the girls should come, too."

Insofar as she had expectations—*no, no, no, please make yourself at home for as long as you like*—what he'd said defied them. A little cock of her head seemed to indicate that he'd got her attention. The film over Flicka's eyes also appeared to clear.

Carol's laugh was more of a hiccough. "You're going to Africa."

The inane punctuation "The handyman can 'cause he mixes cement with love and makes the house work good!" made the proposed journey sound all the more absurd.

"That's right. According to Jackson"—Shep had resolved not to avoid his friend's mention—"you thought I'd never go."

"Well, have a nice time," she said blandly.

"You're coming, too."

However dispiritedly, her famous practicality roused. "Can't. Flicka."

"I know the FD will be challenging, but we'll manage."

"Hot," said Carol.

"Cool towels, fans. When and where possible, air-conditioning."

"Flying. Pressure."

"All she has to do is swallow. She's learned to swallow."

"Drugs."

"Internet."

It was like badminton. The long point ended summarily with a neat smash from the stool:

"I'm going to Pemba."

Carol turned to Flicka and sighed. "You can't go to Africa."

Tipping off her stool, Flicka navigated in a stooped zigzag across the kitchen by gripping a chair, the table, the vegetable storage baskets; lately Flicka made her way about a room with the agile, lateral clamber of Jeff Goldblum in the remake of *The Fly*. She pushed Heather from the sink, filled her water bottle, turned off the tap, and wiped a drizzle of spittle from her chin with her terrycloth wristband in one motion, and set about connecting the syringe to her g-tube for her usual on-the-hour hydration. It was a display of self-sufficiency that said, *See? What about this tiresome business can't be accomplished in Africa?*

Shep had little doubt that previous to Wednesday night Carol would have proven far more adept at concocting irrefutable reasons why a disabled seventeen-year-old with a rare, degenerative disease could not take up residence on an island on the other side of the world with one underequipped hospital staffed by Chinese doctors, none of whom would know anything about managing an exclusively Jewish genetic condition called familial dysautonomia. But that systematic, brisk mother-of-two had been replaced by in some ways a more likeable woman who was utterly lost. Moreover, what she'd just been through must have impelled her to flee. Since so far she'd managed to escape only a piffling thirty miles north to Westchester, the only powerful objection that the New Carol might legitimately have raised to his proposal was that Africa was not nearly far enough away. So she imprudently abandoned her sensible medical line for a tactical error.

"Money," she said. "We don't have any."

"You have less than no money," he concurred. "I glanced at some of the credit card bills lying around Jackson's computer at work. Which is all the more reason to cut and run. MasterCard won't come after you off the coast of Zanzibar. Besides, I have money. Enough, if we're frugal, to last all of us in Tanzania indefinitely. The Wapemba live on a couple dollars a day. We could at least budget five bucks."

Her eyes drifted to the corn flakes, flickering with what seemed a hazy awareness of the dozens, perhaps hundreds of other rock-solid reasons that this preposterous plan was out of the question.

"Dad would want us to go," said Flicka.

"She's right," Shep agreed. "Leave Jackson's parents to arrange a memorial service if it makes them feel better. But I promise you, and I knew the guy almost as well as you did: no memorial to your husband would be more fitting than your getting out of here. If there is an afterlife with a small *a*, he'll be thrilled to know that you took his kids and flew to Pemba."

". . . But there's the inquest."

"Incest?" Heather repeated merrily. "My friend Fiona says her family has incest!"

Yet another reason to leave the country. He asked, "Is there any question in your own mind about what happened?" She shook her head morosely. "Then why worry about an inquest?"

"I'm going with them, Mom," Flicka announced with finality, leaning on the counter for balance as she drained the last of the water into her syringe, "whether you and Heather come or not."

A talented manipulator of other people's pity, Flicka had bossed her parents around for years. Now the facility could be deployed to far more tectonic effect than getting out of her math homework.

There remained one last invitation to issue—albeit the kind extended to folks who you already know can't come to a party but whom you ask anyway as a gesture. Sure enough, when Shep explained about Pemba and how of course she was welcome to join them, Amelia was not about to drop everything: her friends, her job, her boyfriend. But she sounded a little confused, so he was careful thereafter to be crystal clear: "Your mother is dying, sweetheart, and she finally knows she's dying, too. This is your one and only chance to say goodbye. And this time maybe you two can do better than, you know, lumpy versus smooth."

The last time Amelia had driven up to Elmsford, she'd brought her new boyfriend—probably a decent kid, but no match for the awkwardness of the circumstances. His girlfriend's flagging mother didn't have the energy to ask all the solicitous questions that would have filled out a normal introduction: So where do you work? What are your ambitions? Where are your people from? Naturally the Food Channel was on, which must have helped to explain why they ended up spending the entire visit talking about potatoes.

Mashed potatoes, specifically: whether everyone preferred the silky, smooth sort with lots of cream, or the lumpy, bohemian type with chunks and skin. Shep had sat in. After a good twenty minutes of this microanalysis of tuber preparation, it required the full force of his self-control to keep from leaping to his feet and exploding, *Look, Teddy, or whatever your name is, I'm sure you're a nice guy but I'm afraid we don't have time to get to know you right now. So get out of the room; you don't belong here, and your girlfriend only dragged you along to begin with as cover. To hide behind. And Amelia, as you can see your mother is in piss-poor shape, so you have no way of knowing whether this is the very last time you ever talk to her in your whole life. If you end up doomed to remember squandering those final few minutes on POTATOES you will never forgive yourself.*

To the girl's credit, blessed with the opportunity to retake that abysmal scene, Amelia made it up to Elmsford within the hour. She let herself in the front door just as Shep was logging off the British Airways website upstairs. When he hurried down to greet her, he was relieved she'd not brought the boyfriend, nor had she glittered her cleavage, caked her lashes, or plaited her hair. Pale, skinny, and ponytailed, Amelia in loose jeans and a rumpled sweatshirt was recognizably the same kid he'd galloped around the yard on his back, and somehow this de-eroticized version made it easier to embrace his daughter full-bore without embarrassment. Yet that ravaged expression she wore was plenty adult, its etched quality suggesting that a better-than-oblivious relationship to her mother's parlous condition had prevailed for some time.

Forewarned of Amelia's arrival, Glynis had forced herself from bed, and now slipped unsteadily downstairs with a shake of her head at Shep; this was a proper entrance, and she didn't want help. For the first time in weeks she'd put on real clothes, a favorite evening ensemble of ink-black rayon. Over a flowing blouse and matching slacks she wore a rippling floor-length robe trimmed in tiny, tasteful rhinestones. She had drawn on her eyebrows. Her intention, Shep intuited, was not disguise. It was a favor, as Amelia's garb was also a favor: the mother would look her best, and the daughter would look her least adulterated.

As the three of them settled in the living room, Zach sidled into the doorway. At last there was no fevering about the kitchen, no boyfriend, no mashed potatoes. "I'm sorry I haven't come up a little more often," said Amelia, beside her mother on the couch. "It's really hard for me to see you—deteriorated, Mom. I've always admired how beautiful you are, how—statuesque. How you hold yourself . . . above, apart. It hurts me, seeing you not be able to pull off the old class act anymore, no longer being able to act like some—queen. I know that's no excuse. But I have tried to keep up with how you're doing through Z."

The parents turned an inquisitive glance toward their son in the doorway, and he nodded. "Yeah, she, like, at least texts five times a day. Whadda ya think? She's my sister."

"Why not text me?" asked Glynis.

"With Z . . ." Amelia looked away. "Well, from Z I'm sure to get an honest report." She turned back to her mother. "I can't stand the pretending. It's fake, it's gross, it's . . . a violation. We've all been supposed to act as if you were getting better, and I just—I didn't want to remember you that way."

"I'm sorry too, then," said Glynis, taking her daughter's hands. "But we're not pretending now, are we? So I have something for you. To remember me by." Glynis lifted a box from beside the sofa that she must have placed there before Amelia's arrival. Shep recognized his wife's equivalent of his own battered red toolbox.

"I want you to have my old jewelry," Glynis continued. "The things I made before I moved on to flatware. Many of these pieces are very dramatic, and most women wouldn't, as you just put it yourself, be able to 'pull them off.' But you can. You, too, are *statuesque*, and you'll do this work proud."

"Oh!" Amelia cried with a girlish delight as she slid one of the serpentine bracelets up her slender arm. They were all there, the artifacts with which Shep had first fallen in love, including those morbid stickpins, like tiny bouquets of bird bones. "I used to try on these pieces as a kid when you weren't home. In secret. I never told you, but later I started borrowing necklaces to go out, and I was scared you'd take my head off if you knew. I was terrified that I'd, like, scratch the finish, too. But everyone was blown away whenever I wore your work, and I always told them: *my mother made this*. They couldn't believe it. So thank you, thank you! I can't think of anything I'd want more."

Mother and daughter reminisced, and described what they admired in each other; to keep it real, they also dredged up a few memories that were unpleasant. There were silences while they both wracked their brains for whatever they might berate themselves later for forgetting to say. In sporadic, headlong installments, Amelia was delivering one of the very "speeches" that from others had enraged her mother for the last year. Yet for the first time Glynis was able to sit still and listen and accept the compliments. There was nothing insensitive about talking as if she were about to die when she was.

The visit was warm enough and good enough that it didn't need to be overly long.

"Have a great time in Africa," said Amelia, standing. "I hope you make it to Pemba before . . ." She hesitated, then seemed to relish the new lack of pretense. "Before you die. And I hope the end—doesn't hurt too much. I guess it may not have turned out quite the way you intended, but I still think you had a good life, Mom."

Shep feared that his wife would shy away with something worthy of Pogatchnik like, "Well, it was what it was." Instead Glynis shot her husband a long look before turning back to her daughter. "Yes, my dear," she said. "I think I've had a good life, too."

When the two women faced each other at the door, it was an odd moment but strangely simple—elegant, even. They hugged. Neither cried. Their leave-taking was dignified: one of those successful partings at which neither party would leave a sweater behind.

"Goodbye, Mom," said Amelia.

"Goodbye, Amelia." Glynis added with a wry little smile, "It's been nice knowing you."

"Yes," said Amelia, her smile so identically wry, her tone so exactly duplicating the same dry, classy understatement, that these two had to be related. "It's been nice knowing you, too."

Chapter Nineteen

Shepherd Armstrong Knacker
Union Bancaire Privée Account Number 837-PO-4619
Statement for February 2006
Balance: $771,398.22

The journey itself resembled one of those charity events during which a valiant band of the severely handicapped improbably climb Mont Blanc; had they only signed up sponsors, their motley party of seven might have raised thousands for a good cause.

After the ninety-minute drive to Kennedy, Shep ditched his SUV in long-term parking, thinking: *very long term.* (So oriented toward acquisition, Americans cheated themselves of the joys of divestiture, thus far proving much more intense. With every all-in-one printer and pair of flannel-lined jeans he walked clean away from, Shep felt so much lighter that by the time they arrived at Gate 3A he might have flown to Pemba without the planes.) After three hours of loitering, the British Airways red-eye to London was seven hours, followed by a three-and-a-half-hour layover in Heathrow, an eight-and-a-half-hour flight on Kenya Airways to Nairobi, another two-hour layover, an hour-and-forty-minute flight to Zanzibar, a four-hour layover with no air-conditioning, which in hundred-degree heat with Flicka nearly proved catastrophic, a shaky half-hour flight in a twenty-seater prop whose faded appointments dated the plane back to about 1960, an hour's tumble in a minivan, and a twenty-minute speedboat ride, the trip door to door—*door* loosely speaking, since their tented encampment didn't really have one—took thirty-three hours.

Entertainments were numerous: helping his father shit within the confines of an airline head; glaring at fellow passengers who pretended not to stare at Flicka as she lifted her shirt and poured another airline miniature of bottled water into a plastic hole in her stomach; fielding icy offers of assistance from flight attendants who really meant, "Fucking hell, why me?" and "These emaciated cripples have no business flying, and they'd better not die on my plane"; continually moving Flicka's portable oxygen tank out of the way of refreshment carts; trading off with Carol in reminding Flicka to swallow; doling out three complex sets of medications, and having to separate them out meticulously by shape and color when turbulence sent a lap load onto the floor and skittering under other passengers' seats; going begging down the aisle for unused airline blankets to keep Glynis warm; buying *kikois* in Zanzibar's grungy airport to soak in cold water and wipe Flicka down, although it was having remembered to pack the little portable fan that he'd propped on his computer terminal at the swelteringly overheated offices of Handy Randy that really saved the day— thank you, Pogatchnik.

The last bumpy leg on ZanAir was nauseating, the circulation no better than hot breath. Everyone fanned themselves with laminated escape instructions that, given the age of the plane, they should probably have been reading. Clutching his wife's hand, Shep distracted himself by memorizing his first lesson in Swahili—"fasten seatbelts": *fungu mikanda*; "no smoking": *usivute sigara*. Three of these passengers were near enough to it not to worry about imminent demise. Still, as the plane's engines milled in a deafening grind whose fluctuations did not encourage confidence, he prayed to put a first toe on Pemba without freefalling five thousand feet beforehand.

At last the prop plane lurched above the Pemban shallows—a wide alabaster ripple of azures, emeralds, and aquas of a richness one rarely encountered outside computer animation—and then sailed over the lacy rim of a lambent white beach.

"Wow," said Flicka, craning over Heather's lap to gaze out the window.

"Oh, gross, you're getting drool all over me again!" Heather complained, although she'd already dripped guava-banana yogurt down her shirt.

Glynis, too, was glued to her window. "Shepherd, it's beautiful." She sighed. "Maybe you were right."

"Jesum crow, son," said Gabe from the window seat in the next row. "And I thought I'd spend the rest of my days staring at nothing but that cheap reproduction of a Thomas Hart Benton at Twilight Glens."

"Could have found this view on Google Earth without taking four different airplanes," said Zach, who had chosen to sit glumly on his own.

"I always think of Africa as dry," Carol marveled. "But this island looks so lush!"

Indeed, Pemba was densely forested, its terrain lumpy with hillocks, their thick, broad-leafed foliage of banyan trees and banana plants spangled with punctuating palms like asterisks. Tiny, humble patches of cultivation were threaded together with red dirt tracks that would hereafter supplant the West Side Highway. As they passed overhead, roofs of corrugated tin flared silver in the sun, as if the population of Pemba were flashing a greeting to their newest residents in Morse code.

They landed at an airport that Glynis declared "adorable." With a tiny hexagonal watchtower striped in Fanta orange and baby blue, it looked like a toy. The terminal itself was the size of a one-room schoolhouse. After the oppressive seriousness of the last year, Shep welcomed a locale that shrank the accoutrements of Western civilization into playful assemblages that might have been made from Legos.

Lifting his wife, father, and afflicted seventeen-year-old ward from the plane to the three waiting wheelchairs that Fundu Lagoon had thoughtfully organized in advance—they were all so exhausted that even Flicka did not resist—Shep was niggled by his first trace of disappointment. Sniffing the thick, otherwise pungent air as it baked back from the tarmac, he could detect a vague floral sweetness mixing with the reek of airline fumes, but—*no cloves*. Even as their party was loaded by a jovial, muscular driver and the minivan got under way, Shep kept inhaling, sticking his nose out the crack of the van's window with a petulance he could not repress. It was just an idea he'd latched onto, from a snippet he'd read online, but for some reason it had become terribly important to him that the entire island of Pemba would smell like pumpkin pie.

The drive was still enchanting. Between the airport in Chake Chake and the port of Mkoani they traveled one of Pemba's few paved roads, so that if anything the vistas went by too quickly: trees drooping with papayas whose contour reminded Shep with chagrin of his father's aged testicles, immature mangos shaped like lima beans, bulbs of breadfruit spiked like maritime mines. Traffic must have been rare, since as their vehicle passed local women in harlequin *kangas* rose from the shade of their porches to stare. Surveying the housing stock, Shep considered whether to build Chez Knacker with the less attractive cinderblocks of which the newer houses were made, or to go native and learn to construct the more traditional architecture of thatched coconut-palm roofing and mud walls dried on a frame of sticks. The latter, claimed their driver, lasted a good forty years, and their rooms were cool.

Yet as they drew toward the port where Fundu's speedboat would meet them, the roadside was soon lined with straw mats, nubbled with a thin crumble in hues from green to brown. As the mats grew in density—by the edge of town the nubble was spread on the road's meridian, and out onto the tarmac itself—the van gradually infused with the aroma of pumpkin pie. *Cloves*, spread to dry in sun. Inhaling deeply, Shep sat back in satisfaction. The Afterlife had begun.

At $1,250 per night, the "superior suite" at Fundu Lagoon—the very last and most expensive set of tents a ten-minute walk from the main resort, providing maximum privacy—was hardly where Shep planned to hunker down for keeps. At that rate, the Forge Craft settlement would last no more than a couple of years. Yet the resort's comically palatial luxury was perfect for this recuperative pause: catered meals, towels the size of bedsheets in high thread-count Egyptian cotton, and their encampment's generous provision of everything that Shep might have forgotten: floppy straw sun hats, sandalwood shampoo, organic hibiscus teabags, bug spray, mosquito coils, straw carrier bags for beachcombing, and a copy of *Africa Birds and Birding*, not to mention the iced bottle of champagne and chilled glasses that greeted them on arrival.

Indeed, it was the champagne that inspired his immediate solution to what to do about Flicka, whose blood pressure was soaring in the heat. Since the little round plunge pool on their deck was essentially a champagne bucket writ large, it was the perfect place to stick Flicka, who could dangle in the cool blue water through the heat of the day. Snorkeling expeditions to the reef, diving lessons, and dawn speedboat trips to career through cavorting pods of spinner dolphins would keep Zach from grumbling that there was nothing to do; as soon as he'd ditched his bag at their encampment, the kid made a beeline for the computer with broadband in the entertainment tent, having perhaps interpreted the sweat along his hairline as an early sign of Internet cold turkey. Shep's father may have been going through newspaper withdrawal himself, but immediately set up shop in a deck chair in the shade of a wide umbrella, stripped down to his boxers. Sipping champagne and gazing out to the deserted beach while *daos* and *mtumbwis* sailed lazily across the horizon, he seemed sufficiently to savor his miraculous rescue from the lifeless four walls of Twilight Glens to live without *The New York Times*. Instead he drew out the first of the stack of Ruth Rendell and Walter Mosley novels that his son had stashed in his luggage— the very variety of fiction that had been Gabriel Knacker's undoing on the staircase on Mt. Forist Street. After exploring the big main tent and indoor bathroom, playing with the outdoor shower, clambering up to the second floor of the adjoining tent to play with the beaded curtains of mangrove seeds, Heather squeezed into her swimming suit and tumbled to the water. Carol kept an eye on her, but at low tide the girl walked for ten minutes straight out and never submerged deeper than her knees. In her first hour at Fundu, Heather had already got more exercise than Shep had seen the girl take for the last ten days.

He settled Glynis onto the wide white canopied mattress to rest. A staff member arrived promptly with a tall glass of fresh passion-fruit juice and a straw at his request, although he also fed his wife a christening sip or two from his champagne. He eased off the remainder of her velour lounge suit—all that she could stand against her skin these last few months—and tenderly clad her in a soft, thin muslin dress he had snagged from Fundu's gift shop on the way in. Glynis smoothed her hand across the starched and ironed white sheets and glanced overhead at the gathered mosquito netting.

"So this is my death bed," she said simply.

"It's better than that snarl of blankets on Crescent Drive, isn't it? And at least here we don't have to pay any extra to heat the room to ninety."

She smiled. "But whatever am I going to do without the Food Channel?"

"From the sample menus I read online? Grilled wahoo, Thai beef salad, baked lemon soufflé? You're living in the Food Channel."

"Well, it's pretty amazing, Shepherd. Though getting here was horrible."

"I know. I knew it would be horrible."

"I couldn't do that again. I guess not having to is one merit of the one-way trip."

"It's one-way for me, too."

"You're sure you'll stay here?" This was her first tentative inquiry about Shep's real pending Afterlife: life after Glynis. "It's only been a few hours."

"I was sure before the props on the plane stopped spinning. And then on the drive to Mkoani . . . You can tell, they work hard here. They may have cell phones now, but everything is still pretty primitive. More bikes and oxcarts than cars. You want fish, you catch it. You want a banana, you pick it. Suits me. And did you notice all the men by the side of the road—re-soling shoes, fiddling with upended bikes, taking fridges apart? I'm so sick of being told in the States, oh, that would cost more to fix than it's worth, just buy another one. In Pemba, imports are expensive, labor's cheap, and people are poor. So they repair things, keep old appliances running. That's more my nature. I mean, this is a handyman's paradise. I think I could come to understand this life. I don't think I did, the other."

"Maybe I didn't, either," she said sadly. "I got so caught up in . . . You're not an artist, but in my field things can start to seem so—adversarial. Not only with the rest of the world, but with yourself. Wrestling over whether your stuff is any good. But Ruby is probably right. You just make something and then make something else. It's ordinary. Not so different from being a handyman after all. I wish I'd got that from the beginning."

"Worrying about what flatware you did or didn't produce—you can let that go now, too. Look around you. Does it seem to matter?"

The mangrove seed curtains rattled gently in the breeze. A vervet monkey ventured brazenly to the deck and snatched half of Gabe's grilled cheese sandwich. The sun notched closer to the horizon, bathing the encampment in the syrup of a late-harvest Riesling.

"Not especially," said Glynis. "Something about the air, the languor here. It's hard to imagine anything mattering especially."

"I'll tell you what matters," Shep said wistfully. "We should have moved here in 1997."

For the following few days—seemingly an infinity at the time, but less than a week—Glynis miraculously rallied, and Shep allowed himself to hope that Philip Goldman's prognosis had been too pessimistic. They went for dawdling rambles along the beach, bending down for conch shells. They watched crabs skitter to their holes, birds swoop over the banyan trees, schools of tiny silver fish flash into the air beside the pier and patter back to the surface with a rippling plash. Late afternoons when the ruthless sun had softened, he took his wife's hand and led her into the shallow sea, where the sand was fine and clean, the water almost hot from the day's equatorial bask. In the vast, wooden-slatted shower stall, he soaped the salt from her skin and rinsed the grains from between her toes. Making free with the gift shop, he clad her for dinner in filmy cotton shifts, wrapping soft Indian scarves around her scalp. To fend off mosquitoes, he dabbed deet behind her ears like fine perfume. At sunset, they idled at the bar at the base of the pier, where Glynis ordered complicated papaya-and-vodka cocktails for the hell of it. She may not have made it through most of them, but mortality is the ultimate liberator, and one of the many things that didn't matter anymore was her alcohol intake.

Her appetite picked up a degree, and at dinner she would nibble at a crayfish quiche, spear a ring of calamari, fork a flake of Shep's grilled kingfish. They reminisced about earlier research trips; Glynis said Pemba recalled the cove of Puerto Escondido on the Mexican coast. ("Remind me," said Shep. "What was wrong with Puerto again?" "Too many Americans," said Glynis.) Finally she asked about his plans—what kind of house he might build and where. On their third evening, she even raised mischievously, "You're not a monk by nature. I should know. Assuming she stays . . . Do you by any chance find Carol attractive?"

Shep was not so stupid as to imagine that his wife was genuinely playing matchmaker. Virulently possessive and naturally jealous, she hadn't even acknowledged that her husband would survive her until a little over a week ago. So he'd the good sense to aver without hesitation, "Not in the slightest."

"Are you sure?" Glynis teased. "She has the best knockers in the northern—and now the southern—hemisphere."

"I like little ones."

"You've had to."

"Besides, she's too nice," he dismissed. "Not enough of a dark side." Privately he considered that after Carol's last entrance into her Windsor Terrace kitchen, any budding "dark side" must have blossomed apace.

"You don't have much of a dark side yourself," said Glynis.

"Exactly. That's why I need one."

Shep's gratitude for permission to talk about his future without her was boundless. He couldn't help but have thought about it, but always with guilt, and no little superstition, as if he were wishing her gone, hexing her chances. Now that the subject was no longer off-limits, it gave rise to a surprising humor. "You know I plan to bury you in the backyard, don't you," he said lightly over dessert, "like a dog."

Once they bedded down for the night, the squabbling between Flicka and her sister in the adjacent tent was blotted out by the *scree* of cicadas and the wild cackle of bush babies in overhanging branches. He read his wife paragraphs from Hemingway. He sang her the songs he remembered from his childhood, when his mother would tuck him and his sister into bed; his mother's voice had been well pitched and clear, and her version of Taps instilled the tent with the welcome illusion that they were protected: *Day is done. Gone the sun. From the hills, from the lake, from the skies . . . All is well. Safely rest. God is nigh.*

Their fourth night in candlelight, he massaged her feet with lemongrass oil, their soles pumiced smooth from walking on sand. He worked the oil up the shrivel of her atrophied calves. He traced the sharp, classical slope of her tibias, their exquisite line uncompromised even by cancer. He smoothed to her inside thighs, where the skin had loosened with so little flesh to cover. He paused to pool another tablespoon of oil into his palm. But when he reached for her abdomen, she held his wrist. He imagined that she was sensitive about the surgical scar and didn't want him to touch it. But then she pushed his hand further down, pressing the palmful of lemongrass oil into the one part of her body that he had been truly heartbroken to watch go bald. He arched his eyebrows in inquiry.

"This mosquito netting," she said. "It's a lot like a bridal canopy, isn't it?"

Indeed it was.

The remission was precious, and the handful of days when the setting African sun returned the color to his wife's cheeks alone justified the suffering of the journey here. Shep couldn't vouch for their value to the rest of the world, but these few days in Pemba together were worth two million dollars to him. Yet the respite was brief. There came a morning when he woke to find the sheets red. Glynis's menstrual cycle had shut down months before. The bleeding was from her ass.

That was the end of strolls on the beach, for she could no longer walk farther than the bathroom, and then with assistance. She was in pain, and for the first time Shep broke out the liquid morphine.

Shep had been in Morocco with Glynis when his mother suffered the stroke from which she never recovered. Jackson had exited as abruptly as one can, and Shep's other contemporaries were hale. To his mortification, then, his experience of death at close hand had been constrained to cinema and television. On-screen, characters with terminal illnesses lay quietly in hospital beds, mumbled something touching, and dropped their heads. It didn't take very long, and the death itself was as tidy as turning off a light switch.

For filmmakers, death was a moment; for Glynis, death was a job.

Over the course of two long days and nights, his wife's organs slowly shut down. Far from suffering the constipation of chemotherapy, she could no longer keep any substance in, and from every orifice began to leak. Her vomit had blood in it. Her diarrhea had blood in it. Her urine had blood in it. Perhaps it helped that he'd warned the resort in advance, for the staff was kind about the sheets, which they changed twice a day after Shep had carried his wife to a deck chair. The Africans seemed unfazed. He sensed they'd seen this before—and that their own versions of death bore little resemblance to a light switch.

"You want that we bring doctor?" one of the older porters asked, drawing Shep aside. When Shep shook his head, the porter explained, "No, not doctor from hospital in Mkoani. *Uganga*. Very strong in Pemba. A powerful energy line run right under your tent."

"*Uganga*?" Shep had learned the word. "Thank you, but no. We turned our backs on our own black magic. We're not about to throw ourselves on witch doctors of just a slightly different stripe."

Shep and the other five sat vigil. When she was wakeful, churning, crying out, he held her on the bed, or drew her head to his lap. He kept her favorite CDs cycling through his portable player: Jeff Buckley, Keith Jarrett, Pat Metheny. According to his father, what Glynis needed most was simple, animal contact: touch. The steady purr of a human voice, and it didn't matter in the slightest what he said. So to soothe her, he told her about Pemba, all that he had learned from the porters, maids, and waitresses here, who were glad of his interest in their island.

"Cloves," he intoned, keeping his voice even and low. "This island used to be the biggest source of the spice in the world. We don't think about cloves much, except for peaches or pie. But they used to be incredibly important, as a preservative, and as an anesthetic. Did you know that cloves were once worth more than their weight in gold? The government here keeps a tight rein on the crop, and the farmers all have to sell their cloves to the government—at a very poor price, I'm told. So there are clove smugglers, can you believe it? Who run contraband bags in those boats called *jihazzis* to Mambasa, where they can get a better price. It's very dangerous, and you go to prison if you're caught. But the shame is, the market for cloves has imploded. It's not used medicinally much anymore. With refrigeration, it's not needed for a preservative, either. The biggest market is for scenting cigarettes in the Middle East."

She stirred. "If there's no market . . ." she mumbled. "Why risk prison?"

He had not expected her to listen, and he was proud of her for listening; proud of her for trying so hard to still be present, to humor his enthusiasm, to care about conducting a conversation. She had always liked talking—one of those many pleasures that one doesn't consider until they're on the cusp of being withdrawn. Talking, he reflected, was one of life's great delights. He would miss very much talking to her.

"I assume because small money to us, even that fraction of a difference per kilo for a crop that nobody much wants, is large money here. That was always the very basis of The Afterlife, right? Anyway, the funny thing is, the Wapemba don't use cloves in cooking at all. They think it's an aphrodisiac. Or as our driver told me, 'good for home affairs.'"

She chuckled, but that made her cough. He held a handkerchief to her mouth and wiped the pinkened phlegm. "Able was I," she said on recovery, with a sly little smile, "'ere I saw Pemba."

Whatever the allusion, it pleased her with herself, but Shep didn't get it. He felt a rare flash of regret that he'd never gone to college.

Alas, by the second day there was no more talking. Not in the sense of the word that anyone might miss.

"Hurts," she would say, and he would put two more drops of morphine on her tongue. "No," she would say, not in answer to any question. "Fuck," she would say. "Oh, God," she would say, squeezing the sheet so tightly that it retained the clench of wrinkles on release. "Hot," she would say, or "cold." Feeding her ice chips, speeding the revolutions of the ceiling fan, or pulling blankets up or down had to suffice for that farcical ideal of *keeping her comfortable*.

Carol had wondered if they should keep the kids at bay. But Gabe urged her otherwise. Bearing witness to death, he said, should be part of, was perhaps finally the beginning of, their education. It might help Heather to come to terms with her father's fate instead of torturously repeating the theme song to a television ad for his obnoxious employer and stockpiling *pain au chocolat* at breakfast. It might further discourage Flicka from making abusively cavalier references to her own death, and as for Zach—Glynis was his mother. So they involved the children, who took turns sponging her forehead with a cool damp cloth, fanning her with copies of *Africa Geographic*, and plumping her pillows.

Yet there were lulls after a generous dose of morphine during which Glynis sank into a shallow sleep, and two days and two sleepless nights was a long vigil. Too long to remain stricken, to maintain a pitch of grief. So when Carol first scolded her children for giggling, Shep told them, no, it was all right; in fact, it was fine to laugh. In truth, for portions of their deathwatch they had a wonderful time. Carol, Shep, and his father shared a bottle of bourbon the first night, and from then on they kept up a steady stream of cabernet, Kilimanjaro lagers, and more champagne. Fundu's kitchen delivered a groaning board to the tent at every meal—mounds of mangos, pineapple, and papaya; grilled lobster tails, prawn curries, and boiled cassava; whole buffets of chocolate rolls, cream éclairs, and coconut cakes. He encouraged the kids to go swimming, or to join Flicka in the plunge pool during the heat of the afternoon. He admired their beach-combed booty, unusual shells that they arranged as offerings around the bed.

His own offerings were of Glynis herself. Once the sun had set the second day, he lit the dozen tapers that lined the tent. He unrolled the flatware that he'd bundled into his bag on Crescent Drive. He arranged the pieces along the shelves, propping the salad servers with Heather's shells until their inset crimson glass caught the candlelight. He inserted the series of sterling chopsticks in coral from the shore, until they rose in the dynamic attitudes they might have assumed if encased under lock and key in the Cooper-Hewitt. He balanced her forged ice tongs against the champagne bucket, beaded from chilling yet another bottle; he oriented the tongs so that the copper-and-titanium inlay shone from the perspective of the middle pillow. He angled the fish slice so that it writhed in the flicker of a nearby flame, flashing silver like the schools that leapt from the water around Fundu's pier.

He had assured Glynis that her sedulous production of metalwork in middle life was of no consequence, but on his own account he wished there were more of it. She had cannily reincarnated herself in a material far more durable than flesh, and not as fickle. The flatware would outlive her by generations.

Yellowed by candlelight, the gauze of the mosquito netting draped in mellow folds about the bed. The lapping sea lulled not a hundred yards from the tent, and the evening had mercifully cooled. Cicadas surged in and out of the same frequency as the ceiling fan. Appraising the scene, he thought, *I've done the best I can.* Though he was doubtful that Fundu would banner as much on their website, it was a beautiful place to die.

Yet the night was long, a second with no sleep. Carol and his father spelled him holding Glynis's hand while she twisted, but he was fearful of missing the moment, and didn't let them take the helm for more than a few minutes at a time.

Around 2:00 a.m., she slurred drunkenly, "I can't take it anymore," and began to cry. "I can't . . ."

"You don't have to take it anymore, Gnu," he said, turning her head to administer more morphine to her tongue.

Shep couldn't take it anymore, either, though of course he would. To his own embarrassment, he sometimes grew bored, and impatient to get this over. For their lives together as they had understood them had really been over the instant that Glynis announced she had cancer.

Previously convinced that the declaration should be rationed, he had repeated "I love you, Gnu" so many times these last two days that the refrain was in danger of melting into more mumble about cloves. But he was reminded of that cigar box full of foreign currency on his bedside table in Elmsford, in which he'd stashed about a hundred dollars' worth of Portuguese notes. Now that the European Union had converted to the euro, that scrip was no longer legal tender, but a mere souvenir. So just as he should have used up those leftover escudos at Lisbon's duty-free, he spent his passion with abandon while he still had the chance.

"Why is Glynis snoring?" asked Heather at around 5:00 a.m., having crawled from her bed in the adjacent tent.

"Because she's very, very tired," Carol whispered. "Now, go back to sleep."

It would have been difficult for the children to do so. The rattle racked the encampment, and menaced the bush babies away. Shep held his wife and crooned once more about there being nothing to be afraid of, though of course he had no idea. As the sun's first red rim shone over the sea, she seemed to be trying to speak.

"Shuh . . . shuh . . ."

He put his ear to her lips. She exhaled a warmth into the drum that she did not suck back.

There was no final message, no parting avowal, no earth-moving revelation before her head went limp. That seemed fair. Likely most mourners were obliged to forgo a last thing said. You had to make do with the years of their lives that the dead left you instead.

A *knacker* in Old England purchased worn-out and ailing farm animals or their carcasses for manufacture into feed or fertilizer. It may have seemed a morbid moniker, though in its day the trade was respectable, and the surname derived from the medieval tradition of calling a man by his occupation: Baker, Carpenter, Smith. With the caretaking nature of his Christian name, there had always been about Shepherd Armstrong Knacker a great arc: the tending, toiling, and interment that at each stage of life any good man undertook for his brethren, and they for him.

In the years that followed, Shep was true to his christening. It would come as no surprise to those who knew him that the lifelong handyman did not retire to an African island to sip endless tropical cocktails under a beach umbrella. His skills with a wrench and hacksaw were much in demand in Pemba, especially once locals learned that he paid house calls for free. With the assistance of an Arabic charity, he took on the more ambitious project of digging a new community well; the island had a shortage of fresh water. Lending a hand was a good investment, of course. In turn, the Wapemba taught him surefire techniques for catching kingfish, the rules of *bao*, the complications of land purchase in Tanzania, and the optimal bribe for getting another box of Artificial Tears successfully through customs. (Jackson would be pleased to learn that his Mooch-Mug paradigm translated readily to other continents. *Toa kitu kidogo* was so frequently wheedled in Tanzania that it was commonly abbreviated as TKK: "give me a little something.")

Though his relations with the locals were amicable, Shep hailed from a different world, and he would never quite replicate in Pemba the same easy banter and playful jousting of ritual ambles with Jackson around the circuit of Prospect Park. Still, interchanges with their neighbors were good for his struggling Swahili, and being simply different prevented neither party from being warm. Amazingly, Pemba was the only place he'd been to in Africa where everyone wasn't on the hustle— where children and *mzees* alike spotted this conspicuous *mzungu* in the street and cried jubilantly, *"Jambo! Habari yako!"* because they were glad to see him, and not because they wanted his watch.

Hard physical work soon melted away all the cream-laden mashed potatoes that Glynis had left untouched. Yet however busy he kept, Shep always got enough sleep, near the top of the list of pleasures that the ravages of mesothelioma had taught him daily and wittingly to savor. Sleeping joined talking, thinking, seeing, being—as to the last, once in a while doing absolutely nothing and not feeling in the least bit bored—unconscionably long showers, and not-idling-in-rush-hour-traffic-on-the-West-Side-Highway.

After mastering the byzantine socialist property charade—the bureaucrats in Dar bought the land for you, and you bought it from the government, with plenty of TKK to smooth the way—Shep purchased a sizeable coastal plot just outside Mkoani that cost a trifling ten thousand dollars. Securing residency for himself and the five other refugees in his trust may have been a larcenous undertaking, but only in Tanzanian terms; fortunately, the thieves in Dar had no idea how much he would have paid to stay here. Thus even after he sprang for a pickup and small outboard, the wires from Zurich to the People's Bank of Zanzibar in Chake Chake wouldn't significantly deplete his financial reserves for decades. (To his banker's dismay, the monies were conservatively invested in a dumpy savings account that earned a derisory rate of interest. Shep had resisted exhortations that there was a "fortune" to be made in "somewhat" riskier instruments, for he couldn't care less about getting rich when in his adoptive country's frame of reference he was already wealthy beyond measure. Thus he hued to what he called *the principal principle*: above all, keep what you've got.) For that matter, locals were so grateful for rides into town, repairs of their plumbing in the unusual instance that they had plumbing, resolderings of their rickety cookstoves, and his whole family's cheerful assistance picking stems off the clove harvest that they rarely allowed him to pay for anything at the market, and he could go for weeks at a time only out of pocket from volunteering to cover a neighboring child's school fees.

There was some question, of course, about whether Forge Craft's award for compensatory damages was taxable income. According to Mystic, it all came down to whether the settlement "made you whole"—a surprisingly spiritual concern for civil servants, meaning: none of their fucking business. The notion that any amount of money could "make him whole"—could fill the void left by a splendid woman—was every bit as insulting as those Forge Craft lawyers having assessed his wife's value in accordance with how often she did the laundry. In any event, he found himself rather hoping that it *was* taxable income. If the feds wanted to submit to four flights, three layovers, and a minivan ride, they could come and get him.

With Zach's increasingly capable assistance, Shep built a house modest by their own standards, extravagant by Pemba's. Framed with cinderblock for strength, it was coated on the outside with traditional red mud, because he loved the look—baked in the sun, a more casual version of Spain's terra-cotta. The floors were polished mangrove—dark, moody, and kind to bare feet. He roofed the place with proper tarpaper, but topped it becomingly with *makuti*, the dried leaves of coconut palm of local tradition. The very first room he completed was Flicka's, so that she could move from the hotel in Mkoani that, while a vertiginous comedown from Fundu Lagoon, at least had air-conditioning. The island's electrical provision was sporadic, so he imported a generator from Zanzibar, and soon had the little AC unit chugging to cool her bolthole. After his frigid summers at Handy Randy, personally he would have skipped it, but for Flicka air-conditioning wasn't a luxury but a lifesaver.

Shep had never considered his son dexterous or mechanically gifted. Yet once the boy relinquished his surly resistance to Pemba as a losing battle, he threw himself into a level of technology that at last he could understand. It turned out that father and son were constitutionally akin, and Zach thrived with the materials of his father's own young adulthood: timber, stone, cement. Soon a proficient carpenter and mason, he also became a skilled furniture maker with the local mangrove wood. With another burst of height, the boy filled out in the shoulders, at last coming to resemble his father—although Shep was sorry to see the narrower lines of his mother fade. By the time the house was completed, Zach had little taste for idleness. After learning scuba from Fundu's crew, he started working for the resort as a diving instructor. Sadly, the job took the boy a speedboat ride away to the lagoon. Still, Shep was well pleased: his once pale, inward *hikikomori* had left his room.

Meantime, Carol took over the landscaping, a calling she had sacrificed when she switched to IBM for its health insurance. Frangipani, magnolia, eucalyptus, acacia, jasmine, and jacaranda grew rapidly in the equatorial climate. Of course, she had to work around Shep's cocka-mamie fountains; kooky constructs of coconut shells, mangrove roots, conchs, diving flippers, and Africa's ubiquitous plastic shoes, the fountains were an indulgence with the water shortage, but he had dug his own well. She planted fruit trees out front; mangos, bananas, and papayas for the picking facilitated Shep's fiendish experiments in brewing *gongo*, or "lion's tears," the archipelago's lethal moonshine. She tilled a vegetable plot at the back, growing plantains, cassava, and carrots, and grew adept at weaving *coir*, the fibers of coconut husks, into mats and baskets. She returned from marketing trips to Chake Chake with fantastical canvases of hippos, gazelles, and hornbills in the naïve style called *tinga-tinga*. Draped with *kangas*, always full of flowers, and glinting with Glynis's freshly polished flatware, the interior of their little home grew bright.

Carol gave up on homeschooling Flicka, whose protestations that learning to factor equations was a complete waste of time carried more weight on an agricultural island off the east coast of Africa. Flicka made up for her boycott of lessons by inhaling the books that Shep brought back from secondhand shops on ferry trips to Stone Town for provisions. (Shep's own literary ambitions had proven stillborn: he ended his days so wonderfully weary that a page or so put him to sleep. Maybe he wasn't cut out for novels. He'd rather live a good story than read one.) Heather didn't escape her tutoring sessions so easily, but in her free time developed into a remarkable swimmer. They weaned her from the antidepressants. On a diet of fish and fruit, she grew tall and lean, promising to become as beautiful—out of Glynis's earshot, Shep would concede the adjective—as her mother.

No longer repeatedly re-infected by staff carriers in an institution where the bacteria had become endemic, his father defeated *clostridium difficile* and, to both parties' relief, no longer required his son's assistance ten times a day to go to the toilet. With diligent application to the physical therapy exercises he had learned at Twilight Glens, the old man not only regained his original strength but surpassed it, taking brisk daily walks of several miles along the beach. Once he'd run through that stack of detective novels, he started to handwrite a whodunnit himself. He didn't have expectations of publication, he claimed, but if they were now building their own house and catching their own fish and weaving their own baskets, he didn't see why he shouldn't catch the bug of self-sufficiency and write his own books.

The manuscript was never finished. Nevertheless, Shep was relieved that his dignified, formidable father did not meet his end by shitting himself to death in nursing-home diapers. Instead, perhaps overestimating his newfound vigor, he'd been reaching for an enticingly ripe mango and died respectably from the leading cause of traumatic injury in Pemba, according to the local Chinese doctors a far more pernicious medical problem than malaria or AIDS: falling out of trees.

They buried Gabriel Knacker in the back clearing beside Glynis. Shep owed his father for Africa, and the grave site seemed apt. Once the last shovelful was hefted, he said a few words of affection, glad to be spared reading scripture. Gabe Knacker had never regained his faith in God, but he had regained faith in his son, which was probably more important.

It was well he'd left space in the clearing. Like Shep himself, Flicka had fallen in love with Pemba on sight, and never waxed nostalgic about Brooklyn. She'd become a popular local fixture, having learned to make her signature wisecracks in Swahili. Among the Wapemba disabilities, crippling diseases, and genetic abnormalities were common, and they seemed at ease with a girl with a funny hooked nose and protruding chin who crabbed close to the ground while covered head to toe in *kangas* to escape the sun. Yet a sweltering African island was the worst place in the world for a kid with FD, and whenever Flicka reeled into a retching "crisis," Shep cursed himself for his irresponsibility in bringing her here. Still, who was to say that the same thing wouldn't have happened the very same night back in New York? After brushing her teeth, squeezing in her Artificial Tears, smearing her eyes with petroleum jelly, and then swaddling them in plastic wrap, one ordinary night Flicka went to bed to the purr of her private AC and never woke up.

Which reprieved her from following through on her old vow to eventually end a life that was, she often swore, more aggravation than it was worth. Neither Shep nor Carol had ever taken her seriously on this point, until they were dolorously packing up the young woman's things. Hidden away in a little backpack that—come to think of it—Flicka kept with her at all times, they discovered a trove of pills. The rucksack was a grab bag of all the medications that—come to think of it—had mysteriously disappeared: the antidepressants from Twilight Glens that his father had stopped taking, Heather's leftover Zoloft, Glynis's remaining stock of "marzipan," and, most unnervingly, the remains of the liquid morphine. Now they would never know if she'd ever truly planned to call it quits, or if she'd simply kept the backpack at ready hand like a talisman, a magic lantern with one remaining wish. In any event, Flicka had surely relished ongoing access to her own private nuclear option, making the conduct of yet one more day of meds and infections and swallowing lessons not a sentence but a choice.

Thus with three gifts to the soil in the clearing, Shep had *knackered* the whole trio.

That their party of seven would contract to a party of four had been inevitable, of course. With Zach spending more and more time at Fundu Lagoon, in practice they were a family of three. Screamed through Shep's cell phone, Beryl's outrage at the "depraved" and "abusive" kidnapping of their father probably precluded his sister's swelling their ranks any further. (Beryl was livid that she'd been outclassed. Her dull, conformist businessman brother "the philistine" suddenly goes loopy and runs off to an obscure tropical island. Meanwhile, the real artist, the real adventurer of the family, is stuck in the house where she grew up, swaddling down its chill hallways in two sweaters and a secondhand fur coat, trying to design a documentary about "fuel poverty.") By contrast, due to Zach's frequent emails detailing the diving, the dolphins, and the diaphanous dawns, Amelia had grown envious. Forced to take a proper job selling "derivatives"—whatever they were—now that her father didn't subsidize her keep, she had vowed to come out for a visit, if not to *abscond* herself. Shep was uneasy; his daughter's penchant for bare midriffs and jeans slung to the pubic hair wouldn't go down well on a predominantly Muslim island. But so long as Amelia covered her shoulders and wore skirts to the knee, he could see how a pilgrimage to Glynis's grave might help to assuage her sorrow over having missed out on that uncannily celebratory vigil at her mother's bedside.

Oh, the three of them were a "family" only loosely speaking, since Carol and Shep kept chastely to separate bedrooms. Or they did until Carol came out with an astonishing question while lingering after dinner, when Heather was off taking a moonlight swim.

"Do you by any chance have a really, really big dick?"

By morning, after a tearful confidence that he wished she'd got off her lovely chest a long time ago, he would understand the context. At the time he simply laughed and said that there was only one way for her to find out.

Of course, from the very start of this "escape fantasy," Shep had been mindful of its pitfalls. For years people had warned him that there was no escape. Any island "paradise" was bound to disappoint. He would get bored. He would get lonely. He would crave the company of his own kind. He would discover that he was an American through and through, who could never assimilate with natives who believed in voodoo. He would miss movies and fine restaurants and cable television. According to Beryl, he would scurry shamefacedly back to Westchester in no time. Because all along he'd been trying to shed the very rough beast bound to slouch after him wherever he fled: himself.

They were all full of shit. It was great.